SWEET

He grabbed her shoulders, forcing her to look at him. "Corinne," he said in a surprisingly gentle voice, "why do you begrudge me this one night?"

SEETHING

He took her hand and pressed his lips to it, his blue-grey eyes looking deeply into hers. Then he led her to the enormous bed and gently pushed her down on it. The heat from the fire reached them as he began to kiss her.

SURRENDER

Strong hands were easing away her embarrassment and a delicious new warmth spread slowly through her. When he murmured huskily, "I want you," she hooked her fingers through his thick black hair and pulled him to her.

Paradise Wild

Johanna Lindsey

AVON
PUBLISHERS OF BARD, CAMELOT AND DISCUS BOOKS

AVON BOOKS
A division of
The Hearst Corporation
959 Eighth Avenue
New York, New York 10019

Copyright © 1981 by Johanna Lindsey
Published by arrangement with the author
Library of Congress Catalog Card Number: 80-69906
ISBN: 0-380-77651-0

First Avon Printing, June, 1981

AVON TRADEMARK REG. U.S. PAT. OFF. AND IN
OTHER COUNTRIES, MARCA REGISTRADA, HECHO EN
U.S.A.

Printed in the U.S.A.

10 9 8 7 6 5 4 3 2 1

For my home—Hawaii—
and her wonderful people.

Chapter 1

April 9, 1891

THE tall, slender, golden-haired young woman fidgeting by the hall table fastened her startling green eyes on the closed door at the left of the hall. She sighed. The sigh caused her younger cousin Lauren to look away from the window and ask, "For heaven's sake, Corinne, why are you so nervous?" Lauren Ashburn turned back to the window and studied the chilly scene across the way, her brown head tilted back. Boston Common looked so stark—row upon row of ancient trees bending to the merciless wind tearing its way toward Beacon Street and this townhouse.

Even in April, Boston was not an easy place to live. The months of cold, harsh winds and the need to stay indoors much of the time had taken a toll on the cousins. Corinne was harder to please than usual, and even sweet-tempered Lauren found herself gloomy much of the time.

"It doesn't look as though spring is coming at all this year," Lauren sighed as she fingered the rich scarlet draperies.

Corinne glanced up, her golden brows drawing together over the marvelous emerald eyes. "How can you prattle about spring at a time like this?" she snapped. Her glance moved quickly to the closed door and then back to her young cousin.

Following her gaze, Lauren shrugged. "I would think you'd be used to this by now. You've been through it twice in the last year alone."

Corinne's quick temper charged to the surface. "I

1

shouldn't expect you to understand!" she said bitterly. "You have years before suitors will come to speak to your father. Then we'll see how you like waiting while your future is decided by men—instead of by you."

Lauren's brown eyes filled. "I do understand, Cori. I'm sixteen, only three years younger than you."

Corinne instantly regretted her sharp words. Impulsive, she was always having to apologize for angry remarks.

"I'm sorry, Cousin. It's just that I'm so nervous this time. Russell really is my last hope."

"Now why do you say that, Cori? You've had scores of suitors for the last three years, all the most handsome and well-to-do men in Boston. Don't you know how beautiful you are? If Cousin Samuel says no to Russell, there will be plenty more for you to choose from."

"No, there won't be. There are very few men like Russell."

Lauren smiled knowingly. "You mean there are very few men you can twirl around your little finger as you do Russell. Or the way you did Charles, and William before that."

"Exactly. The others just won't do."

"Russell Drayton isn't quite as timid as the other two were. I was really surprised when you chose him. But then, he *has* seemed to conform to your wishes."

"Russell and I have an understanding. He'll do just fine."

"I guess it's fortunate that you don't love him. At least if your father refuses him, you won't be broken-hearted."

"I will never be broken-hearted," Corinne laughed. "But Russell is going to exert himself, show he has some guts. He should be putting on quite a performance right now," she said, nodding toward the closed study door. She frowned. "The interview shouldn't be taking this long."

"Why don't we wait in the parlor?" Lauren suggested. "This hall is too drafty."

"You go ahead. I couldn't sit still. And I want to see Russell the second he comes out."

Corinne rang the bell by the parlor door and the Barrows' butler appeared instantly from the back of the house. "Brock, Miss Ashburn will have tea in the parlor."

"Yes, Miss Barrows," the dour Brock replied. "And Mr.

Drayton? Will he be staying for dinner after the interview, miss?"

Corinne stiffened. It infuriated her that the household staff always knew everything. She had just that morning decided that today would be appropriate for Russell to make his plea, what with her father's congenial mood of the last few days.

"I will let you know, Brock," she replied sharply, dismissing him.

At that moment the front door knocker sounded, startling the three. Brock moved to answer it, but Corinne stopped him, eager for any diversion. She opened the door and shivered as the chill wind swept past her into the hall, molding her blue muslin dress to her body.

The sharp, light-green eyes of a stranger met hers. The man was small and slender, with bright red hair and long sideburns extending below his bowler hat, which he was wise enough to hold in place. He was a curious little ferret-like man with a beaked nose, wearing a tight-fitting brown tweed suit.

"May I help you?" Corinne offered.

Ned Dougherty scrutinized the lovely blond girl carefully with an eye for detail, a habit necessitated by his profession. His mind registered the dark-gold hair, the slightly arched brows, the large eyes of a brilliant, clear, greenish yellow, set perfectly over the modestly curved nose. Long eyelashes fanned high cheekbones. Her lips were not too wide. Her smooth, ivory complexion and gently rounded chin blended beautifully with the lovely face.

"May I help you?" she repeated, a little sharply.

Ned cleared his throat. Hers was a face he would not forget. Nor could anyone ignore the gleaming golden hair with its coppery highlights.

"Is this the Samuel Barrows residence?"

"Yes."

Ned's sharp green eyes continued his examination, noting the slim neck, the high, pointed breasts. The dress tapered to a tiny waist and he could guess at the slim hips and long legs. She seemed about five feet seven, rather tall for a girl.

"Sir, if you do not quickly state your business, I must bid you good day." Corinne was growing impatient.

"Forgive me, miss. I am looking for a Samuel Barrows who, many years ago, visited a group of islands in the Pacific known once as the Sandwich Islands, more recently as the Hawaiian Islands."

"You must have the wrong man."

"Are you quite sure, miss? It was a long time ago, nineteen years. You could hardly have been in Mr. Barrows employ at that time, so you couldn't—"

"I beg your pardon," Corinne interrupted haughtily. "Mr. Barrows is my father."

"Forgive me again, Miss Barrows," Ned said in embarrassment. This girl's beauty had a disturbing effect on him. "I only assumed—"

"I know what you assumed. Now good day!"

Ned Dougherty held up his hand as she started to close the door. "Are you positive you know of all your father's travels?"

"Yes!" she snapped, and slammed the door angrily. But then a distant memory floated into her mind and she quickly opened the door again.

"Wait!" she called, stopping the little man as he turned away. She smiled apologetically. "Now I must ask you to forgive me, sir. My father has been to the Hawaiian islands. He told me about it when I was a child. I'm afraid I had forgotten."

Ned Dougherty's eyes lit up. "This was nineteen years ago?"

"Exactly," she admitted. "He was there when I was born. Did you wish to see him?"

"No thank you, Miss Barrows. Good day to you."

"Wait! I don't understand," she called after him, but he was already hurrying down the street.

"Well, botheration!" she cursed aloud. "What a rude little man!"

Corinne slammed the door shut on the cold evening. Turning, she sighed and faced the empty hall. She studied the many sofas and padded benches against the walls, the large unlit chandelier used for formal gatherings, mirrors, the pictures which were said to have come from England with her ancestors. All these riches and for what? Her father kept the purse strings closed tightly.

Corinne started for the closed door, fed up with waiting.

It opened suddenly, and Russell stormed out. Seeing his angry countenance, she ventured reluctantly, "He said no?"

"He said no," Russell answered tightly. "He said *absolutely* no!"

Corinne grabbed his arm. "I don't understand. Didn't you say what I told you to say?"

"Yes."

"And you stood up to him?"

"Yes, Corinne, yes!"

"Then why?" she pleaded in confusion.

"He saw through me, he said," Russell replied despondently. "God, if he only knew!"

"Knew what? What are you talking about?"

"It doesn't matter, Corinne. He has had us followed for months. Nothing could make him believe I'm not the spineless fool he accused me of being."

"Russell!"

"I don't want to talk about it now. I'll see you later at the club."

He left the house without another word. Corinne stood numbly in the middle of the hall. She genuinely liked Russell. He was by far the most handsome man she had ever seen, even though he was a bit too thin and had a beard that irritated her sensitive skin. But Russell was pliable, ready to bow to her wishes. And they were so well suited. He was tall enough for her own ungainly height, and they enjoyed so many of the same things. They especially enjoyed Corinne's one obsession, which was gambling. Though she really didn't know that much about Russell, he must be wealthy or he wouldn't be able to afford gambling almost nightly. His wealth meant that she didn't have to worry that he was after the money she would inherit when she married.

It wasn't fair. In the last year her father had changed from the loving, tolerant man she had always adored into an obstinant tyrant. He was thwarting her every move.

Corinne's temper, always quick, bubbled now into outraged fury. She marched into her father's study and glared at him across his large desk.

"What are you trying to do to me?" she demanded loudly, not caring who heard her.

"Now, Cori, honey," Samuel Barrows began in a conciliatory voice. "I knew you would be upset, but there's no reason to be."

"No reason!" she countered. "No reason?" She started to pace back and forth before his desk. "When you turned William down, I thought perhaps you had a good explanation. Then when you refused Charles' suit, I thought you were being cautious. After all, Charles was only vice-president of a bank, and though his family was from sound stock and modestly wealthy, they couldn't compare to our family, or the fortune I will inherit." She faced him again. "But what could have made you say no to Russell?"

"He's not the man for you, Cori."

"How can you say that? He's the man I *want* to marry! You've taught me to go after what I want!"

"I should have taught you better judgement," Samuel replied, lowering his light brown eyes. "I've given you too much freedom for a girl. It will have to be a strong man indeed who can control you."

Her emerald eyes sparkled. "But I don't want a strong man. I've lived all my life with a man like that—you! Our battle of wills has been challenging, but I want to live the rest of my life in peace."

"You mean you want everything the way you want it, no matter whether your judgement is sound or not?"

"I want control of my life! Is that too much to ask?" she demanded.

Samuel met her cold stare. "Girl, you have proved over this last year that you're not wise enough to have that control yet."

Corinne started to retort, but quickly remembered Russell saying that her father had had them followed. So he knew about her gambling. And she had taken such pains to be secretive about it, so that he would not guess where her generous monthly spending money went.

"I will admit that my judgement is not always sound, but it will improve in time," Corinne said reluctantly.

"I can only pray that time comes within the next two years," Samuel returned.

Corinne's anger sparked again. "Do you intend to keep me under your rule till then? Are you saying I can't marry until then?"

"No, blast it all!" Samuel finally lost his patience. "I'm

trying to save you from yourself. You're so eager to get your hands on your trust that you don't care who you marry. For God's sake, Corinne, can't you wait just two more years? Then you'll have your grandmother's money and can marry with or without my approval."

"By then I won't need to marry!" she cried in frustration and stormed from the room.

Samuel Barrows leaned back in his velour chair and sighed. No one could say that hot-headed girl wasn't his daughter. Stubborn, determined, impatient, and decidedly short-tempered, she was just like him. It was fortunate that Daneil Stayton had stipulated that her granddaughter couldn't marry without her father's consent until she reached twenty-one. Daneil knew the impulsiveness of youth. She had assumed that Corinne would mature enough by twenty-one to make her own decisions. Samuel wondered.

It was his own fault, he admitted that. He had allowed his only child independence, and at too early an age. He had given her freedom to develop, and had not restricted her just because she was a female. He had been warned repeatedly by his family that he would regret his decision one day, and now he did.

The best thing he could do for his daughter would be to choose her husband for her while she was still under his control. He would see that she married a strong fellow, not some spineless jackass who would let her continue her wild ways. But where could he find a man with a will stronger than Corinne's and find him within the next two years?

Chapter 2

HALFWAY around the world, in the Pacific Ocean, lay the group of islands recently named Hawaii. The awesome loveliness of these islands—considered by some historians to be the site of the Garden of Eden—put visitors in mind of calm, peace, and delightfully easy living. Since the islands' discovery by Captain Cook, many visitors had become permanent residents, unwilling to give up the brilliant colors, the exotic plants and birds, and the delightful ocean in order to return to their less hospitable homes.

Because of the great number of foreign settlers, all was not peaceful in Hawaii in 1891. The Hawaiian natives had just lost their beloved king, often called the Merry Monarch, and his sister reigned in uneasy office in the newly built Iolana Palace in Honolulu. The palace, the first royal residence in the world to be furnished with flush toilets and lit entirely by electricity, was soon to be the scene of a confrontation between loyal monarchists and foreign settlers. In April of 1891, it was the felicitous nature of the Hawaiian natives that kept the peace on Oahu.

Twenty-seven-year-old Jared Burkett had been born on Oahu. He carried the mixed blood of Europe and Hawaii. And though his Hawaiian friends trusted and loved him and his European friends respected his pride in Hawaii, it could not be said of Jared that he possessed the gentle nature of his Hawaiian ancestors. Jared was not an easygoing man. His one weakness was his younger sister, Malia.

Thirty-one years before, Jared's father, Rodney, and Rodney's brother, Edmond, had spent three years building their city home here on Oahu, the island with the greatest number of foreign settlers and boasting the most commerce. Having built the house, Rodney decided to marry. The marriage caused a permanent rupture in his relationship

8

with his brother. Edmond violently objected to Ranelle. Though she was an American and had grown up with American ways, she had Hawaiian ancestors. Edmond felt that his brother was marrying a woman of color. Even the daily sight of Hawaiians could not make him change his harsh attitude.

Edmond Burkett relinquished all rights to the new house he had helped build, and moved into the city, closer to the office of the loan company the brothers had started. Because of their disagreements, Rodney left the running of the company to Edmond and concentrated on other interests, mainly land.

For the most part, foreigners were not allowed to buy land anywhere on Hawaii. But because of Ranelle and her distant Hawaiian relations, Rodney was able to buy tracts of land on the north shore of Oahu. Here he started a small sugar plantation, not to compare with the larger plantations, but big enough to join the island's major industry.

With the profits from his sugar and the loan company, Rodney started a carpentry business. He dealt first in ships' repairs and later included the construction of houses. He made a small fortune. This fortune was lost, however, in 1872, when business and agricultural interests were at a low ebb. The sugar plantation lost money and was eventually abandoned. Only the loan company prospered during those bleak years.

During this time Rodney's marriage deteriorated. His wife's hopeless melancholia affected his business. After Ranelle died, it took a long time for Rodney to pull himself together and put the business back on its feet.

By the time Rodney Burkett died in a sailing accident, leaving all his possessions to his two children, his estate had improved.

His only son, Jared, now occupied the house on Beretania Street. The area was now part of Honolulu, the city having caught up to it years ago. Jared's sister, Malia, younger by ten years, lived most of each year at their beach house on the north shore of the island, on the land that had once been a sugar plantation.

Jared Burkett had proved to one and all that he was capable of taking his father's place. Rodney Burkett had raised a son he could be proud of. Jared was a man who would never succumb to a problem, no matter how difficult it was. The community respected Jared, and feared him a little. He never backed down from a fight.

In the American community, Jared defended his Hawaiian heritage because of his pride in it. Among the Hawaiians, he was worthy to be called a friend.

After his mother's death, he had become withdrawn and moody. That was to be expected, but it never went away. Bitterness grew in Jared, becoming a festering hate. This hate had eaten away at young Jared for sixteen years, since the day of his mother's death.

Today, so many years after that death, the solution for purging himself of that hate once and for all had come to Jared by way of a letter.

Now, on the way to his uncle's office at the Savings and Loan Company, Jared read the letter for what was surely the tenth time.

Dear Mr. Burkett,

It gives me great pleasure to bring you good news so soon after receiving your letter. You employed me to find a Samuel Barrows, who nineteen years ago visited your faraway islands, and this I have done.

Following your instructions, I began the search in my city of Boston and found this man with little difficulty, since he is a very respected and prominent member of Boston society. He resides on Beacon Street in the exclusive residential district in the Back Bay area of the city. His wealth derives from many sources. His most well-known interest is his ship building firm, one of the largest in the state of Massachusetts.

I have no doubt that this is the Samuel Barrows you wished to locate. If I can serve you further, I am at your disposal.

Your servant,
Ned Dougherty

Jared put the letter in the pocket of his white tropical suit as the carriage halted on Fort Street. He looked up at the old two-storied pink building, badly in need of paint. But it looked no worse than the other buildings lining the street in this old section of the city.

Edmond Burkett's office was on the second floor, and Jared climbed the stairs slowly, dreading the encounter before him. There was no love lost between uncle and nephew. For as long as Jared could remember, his uncle had been a stranger to his family. Jared had been seven years old before he met Edmond Burkett, though they lived less than a mile apart. But he knew the reason why Edmond would not associate with his relatives on the island. It was Jared's mother.

Edmond had not been able to adjust to the mixed nationalities of the islands. A man of bitter prejudices, he never forgave Rodney for marrying a woman with Hawaiian blood, even though very little of it still remained in her. His dislike for Ranelle extended to her children, and to Jared in particular because of the boy's pride in his heritage. Though Rodney and Edmond were reconciled after Ranelle's death, Edmond would still have nothing to do with her children. Jared and Malia returned Edmond's animosity.

Now, however, Jared was an equal partner with Edmond in the loan company, and was forced to associate with him. Each of them made an effort to put up a good front. In fact, Jared took particular pleasure in sometimes being overly friendly, knowing how this rankled his churlish uncle.

The secretary in Edmond's outer office smiled brightly when Jared came in. Jane Dearing was an unmarried young woman, recently arrived from New York. She had a special interest in Jared Burkett. Jared's rugged, dark handsomeness made heads turn. His gray-blue eyes contrasted startlingly with his black hair. Jared was very tall, six feet two inches, with a firm, athletic body. Jane was envious of Dayna Callan, the woman he most frequently escorted about the city. So were a great many women. Dayna and Jared had been friends since childhood, and it was assumed that they would marry eventually. But the women of the city were not ready to give up on Jared. Jane Dearing wasn't either.

"Mr. Burkett." Jane's blue eyes sparkled. "It's such a pleasure to see you."

Her interest was obvious and Jared smiled uncomfortably. "Is my uncle in, Miss Dearing?"

"Yes, but he is with Mr. Carlstead right now. The poor

11

man came to see him about an extension on his loan. His tobacco crop wasn't very good this year, I'm afraid."

Jared frowned. Lloyd Carlstead was a good sort, a Swede with a large family of youngsters and a plump, kind-hearted wife. Their small farm barely supported them, but it was on prime land near the city, land Jared knew his uncle would be interested in. Edmond probably would foreclose.

It was well-known that the Burketts did not see eye to eye on running the company. But Jared had relinquished the responsibility of management to Edmond, since his interests were elsewhere. And it did no good to argue for the individual Edmond caused to go bankrupt, for he would always end the argument with, "Either devote your time fully to this company, sell out to me, or abide by my decisions!"

Soon, Lloyd Carlstead rushed out of Edmond's office, his hands clenched, his face beet-red. He passed Jared without even seeing him and ran down the outer stairs to the street. Jared gritted his teeth. The poor man was probably ruined, and all because he had had the poor judgement to come to Edmond Burkett for a loan.

But Jared could not fight someone else's battles today. He needed his uncle's cooperation now, and perhaps some of his money—though he would not ask for it. He hoped Lloyd Carlstead would find help elsewhere.

"I'll just go on in, Miss Dearing," Jared said lightly. "No need to announce me."

"Certainly, Mr. Burkett. I'm sure your uncle will be delighted to see you."

Jared smiled at that. Miss Dearing really did try too hard. He really should take her out to dinner some night, let her find out just how hopeless it was to please him. Then she would turn tail and run. It would be the best thing for her.

Jared strolled casually into his uncle's cool office and closed the door. With windows open wide on both sides of the large room and fans revolving continuously overhead, it really was a pleasant room. Edmond liked to display his wealth, and he did that in his office. Surprisingly, the plush furniture and thick carpeting did not take away from the cool effect.

"How's business, Uncle?" Jared began. Edmond's self-satisfied smirk was his answer.

"Good, good. And I hear you're not doing too badly yourself," Edmond said expansively, and motioned Jared to one of the chairs across from his desk. "The contract you won for that new hotel in Waikiki—now, that was a pretty deal. I always encouraged Rodney to build hotels, but he wasn't up to the challenge, preferring to stick to houses and small stores. You don't get your name remembered that way."

"That wasn't exactly why I went after the hotel job," Jared replied, his gray-blue eyes unreadable. "It means a lot of work for my men over an extended period of time."

"Of course. They'll get lazy if you don't keep them busy."

"No," Jared said coldly. "I don't happen to have that problem."

"Then you're more fortunate than the rest of us," Edmond laughed derisively.

Jared wasn't about to argue. His uncle was set in his beliefs that all Hawaiians were lazy, good-for-nothings. That was ridiculous, but you couldn't tell Edmond anything.

"What brings you here, Jared?" Edmond asked. "Anything important?"

The older man leaned back in his chair. The resemblance between Edmond and his father always amazed Jared. Edmond was forty-seven now, with dark blue eyes and sandy brown hair without a trace of gray. He was six feet tall.

"I'm taking a vacation, Uncle." Jared came out with it smoothly. "I thought you'd like to know."

"That's nothing new," Edmond said blandly. "You take off every year to the beach during the hottest summer months, just like your father did. Can't say I blame you, though. If I owned land over there, I'd do the same thing. Damn hot on this side in June and July."

"You're welcome to visit Malia in the country, Uncle, if you find it too hot here. But I won't be there. I'm going to the mainland."

Edmond's interest was caught. "The States? Well that's a different matter. Funny, though, when you froze your knuckles going to college in the mainland, you swore you would never go back there."

13

Jared grimaced at the memory of those winters. He never did get used to the cold. "It will be summer there too, so it won't be bad."

"I've been meaning to get over there myself," Edmond reflected. "God, it's been fifteen years since I've been off this rock, and that was only a trip to the big island to inspect property offered as collateral. If I could just find an assistant competent enough to take over for me, I might be able to get off for a vacation too, but that seems impossible. Colby, the man I've got now, is about to be fired."

Jared didn't want to talk about company problems. If his uncle only knew how difficult he was to work for, he'd know why he had fired so many assistants.

"Actually, Uncle, my trip won't be just for pleasure. I've been thinking for quite a while about putting some money in a mainland enterprise. They have much more to offer over there in the way of sound investment. Iron, timber, and steel, bigger banks and shipyards than we have, among other things."

"But you can't keep an eye on your money over there," Edmond pointed out.

"True," Jared agreed. "But that wouldn't be necessary if I invested in an established firm. I could just sit back here and reap the profits."

Edmond's blue eyes gleamed at the mention of profits. "Where in the States were you planning on going?"

"The East coast—New York or Boston."

"Good choice," Edmond replied thoughtfully, tapping a finger lightly on his desk. "And how much will you want to take with you when you go?"

Jared waited a moment before answering. "Five hundred thousand."

Edmond sat up and nearly choked. "Good God, man! That's nearly all the cash you have!"

"I know," Jared said with a light grin.

"Wouldn't half of that do?"

"I'm not going to lose money, Uncle," Jared said confidently. "I'm going to make it."

"But still—"

Jared held up his hand. "If you don't think it's wise for me to tie up all my cash, even though I should have ample return in a year, why don't you invest a little yourself?

Say . . . a hundred thousand? It would be safe, since I would guarantee it myself."

Edmond came to a quick decision. "Since you do guarantee it, I will give you half. But you must leave the same amount here to cover it."

"Very well." Jared relented, smiling to himself.

That was more than he had counted on. Now if all the money was lost in what he planned to do, he would not be broke, and he would have a year or more to repay his uncle. He knew that greed was why Edmond was helping him, but nonetheless, he was helping. If only he knew *what* he was helping to do!

"How soon will you need the cash?"

"I sail in five days, on Sunday."

"So soon?"

"I have everything in order, Uncle. All that remains is a quick trip out to Sunset Beach to say good-bye to Malia." Jared grinned mischievously. "You will keep an eye on her while I'm gone, won't you?"

Edmond's eyes widened slightly. "She'll be with all those old relations of yours. I doubt I'll be getting out that way."

"Well, you know how she likes to come to the city for the winter season. Too many harsh storms on the north shore that time of year."

Edmond became flustered. "Look here, Jared. The storms don't come until October or November. Just how long do you plan to be in the mainland?"

"I can't honestly say. Three months, four—but you never know. Possibly six. You don't want me to jump into anything quickly, now do you? It will take time to investigate, to be sure our money is safe."

Edmond sighed. Jared knew damn well he didn't want to be responsible for Malia. His little sister could be quite trying at times and she needed a close watch now that she was almost eighteen.

Jared smiled to himself. He would never trust her to Edmond's care, but it amused him to have his uncle think he was responsible for the young girl. Of course, it would really be Leonaka Naihe who would protect her. But why let his uncle off the hook by telling him that? Jared enjoyed the consternation on his uncle's face.

15

Chapter 3

NANEKI Kapuakele heard the carriage pull off Beretania Street into the driveway, and she ran to the front of the house to peer out the window. It was only the middle of the afternoon, too early for Jared to come home, yet there he was, stepping out of the carriage and coming up the flower-lined walkway.

How he reminded Naneki of her dead husband, Peni—tall and godlike, carrying himself like an ancient warrior. Peni Kapuakele might have been a great chief if he had lived in the old days. He would have been right there beside King Kamahamaha, helping to unite the islands.

Peni was dead. *Ua hele i ke ala-maaweiki.* He has gone on the narrow-stranded way. And Jared was alive. So like Peni, proud, arrogant, forceful. It did not matter that he was not pure Hawaiian as Peni had been, that he had only a small speck of Hawaiian blood left in him. She was *hapa-haole* herself, half white, half Hawaiian. Jared's heart was Hawaiian, and his strength. And he was hers, taking the place of her lost Peni.

Naneki ran a hand through her thick black hair and smoothed down her pink and white floral *muumuu*. She wished she were wearing just a simple sarong, which would cling to her hips and reveal her long, graceful legs. That was all she would wear when she was in the country with Malia. But here in the city, Jared would not let her dress so scantily because of the many visitors who came to his house on Beretania Street.

When Jared opened the door, Naneki was there to greet him. She was a tall girl of gentle grace. She had only to look up a few inches to meet his eyes.

"Hello, Passion Flower."

Naneki grinned. It was what Jared called her when they

16

were alone and he was in good spirits. But this was not often, for this young man was much troubled.

"You home early, Ialeka." She called him by his Hawaiian name as did most of his local friends.

"So I am." He moved into the large living room and threw his wide-brimmed straw hat on a nearby chair. "Would you fix me a rum punch?"

She hesitated, her curiosity aroused. "But why you home so early?"

He sat down on the end of the brown-and-gold sofa and leaned back with his hands hooked behind his head. "The drink first."

Naneki shrugged as if she didn't care, then hurried out of the room and was back in a minute with a tall glass of iced punch. She went to a long bar against the back wall and added a liberal dose of rum, then handed it to him. He drank half, set it down, then pulled Naneki onto his lap.

She giggled and pressed her face to his neck, nibbling softly there. "So this why you come home, eh? You like make love?"

Jared sighed contentedly and kneeded one plump breast through the thin cotton of her *muumuu*. He would miss Naneki while he was gone. She was the perfect mistress, undemanding, there when he needed her. She never complained, except when he left her in the country with his sister.

She was the adopted daughter of his cook, housekeeper, and distant relative, Akela Kamanu, that great Hawaiian woman who had raised Malia since her birth. She had raised Naneki too, taking her in when she was abandoned by her Hawaiian mother because Naneki's father had been a *haole*, white man. Naneki was Malia's closest friend, being only a year older and growing up in the same household, but she also served the Burkett family.

He would not have touched her if she were not a widow. She had been married young, but the marriage had lasted only three months. She had a daughter from that marriage, and little Noelani needed a father. Jared would have to see about finding Naneki another husband someday soon. He was being selfish in keeping her to himself.

He had considered marrying her and raising Noelani as his own. The little two-year-old already called him papa.

But Naneki had loved Peni Kapuakele too much. Peni would always be there, even though he was dead. And Jared would never marry a woman who had had a first love. He knew what that could do to a marriage. He knew what it had done to his parents' marriage.

Jared kissed Naneki's lips tenderly, then with more determination. He rose with her in his arms and carried her upstairs to her room. There he set her down and she pulled her long flowing *muumuu*, her only garment, over her head and tossed it over the wooden bed frame at the bottom of her bed. She lay down and stretched invitingly, her black eyes half shadowed with drooping lids, her full lips slightly parted.

Jared quickly discarded his own clothes and joined her on the narrow bed. While his lips claimed hers again, he ran a hand over the smooth brown skin he knew so well, over the full, large breasts, then down her narrow waist. She was built so firmly, had played in the ocean for so many years, that he did not need to worry about hurting her with his strong hands. She was a match for him. And she welcomed him now, opening her legs so that he could plunge into her.

She received all of his long shaft easily. Jared held back until she reached her pleasure before he gave in to his own. When he was spent, he collapsed on her, resting his head on her shoulder.

"You need bath now," she said softly as she traced her fingers over his sweaty back.

Jared only grunted and rolled over to let her up. The room was intolerably hot. The afternoon sun blazed through the open window, and there was very little breeze. He should have taken her to one of the empty rooms on the other side of the house, one that caught the morning sun and was cooler in the afternoon.

Naneki never asked why he wouldn't bring her to his own room, which was across from hers. He was glad he didn't have to defend his desire for complete privacy there. He did not want to be faced with asking a woman to leave his bed after he had finished with her, but his need for solitude soon would force him to do so. It was much easier for him to simply slip away afterwards.

While Naneki left to run his bath, Jared wondered if his

desire for privacy had anything to do with those terrible dreams that sometimes made him cry out in the night. It was likely. He didn't want to share those vivid memories with anyone.

He guessed that the women he had known didn't consider him a determined lover. He came to them only when he needed them, and he never attached himself to any one woman. He was careful in his choices, having nothing to do with virgins, and staying away from whorehouses for health reasons. Widows were his first choice, and then the promiscuous daughters of acquaintances who asked for what they got. Nothing infuriated Jared more than a tease, or gave him more pleasure than showing one that she couldn't trifle with Jared Burkett. He considered himself fortunate that no particular woman had a hold on him. He knew what love could do to a man, how destructive it could be.

He would probably marry Dayna Callan one day—they had never spoken of it, but Jared assumed she was waiting for him. They were friends now, not lovers, and Jared was hoping he might find a woman with more passion than Dayna seemed to have. At twenty-five, she was lovely, quiet, and unassuming. She had never been in love. Jared was sure of this and it was why he considered Dayna for his wife.

Leonaka, Jared, and Dayna had been a constant threesome as children growing up on the north shore together. The two friends always knew how to bring Jared out of his dark moods. But to marry Dayna? Ah, would he ever make up his mind? It would be like marrying a saint, and he wasn't quite sure he could stand that. He had never even embraced her in anything but friendship. How could he bring himself to make love to her? But she was probably just what he needed. With Dayna, there would be no strife in his life other than that of his own making.

Naneki came back into the room. "Water ready, big boss man."

She was still in a playful mood, so he asked, "Will you join me?"

She nodded and started to pull him up from the bed, but let him go before he sat up completely. "Why else you come home so early, Ialeka? I never see you this time of day before unless we in country."

19

Jared got up and whacked her on the behind. "After we bathe we have some packing to do."

She brightened. "We going home?"

"You are. You came to Honolulu for some shopping and you stayed three months. How will you explain that when you get home?"

"Akela knows. She happy I take care of you."

Jared grunted. "Malia doesn't know."

"Malia is my friend. She not think bad of me," Naneki said with a slight grin.

"Regardless, I don't want her to know." Jared frowned. "You understand that, Naneki?"

She nodded, but she warned him again, "You always spoil Malia. You no let her grow up." When Jared's eyes turned a steely gray she added quickly, "But I understand. Come."

Jared's mood had changed. "There's no more time to play, Naneki. We will leave first thing in the morning. I have to be back in Honolulu by Friday. I'm leaving Sunday for the mainland."

"Like when you went college?"

"No, this is business."

"How long? You will miss your summer months in Sunset?"

"Yes. But I will try to be back by Christmas."

Naneki tried to hide her disappointment. "That is very long time away."

Jared came to her and kissed her lightly. "While I'm gone you should start looking for a new husband. Noelani needs a father."

She grinned. "When *you* marry? I no see *you* running to church."

"One of these days, I will."

"With Miss Callan. I like her. I no mind share you with her."

Jared sighed in exasperation and pulled her along with him to the bath. "Just remember what I said. Start looking for a husband."

Chapter 4

NED Dougherty's office was on the south side of Boston. Hardly an office, it was just a small room above a tavern. There were a cluttered desk, two chairs, and file cabinets crammed into the small space. As Jared sat across from the red-haired man, he began having second thoughts about being there. Whatever he had expected to find, it certainly wasn't this.

Ned's appraising look took in Jared's expensive suit, his aura of strength, and he noted a bit of ruthlessness in the sharp blue-gray eyes. This was a man who got what he wanted, and Ned anticipated profiting from whatever he wanted.

"I can honestly say, Mr. Burkett, that I didn't think I would hear from you again. And I certainly didn't expect to meet you. Your business must be pretty important to bring you here all the way from Hawaii."

Jared decided to be frank. If this man could accomplish what he wanted, then he didn't mind paying an outlandish fee for it.

"What I plan to do in Boston is very important to me," Jared said as he glanced about the office. "But I'm not quite sure you're up to it, Mr. Dougherty."

"Don't let the size and location of my office fool you," Ned replied defensively. "The larger investigating firms have bigger expenses and charge their clients more. I get more clients."

"Do you work alone?"

"I get help when I need it." Ned leaned back and smiled. "I can see by that wary look that you have doubts about me. Let me assure you that I have never disappointed a client. Whether I am investigating a firm, finding a missing

21

person, or trailing a wayward wife, I do get results. I've even helped solve a few murders."

Jared was not impressed. "I need not only information, Mr. Dougherty, but publicity as well."

"I have a cousin and a few friends who work for the newspapers."

"I will need to be well-known in this city within a very short time—in about a month."

"No problem, Mr. Burkett."

"Very well, then, I will take a chance on you, Mr. Dougherty. But I wouldn't like to be disappointed."

The threat was obvious and Ned felt a slight chill race down his back. He shrugged it off.

"I'm curious to know how you found me, Mr. Burkett. Have you been to Boston before?"

Jared began to relax. "No. I got your name from a college friend in the States. He told an amusing story around school about his grandfather hiring you to follow his grandmother, suspecting her, at seventy-two, of having an affair."

Ned laughed, relieving the tension. "I remember that old man quite well. It was the most ridiculous case I ever worked on."

"I imagine so. But I never forgot your name," Jared admitted. "I knew even then that I would have need of you one day."

"Well then, Mr. Burkett, I'm sure we will accomplish what you want done, if you'll just tell me what it is."

Jared's eyes held a cold gray glint. "I want information on Samuel Barrows, especially about his business interests, the extent of his wealth, and how much reserve he has. I want to know everything about the man, his associates, and his family. I want to know his future plans, how he works, his weaknesses, and his habits."

Ned nodded. "It will probably take about two weeks to get what you want. Since gathering information is pretty routine, I don't foresee any problems."

"Fine. Now, about the publicity. You will start on that immediately. As I said before, I want to be well-known about town. I want to be talked about in the highest financial circles, especially in Samuel Barrows' circle."

The little detective picked up a notebook and pen and leaned over his desk. "I'll need facts about you, then."

Jared grinned. "Jared Burk, millionaire from the West Coast, here to invest money. That's all you need to know."

"I don't understand."

Jared rose from his chair. "You don't have to understand. The name and facts I just gave you are false. I don't want my real identity known. But I do intend to invest some money if the circumstances are right. You might recommend a good lawyer."

Ned's curiosity was aroused. "You want to be a man of mystery, then?"

"Exactly."

"Very well." Ned came around his desk to shake hands. "I'll get the name of a lawyer to you in a few days. Where can I reach you?"

"I checked into the Plaza this morning as Jared Burk."

The ride back to the hotel was pleasant. Jared had the driver take a short tour of the city first. The weather was a brisk sixty-five degrees on this early June day, warm for Bostonians, but chilly compared to Hawaii. Jared hoped he would not have to stay here too long, especially into the colder months.

The carriage entered the Back Bay area. When Jared saw the Beacon Street sign, his whole body went stiff. Which one of these tall townhouses belonged to Samuel Barrows? Whichever one it was, Jared would be invited to that house soon. He would make Samuel Barrows' acquaintance. And then somehow, in some way, he would break the man, ruin him. Killing was too quick. Jared wanted him to live a broken man, to know what had happened, and why.

Jared remembered the first time he had heard the name Samuel Barrows spoken from his mother's lips. He had been seven years old. Life was good. He lived in the country with his mother, while his father tended business in Honolulu many miles away, making frequent visits to his family.

Jared and Leonaka were just beginning to learn responsibility, being allowed to help plant sugar cane. But they were quick to slip away to the beach and meet Dayna. The beach was their playground, surfboards their toys. One day when Jared stole away to the beach by himself he found his mother there, walking hand in hand with a tall man he had never seen before. That night he asked his mother who the strange *haole* was, and she told him. Samuel Barrows, an old friend from Boston, where his mother came from.

A week later his father came home and for the first time in his life Jared heard his parents fighting. They were in the enclosed patio at the back of the house and were unaware that Jared was in the back yard, only a few feet away.

"Who in damnation is this man John Pierce saw you embracing?" Rodney Burkett had begun.

"John?"

"Yes, our neighbor! He came all the way to Honolulu just to tell me what he saw—you and another man behaving in an unseemly manner on the beach!"

"There is no reason for you to be upset," Ranelle answered in a quiet voice. "It was just Samuel Barrows, and we embraced only to say good-bye."

"Barrows? The man you were supposed to marry? The man who married an heiress instead, because his family needed money?"

"Yes, I told you about him."

"What in God's name was he doing here?"

There was a long pause. "He—he came for me. He said he still loved me."

Something shattered against a wall, a glass or a vase. "He still loves you! What about his rich wife? Did she conveniently die?"

"Rodney, I told you there is no reason to get upset." Ranelle started crying. "He's gone now, gone back to Boston."

"You didn't answer my question, Ranelle. Is he a free man now?"

"No, he's still married. But he would have left her if I were free, regardless of the disgrace. There are no children in that marriage, and his family is solvent again. But he didn't know that I had married, that I have a son."

Quietly, in a torn voice, Rodney asked, "Did he ask you to leave me?"

"Rodney, stop it!" Ranelle pleaded. "There's no point in it. Samuel's gone—he won't ever come again."

"Did he?"

"Yes, he wanted me to go with him. He said he would

24

take Jared, too. But you can see I'm still here. I told him no!" Ranelle began screaming hysterically. "He is eight years too late! Too late!"

Jared ran down to the beach then, to get away from the sound of his mother crying. He had never heard her cry before, never heard his father's voice raised so angrily or with such pain.

Ranelle Burkett was never the same after that. She had always been a gentle and loving mother, devoting her life to her son and husband. Now she was distant, withholding her love. She no longer smiled or laughed. She began to drink heavily, and frequently cried silent, hopeless tears.

For two years Jared lived in a state of confusion. He didn't understand why his mother didn't love him anymore. He didn't understand why his parents fought all the time. And then Ranelle was expecting a baby. Rodney had first been delighted, but then things between them got even worse. Ranelle turned from melancholy to bitterness. She didn't want the new baby. Rodney stayed away from the house, but the arguments didn't stop. Now Ranelle also fought with Akela, who warned against her heavy drinking. Jared stayed away from his home as much as possible.

When Malia was born, Ranelle wanted nothing to do with her. She gave the baby over to Akela, took to her bottle again, and was hardly ever sober. Jared finally came to understand why his mother had changed. She was still in love with Samuel Barrows. He had overheard many fights between his parents, but one in particular explained much.

It occurred early one morning, just after Malia's birth, before Ranelle had a chance to find her rum. Jared was still in bed, but his room was next to his parents' and their loud voices woke him.

"For God's sake, go to him then!" Rodney was shouting. "You're no good to me anymore, you're no good to your children. You haven't been a wife or mother since that bastard Barrows came here. Yes, you gave me another child, but only because I forced myself on you."

"Please leave me alone, Rodney," Ranelle replied. "I can't help the way I feel."

His father's voice was filled with pain. "Why, Ranelle? Just tell me why? Our first eight years were good. We were happy. How could we have been so happy if you still loved him?"

"I had given him up. I thought there would never be a chance for us, don't you see? I made myself forget him. I should have waited for him. He had always intended to leave his wife after a few years, but I didn't know that. I should have waited."

"Did you ever love me, Ranelle?"

"Oh, Rodney." Ranelle started to cry. "I never wanted to hurt you. I did love you. But Samuel was my first love, and I can't help loving him still."

"Then go to him," Rodney said brokenly. "I will give you a divorce."

Ranelle laughed, but it was not a happy sound. "It's too late! He wrote me after he returned to Boston. His dear wife had a baby while he was gone, six months after he left. Now he'll never leave her."

"Ranelle, Ranelle, forget him. Can't you do that? You did it once before. Forget him again."

"How can I when I know this time that he still wants me? He proved that by coming here to find me. He loves me and I love him!"

"You must do something, Ranelle. We can't go on like this. I can't work anymore. And it's affecting Jared. He's withdrawn, he's become moody. You have got to stop drinking and start acting like a wife and mother again."

"Leave me alone, Rodney."

"Ranelle, please."

"Just go away. I don't want to talk anymore."

There was silence. But now Jared knew why his life had been turned upside down.

And when Malia was one year old, Ranelle Burkett died.

It was a stormy night, the night Jared still had nightmares about. His father was in Honolulu, and Akela had taken Malia and two-year-old Naneki to visit relatives in Kahuku for a few days. The eleven-year-old Jared had become very protective of his mother, and would not leave her alone in the house. Just the two of them were there that night.

Jared heard the patio door leading to the beach open and close, and he got out of bed to see if Akela had returned. When he found no one in the house he ran to his mother's room but found it empty, a half-filled bottle of rum lying in the middle of the bed.

He panicked, for his mother never left the house at night. He raced outside and down to the beach, screaming *Mother* over and over again. There was no answer. He wasted time searching along the shore before he saw her in the water. She was wading quickly away from the land.

Ranelle Burkett couldn't swim. All those years with the ocean at her back door, yet she'd never learned to swim. The surf was high because of the approaching storm, and Jared dove into five-foot waves to reach her, but it was as if the hand of God just swept her away. The moonless night was too dark. He couldn't see. The tears blinding his eyes hindered him, too. But he stayed in the ocean all night, looking, hoping, praying.

Dawn brought the storm, but also enough light to see by. And Jared found his mother, half a mile down the beach, washed up on the cold, wet sand. She was dead.

It was many hours before they were found, Jared sitting in the sand staring out to sea, his mother's head cradled in his lap. He couldn't keep the truth a secret, that she had killed herself, for it was well-known that she couldn't swim, that she never went into the water even to wade.

It was many years before Jared stopped blaming himself for not being able to save her. She would only have tried again, he finally realized. She had wanted to die. And Samuel Barrows had driven her to her death. By coming into her life when it was too late, he had pushed her into the sea. He was responsible for her misery and her death, and Jared would see to it that he paid.

Chapter 5

THE townhouse on Beacon Street was brightly lit and filled with fresh-cut summer flowers from the Barrows' garden. Maids in stiff black uniforms and white aprons circulated drinks among the early guests. This was to be a formal party, and guests would mingle in the large reception hall until dinner was announced.

Upstairs in Corinne's bedroom, Florence worked on her elaborate coiffure while Corinne's cousin Lauren paced nervously across the room behind them, her slippers with their tiny heels clattering noisily as she moved back and forth. This was Lauren's second formal party, and she was anxious about the impression she would make.

"Are you sure this gown is suitable?" she asked for the third time.

"Yellow becomes you, Cousin. After all, you don't want to wear anything darker at your age," Corinne said as she watched Lauren through her mirror.

"But your gown is so daring, Cori, with only those thin sequined straps to hold it up. And rose silk is so beautiful. Mother wouldn't let me have a gown like that. I'm sure I look old-fashioned."

"Oh, stop fretting. I am a bit older than you, remember," Corinne remarked impatiently. "But I suppose I forget what it was like to be sixteen. You really will be the prettiest girl at the party, so stop worrying."

Lauren smiled. "Maybe if you don't come I'll be the prettiest."

"Don't be silly. And looks aren't everything. You know most men won't look at me twice because I'm too tall for them. Small, delicate women like you are all the rage."

Lauren blushed and changed the subject. "I wonder why

28

Uncle Samuel didn't have this party on July Fourth, just a few days ago. And why didn't he give us more warning?"

"I don't know, but I don't care, either," Corinne smiled. "A party is a party."

"I suppose so. But this one was planned awfully fast. Mother had a fit because her dress wasn't finished in time and she had to wear an old one. What was the hurry, do you know?"

"There is some man Father wants his friends to meet. He decided to do it this way with a party, to please me. We haven't been getting along too well lately."

Florence gave a *humph* to that as she slid ruby pins into Corinne's hair. Florence Merrill had been with Corinne since she was a child, and she knew what was going on. The maid fastened the last pin in place, then left the room. Corinne fussed through her large jewel case.

"Will Russell be coming?" Lauren asked.

"Of course."

"Still no luck in getting your father's permission to marry him?"

"No. I haven't given up yet, but I'm beginning to think it's hopeless. Father won't even discuss it anymore. I just might have to find someone else pretty soon if Father doesn't show some signs of coming round."

"Have you anyone in mind?"

"No. It's going to be very difficult to find the man my father will approve of. He wants me to have a husband of strong will—'A man you can't boss so easily,' were his exact words. But that kind of man would defeat my whole purpose."

"I still say you should wait for love," Lauren sighed.

"No, my dear," Corinne said, her stiff lip showing her determination. "Marriage will be my life, so I must have control of it. I can always find love on the side."

"Corinne!"

"Well, it's true. In fact, I thoroughly intend to have discreet love affairs. I feel there's nothing wrong with that since I know full well that every married man does the same."

"Not *every* man."

"But most of them. So why shouldn't I?"

29

Lauren shook her head sadly. "You have such a cold outlook on life, Corinne."

"No, I'm realistic. I know what to expect from a marriage, and I know the way I want it to be. And what I don't want is a man who will try to assert his will over mine."

"Would that really be so bad?" Lauren asked. She just couldn't understand her cousin's need to rule in her marriage.

"For me it would, yes. Now help me with this necklace, will you?"

Lauren came over to fasten a tear-drop choker of rubies and gold about Corinne's neck. A matching bracelet was added, and Corinne chose a small ruby ring instead of her large one. She didn't like to overdo it. The older matrons all wore many eye-catching rings at once. Corinne liked to wear only one at a time, though she had many to choose from. She decided against ruby earrings. The glittering pins that held her long dark gold hair in place were enough.

"Who will be here tonight?" Lauren asked, nervous again now that they were ready to go downstairs.

"Just the usual crowd, though Edward and John Manning will be here with their father," Corinne said absently. "And Adrian Rankin."

Lauren smiled. These handsome young men were part of Corinne's crowd of intellectuals and artists. "What about this man your father is giving the party for? Is he young?"

"The party is for me," Corinne reminded her. "Father just decided to combine business with pleasure. But about Mr. Burk, I have no idea. But he probably isn't young."

Lauren's face changed to a look of excitement. "Did you say Burk?"

"Yes, I think Father said Jared Burk."

"Why, that's the man everyone is talking about. Haven't you heard about him?"

"No, I haven't been attending the daily social functions lately."

If Lauren only knew why I haven't, she thought. Corinne hardly ever went out in the day anymore. She spent her days sleeping because she sneaked out each night to meet Russell and a few other friends at their favorite gambling house. Her father probably knew, but he hadn't come right out and forbidden her to gamble, not even when the last club she attended asked him to pay off her debts.

Her luck had changed recently. Why, just last week she had won a considerable amount. But it was nothing compared to what she would win if she could just play in a no-limits game. Corinne's greatest desire was not to have to worry about I.O.U's that might reach her father, to be able to risk a thousand, two thousand, even fifty thousand on the turn of a card. But that day wouldn't come until she married, or until she reached twenty-one. And she was too impatient to wait.

"I overheard our fathers talking about Mr. Burk," Lauren was saying. "And my mother's friends have been gossiping about nothing else."

Corinne's interest was aroused. "What is so intriguing about this Mr. Burk?"

"That's just it. No one knows anything about him except that he's terribly rich. They don't even know where he comes from. People say he's from somewhere out West, but nobody knows for sure."

"Is that all?" Corinne was disappointed. "Just that he's rich and from somewhere out West?"

"Well, it's been rumored that he's here to invest a few of his millions."

"That would explain why my father is interested in him. What other rumors have you heard?"

"Only that he throws money around as though he had it to burn. It must be nice to be that rich."

"I wouldn't know," Corinne remarked bitterly. Someday she would have money to burn, but it wasn't fair that she had to wait.

They left Corinne's bedroom and stopped at the top of the stairs to view the brightly lit hall below. The room was filled with richly dressed people of all ages. Most had drinks in their hands, and had formed small groups. As usual, the matrons had taken to the padded benches against the walls to watch the younger people and to gossip without being overheard.

The attractive tall stranger in white evening attire stood out. "Do you think that's him?" Lauren asked.

"I don't know," Corinne admitted. "I can't see his face."

"Well, who do you know who is that tall?"

"I guess you're right. Who is he talking to?"

Lauren moved off to the left. "It's Cynthia Hamill," she called softly, returning to Corinne's side. "You should see her face. She's positively glowing."

"You know Cynthia," Corinne said drily. "She's at her most charming whenever she meets a new man."

Lauren replied with distaste, "If you ask me, she's a bit too flighty. And she flirts outrageously."

"There's nothing wrong with that, as long as you know what you're doing. It's fun. After all, it doesn't go any further than a few innocent kisses."

"Really, Corinne!"

Corinne smiled. She didn't really like Cynthia, either.

"Give yourself another year or two, Cousin, and you'll see there's nothing wrong with a little flirting."

But Lauren wasn't listening anymore. "Look! He's turning around." And then she added breathlessly, "Good heavens! Have you ever seen such a good-looking man?"

Corinne was equally surprised, not by the stranger's striking handsomeness, but by his youth. "If you like that rugged, outdoor type, I suppose not. He's younger than I imagined he would be."

"Yes. Young and rich and gorgeous!"

"Lauren, honestly! He's just another man."

Lauren couldn't take her eyes off the stranger. "Look how dark he is. He must have spent most of his life under a hot sun to get that dark."

"Not necessarily. Maybe he's a foreigner."

"A rancher, probably. They have lots of cattle ranches out West. Or maybe he's a ship's captain, or even—even a pirate! He does look like a pirate, doesn't he?"

Corinne was getting annoyed. The stranger wasn't her type. She had found that all men with superb, powerful bodies generally had strong wills to match. You couldn't dominate such a man.

"Why don't you go ask him, Lauren. Then you can stop guessing and—"

Corinne stopped abruptly and caught her breath. The stranger was looking directly up at her. His stare was magnetic, and Corinne felt a chill race down her back. His eyes penetrated hers as if he were reading her thoughts, and for a moment she couldn't move, couldn't breathe.

She finally managed to turn away. What on earth was the matter with her? She signaled to Lauren that it was time to join the party.

Jared watched with keen observation as the two young women moved languidly down the stairs in the manner of a grand entrance. The smaller, brown-haired girl with the pink complexion was pretty, but too young. Obviously shy, she kept her eyes downcast. The dark blonde was exquisite, though, an outstanding beauty. She seemed quite self-assured. Tall and stately, she was superbly proportioned, more perfect than a finely chiseled statue. Had he ever seen such ethereal beauty before? But he had to doubt such perfection, and wondered if corsets were responsible for the ideal figure.

There was something extremely compelling about this girl, and it wasn't only her beauty. There was haughtiness about her, an arrogance unusual in a woman. It would be a challenge to make this one purr!

Could she possibly be Corinne Barrows? He frowned. Ned Dougherty's report had said that she was extremely beautiful. The more he looked at this young woman, the more he thought how well she would fit in his arms. Jared fervently hoped he was not Miss Barrows, for that young woman was as much his enemy as her father was.

Corinne noted the changing expressions on the stranger's face as he watched her approach. She had seen appreciation in his eyes, even desire, but something else as well. It was as if he liked what he saw, but didn't want to. This amused Corinne. Was he married?

"It's good you could come, Cynthia," Corinne smiled as she and Lauren reached the couple. "This party was so sudden I was afraid you might have had other plans and couldn't make it."

"I almost didn't make it," Cynthia replied. "But then Father told me who the guest of honor was going to be and, well—I just had to meet him."

Cynthia was a small woman with a baby-doll prettiness. Corinne imagined that she would have fit perfectly in the Old South. But Cynthia was also very vain and did nothing to hide her vanity.

"And have you met him?"

Cynthia laughed, a tinkling sound that grated on Corinne's nerves. "You're teasing, of course. Really, Corinne, I don't know why you didn't tell me he was such a handsome and charming gentleman."

"Is this by any chance the gentleman we're discussing?" Corinne coolly nodded to Jared.

"You know it is."

"Well, you see, I haven't yet met Mr. Burk."

She was stunned by the icy gray eyes. He seemed to dislike her, yet he had never even seen her before. He quickly masked his feelings and, with a fixed smile, bowed to her.

"I don't think introductions are necessary," Jared Burk said in a deep voice. "We know each other's names."

"That is hardly proper, Mr. Burk."

"Since when are you proper, Corinne?" Cynthia laughed, getting a stabbing look in return. Cynthia recovered quickly. "You don't know Corinne's cousin, Mr. Burk. This is Lauren Ashburn."

"A pleasure, Miss Ashburn." Jared smiled at her, but she was too tongue-tied to answer and just stared at him.

A maid passed with a tray of drinks and Corinne took one. It wasn't like her to feel so ill at ease, but Jared Burk kept staring at her. Though his eyes held only interest now, she couldn't help but remember the cold look he had given her before. She was still stunned by it, and piqued that he had deprived her of a proper introduction.

"Are you aware of the rumors making the rounds about you, Mr. Burk?" Corinne asked him pointedly.

"If there are rumors, they are undoubtedly exaggerated," he replied smoothly.

"The good ones or the bad ones?" When he did not answer immediately, Corinne grinned slyly. "Have I embarrassed you, Mr. Burk?"

Cynthia was annoyed by Corinne's obvious attack, sensing Jared's discomfort. "Corinne, what's gotten into you?"

"I'm just trying to get at a few facts," Corinne replied innocently. "I only just heard about Mr. Burk today, but undoubtedly what I heard is only rumor and speculation."

"I assure you there is no great mystery about me, Miss Barrows," Jared said in a congenial tone.

"Then you won't mind answering a few questions?" Corinne ventured, no longer keeping the sharpness from her voice. "After all, you are a guest in my house, yet I know nothing about you."

"Not at all—if you will be equally frank," he countered.

Cynthia moved between them before more was said. "I haven't seen Russell yet. Isn't he coming?"

"Yes, he's coming."

"Russell Drayton is Corinne's unofficial fiancé," Cynthia offered for Jared's benefit, then beamed at Corinne. "Mr. Burk isn't married yet, either."

"Are you one of those confirmed bachelors, Mr. Burk?" Corinne questioned. "Or have you come to Boston in search of a wife—among other things?"

"I'm here on business, Miss Barrows."

"Not looking for a wife? That's too bad, isn't it, Cynthia? Why, we have some of the most refined, intelligent, sophisticated women in the world here in Boston."

"If I didn't know better, I would swear you just described yourself, Corinne," Cynthia said. "Haven't you obligations to attend to—like seeing to the rest of your guests? We would not want to detain you."

"Yes, of course. We will talk again, I'm sure, Mr. Burk. I see Russell and I really must go and greet him," Corinne said smoothly. She couldn't resist adding, "You know, Cynthia, you really shouldn't be so obvious. You might make Mr. Burk nervous. He might not be used to aggressive women like you and me."

Corinne left Cynthia blushing and heard her say, "I am not! My God, she *can* be rude when she chooses."

Corinne smiled and moved to the front of the hall. She greeted Russell with exaggerated pleasure and kissed him lingeringly before everyone, which embarrassed him considerably.

"Was that exhibition necessary?" he whispered as they walked arm in arm to join the other guests.

"It was for my father's benefit, though I doubt he was around to see it."

"He saw it, all right," Russell said tightly, looking directly at Samuel Barrows' disapproving stare.

"So there you are, Father," Corinne greeted him. "Where have you been hiding? I didn't see you earlier."

Samuel's arm slipped possessively around his daughter's waist. "There was some trouble at the shipyard. Nothing serious, but it did require my attention. I didn't think it would take so long, though."

"Well, at least you're back before dinner," Corinne teased lightly. "I wouldn't have forgiven you if I had had to act as both host and hostess."

"You would have managed superbly."

"I know, but you would never have heard the end of it," she smiled.

Samuel nodded stiffly to Russell, then ignored him. "Have you met Jared Burk yet, Cori?"

"Yes, though I can't say I like him."

"Oh? Did he say something to upset you?"

"No, it's just a feeling. I can't explain it, but the man seems—well, dangerous."

"Come now, Cori," Samuel laughed. "He's interesting, but I wouldn't say dangerous."

"Why have you taken such a liking to him, Father? You can't know very much about him."

"I don't, to tell the truth. But I do have it on good authority that he's here to invest a sizeable sum of money. His lawyer has been all over town making inquiries."

"So? What has that to do with you?"

"Will you excuse us, Mr. Drayton?" Samuel said curtly. "This conversation has become rather personal."

"Father, really!" Corinne complained.

"That's quite all right," Russell said. "I could use a drink, anyway."

Corinne fumed as Russell walked away. "That was uncalled for, Father."

"I suppose so, but I'm not going to pretend I like Russell Drayton."

"Obviously, but he's going to marry *me*, not you!" Corinne snapped furiously. "You don't have to like him—just approve of him."

"I can't do that either, nor will I discuss it anymore. Now about Mr. Burk—"

"To hell with Mr. Burk!" Corinne cut him off in fury and stalked away to find Russell.

The party progressed successfully without much attention from Corinne. Dinner, served in the formal dining room, was superb. There was roast chicken in a glazed orange sauce, and three varieties of beef, as well as a variety of vegetables and sauces.

Corinne, annoyed with her father, ignored him throughout the meal. Mr. Burk, however, she couldn't ignore. She often found him staring curiously at her, and despite her first reaction to him, her own gaze was drawn to him again and again. She began to feel guilty about her earlier behavior. After all, she really had no excuse for being so rude to him. She could have misinterpreted that look he gave her. And the more she thought about it, the more she was convinced that she must have been mistaken. It could have been any number of things unrelated to her that caused the venom in his eyes for that one moment.

After dinner the guests gathered in the parlor to be entertained by a well-known singer, with Lauren accompanying at the piano. A few of Samuel Barrows' friends and Jared Burk were not present, however, having joined Samuel in his study. Corinne couldn't help wondering what her father was up to.

Later, after all the guests except Russell had departed, Corinne, saw a chance to speak with her father again. She saw Russell to the door, endured his amorous embrace, then promised to meet him the next night at the club. The party preparations had kept her busy for most of the week and she was eager to try her luck again.

Now with the hall quiet once again, Corinne crossed slowly to the closed door of her father's study. The light coming from beneath the door showed her he was still there. She supposed she owed him an apology. She was sorry she missed seeing Mr. Burk again before he left, for she owed him an apology too. She felt like a small child again, with all the misbehaving she had done in one evening.

Just as Corinne reached for the doorknob, the door opened and her father and Jared Burk emerged from the room. Corinne was quite surprised, but glad to see she had not missed Burk after all.

"Still up, Cori?" Samuel observed. "Good, you can see Mr. Burk out."

"That is unnecessary," Jared said.

Corinne shrugged aside his objection as her father went back into his study. "Come along, Mr. Burk. I had hoped for a few minutes alone with you. I'll just get your things from the cloak room."

She returned in a moment with a satin-lined evening cloak and a tall silk hat. "These must be yours," she said, rubbing her fingers over the soft satin. "Very nice."

He smiled at her as he threw the heavy cloak over his wide shoulders. "We are alone, Miss Barrows. What did you have in mind?"

His tone of voice implied a great deal, but she let it pass and kept her temper.

"I just wanted to let you know how sorry I am for my behavior earlier. There was no excuse for asking you questions that were none of my business."

"You did seem to attack me with a purpose in mind," he recalled. "Perhaps if I knew why?"

She laughed and blushed at the same time. "I suppose it did seem that way."

"And the reason?"

"I'm afraid I took offence at the way you looked at me when I first joined you this evening—as if you wanted to throttle me. I don't usually get that kind of reaction from men."

Jared frowned. "If I gave that impression, then it is I who must apologize to you. I had other things on my mind at the time."

"Yes, after I thought about it, I realized that must have been the reason."

"We've gotten off to a bad start, Miss Barrows," Jared said as he walked slowly to the entrance door. "Perhaps we should start again. Tomorrow, over lunch? That is, if your Mr. Drayton won't mind."

He said it in the way of a challenge, and Corinne couldn't resist that. "Lunch would be nice. You can call for me around noon."

"At noon, then."

He paused for a moment and stared at her, and Corinne felt goose bumps spread over her arms. She quickly rubbed them.

"Good evening, Miss Barrows."

She nodded. "Mr. Burk."

He was gone and she sighed in relief. Something about that man disturbed her, but she didn't know what. She shook off the feeling and went back to her father's study. She found him still at his desk, going over papers.

"You're not supposed to work after a party, Father," she scolded as she came into the room.

"I'm not working, my dear," Samuel replied, putting the papers down. "Actually, I was looking over your grandmother's will."

"Whatever for?" Corinne frowned. "This hasn't anything to do with Mr. Burk, does it?"

"In a way, yes. He asked about the owners of the shipbuilding firm. I was just checking to be sure I gave him the correct facts without giving him all of them."

"Just what are you talking about?"

"Sit down, Cori. As you know, my father founded the shipyard, but it was on its last legs when I married your mother. Your mother's money helped, but it was your Grandmother Daneil who saved the shipyard. She became a full partner, but left the running of the yard to me. Later, when we expanded, Elliot invested, and now he and I run it together."

"What has this to do with Mr. Burk? You're not thinking of letting him invest in the firm, are you?"

"Yes," Samuel said frankly. "Elliot and I have been considering enlarging the yard for many years. We just can't meet demand as it is."

"Then use your own money," she suggested. "Why bring someone else into it?"

"By taking another partner, we will increase profits, our customers will get quicker results, but it will cost us nothing."

"And where does this put Mr. Burk?"

"He will be a silent partner, not an active one. After all, the man isn't planning on settling here in Boston, not as far as I know. He will own shares in the firm which will double his investment in a few years, but he will have no control and very little voting power. Elliot and I own equal shares, but you are the major stockholder, since your grandmother left you all her shares."

"Why not get an investor that you know, then? One of your old cronies. Why Mr. Burk?"

"Because I'm sure he doesn't plan to stay here. He won't be underfoot, constantly inquiring about his interests. And there is no way Mr. Burk could ever get control of the firm, just in case he has that in mind."

"He could marry me," Corinne teased. "That would put him in control."

Samuel grinned. "You like him, then? He's a very intriguing fellow."

"I was only speaking hypothetically, Father," Corinne answered quickly, appalled.

She could just see herself married to a man like that. He would rule with an iron hand, worse than her father did.

"Well, even if you did marry Mr. Burk, he could not have control of your shares unless I decided he was trustworthy. And I doubt that I would decide in his favor until the day I died."

"I thought when I reached twenty-one that I would be in control. Are you saying I won't be?"

"That's why I was looking over your grandmother's will. The money will be yours when you become of age or marry, but control of your shares is still left to me, until I feel you are ready to take over. And if you are married then, I will have to have confidence in your husband, also."

"Why? I don't understand why grandmother gave you that power. She didn't even like you."

"I know," Samuel chuckled. "She knew I married your mother for her money, which was and still is a common practice. Not that I didn't care for Mary, mind you. But Daneil knew that I would look after your best interests, and that's what she wanted to ensure."

"Why didn't you ever tell me about this before?" Corinne asked.

"Because it doesn't really affect you, Cori," he answered easily. "You're not planning on participating in the running of the firm, are you?"

"Of course not."

"So you see, it makes no difference. I maintain control of the firm, but the profits from your shares still go to you as they always have."

"I haven't seen any of these profits!" Corinne remarked bitterly.

"They have gone into your trust, more than doubling it since your grandmother's death. They will come directly to you when you are of age."

"Or when I marry?"

"Yes."

"You know, if you could just give me some of that money now, Father, I wouldn't be in such a hurry to marry," Corinne suggested.

"And have you lose it all? No, my girl. I just hope when you finally do get your money, you show some sense in what you do with it. The two hundred you get monthly now comes from your trust, but what do you have to show for it?"

"I spend money on clothes," she said defensively. "And jewels."

"You charge those to *me!* You throw your own money away."

"This conversation has become boring. Good night, Father." Corinne rose stiffly and stalked from the room.

Chapter 6

JARED Burk called at the Barrows' townhouse promptly at noon, but was kept waiting for thirty minutes. Corinne didn't do it on purpose, as she sometimes did with her other callers. She had actually overslept, forgetting to tell Florence to wake her early.

When she finally came downstairs to meet him, Jared's eyes showed that he didn't mind the wait. She wore a simple dress without frills, elegant because of the rich silk poplin material. Bottle-green, it was a few shades darker than her eyes. The high collar was ribboned in a darker green, with an ornate diamond broach. A large diamond and emerald ring was her only other jewelry.

After a few words of greeting and the customary compliments on Jared's part, they left in Jared's hired carriage. He allowed her the choice of restaurants, since he was not acquainted with the better establishments, and she chose a small cafe that she often enjoyed. The food was excellent and the atmosphere friendly.

Jared ordered lunch for them both, making a choice Corinne silently approved of, and a light wine was served immediately. After taking a few sips, Corinne relaxed a bit and observed her escort boldly.

He was smartly dressed in a dark blue suit, opened to reveal a light blue silk vest with mother-of-pearl buttons. His rugged good looks, his expensive clothes, his entire appearance commanded attention. His face was smoothly shaved, and she still wondered how he had acquired such a deep tan. Corinne felt the envy of the other women in the room, and this pleased her vanity.

"Is something wrong, Miss Barrows?" Jared finally asked, after he had allowed her scrutiny to continue for several moments.

She blushed slightly. "I didn't mean to stare. I've just never met anyone as darkly tanned as you are. It must be terribly hot where you come from."

"You get used to it," he replied noncommittally, and quickly changed the subject. "I must say I expected a chaperone to join us today."

Corinne laughed. "Whatever for? We live in a new age, Mr. Burk. Chaperones are old-fashioned."

"Not everyone feels that way."

"You, for instance?"

"Yes," he admitted. "Frankly, I'm surprised your father doesn't insist on a chaperone for you."

"My father is quite tolerant where I am concerned. He has always given me complete freedom, so I have learned to be cautious. I avoid dangerous situations. Have I something to fear from you, Mr. Burk?" she asked coyly, thoroughly amused by his archaic ideas.

He grinned before answering. "That depends on what your fears are."

"Meaning?"

"Some women fear what others don't."

Lunch was served. Though Jared never gave her questions direct answers, he asked her many. He quizzed her about Boston, and she proudly related some of its history.

She relaxed and enjoyed his company. He could be charming and witty, and when he laughed, his eyes were more blue than gray. But afterwards, on the ride home, she was taken by surprise when he began questioning her again, and in a personal vein.

"I find it unusual that your fiancé didn't object to our meeting today."

"He didn't know about it," she admitted. "But he wouldn't have said anything if he had."

"You intend to tell him?"

"Our lunch was perfectly harmless, Mr. Burk. And besides, I am not answerable to Russell."

"But you are engaged to marry him?"

"Not officially—not until my father gives his approval, that is."

"Then Mr. Drayton hasn't asked for you yet?"

Corinne became uncomfortable. "Really, Mr. Burk. That is none of your business."

The carriage stopped on Beacon Street, but Jared didn't move to open the door. "You're quite right, of course. I just find it strange that a man who plans to marry you would allow you to see other men."

"Allow?" Corinne felt her temper rising. "No one *allows* me anything. I do whatever I please, Mr. Burk. Russell wouldn't presume to put restrictions on our relationship."

"You're very independent, aren't you?" he commented.

"Yes, I am," she said proudly. "I value the freedom I have gained."

"But you are willing to give it up when you marry. You must love Mr. Drayton very much."

"Of course I love him," she lied, knowing how callous it would sound if she admitted the truth. "But Russell and I have a very agreeable relationship, Mr. Burk. I won't be giving up my independence when I marry him."

"Then he is a very . . . unusual fellow."

"Yes, he is—quite different from most men."

"You mean he's weak, don't you?" he asked contemptuously.

"Certainly not!" she replied indignantly, wondering why she had allowed this inquisition to go on so long.

"Then he loves you enough to give you whatever you want, including the independence you value so much?"

"I think, Mr. Burk, that your boldness has gone far enough. I have told you much more than you have a right to know."

He grinned. "I apologize, Miss Barrows. But I have never met anyone quite like you. I find your ideas fascinating."

"You are teasing me now, and I don't like it," she said icily. "I know you don't approve. Your type never does."

"My type?" he raised a brow in amusement. "Have you put me into a category, Miss Barrows?"

She ignored the question. "I enjoyed lunch, Mr. Burk. Thank you for inviting me."

Corinne reached for the door handle herself, but Jared stopped her by placing his hand over hers. A strong current seemed to pass between them. The strength in his fingers seemed to drain her own.

She was shaken. She looked at him questioningly. "I—I wish to go in now," she said weakly.

His gray-blue eyes probed her face as if he were trying to read her thoughts. "I know. But I want to see you again."

"Why?"

"I find I like you very much, Miss Barrows."

"I'm afraid I can't return the compliment," she said frankly.

"I have offended you and I'm sorry. But I really would like to see you again. Tonight for dinner? And the theater, perhaps?"

"No, Mr. Burk. After last night's party, I have decided to spend a quiet evening at home tonight."

"Then tomorrow?"

"I hardly see the point. We really have nothing in common. And Russell might not understand."

"I thought you weren't answerable to Mr. Drayton?"

"I'm not."

"Then you will see me again?"

"I will have to think about it, Mr. Burk." This time she did not accept the bait. "Good day."

He opened the door for her then, and Corrinne rushed out of the carriage without waiting for him to help her. Nor did she wait for him to follow and escort her to her door, but ran quickly up the steps and into the safety of her home without looking back.

Her heart pounded frantically as she leaned against the door. She didn't know what had frightened her so about those last few moments in the carriage. Jared Burk had stopped her temporarily from leaving, but that was not the reason. Was it Jared Burk himself? More likely it was his touch, for she had never felt so drained of will and strength as she did when his strong fingers closed over hers. She was stunned by her own reaction, for nothing like that had ever happened to her before.

What was wrong with her? He was just another man, the kind of man she avoided. She had sensed a dangerous quality about him when she first met him and she had been right. He had made her lose control of herself, if only for a moment, and that was extremely dangerous.

Jared had started to escort Corinne to her door, but before he even stepped from the carriage, she was inside the imposing townhouse and the door was closed. He sat back down and then noticed the green silk purse on the opposite seat. He picked up the purse, thinking to return it, but abruptly changed his mind and signaled the driver to return to his hotel.

Jared leaned back and stared thoughtfully at the silk purse, picturing it attached to that slender wrist. He frowned as he wondered what had caused Corinne to run into her house the way she did, as if she were frightened of him. She had good reason to be, but she couldn't possibly know that. Oh, he had baited her, antagonized her even, in order to judge her character. And it had worked.

He had the haughty Corinne Barrows halfway figured out. He knew she took offense easily. She was spoiled, and was allowed much too much freedom. Someday that would get her into trouble, but that didn't concern him. She was a cool one, sure of her beauty and the effect it had on men.

No decisions had been reached yet, but Jared had only a few options left out of all those he had considered. He had all the facts he needed about Samuel Barrows, and some surprising ones about his daughter. All that remained was to decide what to do with the information he had.

He was hoping that his investment in Barrows' shipyard would yield him a certain amount of control in the firm, enough to block major decisions and ultimately destroy the firm. It was Barrows' major source of income. His other interests amounted to nothing in comparison. Of course, Jared's money would also be lost when the shipyard went under, but nothing mattered except ruining Samuel Barrows. That shipyard meant everything to him. He had devoted most of his life to it. He had turned away the woman who loved him in order to save it. Now Barrows would lose all he had worked for.

Out of mild curiosity, Jared opened the purse he held. He removed a silk handkerchief with lace edging, a few dollars, a compact of light powder. He opened the lid from a small vial of perfume and smelled the delicate fragrance Corinne had worn.

One item startled him—a tiny knife with a short, sharp blade, encrusted with jewels, no less! He couldn't imagine the sophisticated Corinne ever using it.

The last thing he took from the purse was a slip of paper with an address on it. The paper was crumpled as if it had been read many times. Jared had learned this address from Ned Dougherty.

Sure, he had doubted Dougherty's assertion that Corinne Barrows went to this place two or three times a week in the middle of the night. But wasn't he looking at the proof right now, the address of a private gambling house in Cambridge across the Charles River? And not just a gambling house, but a place where gentlemen brought their lady loves for a little dalliance on the second floor. A little luck with the cards, a little lust upstairs.

Jared's opinion of Corinne Barrows decreased even more. Regrets? He would have absolutely none now, if he were eventually forced to use her to accomplish his plans.

Chapter 7

CORINNE glanced at the clock on the mantle and impatiently began to tap her foot. One o'clock in the morning. She hated to be rushed.

"Florence, please hurry," Corinne said petulantly. "Russell will be down the street any moment now."

"If your hair wasn't so silky, it would be easier to put up," Florence replied, unperturbed. "And it won't hurt Russell Drayton to wait a spell. He shouldn't be out there anyway," she added disapprovingly.

"Now don't start on me tonight," Corinne returned. "I'm in no mood."

"You're never in a mood to listen to reason," Florence reminded her, though she never tired of trying. "Sneaking out in the middle of the night! One of these days you're going to regret these little adventures, you mark my word. A lady just doesn't do these things."

Corinne grinned mischievously. "Would you like to come with me to see I don't get into trouble? I'm sure Russell won't mind."

Florence actually looked shocked. Though she was only fifteen years older than Corinne, her morals were those of a much older generation.

"I can just see me in that fancy gambling house. Why, my mother, God rest her soul, would come back to haunt me. And your mother's probably been turning in her grave for quite a while, knowing what you're about."

"Now don't you try and make me feel guilty, because it won't work, do you hear?" Corinne snapped. "Lord, is it a crime to put a little excitement in my life? Gambling is fun, Florence. It's thrilling," she tried to explain. "And it's not as if I didn't know what I was doing. I've learned how to play the games, and I'm really quite good."

48

"You know you're doing wrong or you wouldn't be sneaking out of the house, and by the servants' entrance, no less. Nor would you be wearing that special cloak to disguise yourself." She gave an indignant snort. "Cheap pauper's wool, as if you couldn't afford better."

Corinne looked at the dowdy cloak lying across the foot of her bed. "No one will recognize me in it."

"You're going to disgrace this family yet, Corinne Barrows. A scandal, mind you, and one you'll never live down, because it will be the first to touch the Barrows name."

"I'll never bring scandal to this family!"

"And just how—"

"You didn't let me finish," Corinne interrupted. "Why do you think I pick clubs so far away? Because I won't be known there. In all the time I've been going, I've seen only two people I recognized at the clubs."

"You see!"

"But they won't spread rumors about me, because they have their own secrets to hide."

"Your father found out, didn't he?" Florence reminded her. "Lord knows why he didn't put his foot down then and there. I thought for sure that would be the end of it."

"Well, he didn't. I suppose he thinks I'll outgrow it. And I will stop, just as soon as I can play in that one no-limit game I've been dreaming about for so long."

"You're obsessed, Cori. You've got to stop soon. Gambling can be a disease for some. They just can't ever quit."

"That won't happen to me," Corinne said with confidence.

With the last pin in place, forming a severely tight coiffure, and dressed in lavender velvet with long sleeves and a high collar, Corinne was ready to go. She withdrew her money from a locked drawer, then looked about for her purse. When she couldn't find it, she frowned. Her expensive little knife was in that purse, and she always liked to carry it with her, especially at night.

"Have you seen the green silk purse I had with me today, Florence?"

"No."

"Then I must have left it in the carriage today. I'm sure I had it when we left the cafe."

"You haven't said very much about what happened today," Florence remarked.

"Because there was nothing to tell. I had a very boring time."

"Oh?"

"Don't 'oh' me," Corinne said irritably, hearing the doubt in Florence's voice. "Just get me another purse. I'm late enough as it is."

Soon, concealed to her satisfaction, Corinne tiptoed through the house as she had countless other nights, and slipped out the servants' entrance. And there, waiting a block down the street, was faithful Russell, ready for tonight's escapade.

Smoke gathered above the room like a heavy blanket, from the many cigars, cigarettes, and pipes of the gentlemen present. The smoke could not escape the room, for the windows were tightly closed and heavily curtained. To the passerby, the house looked like any other, but to the occupants inside, it was a hotbed of excitement. Fortunes could be won or lost here, and love affairs could continue in the strictest of privacy.

Corinne had never investigated the upper regions of the house. She sometimes wondered what it was like up there, but she had never found out. Russell had tried to get her to go up with him a few times—for a private drink, he would coax. But she was no fool. She knew what he wanted. But he just didn't have the power to make her want it too.

It made Corinne sick one night when a girl's screams were heard from upstairs, yet no one downstairs moved. No one had gone to the poor girl's rescue.

Why, anything could happen on the second floor, even murder, for the two parts of the house were completely separate. It was a rule that no two couples could leave the gambling hall at the same time. That way, if a couple wished to slip upstairs for a few hours before going home, no one could witness it.

Corinne could see the sense in that rule, but it irked her, for she could just imagine the men in the gambling room speculating, when she left, on whether or not she went upstairs with her escort. It was a constant embarrassment to her.

Nine round tables filled the brightly lit room. The house did not supply dealers at each table, but the house did very well by collecting money from each player before each new game was played. Different games of chance were played at different tables. Corinne often preferred faro, a game in which each player took turns being the banker, or blackjack, the deal passing with each new twenty-one. She had learned to judge the odds well in the latter, and was ecstatic whenever she was dealt a blackjack, the desired ace and face card which paid double and gave her the deal. But though she did well in blackjack, she liked the poker tables best of all. With a little trickery, she could bluff herself a winning hand.

Corinne loved to bluff in poker. She wore elegant, yet prim gowns for the express purpose of keeping her figure from distracting from her face. Her expressions fooled many a player. Once they caught onto her, though, she would change tactics and fool them again. Even Russell could not tell when she was bluffing.

Tonight Corinne felt lucky. She had already won three hands out of the first five. The others at her table, three gentlemen and a brashly dressed young woman, did not show exceptional skill. Russell went to play blackjack once he was assured that the men at Corinne's table were interested in cards, and not in her.

"Draw poker," the dealer called, and dealt five cards to each player.

The other gentleman next to Corinne opened, and after she examined her cards and found a straight possible, she called. One other player called, and when it was Corinne's turn to draw, she took one card to fill her straight. It was not the card she wanted, but a slight raising of her eyelids said it was. The opener checked to her one card draw and Corinne bet the limit, then sat back and waited. The other player did not hesitate to fold, but the opener took a few minutes to make up his mind before he, too, dropped out.

Corinne threw in her cards and raked in the chips. She won quite a bit during the next hour, though with good cards rather than bluffing. She was enjoying herself immensely until Jared Burk sat down at her table.

She was stunned to see him sitting there across from her, dressed in black evening attire, grinning sardonically. Corinne was mortified that he had found her here, after she had told him she would be spending a quiet evening at home. What must he think? Was that why he was grinning?

"Maybe my luck will change now, with new blood in the game," said one of the players.

"Perhaps," Jared replied smoothly. "But it is hard to entice lady luck away from a—lady."

Corinne felt her cheeks flaming. She had detected the sarcasm in his voice.

"Five card stud," Corinne called in a stiff voice that was not lost on Jared. She dealt the cards quickly, putting an end to conversation.

From that moment on, Corinne lost. Every bit of her winnings and the money she had brought with her was transferred across the table as the hours passed. Corinne became furious with herself. No matter how hard she tried, she just couldn't concentrate on the game. She didn't look at Jared, but she could feel his eyes mocking her. It infuriated her so that she could hardly see the cards she held, and had to be repeatedly reminded when it was her turn to bet or call. What must he think?

The final straw was looking at three kings in her hand, knowing she could finally beat Jared, and not having the chips left to bet with. She would not give Jared Burk the satisfaction of seeing her sign an I.O.U. to finish the hand.

"This hand is not worth betting anyway," she lied, with a smile to cover her frustration. "I think I've had enough for tonight."

Feigning boredom, Corinne left the table and crossed to the long bar built against a wall. She ordered a straight whiskey. She wasn't used to hard liquor, but why not? There was a first time for everything.

She had nothing better to do than sit there and get drunk. Russell was winning and would not want to leave yet.

"So this is how you spend a quiet evening at home, Miss Barrows?"

She turned to find Jared beside her, leaning smugly against the bar, his winnings in his hat. He swung the hat slowly to and fro.

"It's not evening, Mr. Burk," she said caustically, her temper surfacing. "It's almost morning."

"So it is."

She glared at him, but he was not deterred. "I see you're angry with me," he said. "I'm not surprised, though. Most women are poor losers."

"And most men!"

"True. We have that in common, don't we? For I'm a very bad loser myself."

She knew that he did not mean only at cards. She took a swallow of her drink, then nearly gagged as the fiery liquid seared her throat.

"So now you will drown your sorrows?" he taunted her. "I thought you had more spirit, Corinne."

She frowned. "I did not give you leave to use my first name, Mr. Burk."

"Isn't it time we stopped being so formal?"

"I think not," she replied haughtily.

Jared smiled. He looked away from her for a moment and his eyes fell on Russell. The man was obviously an utter fool, Jared thought contemptuously. He should have more sense than to bring his intended bride to an establishment like this. And then to leave her to her own devices! Why, anyone could whisk her out of here, and Russell Drayton wouldn't know of it for some time.

"Would you like me to escort you home?" When Corinne glanced at him suspiciously, he added, "Since your fiancé is otherwise occupied."

"No thank you," Corinne said coldly. "I don't mind waiting for Russell."

"Perhaps you would like a small loan, then," he offered. "So you can continue to play? I did so enjoy your company at the table."

"You mean you enjoyed winning my money!" she replied bitterly.

He shrugged, then grinned, his eyes dancing. "That, too."

"I never borrow money when I come here, Mr. Burk." She lied convincingly, but kept her eyes averted. "I set my limits and stick to them."

"Very commendable," he said drily. "Is that why you're wearing no jewels tonight? Afraid you might be tempted to gamble them away?"

She couldn't help smiling at his perception. Did the man know everything?

"I did get a bit carried away the first time I came to an

53

establishment like this," she admitted. "I lost a valuable diamond broach on the turn of a card. Since then I have left my jewels at home."

"You talk as if you come here often."

She was stung by the condemnation in his voice. "I do," she replied defiantly. "I can afford to."

"But can you afford to have it known?"

Corinne frowned. "Is that a threat, Mr. Burk? Are you implying that *you* will make it known?"

"I wouldn't dream of tarnishing your good name," Jared assured her.

"But you feel that I am doing so by coming here?" When he shrugged, she continued angrily. "No one knows me here, Mr. Burk. And if someone did, they would say nothing out of respect for my father."

"But you take that risk?"

"I come here to gamble. I gamble in that respect as well. Besides, it's really none of your business, is it?"

Jared acquiesced with a slight nod. "I will say no more. But I still offer you a ride home." When she started to refuse him again, he added, "Once I leave, Miss Barrows, you will be swarmed by gentlemen wanting to make the acquaintance of a beautiful woman whom they will presume is alone. There is no need to put yourself through that."

"I can take care of myself," she said, her proud nose rising in the air.

"Forgive me. I only assumed you wouldn't want that kind of attention. Perhaps I was wrong."

He was utterly infuriating.

"I don't relish being bothered, Mr. Burk. I just feel I should wait for Russell."

"Why?" he asked pointedly. "He's not even aware that you are waiting." Then he conceded graciously, "Though I'm sure he would come to you if he were aware of it." She knew he didn't mean it.

"Is it my presence that is stopping you from accepting my offer?" Jared suggested in a soft tone. "You're not afraid to be alone with me again, are you?"

"Certainly not!"

"Well, then?"

Corinne looked at her empty glass. She had convinced

herself earlier that she had nothing to fear from this man, so why was she hesitating?

"Very well," she smiled agreeably. "If you will just give me a few minutes to tell Russell that I'm leaving."

"Is that really necessary?"

"Why, Mr. Burk," Corinne teased lightly. "You wouldn't want my fiancé to think I had deserted him?" She leaned closer and whispered, "He might think I've gone upstairs, and then cause quite a scene looking for me."

Corinne laughed softly at the startled look on Jared's face before she moved to Russell's table. Let Jared Burk think whatever he wanted, she didn't care for his opinion anyway. And it had been such a pleasure to shock him, to see that arrogant look leave his face for a moment! She felt much better now.

She waited patiently for Russell to finish his hand before she attracted his attention. He was reluctant to leave his table, but he came to her anyway.

"Russell, dear, I didn't want to interrupt you and take you away from your game, but it would be remiss of me not to tell you that I'm leaving."

"Leaving? Why?"

"I lost my money rather quickly."

Russell looked back at his own winnings. "I can't leave yet, Corinne. My luck's been too good tonight. If you need some more money—"

"No, Russell, you know I never borrow from you. Besides, I am rather tired. And you needn't leave your game. Mr. Burk has kindly offered to take me home."

"Burk is here?" Russell frowned, and looked about the room, spotting Jared waiting at the bar. "I don't like that man, Corinne. He seems too much the adventurous type to me, or more like a mercenary."

"Don't be ridiculous, Russell," Corinne scoffed. "He may give the impression that he's ruthless, but he's perfectly harmless. And he *is* going to be a partner of mine very soon. Father feels we need his money, so I can't very well be rude to him, now can I?"

Russell looked back at his winnings once again, an avaricious gleam in his dark gray eyes. "I suppose not. But do be careful, Corinne."

"What do you mean?"

"I know how you flirt when the mood suits you. I wouldn't trifle with Burk if I were you."

She ignored his warning. "It's strictly a business relationship, Russell, no more."

The enclosed carriage Corinne found herself in was not quite so large as the one Jared had used to take her to lunch in, nor was it as comfortable. Corinne nearly swore aloud when a bump in the road almost unseated her.

"I must apologize for this conveyance." Jared spoke from the dark interior. "But it was the best I could find on short notice. To tell you the truth, I wasn't too sure the driver would wait as I had paid him to do."

"You should consider hiring your own driver," Corinne suggested impulsively. "That is, if you plan to be here much longer."

"I don't," he replied.

"So you plan to invest your money and run?"

"If you wish to put it that bluntly, yes," Jared answered without hesitating.

"And have you made a decision about our firm yet? Or if you'd rather not say, I'll understand."

Jared smiled, though Corinne could not see it in the dark. "Would I be making a sound investment if I did?"

"Certainly." Pride slipped into her voice. "I've made a fortune over the years myself, so I've been told."

"Don't you know?"

"My money is in a trust, Mr. Burk, that my grandmother arranged for me. It contains the money she left me, plus all the shares she owned in the shipyard. But my father has control of it until I marry."

"With his approval?"

"Yes."

"I take it you don't care for those terms?" Jared asked casually. "I mean, considering how fond you are of being independent?"

"I don't mind having to get my father's approval to marry," Corinne replied. "What I mind is having to wait for my money in the meantime. I mean, there is all that money just sitting there, and my father doesn't give me enough to meet my needs."

"I find that hard to believe."

"My spending money would be sufficient for most women, but it isn't for me."

"Because of your gambling?"

Corinne gasped. He was so perceptive it was frightening. "I just want control of my own money, Mr. Burk. Wouldn't you?"

"Yes, but when you marry, you still won't have control. Your husband will."

Corinne laughed softly. "No, he won't."

"I don't understand."

"It's quite simple, Mr. Burk. You see, that's one of the agreements Russell and I have. He understands that I can't tolerate restraint. When I marry, I will be free."

"I see."

And Jared finally did see. In Russell Drayton, she had found herself the perfect husband. Perfect for her.

"If it only takes getting married to get what you want, why haven't you done so yet?" Jared asked curiously, hoping Corinne would continue to talk on this personal level without getting suspicious. "Is Mr. Drayton afraid to confront your imposing father?"

Corinne could see Jared's face only when the carriage passed a street lamp and light filtered in. She couldn't see his expression at that moment, but he did not sound as if he were baiting her.

"The truth is, Mr. Burk, Russell has seen my father about me, but my father refused him."

"I'm sorry."

"Don't be. My father will come around."

"He doesn't strike me as a man who changes his mind easily," Jared remarked.

Jared had touched on a sore subject. And he was right. Samuel Barrows hardly ever changed his mind. He had put very few restrictions on Corinne's life, but when he did, there was nothing that could make him reverse his decision. This would be different, though, Corinne told herself. He just *had* to give in this time.

"When he sees how set I am on this marriage, he will relent," she said with more confidence than she felt.

"Then perhaps I will be invited to the wedding?"

"If you are still here," Corinne said lightly.

"By the way, you left your purse behind today, or rather,

yesterday. Had I known I would see you again so soon, I would have brought it along."

"I was afraid I had lost it for good." Corinne was relieved. "I will send someone around to pick it up at your hotel tomorrow, if that will be convenient?"

"It won't be necessary at all. I will return it when I pick you up for dinner tonight."

"I haven't said I will dine with you, Mr. Burk," Corinne replied saucily.

Jared grinned slyly. "Isn't that the least you can do, after I left a perfectly good winning streak back there just to bring you home?"

Corinne laughed, actually enjoying the banter. "You make yourself sound like a martyr. I didn't ask for your services, you know. In fact, you were quite persistent."

"I suppose I'm just chivalrous at heart, unable to resist a lady in distress."

"Is that what I was?"

"Weren't you?" he countered.

"Very well, I will have dinner with you tonight—if you tell me how you happened to be at the club. It's not exactly a public spot."

"My lawyer told me about it," Jared replied easily. "In fact, if he hadn't been along, I probably would not have gotten in."

"You mean he was with you, and you just left him?"

The carriage came to a stop just then. "I'll go back for him."

Corinne smiled. "You really have gone out of your way just to bring me home, haven't you?"

"I enjoyed it," he said casually, and opened the door. He made sure he got out first to help her down.

Corinne felt strangely happy all of a sudden. He had gone to so much trouble for her.

He held her elbow until they reached the front door of her house. Dawn was just creeping over the horizon, but Corinne felt wide awake.

"I'm going to kiss you, Corinne Barrows," Jared said suddenly.

Before she could react, he had pulled her into his arms. It was a gentle yet forceful kiss, and Corinne didn't have the will to resist for more than a moment. He did not press her tightly against him as Russell often tried to do, but just held her firmly enough so she couldn't escape.

He released her. "Before you bite my head off for taking such a liberty, you have to know that nothing could have stopped me just then. Not you, nor my own will. I felt compelled to kiss you and couldn't resist doing so."

Corinne smiled. "You disappoint me—Jared. I wouldn't have expected you to apologize."

She left him like that, completely surprised and pleased by her response.

Chapter 8

CORINNE sauntered into the parlor. "So there you are, Father. What are you doing, sitting here in the dark?" Samuel was slouched in a large, comfortable chair with a brandy in one hand. "The fire gives enough light, and it's more peaceful this way," he replied, turning a speculative gaze on his daughter. "You're all dressed up? Have you plans for this evening?"

Corinne went to stand by the fireplace, lifting her skirts a little to warm her legs. September nights were getting much too chilly. She made a mental note to wear something warmer later that night.

"Jared is taking me to a recital. He should be here shortly."

"Jared, is it?" Samuel raised a brow. "I didn't know your relationship with Mr. Burk had become so intimate."

"Don't be silly," Corinne admonished. "It's just that I feel foolish calling him Mr. Burk after he has been my escort more than a dozen times in the last two months." She did not include the many times he had taken her to the gambling club. "We've enjoyed dinners, luncheons, the theater. He even took me to the Compton's ball, which you were too busy to attend, and we've gone upstate for the races."

"My, my," Samuel mused, pretending he didn't know his daughter's every move. He knew all about her dates with Burk. "What has happened to Mr. Drayton? Is he no longer in the picture?"

Corinne stiffened. "Russell had to go to New York in the middle of summer."

"Business—or pleasure?"

"Neither," Corinne snapped. "His mother's people live

60

there. His grandfather is ill and the doctors warn that he might not recover. Russell says he's really quite old. Anyway, it was only proper that he go."

"And so you have turned to Mr. Burk in his absence?" Samuel asked pointedly.

"You really can be exasperating at times, Father," Corinne retorted. "Russell will be back any time now, and he will be my husband eventually. I simply see no reason to confine myself while he's gone."

Samuel frowned. "You're not leading Jared Burk on just because you need an escort, are you, Cori? He's not a man to trifle with."

"I've been told that before," she laughed. "But no, Father. Jared knows how I feel about Russell, that I intend to marry him. We enjoy each other's company, that's all. He really has turned out to be quite likeable."

"You thought differently when you first met him," Samuel reminded her.

"First impressions aren't always accurate. I was wrong about him. I admit it."

"Is there a chance that's not all you're wrong about, Cori?" he ventured.

"What do you mean?"

"Are you sure Burk considers your relationship as innocent as you say it is?" Samuel asked in a serious tone.

Corinne shrugged off his concern. "Of course he does. Oh, I may flirt and banter with Jared, but that adds spice to our encounters. Life would be utterly boring without a little flirtation. He knows I don't mean anything by it."

"He knows you so well, eh? Can you say the same? Have you learned anything about him during all these innocent outings? Where exactly does he come from? Who are his people? You don't know if he comes from good stock, do you?"

"I have asked him, but he always evades my questions," Corinne replied, then grinned. "I do believe he likes his role as mystery man."

"Aren't you curious, though?"

"Not especially, but you certainly seem to be," Corinne said. "Why haven't you asked him where he comes from?"

"I did."

"And?"

"And he evades answering me as well. He said it wasn't important, that it didn't concern our negotiations. And he was right."

"Well, if he invests with you, then you will find the answers when he leaves Boston. He will have to give you a forwarding address if he intends to collect his profits."

"Well, then I should know any day now."

"Why?"

"He made his investment with our firm last week," Samuel answered, amused by his daughter's surprise. "Didn't he mention it?"

"No, he didn't. He didn't say a thing to me about it," Corinne said, suddenly quite annoyed. "Why didn't you tell me sooner?"

"I haven't seen very much of you lately, my dear. Either I'm working, or you're nowhere to be found."

"So he's a partner then?" Corinne said, more to herself than to her father. She couldn't understand why Jared hadn't said anything to her about it.

"Yes, he's a partner, all right," Samuel returned with a chuckle. "He invested much more than we anticipated, almost a half million."

Corinne let out a slow whistle. "You didn't need that much for the expansion, did you?"

"No, but Mr. Burk insisted. It was the only deal he would agree to."

"And that gave him more shares than you intended he have, didn't it?"

"Yes. He now owns as many shares as Cousin Elliot and I own. If he wanted to, he could counter our votes. Which would leave your vote as the deciding one."

"But you control my vote."

"Yes, I do," Samuel smiled.

Corinne gasped at the sly look in her father's eyes. "You didn't tell him that, did you?"

Samuel shook his head slowly, savoring his business judgement. "He will find out at the first board meeting—if he is here to attend it."

"You deceived him, then!"

"Hardly. I just wisely withheld a few facts. Do you think I didn't know he has been paying court to you? If he hadn't paid so much attention to you, then I wouldn't have felt the need to conceal those facts. As it is, I have to consider all possibilities, and one is that he may have hopes of taking over the firm. If not, then why such a large investment?"

"That is ridiculous," Corinne replied doubtfully. "What does he know of shipyards?"

"Must I remind you that we know nothing about him, Cori? If he hadn't been so secretive, then perhaps I wouldn't have either. But regardless, if it was his intention to control the firm by manipulating you, then he's in for a big surprise and it's only what he deserves. And if he had no such plans, then it won't matter one way or the other."

"Jared is not as devious as you imply," she said angrily.

"No, he's probably not. But it doesn't hurt to be cautious. And time will tell."

"Yes, time will prove that your imagination has run rampant," she rejoined.

"You're very defensive of him," Samuel observed. "You haven't by chance been fooling yourself about your involvement with him, have you, Cori? He's a very attractive man, the kind women fall in love with easily."

"You would like that, wouldn't you?" Corinne accused him, her eyes suddenly darkening to deepest emerald. "He's just the type of man you would approve of!"

"Well, I doubt he would let you run wild the way I have," Samuel chuckled.

"You can get thoughts of matchmaking out of your head right now!" Corinne snapped hotly. "I'm going to marry Russell!"

"Not as long as I have anything to say about it!" Samuel raised his voice to match hers.

Corinne glared at him. He would never give in, she could see that now. She would just have to find someone else. But not Jared Burk, definitely not him. Oh, he was charming enough, handsome and rich enough, and when he kissed her, as he had many times, she felt a thrill all through her body. Without any effort he sucked her will away, and for just that reason he would not do for a husband.

"Very well, Father," Corinne said coolly. "When Russell returns, I'll tell him I won't see him anymore."

"Good. Then you're going to consider Burk?" he asked, unable to hide the hopeful gleam in his eyes.

"How can you even ask that after you practically accused him of trying to take over our shipyard?"

"I said no such thing. I said it was only a possibility, and not a very likely one."

She glared at him. "You would let him marry me, though, wouldn't you?"

"I think he would make a good husband, yes," Samuel said truthfully.

"Well, I don't. And he will be leaving soon anyway," she said, killing her father's hope.

"Where is he? Didn't you say he would be here shortly?"

Corinne looked at the clock on the mantle and frowned. "He's late."

Samuel chuckled. "Well, that's a change. For once someone has kept you waiting."

"Well, it will be the last time!" she replied stiffly, and started pacing the floor. "I won't be seeing him again after tonight."

"Just because he's late?"

"No, because I can't very well find my future husband if Jared Burk is monopolizing my time."

"You're very cold, daughter," Samuel said disapprovingly. "I pity the man you do finally marry."

Chapter 9

JARED was thirty minutes late, which put Corinne in an even worse mood than her conversation with her father had done. She greeted him coldly, and said very little to him the entire evening, except to confirm his promise to pick her up again after midnight. Jared did not question her silence, assuming she was pouting because of his tardiness. Corinne let him think so. She would explain later, before he brought her home from the club.

Corinne was not really angry with Jared, but with her father for his unreasonable stubbornness. All that time wasted on Russell. And now time would be wasted in finding another man to suit her needs. But to wait another two years for her money was even more unthinkable.

That problem was not enough, for Jared posed another. She did not look forward to telling him that she wouldn't see him again, and explaining why. She hated having to break off a relationship, to suffer the hurt looks and pleadings as she had with William and Charles. She was not so cold-hearted that the scenes did not affect her, but she was too strong-willed to let them sway her.

With Jared she did not feel quite so much guilt, for she had not instigated their relationship, as she had the others. He was the one who insisted she see him again and again. Granted, she used him as an escort, but he used her for a diversion during his stay in Boston. So he would have no right to be upset when she talked to him later.

Corinne built up more resentment against Jared after they reached the club that night. Each time he brought her here, he insisted she play at his table so he could keep an eye on her. And each time she played with him, she lost to him. It was infuriating.

Tonight was no different. They had been at the club for

three hours. It was not crowded, for this was a week night and many of the earlier gamblers had gone home long ago. Only three tables were still occupied. Corinne was about ready to quit. Again, Jared had won all her money.

"This will be my last hand," Corinne announced.

"I think mine, too," said the sandy-haired man on Corinne's left.

"We might as well all quit, then," responded the only other player besides Jared.

Jared nodded in agreement and Corinne dealt draw poker. She had just enough chips to finish this hand, as long as there were no raises. She prayed this last time for that one hand that would give her a sure win. This would be the last time she would come here with Jared, the last chance she had to beat him—just once, only once was all she asked for.

She spread her cards slowly, and held her breath as the queen, jack, nine and eight of clubs appeared one at a time to tantalize her. She squeezed off the last card slowly, but her heart fell when she saw the three of diamonds. However, there was still the draw, and though she would have to fill an inside straight for the best hand of a straight flush, a regular flush was also possible and not a hand to scoff at.

Jared opened the betting, and Corinne and one other player called. The other player took three cards; Jared asked for two, leading her to believe he was drawing to three of a kind. She took her one card and was almost afraid to look at it. Jared bet again, the limit for their table, fifty dollars, and Corinne gently lifted her draw card from the table and put it in her hand. She did not bat an eye as she stared at the ten of clubs. A queen high straight flush, just two cards under a royal, the best hand possible! She couldn't believe it. It was the best hand she had ever held, yet she had no money to bet it! She didn't even have enough to call, since Jared had bet the limit. She wondered furiously if he had done it on purpose, knowing she couldn't call.

"It's up to you, Corinne," Jared said.

She looked at him icily, and then addressed the other players with a most beguiling smile. "Would you mind if I left the table for a moment before we finish this hand?

66

I know it's not usually allowed, but this is the last hand and I would like to see it through."

"Go right ahead," said the man who had folded.

"Don't matter to me, either," said the other man, and threw in his cards. "I'm not going to call anyway."

Corinne glared at Jared, daring him to object. "Do *you* mind?"

"I hardly think it's necessary to see the owner about more money, Corinne, when this is the last hand. Why don't you just throw in too and we'll call it a night?"

"I would rather finish," she said stiffly. "Or are you afraid I might finally beat you?"

He shrugged and leaned back in his chair. "Very well, I will wait. But don't be too long."

She left the table, but returned after only a few minutes in bitter disappointment. The owner had refused to give her any more credit.

"Well?" Jared questioned upon seeing her forlorn expression.

She looked at him speculatively. "Would you take my I.O.U.? You know I'm good for it."

Jared waited a few moments before answering. "If that's the case, why don't we raise the limit? As you say, you're good for it, and it's just the two of us now."

The other two players had gone. They were alone, and now she felt the old thrill of the game that she hadn't felt since she started playing with Jared. She was going to beat him, and for high stakes.

"Five thousand?" she suggested.

She noted his look of surprise and grinned. That was more money than she could afford to pay without going to her father. But she wouldn't have to do that, for she was going to win this hand, and win it big.

Jared nodded, and withdrew pen and paper from his pocket. "You haven't called my bet, Corinne."

She took the paper and wrote an I.O.U. to cover his bet and her raise. "And five thousand," she said confidently, never more sure of a winning hand.

Jared reached into his pocket again and took out a wad of bills and peeled off some. "There's your five." He paused and counted off more money. "And five more."

Corinne was delighted. She reached for the paper to match his bet and raise him again, but Jared stopped her.

"I won't accept another I.O.U., Corinne."

"Why not?"

"Because I know where you will have to go to honor the debt, and I don't think he will be too pleased."

"My father will never know, Jared, because I don't intend to lose."

"This is a game of chance, Corinne," he warned her in a level tone. "Only one hand is unbeatable, and the odds are you don't have it."

"Are you afraid I might have beat the odds?" she challenged him.

"You're that sure of your hand?"

"I am."

"That's too bad, then, since you can't afford to call," he said offhandedly.

Her temper exploded. "Why did you raise me, then, if you didn't intend to let me cover it?"

He completely ignored her outrage. "You are the one who left the pot open to another raise by raising me. You also suggested a five thousand limit. I agreed to no more," he reminded her casually.

"I meant per bet!"

"Well, I didn't."

"You're contemptible, Jared Burk," she said hotly. "It's just as well that I decided not to see you again after tonight."

"You do take defeat graciously, don't you?" he said with heavy irony.

"That has nothing to do with it!" she snapped, her expression furious. "I was going to tell you on the way home. It's nothing against you—at least, it wasn't until now! But you have just proved yourself beneath me. I wouldn't see you again if you begged me to!"

He shocked her by smiling. "By God, woman, you actually expect me to, don't you? I don't think I've ever met anyone quite as vain as you are."

Corinne turned bright red, but stiffened her back and rose with dignity. "So now you insult me. Well, I don't have to listen to any more."

She started to leave, but Jared reached across the table and grabbed her wrist. "Sit down, Corinne."

"I will not!"

"Sit down!" he commanded in a voice she had never heard him use before.

She did so, but first jerked her arm free. Then she waited, her eyes like fiery emeralds as she glared at him.

Jared leaned back in his own chair and reached into yet another pocket and pulled out several small pieces of white paper. He tossed them across the table at Corinne and met her murderous stare.

"Since neither of us has any intention of seeing the other after tonight, you can honor these now."

She picked up the notes and was aghast to recognize her I.O.U.s to the club for two thousand dollars, now payable to Jared Burk. Her eyes turned on him accusingly.

"How did you get these?"

"I bought them."

"Why?"

"That doesn't matter. What matters is I am collecting on them now, including the one you signed only a few minutes ago. Seven thousand, lady."

He said lady with such contempt that she flinched. "If my debt was paid in full here, why wouldn't they give me more credit tonight?"

"Because when I bought your notes, I told them you were not a good risk," he said smoothly, as if he did that sort of thing daily. "It was not hard to persuade them, since you had not come to claim the notes yourself."

"How dare you?"

"I thought I was doing you a service, since they would have gone to your father soon for payment. I will settle with you, not your father."

"And just how do you expect me to pay you tonight, when you know damn well I don't have any more cash on me?"

"But you do have something to sell."

"So my father was right!" Corinne gasped. "You're after control of the shipyard. And to think I actually defended you!"

Jared frowned. "Your father said that?"

"He most certainly did. He told me this evening that

69

you might try to manipulate me to get control of the firm, and he was right."

"Is that why you decided not to see me again?"

"Yes," she lied, taking that excuse rather than trying to explain the other.

"Well, your father was wrong, Corinne." Jared lied also, in a surprisingly soft tone. "And you do yourself an injustice to believe it."

"What do you mean?" she asked suspiciously.

"I did not intend to buy your vote. That's not what I want from you."

"What, then? I have nothing of value on me."

Jared's eyes were inscrutable. "You have yourself, and one hour of your time upstairs."

Corinne couldn't help but laugh. "You can't be serious." When he said nothing she jumped to her feet, her temper bubbling with indignation. "I have *never* been so insulted!"

"You don't feel you're worth seven thousand dollars?" he asked calmly.

"My worth is not in question!" she hissed, holding onto the table to stop her hands from trembling. "You are despicable to even suggest such a mode of payment!"

"It is the only alternative you have."

"I will get your money tomorrow, every cent of it! You will just have to wait until then."

"I don't intend to wait that long."

"Nor do I intend to agree to your terms!" she snapped defiantly. "And there is nothing you can do about it, now is there, Mr. Burk?"

There was a malevolent gleam in his eyes that should have warned her. "On the contrary. I will collect payment in full, whether you are agreeable or not."

"You wouldn't dare," she said tightly. The others in the room would protect her if need be.

"Is that a challenge?"

Corinne faltered when she met his determined look. "No, it's not."

My God, he *would* attempt to collect, she thought fearfully. Of course, someone would stop him, but it would cause such a scene that she couldn't hope to keep it secret. Rumors about it would run rampant through the city.

"Why do you hesitate, Corinne? In effect, you will receive seven thousand dollars for just an hour of your time. I don't imagine many women could command such a price." His lips curled ever so slightly. "Or do you object to being paid for what you usually give away free?"

She gasped. Could he really think that badly of her? Well, she didn't give a damn for his opinion. She wasn't going to give in to his demands, one way or the other. But she did need to get out of this situation without causing an embarrassing scene.

"You haven't made it worth my while," she said in a deceptively pouting tone. "Nor have you given me a sporting chance." She looked down at the pot in the center of the table, and then at the cards on the table before her, and smiled enticingly. "Now if you would make my debt twelve thousand, and allow me to call your raise, then I might agree to your terms."

"Might?"

Her smile widened, for she knew she couldn't lose. "I will agree."

He leaned forward. "So there is no misunderstanding this time, let me make my terms clear. If I win this hand, you will go upstairs with me for one hour. And that is not an hour of conversation I am talking about, Corinne, but an hour in bed. Is that clear?"

She drew herself up. "You don't have to be so vulgar, Mr. Burk. I understood what you had in mind."

"Then you agree?"

"Yes, do you?"

He nodded, and she grinned triumphantly. She turned her cards over with a flourish and waited with anticipation for his look of defeat. But it didn't come. Instead he grinned back at her and shook his head.

"Not good enough, Corinne."

She stared in disbelief at the cards he turned up. A high straight flush in diamonds, beating her by one card. It was impossible.

When she met his eyes, her own sparkled murderously. "You cheated!"

"How could you prove it?" he asked as he pocketed the money and the notes.

"You did, didn't you? When I left the table you changed your cards!" she accused him furiously.

71

"I repeat, how could you prove it, Corinne?"

"I don't have to prove it—*I know it!*"

"That makes little difference. The cards say I won and now you will pay up."

"Not on your life!"

Corinne grabbed her purse and ran from the room.

The dark hall outside the gambling room was empty. The stairs leading up to the second floor were conveniently right next to the entrance door, so that nongamblers could just slip upstairs without being seen. Corinne had never been as aware of those stairs as she was right now. She shuddered as she passed them, hearing a woman's high-pitched laughter from somewhere above.

Should she hide up there and let Jared search fruitlessly for her out in the street? That was where he would assume she had gone. But she couldn't bring herself to go up those stairs. If she could convince Jared's driver to take her home, then she would leave him at the club. That was better.

Corinne opened the entrance door, only to have it slammed shut in front of her, Jared's large hand pressing against it. His arm stretched over her shoulder, and she turned to him.

"I will scream, Jared. I will! You can't stop me from leaving here!"

"Yes, I can," he said coldly, "until you've paid your debt."

"I wouldn't go upstairs with you if my life depended on it. I want you to move!"

She tried to shove him away from the door, but she couldn't budge him. He let her try for only a moment before he picked her up and started up the stairs.

"No!" Corinne screamed. "No, I won't!"

"You no longer have a choice," he said as they reached the top. "Now which room would you prefer, my dear?" he taunted. "One you've occupied before? Or would that make you uncomfortable?"

Corinne's stomach churned with fear. The long corridor before her was very dark, wallpapered in deep royal blue, with only a single lamp at the opposite end giving the tiniest speck of light.

"I have never been up here before," Corinne whispered,

hearing the terror in her own voice. "You have got to believe me, Jared."

He laughed cruelly and moved down the corridor to the first open door. "But you don't expect me to, do you?"

"What have I done to make you think otherwise?" she demanded.

He entered a room decorated entirely in green, from the carpet to the furniture to the sheets on the large bed. Everything was green.

Jared shut the door, but didn't set her down yet. His eyes glowed in the dim light as he looked down at her. "Our room matches your eyes," he mocked.

"You've teased me for more than two months now," he continued. "You had to pay the consequences sometime. I don't usually wait this long."

"I never teased you!"

He raised a dark brow. "Do you deny flirting outrageously with me? Do you deny returning my kisses willingly?"

"I may flirt a little, but I mean nothing by it," she said defensively. "I thought you understood that. And I didn't ask you to kiss me, did I?"

"But you didn't try to stop me, did you? A real man won't settle for just kisses, lady," Jared said contemptuously.

"Most will!"

"Not this man," he told her coldly. "Not when you've led me to expect more."

He set her down and turned to lock the door. While his back was to her, she quickly opened her purse and took out the small knife he had long ago returned to her. It would be the first time she had ever used it other than in practice. She just prayed she could remember all that Johnny Bixler had taught her when she was only a child of ten.

Jared turned around sharply as he heard her slide the knife from its sheath. He laughed heartily at the picture she presented. She was dressed in gold velvet with pearl buttons and lace trimmings. Her dark gold hair was arranged on top of her head with gold velvet ribbons, a few curls escaping on her temples. She held a purse in one hand and the knife in the other.

"Just what do you plan to do with that pretty toy?" he asked, chuckling.

"I'm going to use it if I have to. If you come near me, I will."

"Didn't anyone tell you that you can get hurt playing with knives?"

"I happen to know how to use this one. If anyone gets hurt, it will be you," she said with more confidence than she felt. "Now unlock that door."

He ignored her demand and stood, his feet planted apart, before the door. "I wondered why you carried a weapon in your purse. Do you often feel the need to protect yourself? Or is it just me you refuse to give in to?"

She glared at him. "So you looked in my purse before you returned it? A gentleman wouldn't have done that."

"Well, we both know I'm not one, don't we?" he replied and began removing his coat.

"What are you doing?" she demanded.

"I'm preparing to transact our business," he answered lightly. "After all, you bet only an hour of your time and that time is wasting away."

"Damn you, haven't you heard anything I've said? You're not going to touch me. I would sooner make love with the devil than with you!"

"The devil and I are on good terms," Jared said coolly. "I'm sure he won't mind."

"I hate you, Jared Burk!"

"That hardly makes any difference. Now be a good girl and stop acting as though you've never done this before. If you cooperate, you will enjoy it as much as I will."

Before she could reply, Jared threw his coat in her face, taking her by surprise. He had her wrist in his grip before she could yank the coat away. He jerked her up against his hard chest, bending her arm behind her back and applying pressure until they both heard the knife hit the floor. He stared into her frightened eyes for several moments before he brought his mouth down over hers savagely.

Corinne had never been embraced so tightly before. Her body was molded to his. Even with the pain in her shoulder, for he had not released her arm, her body tingled with feeling, revelled in it.

Jared released her arm and stepped back. "You want me as much as I want you. Why are you pretending otherwise?"

His words were like a slap and Corinne turned crimson. He was right. She hadn't even struggled to fight his kiss, she had returned it wholeheartedly. What was the matter with her?

She wrung her hands. God, she had to make him believe her! "I can't, Jared. I'm not what you seem to think I am. I have never been with a man before—I swear I haven't! I may do some wild things, but that's not one of them."

"You're lying, Corinne. You're no more virginal than I am."

"Don't you care if I'm telling the truth?" she cried. "Are you so bent on having me that you won't listen? My God, you're my father's partner—*my* partner. Do you think we can ever work together after this?"

"This has nothing to do with the business. You're paying your debt, Corinne. That's all."

"Damn your blackhearted soul!" she stormed. "I owe you nothing!" She had forgotten her fear.

"That's what this is all about, isn't it, Corinne?" He grinned sardonically. "You're just mad because you think I cheated you."

"You did! But regardless of that, I'm not about to give myself to any man until I marry."

"Then you shouldn't have agreed to it downstairs," he replied, and reached for the buttons on her dress.

Corinne slapped his hand away furiously and bent to retrieve her knife, but Jared kicked it out of her reach. He lifted her up and tossed her on the bed, not too gently.

Corinne started screaming, but Jared fell on her and covered her mouth with his hand.

"Don't get me angry," he said in a deadly voice. "I can be very cruel when I'm angry." He used his free hand to rip her dress open. "It won't do you any good to cry rape, because no one here is going to give a damn. The opinion of the house is, if a lady comes here, then she's no lady. I'm of the same opinion, so don't try my patience anymore. Is that clear?"

As Jared uncovered the firm mounds of her breasts, some of the coldness left his voice. "You really are beautiful," he murmured. "I've never seen such soft, white skin."

He bent his head to her breasts and kissed each peak in

turn. He lingered there for a long while before he looked up into her wide, tear-filled eyes.

"I won't hurt you, Corinne, as long as you don't fight me," he said almost tenderly. "I promise you that."

He moved his hand from her mouth and bent to kiss her. He kissed her deeply, ravishing her mouth with his tongue, but she did not respond at all. He shrugged indifferently.

"If you want to be stubborn, that's up to you, Corinne. It won't stop me."

Corinne wouldn't answer. She was so ashamed she wanted only to die. She couldn't stop him. He would hurt her if she tried, he had said so. And he would rape her anyway, so why should she suffer more than she had to?

She prayed for him to finish quickly. When he lifted her to remove the rest of her clothes, she didn't resist. When he spoke to her tenderly, she didn't hear. When his strong, powerful hands caressed her gently, she felt nothing but her shame.

Tears fell silently down the corners of her tightly closed eyes. When a sharp, ripping pain made her jerk, she bit her lips to keep from crying out. He had promised not to hurt her, but she knew he would. Florence had not let her grow up entirely ignorant. Now Jared Burk had taken her innocence, the innocence she had always expected to give her husband. He had forced it from her with brute strength. Corinne had never known such hate as she felt now for Jared.

Jared's exhausted body became very heavy, and Corinne guessed it was over.

"You have been paid in full, Mr. Burk," she said tonelessly. "If you will kindly remove yourself from my person, I would like to leave."

"You're certainly a cold bitch," he grunted, then left the bed to dress.

"I was told that once already this evening. I don't need you to tell me again."

"What you need is someone to warm you up. I pity the man you marry if he has to put up with that kind of performance in bed."

"He won't," Corinne replied tightly, and sat up on the edge of the bed, swaying a little. "What if I get pregnant?"

He shrugged. "Odds are you won't, since this won't happen again. But it is your risk, not mine. It comes with being a woman."

Jared finished putting his clothes on and casually stepped around the bed to retrieve her torn dress. Corinne heard his sharp intake of breath and turned to look at him. She followed his gaze to the center of the bed and the stain of blood that looked black on the green sheets.

"What's the matter, Mr. Burk?" she asked bitterly. "You seem surprised. Didn't you know that virgins bleed?"

His eyes met hers and they were a bright gray, without a trace of blue. He stared at her for a long time.

Finally he marched to the door, her clothes gripped tightly in his hands. He turned and glared at her across the room.

"You stay here until I return," he ordered harshly. "Do you hear me?"

"Where are you going?"

"Just stay here, Corinne," he answered. "I will be back before noon."

"Noon!" she gasped. "It's almost dawn now. You know I have to be home by dawn or I will be missed!'

"I will take care of that."

"How?"

But he was gone. And he had taken her clothes. What evil was he up to now?

Chapter 10

WITH two blankets wrapped about his legs and a heavy cloak about his shoulders, Jared waited impatiently in his carriage outside the old brownstone townhouse on Beacon Street. It was just dawn, and the chill from the autumn night still invaded his bones. It would be hours yet before the sun would dispel the infernal cold.

It would also be a while yet before it would be appropriate for him to call on Samuel Barrows. The older man would still be asleep in his warm bed, unaware of his daughter's whereabouts. Jared had enough to tell him that would arouse his ire without making things worse by waking him up.

Damn! Nothing had gone right since yesterday. And he had thought he had everything worked out perfectly. With Corinne's debts from the club in his possession, and their agreeable relationship, it would have been a simple matter to sway her to his side. After all, she was not on good terms with her father right now, not since he opposed her marriage to Drayton. She would easily have voted her shares in the shipyard with his, if just for spite. Or so Jared assumed.

But she blew his plans to hell by casually informing him that she wouldn't see him again. And after he had wasted two months dancing attendance on her! And if his failure with her were not enough, Samuel Barrows suspected his plans for the shipyard.

Now Jared was feeling guilty—guilty and furious. The bitch had deserved what she got. She had no business pretending to be an experienced woman. A virgin—a damnable virgin! She had tried to tell him, but he wouldn't believe her, which made it even worse.

Jared couldn't stand waiting anymore. If he had to

pull Barrows out of bed, that was too bad. But a few more minutes of these recriminations and he would say to hell with it all. There was one more course of action—the last one—but he certainly didn't relish it. It was either that or give up and go home. At this point, he was just about ready to go.

Brock opened the door to Jared's knock after only a short wait. Jared had gotten used to this sour-faced butler, but he had never before seen him quite so put out.

"Really, sir." Brock was indignant. "Are you aware of the hour?"

"Of course I am," Jared answered impatiently. "I wouldn't be here if it were not an urgent matter."

"But Miss Corinne never rises this early," Brock replied, casting a look behind him at the stairs. "And her maid lets no one disturb her."

Jared wondered if the butler assumed she had only just come home. She had said her servants were aware of her escapades. You couldn't hide anything from servants for very long.

"I don't wish to disturb Miss Barrows," Jared said with some amusement. "It's her father I wish to see."

"Well, sir, that is different. Highly irregular at this hour, but Mr. Barrows does happen to be up and dressing at this moment. If you would care to wait in the study, I will inform him of your presence."

Ten minutes later, a welcome cup of coffee in his hands, Jared rose to greet Samuel Barrows as he entered his study.

"I understand there is some urgency," Samuel stated as he took his place behind his large desk. "I can't imagine what it could be unless you've decided to terminate your stay in Boston. Have you come to finish our business before you leave, Mr. Burk?"

"This has nothing to do with business," Jared replied, wondering how he should begin.

"Just what is so important, then?"

"I've come about your daughter." Jared jumped right into the heart of it. "To get your approval of our forthcoming marriage."

Samuel stared incredulously at Jared for several moments before he blustered, "Good God, young man! I don't

79

know how you do things where you come from, but here we usually discuss these matters at a civil hour."

"You will understand shortly why I couldn't wait, Mr. Barrows. But first, I want to know if you will give us your blessing."

"Please, Mr. Burk. Not so fast." Samuel held up his hand to slow things down. "I was under the impression that Corinne wasn't exactly attracted to you. No offense meant, but perhaps you're not aware that she prefers men she can dominate. Was I wrong about you? Does my daughter find you easy to—er—deal with?"

"No."

"Well, why would she agree to marry you?"

"I haven't asked her yet."

Samuel couldn't help laughing. "But you think she will say yes when you do?"

"She will, with the proper persuasion. And I can be very persuasive."

"I'm sure you can be, but Corinne is not easily persuaded. She knows what she wants out of life and she has the stubborn will to see it through. And you're not exactly what she has been looking for."

"Perhaps not," Jared shrugged. "But I am the man she is going to marry."

"You sound as if you are telling me, not asking me," Samuel observed with a raised brow.

"I am. I would rather have your approval, but it won't make that much difference."

Samuel chuckled, his brown eyes alight with pleasure. "I like a man with determination, Mr. Burk. You must love my daughter a great deal."

Jared scowled. He had hoped to avoid this aspect of things.

"To be frank, Mr. Barrows, love hasn't entered into it. Your daughter is extremely beautiful, as you know, and desirable as a woman, but she is going to make a difficult wife. I don't need to tell you how radical her thinking is, for I'm sure you know that already. She considers marriage her ticket to freedom. She gives no thought to the responsibilities involved. But with guidance, she will learn."

Now Samuel's paternal instincts were aroused. He stood

up stiffly, placed his hands flat on his desk, and leaned forward with an angry gleam in his brown eyes.

"Let me get this straight, Mr. Burk. You don't love my daughter and, in your opinion, she won't make you a good wife. So why in damnation are you here telling me you're going to marry her?"

Jared did not hesitate. "It's a matter of honor, sir."

"Honor? Just what the hell are you talking about?" Samuel blustered, thoroughly confused.

"Before I explain, let me ask you this. Are you aware of your daughter's predilection for gambling? Do you know that she leaves your home late almost every night to frequent an unsavory establishment across the Charles?"

"I know everything my daughter does, including that you have been her escort on these late night ventures ever since that weak-kneed Drayton left town."

"If you knew, why didn't you put a stop to it?" Jared demanded.

"The only way I could have done so would have been to lock her in her room. The girl is headstrong and will do what *she* wants, not what I tell her to do. I felt she would lose interest soon. I still think she will."

"But in the meantime, you don't mind that she is seen in that place?"

"Of course I mind. But I can't stop her from going there."

"You really should have, Mr. Barrows," Jared said ominously. "That place is not just a gambling house. Any patron who goes there knows what the second floor of the house is used for. Do you?"

"Yes." Samuel looked away, embarrassed. "Yes, yes, I know. But Corinne is a good girl. I don't worry on that score."

"Perhaps *you* knew how innocent she was," Jared remarked sardonically. "But I didn't. In my opinion, no decent woman would go to such a place."

"Here, here!"

"Let me finish. That is not the only reason I . . . assumed certain things about her. In case you didn't know, your daughter is an outrageous tease. She gives the distinct impression that she is worldly in all matters. Do you understand what I am saying, Mr. Barrows? Because of her

81

flirtatious manner and the infamy of the gambling house she frequents, I did not believe her innocent, not even when she swore to me that she was."

Samuel's face turned a bright red. "Just what have you done to my daughter?"

Jared felt every muscle in his body come alive. He had put himself in a dangerous position. But he was going to tell the truth.

"I won Corinne in a hand of poker, in a game involving only the two of us. The terms were established beforehand. She was determined to finish the hand, but she didn't have the money to do so. So she wagered herself."

"I don't believe it!" Samuel stormed.

"She was positive she would win, Mr. Barrows. Otherwise I'm sure she wouldn't have agreed to the terms. But she did agree—and she lost. And then she refused to honor her wager. But I'm afraid I didn't feel quite gallant enough to accept her refusal."

"What are you saying, Burk? If you—"

"I raped your daughter," Jared cut him off coldly. "I regret it, but it doesn't alter the fact—I raped her. If I had had the slightest belief in her innocence, then it certainly wouldn't have happened. But she did wager herself. I could not believe a virgin would take that risk."

Samuel sat down heavily in his chair. "I don't know what to say to you, Burk. I should have you thrown in jail, but the trouble is, I understand how this could have happened. My God, was my daughter really fool enough to gamble herself in a game of chance?"

"Yes."

"And now, because she was indeed a virgin, you feel obliged to marry her?"

"I will not take full blame for what happened. But because of her innocence, I do regret it. I feel like a complete idiot for having judged her so incorrectly. But what's done is done. She has paid for her mistake. Now I feel honor-bound to pay for mine. I will do right by her, Mr. Barrows. In fact, I insist on it."

"This must have happened last night?"

"Yes. She isn't hurt, sir." Jared anticipated him. "She's

not too pleased with me, however. In fact, I left her in a fine temper."

"You left her? Where?"

"She's still across the river, in a cozy bedroom, probably sleeping right now."

"Not if I know my daughter. She'll come storming in here any moment, demanding your head on a platter."

"I don't think so. I didn't leave her much choice in the matter of her staying or leaving. I have her clothes with me."

Samuel took a deep breath. He couldn't hold Jared entirely to blame for this. Corinne had brought it on herself. Who knew her better than he did? And he had warned her not to trifle with Burk.

He cleared his throat. "I will say truthfully, Mr. Burk, that I wish to God none of this had happened. But it has, and at least you have offered to do the right thing by my daughter."

"Then you will approve the marriage?"

"I will, if Corinne agrees to it. But if she doesn't, and quite frankly, I doubt she will, then you will not be obliged to make further restitution."

"That is very charitable of you, under the circumstances. But she will agree," Jared said confidently.

Samuel scowled. "If you think to use force to get her to marry you, you can abandon that plan right now. I will not allow Corinne to be abused again."

"I had not even considered that, Mr. Barrows," Jared replied smoothly. "I give you my word. I will not mistreat Corinne in any way."

"I hope I can trust you to keep your word," Samuel returned with a stern look.

"You can."

"Very well, then, you have my permission to propose marriage to her. But when you speak to her, I would appreciate it if you wouldn't mention that I approve the marriage. In fact, it would be better if she didn't know that I am aware of what has happened. I don't want to cause her any further shame."

"I understand," Jared said uncomfortably. "But I'm afraid I need one of her dresses from here. The one she was wearing was—damaged. She will know I have been here."

Samuel almost flew into a rage again. "No problem, Mr. Burk," he said tightly. "Get the dress you have with you fixed. Find a seamstress and have it repaired, it's that simple. I will see that my butler forgets you have called."

Chapter 11

CORINNE was asleep when Jared returned. He wanted nothing more than to get some sleep himself, but he couldn't yet. He had to get things settled with Corinne first.

He laid her clothes out on the foot of the bed and stood looking down at her. Her dark-gold hair had come unbound and lay spread out over the pillow in soft waves. It was so long and luxuriant, like spun silk.

She really was so damnably beautiful. If only she weren't Barrows' daughter. . . . But she was, and Jared couldn't allow himself to forget that. To Jared, she was only a means to an end. And once that end was accomplished, he would never see this wild, green-eyed beauty again.

"Corinne, get up," Jared said softly, and shook her shoulder. "We have to talk."

"Go away," she mumbled, and turned her head into the pillow.

"Come on, now," he coaxed good-naturedly. "It's almost ten o'clock."

She glared at him, sleep vanishing instantly now. "You! So you came back after all?"

He grinned. "You didn't think I would just leave you here, did you?"

"Yes," she said bitterly, pulling the sheet up tightly to cover herself. "I wouldn't put anything past *you!*"

"I went to get your dress repaired. And I needed time to think, to make decisions."

"About what?"

"About last night. Corinne—"

"I don't want to talk about it!" she cut him off furiously. "I just want to forget it!"

"It's not that simple."

"Isn't it? If you will just get out of my life, I will forget you quite easily."

"I would like to forget, too, but I can't," Jared replied. "What I did was unforgiveable."

"Are you trying to say you're sorry?" Corinne asked caustically.

"Yes."

"Don't you think it's a bit late for regrets, Mr. Burk? The damage is done."

"It's not too late for me to make amends."

"Are you a magician?" she asked in a sarcastic tone. "Can you give me back my innocence?"

"No, but I can see to it that you don't suffer further because of what I did to you."

"Suffer further? What are you talking about?" she demanded. "The only suffering I'm enduring is being in the same room with you!"

"I wish you would calm down, Corinne, so we can talk seriously."

"Why should I?" she snapped.

"Because you are as much to blame for what happened as I am," he said sharply, then lowered his tone before continuing. "I was wrong, Corinne, but I was angry with you for leading me on. You had no business acting the way you did if you were a virgin."

She turned away, unable to look him in the eye. She knew she was partly to blame—*she knew it*. But it didn't stop the rage she felt at being used so callously.

"You didn't have to treat me like a whore," she said in a small voice.

Jared sat down on the side of the bed, strangely moved by her pitiful statement. He reached out and turned her face to his.

"I am so sorry, Corinne. I swear I never meant to cause you so much pain." His eyes searched hers deeply. "If I had known you were innocent, I wouldn't have touched you. You do believe that, don't you?"

"I don't know," she said weakly. Tears formed, making her eyes shimmering pools of green. "I don't know what to believe about you any more."

"I can't blame you for not trusting me now. But I swear I will never hurt you again, Corinne."

"Just go away, Jared." She pushed at him. "I don't want to talk anymore."

Her words shook him more than he let on. They were the very words his mother had said to his father so long ago. The sharp reminder shocked him deeply.

"You *will* talk to me, Corinne. You have to, for your own sake." He added, "A child might have been conceived last night. Will you take that risk all alone?"

"Just what are you getting at, Jared?" Corinne demanded wearily. "Just tell me, and get it over with."

"I want you to marry me."

There was a moment of complete silence.

"Do you?" She laughed without humor. "Do you really? Tell me why?"

"I am serious, Corinne."

"I asked you why, Jared," she said coldly. "You don't love me. Are you sacrificing yourself because you feel guilty?"

"I don't feel I am sacrificing anything. I am only trying to solve the problem I have created," he replied, keeping his tone calm.

"Well, I don't see any problem. What's done is done. I'm not going to go and kill myself because of last night. I'll survive, you can be sure of that."

"And if there is a child?"

"If that happens, I will give it away," she said harshly, intending her words to cut him. "I certainly wouldn't keep a child of yours."

Jared gritted his teeth. She certainly hated him.

"I am not offering you only marriage, Corinne, but also what you want out of life. I know that you love Russell Drayton, but I also know that your father won't let you marry him. But if you marry me now, you will not only protect yourself in case of a possible pregnancy, but you will have what you want. After a reasonable time, you can divorce me and have Drayton."

Corinne started to explain that there could be no divorce in her family. It wasn't acceptable. But her curiosity was aroused. "What did you mean, I would have what I want out of life?"

"You want freedom, don't you?" he reminded her. "You want independence?"

87

"Are you saying that if I married you, you wouldn't try to control me? You wouldn't set down any rules, or try to restrict me in anyway?"

"That's exactly what I'm saying," Jared replied, knowing that he had finally swayed her.

"And my money? Would you try to regulate it?"

"I don't need your money, Corinne. You can do whatever you want with it."

She couldn't believe he was willing to give her exactly what she wanted. It was too good to be true. Why was he being so cooperative?

"How can I trust you?" she asked skeptically.

"I will sign an agreement in writing, if you wish," he offered.

"Before marriage?"

"Yes."

She looked away from him. "What you propose is very tempting, Jared," Corinne admitted after a while. "But I wonder if you will still want to marry me after you hear my last condition."

"I'm listening." Jared grinned slightly, sure that he had won.

"Last night was very humiliating for me. I found making love thoroughly repugnant. If I agreed to marry you, I would be your wife only for appearances' sake."

"You're saying your bed will be off limits?"

"Yes."

The muscles in Jared's jaw twitched. Why did he mind? He could never grow to love her anyway. Why was he hurt?

"You didn't give yourself a chance last night, Corinne. Making love can be very enjoyable for both partners, when both participate."

"I don't intend to let you prove that, Jared," she returned stubbornly.

"Very well," he said. "As long as you don't object to my finding satisfaction elsewhere."

Corinne laughed, to Jared's further chagrin. "I would be surprised if you didn't. No, I have no objection."

Jesus, she really didn't give a damn about him, did she? Jared kept his expression controlled. "There will have to be one night, though, the wedding night—to consummate the marriage."

Corinne considered that. One more night like last night. How could she? But here was everything she wanted, and not two years away. She would be able to stand just one night.

"I agree," she said finally. "You're getting an awfully poor bargain, Jared. Do you think it's worth it?"

Jared relaxed completely. Not once did she mention her shares in the shipyard. He didn't know how he would have handled that if she had brought it up.

"My part of the bargain is not so bad, Corinne. I will be making amends to clear my conscience. Yes, it's worth it. And besides, it won't be for all that long. Once you get a divorce, we will go our separate ways."

Corinne's eyes danced with laughter. He thought he knew why she was happy, but he didn't know the real reason.

There will be no divorce, Jared Burk, thought Corinne. This bargain will be till death do us part. But she wouldn't tell him that just now. God, what magnificent revenge!

Chapter 12

THE marriage banns were posted and the wedding date set for October 10, a Sunday less than four weeks away. Invitations were dispatched immediately, and Corinne started fittings for her wedding gown. Her days were filled with making preparations and shopping for her trousseau. The four weeks passed quickly.

She didn't see much of Jared during this time, and had little opportunity to talk to him. He sent over the written agreement he had promised her, and that removed all trace of doubt.

Her father didn't know about the paper that guaranteed her independence. If he had, he would never have let her marry Jared. Corinne sometimes wondered why her father had agreed to the marriage so easily, without questioning her about her change of mind concerning Jared. But she gave the matter little thought.

During the final hectic week before the wedding, only one thing happened to disturb Corinne. Russell returned to Boston. He already knew that Jared had replaced him, so she didn't have to break that to him. But he did demand explanations.

It was the middle of the afternoon when Corinne was informed that Russell was waiting for her in the parlor downstairs. She had been trying on her finished wedding gown, delivered just that morning, and had been in a bubbling mood, for the gown was exquisite. Now her spirits were dampened.

Seeing Corinne's expression, Florence asked, "Did you think you wouldn't have to face the poor man?"

"No, but I had hoped I would be Mrs. Jared Burk first," Corinne replied. "Now quickly, help me change."

"It would be even worse if you didn't see him until after

the wedding," Florence said as she began unhooking the back of the gown. "The man expected to marry you. He deserves to know why you choose another instead."

"I know. But at least if I were already safely married, Russell couldn't try to talk me out of it."

Florence shook her head. "You treat a man's feelings so lightly, Cori."

"Russell knows I didn't love him," she said defensively.

"But *he* loved *you*."

"Whose side are you on, Florence?" Corinne demanded petulantly.

"Yours, my girl. I've known you since you were born. My mother was your nurse, and then I took care of you after she died. You've been like a daughter to me."

"Oh, stop it," Corinne giggled. "You're not old enough to be my mother."

"I'm close enough. And when I can't speak my mind to you, then it's time I left."

"Don't be silly."

"Well, you have to listen to someone, Cori. And who else will tell you what you're doing is wrong? I never cared for Russell Drayton, but you used him. That was terrible. Now you're using Mr. Burk to get what you want, and you don't love him any more than you loved Drayton."

"Jared is aware of that. Our marriage will be one of convenience."

"Convenience only for you. Heavens, Cori. You told me you won't even be sharing the same bedroom. What is he going to get out of this marriage?"

"He owes me!" Corinne snapped, forgetting that Florence didn't know about Jared's mistreatment of her.

"Owes you? Owes you what? What haven't you told me, Corinne Barrows?" Florence asked sternly.

"Nothing." Corinne nervously laughed it off. "Nothing, really."

She couldn't tell Florence. She was too ashamed of her own part in it. Worse, no one would understand how she could agree to marry the man who had raped her. No, she couldn't explain.

When she came downstairs, she found Russell in a furious mood, made worse by his having been kept waiting.

"I was beginning to think you were afraid to face me!" Russell nearly shouted as she came into the room.

Corinne ignored the accusation and inquired softly, "Did your grandfather recover, Russell?"

"He died."

"I'm sorry."

"I'm sure you are," Russell replied cuttingly. "Just as I'm sure you're sorry you didn't let me know you had dropped me for someone else the moment my back was turned!"

"Don't be bitter, Russell. You know my father wouldn't have let us marry."

"You said you would convince him!" he reminded her, his blue eyes dark with anger.

"I tried, but he just wouldn't change his mind."

"You know I would have waited until you no longer needed his permission," Russell said, a little less harshly now.

"And you know I had no intention of waiting that long." Corinne's annoyance was building. "Be reasonable, Russell. I never pretended to love you. I made that clear. I was honest with you from the beginning. It just didn't work out the way we wanted."

"Do you love Burk?"

"No. I have the same agreement with him as I had with you. The only difference is that my father didn't refuse Jared. And if it's any consolation, Russell, Jared and I will be married in name only."

Russell crooked a brow. "That wasn't one of our agreements."

"No, it wasn't."

"Why would a man like Burk accept such preposterous terms?"

"*I* don't think they're preposterous." Corinne brushed away the question indignantly.

"What does Burk get out of this?"

"A wife for appearances' sake only," Corinne lied. "Which is what he wants."

"And that's all?"

"Yes."

Russell sneered. "So he's using you just as you are him. He'll have his fun with the ladies, but needn't worry about being pressured into marriage, since he will have a legal wife. How very tidy. The man really is a cad, isn't he?"

"I suppose that's what he has in mind," Corinne remarked with some irritation. She hadn't considered Jared's plans.

"Then will you still see me, after you're married?"

Corinne frowned. "I don't know, Russell."

He hurried over to her and grabbed her shoulders. "Don't shut me out completely, Corinne."

"If you're still hoping I will fall in love with you, don't. I doubt I will ever lose my heart, Russell. I would have to depend on someone else then, to trust them. I much prefer relying on myself. I can count on me."

"I can't give up hope, Corinne, not yet." He pulled her closer and sought her lips for a long kiss. "Don't ask me to."

Corinne hated the pleading in his voice, the hurt look. It was the weak men who could not give up gracefully.

"I suppose we could remain friends," she suggested briskly. "But I really can't see you again until after I'm married."

"Very well, Corinne. Whatever you say," he eagerly agreed.

It was so like Russell to bend to her every wish. It was really too bad her father had refused him. At least she liked Russell. She couldn't say as much for Jared Burk.

Chapter 13

OCTOBER 10 dawned with a misty rain that built to a thunderous storm by mid-afternoon. From her bedroom window, Corinne looked miserably out on the rain-drenched street. Streams of water ran along the gutters. The park across the street was flooded.

Corinne glanced over her shoulder at Florence and asked dismally, "Isn't it suppose to be bad luck to have it rain on your wedding day?"

Florence was searching through the dressing table for Corinne's pearl-studded hair pins. She turned and made a disapproving sound.

"Now, that's only superstitious nonsense. And besides, it sounds to me like it's letting up. The sun may shine yet before four o'clock."

Corinne looked once more at the dreary park scene. "It won't," she sighed, and turned away from the window. "And my hair will probably be ruined going to and from the carriage. Not to mention my gown."

"Maybe we should go to the church early and dress you there," Florence suggested.

"Yes, maybe," Corinne replied automatically, her thoughts already drifting to other matters. From the moment she had awakened that morning she had been assailed by doubts. Suddenly she turned wide, fearful eyes on her maid. "Oh, Florence, what have I gotten myself into?"

"Don't you look at me as if I had answers," Florence said austerely. "You should have thought of that sooner, my girl."

"I don't know this man I'm marrying," Corinne went on. "My God, I still don't even know where he comes from!"

"Does it matter?"

"Nor do I know where we will live. We can't very well stay in his hotel."

"I'm sure he has made some kind of plans, Cori," Florence tried to reassure her.

"He'd better not. Not without my approval!" she snapped childishly. "And if he thinks I am going to leave Boston to go live wherever it is he comes from, well—"

"I don't know why you didn't talk these things out with the man. What have you been thinking of?"

"It didn't occur to me until now," Corinne admitted, and then cried in a burst of panic. "Oh, Florence, I won't marry him! I can't!"

"That would be a scandal—one to set all of Boston on fire. Corinne Barrows doesn't show up at the church!"

"But—"

"No buts." Florence cut her off, though gently. "You're just nervous, Cori. It happens to all brides. This marriage is what you wanted. And you're getting a fine, handsome devil for a husband."

"Devil is right."

"Tsk! From what I've seen of Jared Burk, he's nothing but a pussycat. He's a charmer, that one."

"Well, I've seen another side to him, Florence. He's like two completely different men."

"What are you talking about?"

"Nothing," Corinne answered quickly. "It must be nerves. Maybe I'm just worried about tonight and what will happen after the reception."

"Ah, that will go smoothly," Florence chuckled. "You know what it's all about because I told you so myself, since your poor mother wasn't around to do so. Not that she would have, with her upbringing. Lord, but you're not like your mother at all."

"I remember so little about her," Corinne reflected, feeling herself slowly relaxing. "Only that she and Father never really got along."

"Well, their marriage was one of convenience too, just like yours will be."

"I know," Corinne said and glanced at the clock. "We had better be going if I'm going to dress at the church. I'll tell Father while you get my things ready. And don't forget my grandmother's pearl necklace. It will go so well with all that white lace on my gown."

"I know, I know," Florence smiled. "Are you feeling better now?"

"Yes. I don't know what got into me, but I'm fine now. Let's get this wedding over with."

Parked at the end of the street, a few houses away from the church, was an old-fashioned coach with two spirited mares harnessed to it. The coach was empty and facing away from the church, but a heavily cloaked driver sat up on the box, turning to look back at the church every time he heard a carriage pull up near it.

Thunder sounded often, and lightning lit the darkly clouded sky. The rain came down in sheets, but the driver didn't seek the dry interior of the coach.

He waited, waited for one particular carriage and the occupant who would step down from it. A brand new rifle was held tightly in his hands, concealed beneath his cloak.

Jared was in a foul mood. He rode to the church with Willis Sherman, the lawyer Dougherty had recommended to him. Sherman would be his best man, and sat across from him in the carriage. Jared hid his agitation from Sherman.

What in damnation was he doing marrying Barrows' daughter! Every time he looked at her he was reminded of her father and how much he hated him. But it wouldn't be for long, he told himself. As soon as he used Corinne's shares to destroy the firm, she would divorce him. But how long would that take? And was it worth marrying her for?

So much time had already been invested. He had left home five months ago. But at least no one at home would know that he had married and divorced during his trip to the mainland. He wished it were over, that he were on his way home right now.

The carriage stopped and Jared waited for the ushers to bring umbrellas before he stepped outside. A fine day for a wedding, he thought grimly. Suddenly, thunder cracked like a shot from a gun and it was several seconds before Jared realized it had indeed been a shot. And he soon spotted a hole in the carriage where the bullet had struck only inches from him. Jared watched as a coach took off quickly down the street.

"Strange-sounding thunder," Willis Sherman remarked as he followed Jared to the church.

"Yes, it was," Jared replied, saying nothing more.

His instinct was to follow the disappearing coach. But Corinne would never tolerate being stood up at the altar. He was stunned, not so much because he could have been killed, but because he couldn't figure why someone would try to shoot him. He had no enemies here in Boston. It didn't make any sense. For that reason, he concluded that the shot had not been meant for him. It was probably a madman run amuck.

"Come on, before we get soaked," Willis urged. "It's coming down hard and these umbrellas aren't any help."

Jared nodded and hurried up the steps to the church. He dismissed the shooting. Right now, he had to get married.

A few minutes later, Samuel and Corinne Barrows slowly followed Lauren, the maid of honor, down the aisle. Jared stood waiting at the altar with an impatient look about him that made Corinne all the more nervous.

He was superbly fitted in black pants and a white formal jacket with black velvet lapels. He was extremely handsome. Corinne couldn't help feeling a little proud because of it. Lauren was happy, and also envious. And Cynthia had refused to come to the wedding. She had had such high hopes about Jared, and wouldn't even talk to Corinne. Russell hadn't come, either. But many others from her crowd of friends and her father's friends were there to wish her well. The guests were richly and colorfully dressed.

Her father pressed her arm reassuringly, but his presence didn't help her panic. Her hands were sweating. Her heart pounded so furiously she could hear it above the music and the roaring rain outside.

When Jared took her hand, she knew he could feel the cold clamminess of it. He would know how frightened she was. When he smiled at her she blushed hot pink beneath her veil. She couldn't know that he was admiring her despite himself. In the lace-covered white silk gown and hem-length matching veil, she was lovelier than anyone he had ever seen. What a peculiar twist of nature, Jared considered, that anyone as heartless as Corinne Barrows should look so much like an angel. Her dark-gold hair was piled high and pinned with pearls, then covered by the veil. She carried New England fall flowers, the deep red and orange chrysanthemums accenting her lovely hair perfectly. Jared shook himself from his reverie as the minister began. The gaunt old man in white robes began the traditional wedding service, but Jared paid scant attention, and Corinne barely heard what was said. She had just realized that she was utterly alone, and likely to stay that way. After today, her father would not play a large part in her life, and Jared had promised not to interfere in her life at all. He had signed a paper agreeing to that. She had in effect made him state that he didn't give a damn about her. And he didn't. She would have only herself to depend on from today on.

"I now pronounce you man and wife."

Corrine gasped. She couldn't run away now. It was over. She had said yes without even knowing it. She stood paralyzed as Jared lifted her veil and touched her cold lips with his.

"Smile, Mrs. Burk," he whispered as he took her arm to escort her down the aisle. "This is supposed to be a happy occasion."

She fixed a smile on her lips for the benefit of the guests, and was soon lost in a whirl of congratulations. She was passed from one man to another for the traditional bride's kiss. Eventually Jared maneuvered her through the crowd and out of the church. They dashed to the waiting carriage that would take them to the photographer's studio and then the reception at her home.

Riding in the carriage, avoiding Jared's eyes, Corinne kept repeating to herself, it's done, it's done. She had her marriage certificate, which she had signed without even looking at it. And at home she had the document that would make Jared honor his promises to her. It would be all right. She just had to get through tonight.

She sat through the picture-taking with an outward show of calm. Jared no longer seemed impatient. The pictures were taken quickly, and they left. They had not spoken more than a dozen words to each other.

The reception was in full swing when they arrived at the Barrows' townhouse. Again they were bombarded with good wishes by a jubilant crowd. The party was gay. Samuel

Barrows had ordered the best foreign delicacies and the most expensive champagne. Boston society could always unbend for a wedding party. Frequent toasts were made, and Corinne was seldom without a glass in her hand. But much sooner than she expected, Jared suggested they leave. Corinne refused and refused again, but finally Jared cornered her by the stairs.

"Go up and change, Corinne."

There was a determined note in his voice, but she wasn't nearly drunk enough yet to go with him.

"Won't we be staying here for the night?"

"Under your father's roof? Hardly," he replied derisively. "We shall spend our short honeymoon at my hotel."

"Not yet, Jared. It's still early."

He grabbed her elbow and his grip was unduly harsh. "I know what you're trying to do, Corinne, but it won't work. This night is mine, and I intend that we both enjoy it."

"You can enjoy it all you want, but I certainly won't!" she hissed, furious that he saw through her plan.

"I wouldn't be too sure," he said with a devilish smile that made her shiver.

"I don't want to go yet, Jared." She tried pouting, but it didn't work.

"I will take you upstairs myself, Corinne, if I have to," he warned her. "And if you're not back down here in twenty minutes, then—"

"Very well!" She glared at him before she went upstairs in a huff.

Florence was waiting for her. A burgundy dress and cape were laid out on her bed. "I only just laid your clothes out. I didn't think you would be up this soon."

"Neither did I!" Corinne replied angrily.

"The other things you will need have already been sent to his hotel."

"By whose orders?"

"Mr. Burk arranged it."

"Did you know about this?"

"Come now, Cori. You didn't really think you would spend your wedding night in your own home, did you?" Florence admonished.

"I just don't like having things arranged for me without my knowledge."

"Well, if you had taken the time to discuss things with your husband before today, you wouldn't be surprised."

"My husband? Yes, well, speaking of *him,* we had best hurry. He had the nerve to threaten to come up here and get me if I take too long."

Florence chuckled. "He's impatient, is he?"

"He'll have his one night—but that's all he'll ever have!"

The ride to the hotel was accomplished in total silence. Corinne was feeling only a little light-headed from all the champagne she had consumed, but that was slowly slipping away because of her anger and, she had to admit, her fear. She had hoped not to be aware of one minute of the ordeal, but Jared had thwarted her.

His hotel suite was large and luxurious, one of the best the management offered. There was a burgundy and gold living room, with a balcony overlooking the city, and a bedroom hidden by double doors. She eyed those doors warily as Jared took her cloak from her and tossed it on a sofa. Then she saw a bucket on the table with a bottle of champagne chilling in it.

Nodding towards the bottle, she smiled. "We haven't toasted each other yet."

"Let's not be hypocritical, Corinne."

"For God's sake!" she snapped. "One more glass isn't going to knock me out!"

He came over to her and lifted her chin to stare into her dark green eyes. "Very well, if you go and change while I fill the glasses."

She turned away from him. "Can't that wait a bit longer?"

"No."

"Please, Jared."

He grabbed her shoulders, forcing her to look at him again. "Reluctance was not part of our agreement, Corinne," he said in a surprisingly gentle voice. "Why do you begrudge me this one night? I'm not going to hurt you again, I promised you that."

She knew she was being unreasonable. She had demanded so much, yet this was all he had asked for in return.

"I'm sorry," Corinne said weakly, lowering her eyes. "I guess I'm just—frightened."

He drew her into his arms and held her gently for several long moments before he spoke. "I know. But you have nothing to fear from me." He lifted her face to his and kissed her tenderly. "Tonight isn't going to be like the last time, Corinne. I'm not angry with you, and I promise not to lose my temper, so there is no reason for you to be afraid."

He spoke so softly that she almost trusted him. Almost. She remembered the feelings that used to soar through her when he kissed her before. Perhaps she might enjoy tonight after all.

"I won't be long," she said shyly and walked to the bedroom.

Jared smiled as she closed the doors behind her. How easy to manipulate Corinne was, when he made the effort. He would give her something to remember tonight, something to make her wish she hadn't demanded separate bedrooms.

Corinne found her traveling case open on the foot of the bed. She withdrew the negligee and robe that she had bought for tonight. The gown was a delicate lime green lace over a dark emerald silk. It wasn't overtly sexy, but it was provocative nonetheless, with its form-fitting lines and deep cleavage. There were long, filmy silk sleeves, and the back dipped as low as the front. Pearl buttons held it from hem to cleavage.

She changed into the gown and then began taking the pearl pins from her hair. She wasn't quite finished when Jared came into the room with two glasses of champagne deftly balanced in one hand while he opened the door. He had removed his jacket and tie, and his white frilled shirt was opened to the waist, displaying a chest of curly black hair.

"Go on with what you were doing," he said as he handed her one of the long-stemmed glasses. His eye roamed over her appreciatively before he continued. "I just wanted to start a fire to get this room warmed. Your Boston weather is a bit colder than I'm used to."

Corinne took a sip of the champagne, then put it down and started combing out her hair. She watched him covertly as he walked to the fireplace. So he was used to a hot climate. But of course, with that rich tan.

"Just where do you come from, Jared?" She saw his back stiffen as she asked him. "Isn't it about time you stopped avoiding that question?"

"It's just not important," he replied, not facing her.

She smiled beguilingly. "Maybe not, but satisfy my curiosity anyway."

"I was raised on an island in the Pacific, Corinne."

She was genuinely surprised. Why had she assumed he was from out West?

"What's it called?"

"Oahu," he said truthfully, omitting the name of the island chain.

"I've never heard of it."

"I didn't think you would have," he replied as the fire started crackling. He turned to grin at her. "Now no more questions."

"Just one more?" she asked cajolingly.

He shrugged and started to take his shirt off. "Go ahead."

Corinne turned around quickly, embarrassed to watch him undress. "What do you do there?"

"I build houses."

Again she was surprised. She hadn't pictured him as a builder. A rancher or miner, yes, even a gambler—he did that so well. But certainly not a builder. It seemed so unchallenging, so unlike him.

"You have a business there?"

"Yes."

"And you plan to return to it?"

"I thought you were going to ask only one more question," he reminded her.

"Do you, Jared?" she persisted.

He sighed. "Eventually." She turned away as he shucked off the rest of his clothes.

They really would live separate lives, Corinne thought. Thousands of miles separate, for she wasn't about to live on some obscure island. But she had no more time to think about it as Jared came up behind her and his lips found the smoothness of her neck.

Corinne molded herself to him, enjoying the exciting feel of him. When his mouth moved to the sensitive area of her ear, she grew hot with pleasure. She didn't protest as his fingers unfastened the buttons down to her waist and the gown fell to her feet.

The heat from the fire reached them, but Corinne was feeling a different kind of heat as Jared turned her around in his arms and kissed her hungrily. She was startled as his hard manhood pressed against her, but she hesitated only a moment before she turned to face him, raised her arms around his neck, and returned his kiss with abandon.

Corinne had never felt such thrilling sensations as she did now with her body pressed against his. She was actually disappointed when he released her. He took her hand and pressed his lips to it, his blue-gray eyes looking deeply into her dark-green ones. Then he led her to the large bed and gently pushed her down on it. For the first time she saw him completely, and was amazed at the sight. All his power and strength was there for her to see, in the long legs, the hard muscles across his chest and arms, and the animal grace. He was a superb, rugged, hard man, and it thrilled her just to look at him.

When she caught him grinning at her she blushed hotly. Had he seen her admiration?

"I—I didn't mean to stare," she stammered and became even more embarrassed.

"Have you never seen a man before?" he asked softly.

"No."

"But you must have seen me when—"

"No, I didn't," she admitted quickly. "I kept my eyes closed."

Jesus, even though he had taken her once, she was still really a virgin. Jared laughed kindly, and lay down beside her.

"You are so innocent, Kolina, so very innocent," he said as he placed soft kisses over her face. "And so beautiful, so exquisitely soft and sensual."

His eyes moved slowly from her waves of gold hair, over the entire length of her supple body. His hand followed, then his lips. Corinne began forgetting her embarrassment as she felt every part of her being explored and delighted. Had he done this before? But, no, she wouldn't think of that other time. This was all different.

When he opened her legs and moved on top of her she

103

was ready for him. His lips sought hers again before entering her, and the kiss left her trembling.

"Do you know how much I want you, Corinne?"

She looked into his blue-gray eyes, hazy and half-closed, and she knew. "Yes."

"And you want me?"

She felt no shame in answering, "Oh, yes, Jared."

"Now?"

"Yes, now!"

She hooked her fingers in his thick black hair and pulled his lips to hers, kissing him with a passion she hadn't known she possessed. At the same time, the top of his organ probed for entrance, found it, and glided smoothly into her, deeper, until she felt all of him pulsating in her. He was exquisitely tender at first, moving in her slowly, giving her time to savor each new sensation to its fullest. It was she who quickened the tempo when a sweet ecstasy suddenly surged through her whole being. She met his every thrust with a savage fury, feeling this had to be the height of bliss, but there was more, and she held her breath as the feeling intensified. All too soon, those final thrusts sent her soaring into the most glorious throbbing esctasy imaginable.

Some time later, Corinne floated back to reality. To think she had looked with dread on that magnificent experience. What a fool she had been! But Florence never told her it would be like *that!* And dear Lord, she had made Jared promise it would not happen again!

Corrine opened her eyes to gaze into Jared's. He actually looked as stunned as she was.

"Is it always like that?" she asked dreamily, her fingers running through his hair. She felt so good she didn't want to move ever again.

"No, love," he answered huskily. "It depends on the partners, if their passion is equally matched."

"Ours was, wasn't it?" she grinned.

He touched his lips to hers ever so softly. "Perfectly," he agreed.

Jared wouldn't admit that it had never been better for him. He couldn't believe what had happened. He had never had a woman abandon herself so passionately before. Oh, there had been savage meetings of the flesh, but none quite so satisfying. Why did it have to be this woman who set his blood on fire and had the power to make him want her again, even now?

"Oh, Jared." She snuggled her face against his neck and heard him groan. "I loved it. Did you?"

He cupped her face in his hands and grinned down at her. "Are you fishing for compliments?"

"I suppose so," she giggled.

"You were magnificent, Kolina, but then you must know that."

"Kolina? You said that before. What does it mean?"

"Your name in my language."

"Oh." she said, disappointed. She had hoped it was an endearment.

Jared started kissing her again. Maybe she wouldn't have to tell him how foolish she had been to insist on separate bedrooms. Maybe he knew and wouldn't make her bring it up. And as he started to move in her, she felt sure that he, too, would want this again and again.

Chapter 14

"ARE you awake, Corinne?"

She rolled over under the sheets, half asleep, and found the space beside her empty. She looked about the room until she saw Jared standing by the fireplace. He had donned a black robe and held a glass of champagne in his hand.

Corinne frowned. "Aren't you going to sleep tonight?"

"A man doesn't get married every day," he replied offhandedly. "I'm too wound up yet to sleep."

She grinned impishly. "You want to—"

"I can only do so much in so short a time, Corinne."

"Have I exhausted you?" she teased.

"For the moment, yes."

"Well, come back to bed and I'll make you feel different."

"My God, you're insatiable!" he exclaimed incredulously, and shook his head. "But I want to talk right now."

"I don't," she pouted and turned over on her stomach.

Jared sauntered over to the bed and sat down beside her. "Appease me," he said, and rubbed a hand over her behind. "When is the next board meeting, Corinne?"

"Why on earth would you want to know that now?" she asked into her pillow without looking at him.

"It's a matter that concerns me."

"I don't know, Jared. I've never gone to the meetings."

"Why not?" His hand moved up to her back, and then back down to her thighs. "You're the largest shareholder. Don't you have any interest in the firm?"

"Why should I? My father won't let me vote my shares anyway."

"But you're married now," he reminded her. "He no longer controls your trust."

"My money, no, but he still has control of my interests in the firm. He will control my shares until he feels I am capable of taking over my interests."

"But you have a husband now who can look after your interests for you."

"My father would have to trust you completely, Jared, before he would turn my shares over to you."

Jared's hand stopped moving. "You're my wife. Our vote should be the same."

She turned around to look at him. "Why are you making so much out of this, Jared? My father knows what is best for the firm. He isn't going to misuse my vote."

"But that gives him complete control of the firm."

"He should have that control. After all, his family founded the shipyard. What are you worried about? You will make a handsome profit from your investment. The firm isn't about to go bankrupt."

"What if you told your father you were ready to take responsibility for your shares?"

Corinne laughed. "He wouldn't believe me. He knows I don't want to be bothered."

"But if you tried."

"Jared, he would know it was your idea," she said seriously. "He would revert to his absurd assumption that you wanted control of the firm. But you don't, do you?"

He stood up stiffly. "Of course not," he said in a barely controlled voice and started to walk from the room.

"Where are you going?"

"I have a letter to write. Go to sleep, Corinne."

It took every effort for Jared to close the bedroom door quietly. He stood there, so filled with blind rage that the stem of his champagne glass broke in two. Blood flowed unchecked from his palm. He started to throw the glass across the room, but caught himself in time and let it drop soundlessly to the carpeted floor.

Damn Barrows to hell and back again! The sly, suspicious bastard! Why had he kept those facts a secret? Jared had married Corinne for *nothing!* He had had doubts before the wedding—he should have acted on his instincts. Now . . .

He sat down at the writing table and began a letter. Nothing had gone right on this trip, but he would not go home without letting Barrows know why he had come. The man would not feel his wrath fully, but he would never forget the encounter.

Two hours had passed before he finished the letter to Samuel Barrows and also wrote out a notice for the newspapers. His anger had not cooled. He looked toward the bedroom and did not feel the slightest twinge of pity for the woman there. She would suffer the most for what he was going to do, but Barrows would also feel her shame. She was her father's one weakness. What hurt her hurt him.

Jared entered the bedroom and crossed quietly to the bed. The fire had not quite died out, and he could see Corinne's sleeping figure clearly. His face softened as he looked down at her delicate beauty, the soft waves of gold hair. He started to reach out and touch her, but stopped himself.

He became furious all over again. He would not have regrets, damn it! She would recover eventually, he told himself. She was resilient.

Forcing himself not to look at Corinne again, Jared dressed and packed his things quickly, then left his hotel. He stopped off at the newspaper office and arranged for his notice to be posted the following morning and printed daily for one month. Then he went directly to Beacon Street, his last stop before he caught the first train West.

It was three o'clock in the morning when the butler answered Barrows' door and said dryly, "Another matter of urgency, sir?"

Jared would not be put off. "I wouldn't be here on my wedding night if it weren't."

Brock straightened his back. "Yes, sir. I will wake Mr. Barrows at once."

"I will wait in his study," Jared said and crossed the dark hall.

In less than ten minutes Samuel Barrows burst into the room wearing robe and slippers, his blonde hair touseled from sleep. But he was wide awake, and upset.

Jared saw his fearful reluctance to ask what had happened. "Before you waste time with questions, there is nothing wrong with Corinne. She is sleeping peacefully and doesn't know I am here."

"Then why—"

"Sit down, Barrows," Jared interrupted him coldly. "I will ask the questions this time, and one in particular. Why the hell didn't you tell me you controlled Corinne's shares in the shipyard and would still have that control even after she married?"

Samuel was not only surprised by the question, but a bit shaken by Jared's icy tone. "It was not pertinent to our dealings."

"In your opinion! And you still felt those facts weren't pertinent even after I offered to marry your daughter?"

"*Is* that why you married her, Burk?" Samuel began to despair. Why hadn't he realized there was something strange about the marriage? "To get control of the firm?"

"Yes! And my name is not Burk, it's Burkett."

"Burkett? Why would you use a false name? I don't understand any of this. You have married an extremely wealthy woman. You could buy a half dozen shipyards."

"I don't want her or her money—I never did," Jared said venomously. "And you could have spared her a lot of pain and humiliation if you hadn't seen fit to hide those facts from me when I made my investment."

"Why are you so obsessed with this shipyard? Why do you want it so badly?"

"I don't want it, Barrows! I wanted to *destroy* it, to bankrupt it and you!"

"Damn it, you're not making any sense!"

Jared threw the letter on Samuel's desk. "Read it. If I have to say any of it aloud I am going to lose what little control I have left and kill you!" Jared said in a deadly calm voice. "Now read it!"

Samuel stared at Jared in amazement. He had never been threatened before. And there was such underlying rage in this young man that was demanding release. There was a great deal he didn't understand.

Without further hesitation, Samuel picked up the bulky letter and read it quickly. When he finished, the letter dropped to his desk and he sat for a few moments, staring straight ahead. Then his eyes met Jared's. "Is it really true? Ranelle is dead? And all this time?" When Jared didn't answer, he said, "All these years I thought of her as living. I have been waiting for the day Corinne married and left home, before I . . . I meant to try again, Jared, to persuade your mother to come away with me."

"You meant to destroy her life *again?*" Jared said in that deadly quiet voice. "You did a thorough job the first time!"

"I loved your mother."

"You couldn't have," Jared replied with bitter contempt. "If you had, nothing would have stopped you from marrying her!"

"You don't under—"

"I said *nothing!* I know of your family obligations, your so-called duty to save the family business. Well you saved it, didn't you—at my mother's expense!"

"I'm sorry, son."

"I'm not your son! I might have been, and I almost wish I were, then my mother might still be alive. She loved you so much that she couldn't bear life without you. She became a drunk. You did read that in the letter, didn't you? A drunk! It was the only way she could forget that you still wanted her!"

"I didn't know."

"Of course you didn't," Jared sneered. "After tearing my mother's world apart, you simply went back to your wife and daughter. It didn't matter to you what happened after you left Hawaii, what affect your visit had on my mother. She no longer cared about me or my father. We didn't exist for her anymore. And my father was nearly destroyed by it. He loved her, you see. She had been his for eight years, until you took it upon yourself to ruin our lives."

"I never meant to."

"I didn't tell you yet how she died, Barrows. You haven't asked. Don't you want to know?" Jared asked cruelly, beginning to relive the nightmare. When Samuel said nothing, he went on. "She walked into the ocean one night and took her own life. I saw her disappear under the waves, but I couldn't reach her in time. I couldn't find her at all until morning, when I finally saw where her swollen body had washed up on the beach."

"Surely it was an accident, Jared!"

"You would like to think that, wouldn't you? But you see, my mother couldn't swim, she had never learned. She never went near the water, not even to wade in it."

After a long silence, Samuel whispered, "And you blame me for all of this."

"I wanted you to know why I came here. I wanted to

ruin you, Barrows, but I failed. I would kill you now, but I think I've already suffered enough because of you."

"So you used my daughter to get at me. What about her? She is your wife, and need I remind you there was a matter of honor involved?"

Jared laughed bitterly. "There isn't a shred of honor in me. Haven't you realized that by now? And your daughter got what she asked for."

"Have you no conscience?"

"Have you?" Jared demanded. "Where was your conscience when you wrote my mother telling her about your baby daughter and that it was just as well she had decided not to go with you?"

"She did make that decision, Jared."

"Yes, she did, and she regretted it. She blamed me and my father because she felt obligated to stay with us. But none of it would have happened, Barrows, if you had stayed out of her life. What right did you have to seek her out after so many years? Did you really expect her to throw away the life she had made for herself and run away with you?"

"But I expected to find her free."

"But you didn't, and yet you still asked her to leave with you. You killed my mother. Indirectly, but the fact remains that she would be alive if it weren't for you. I hope that weighs on you forever. At least then my coming here won't be a total loss."

"Jared, please," Samuel began. "You have got to believe I—"

"No!" Jared cut him off sharply. "Nothing you could say would ease the hatred I have for you."

"And now?"

"I'm going home. Your shipyard is safe again. But at least I'm not leaving your family unscathed," Jared said with a vicious grin. "Your daughter isn't going to let you forget our meeting."

"What do you mean?"

"Corinne won't be too happy in the morning, nor will you be. And if you think you can retaliate by trying to cancel our business deal, don't. It would give me great pleasure to take you to court. So I will expect my profits on a regular basis, and I will retain my lawyer here to look

111

after my interests. I couldn't ruin you, Barrows, but I'm going to make money from you."

"I don't wish you ill, Jared."

"You will in the morning. It really is too bad Corinne has to suffer for what you did before she was even born. You can tell her I'm sorry for that. But it probably won't make a difference." With that, Jared stalked from the room without another word or a backward glance. He saw himself out.

Samuel heard the carriage drive away. Many emotions clouded his mind as he slouched back in his chair, but foremost was grief. His first and only love was dead. God help him, how could he live with that . . . and the fact that he was responsible?

Chapter 15

THE storm abated Monday morning, and by midday all traces of it were gone except for a few puddles here and there. The sky was bright. Boston was pleasantly warm for October. The city sparkled. But in the Back Bay section of Boston, on Beacon Street, the mood was not so cheerful.

Corinne came home alone at noon. Spending the entire morning sitting in Jared's empty hotel suite had made her more confused than angry. She waited hours before going down to the lobby to inquire if he had left a message. That was how she found out that Jared had checked out of the hotel in the middle of the night, without explanation.

At home, she learned that her father had locked himself in his study ever since Mr. Burk had called in the middle of the night. What was going on?

She found Samuel slumped over his desk, his head resting on his folded arms. There was an empty liquor bottle beside him.

"Father?"

Samuel raised his head groggily. Corinne gasped at the sight of his haggard face. She had never seen him look so old.

"Are you ill, Father?"

"Just tired, Cori," he answered, running a shaky hand through his hair. "I have been waiting for you. I rather expected you would be here sooner."

"Then you know I woke up alone this morning. Where is he, Father?"

"He's gone, Corinne. You won't be seeing your husband again—if he is your husband. Christ, the marriage may not even be legal!"

"Are you drunk?" Corinne demanded.

"I wish I were drunk, but unfortunately I'm not. I went

113

through a whole bottle, but it didn't help at all. Nothing is going to drown the truth."

"What truth? What do you mean 'if he is' my husband?" She held out her purse. "I have the certificate right here."

"Have you looked at it?"

Corinne frowned and quickly took the document from her purse. When she saw the name written next to hers, she drew in her breath sharply.

"Burkett? He used a false name for this!"

"No," Samuel sighed, having hoped that the name Burk would appear on the document. "It looks as though your marriage is legal after all. Jared Burkett is his real name."

"What is this all about, Father? Who the devil have I married?"

"A young man so full of hate that he came here just to destroy me. He thought he had failed, but he didn't. God help me—he didn't."

Her father was near tears and it tore at her heart. "What happened? What did he do to you when he was here last night?"

"He didn't do anything except tell me the truth, the truth of which I had been mercifully ignorant for nineteen years."

Samuel pushed the worn letter across his desk. "Here. That explains most of it. You have a right to know why he used you to hurt me."

Corinne read the letter, her back becoming stiffer as she did so. "He says you killed his mother," she gasped, her green eyes wide. "What does he mean?"

"My beautiful Ranelle took her own life. My God, if I had only known what my going to Hawaii would do to her!"

"You loved her?" Corinne asked quietly.

"She was my first love, and I hers. We expected to be married. There was no question in our minds. But then the damn shipyard was near ruin, and my family urged me to marry for money, in order to save it. God, if only I hadn't felt it was my responsibility to do it. But I did, and I married your mother instead. Ranelle ran away to Hawaii before I could ask her to wait for me. Many years passed before I found out where she had gone. Your mother and I had never got along well together, and we had no children. I felt the time was right to go to Ranelle and beg her to come back to me."

"You would have divorced mother?" Corinne asked in surprise.

"Yes. Ranelle and I belonged together—we were meant for each other. But I never dreamed she would also have married, and that she might have a child."

"Jared?"

Samuel nodded. "But even after I knew this, I still begged her to leave with me. I should never have let her know how much I still wanted her. It was that knowledge that she couldn't bear to live with once I had left Hawaii. She was never a strong woman."

"But she didn't go away with you—*she* made that decision," Corinne reminded him.

"Could you tear your seven-year-old son away from the father he adored, or desert that son? Could you so easily break the heart of a man who adored you and thought you loved him as much? Ranelle couldn't. But she regretted that decision. And then I disappointed her again. Before Ranelle could write to me, I wrote her to tell her I would stay with my wife, since she had given me a daughter. I told her it was just as well that she had made the choice she did. That destroyed Ranelle completely, though I never knew it until now."

"I am to blame," Corinne said sadly. "If I hadn't been born—"

"No! It had nothing to do with you. I was fool enough to think I could finally have what I wanted most, the one love of my life. But life had gone on, we were not the same people anymore. It was too late for us. If only I had realized that before I tried to recapture the past—I shouldn't have gone to Hawaii."

"I can see why Jared might blame you, but he's wrong. And you can't blame yourself, either. You couldn't have known what would happen. He blames me so much that he came here to destroy me. I've never met anyone so filled with hate."

"So he used me to get at you." She shrugged as if it didn't matter to her any longer. "But he gave me what I wanted, and if he thinks I will divorce him because he has deserted me, he's wrong. We will just have to hide the fact that he's gone, at least for a while. And then, to explain his continued absence, we can say he had to leave on business. Eventually I will say he died."

"Corinne," Samuel sighed. "Jared Burkett was after revenge. Though he failed to ruin me financially, he still got his revenge. Jared struck a final blow before he left. Here." He pushed the morning paper at her.

Corinne took the paper warily, a gnawing apprehension growing. In the lower right hand corner of page ten was a notice in bold black letters. It seemed to jump off the page at her.

DECLARATION OF DESERTION

Jared Burk hereby acknowledges
that his new bride, formerly
Corinne Barrows of Beacon Street,
has proved an unsatisfactory
wife. On these grounds
he has deserted her.

The numbness lasted only a moment. Then she stood up and began ripping the paper.

"How dare he!" she shouted, her temper unleashed fully. "And how dare that paper print such a crude notice? I will take them to court!"

"That would be even more embarrassing for you, Cori," Samuel said softly. "And the damage is already done. We'll just have to weather this."

"He's going to pay for this! My God, he made it sound as if I—I—" Tears sprang to her eyes. "It's a lie! I wasn't unsatisfactory—I wasn't!"

"Corinne, honey, no one is going to think otherwise."

"Won't they? He's gone—that much is true—and he made sure everyone would know that he left me!"

"If it's any consolation, Cori, Jared told me before he

116

left that he was sorry for having to use you to get to me. I think he really regretted that."

"Sorry?" she said furiously. "How can I face people? I won't be able to leave this house without dying of shame."

"It won't last forever, Cori. Gossip only runs its course so long, and then it is forgotten. It might be better if you went away for a while. I can start the divorce proceedings while you are away."

"Divorce? And bring further scandal on this family?" she glared at him. "No! There will be no divorce."

"But surely—"

"No! That's what Jared wants. I will die before I give that despicable cur what he wants. Let him wonder why he doesn't receive divorce papers. I hope it drives him crazy wondering. I hope he finds someone he loves and wants to marry. He won't be able to because I won't release him. Believe me, Jared Burk will pay for this—one way or another."

Chapter 16

CORINNE's anger had been a show, a disguise to keep private the terrible hurt she really felt. From that morning, she refused even to think about her wedding night. She would not allow herself to remember anything of Jared except the unpleasant elements in the man. She hid herself, refusing to go outside at all and receiving no one.

Florence was the first to see the changes taking place in Corinne, and Samuel also became disturbed. She was pale, she had none of her old humor, and she took no interest in anything. What distressed her father the most was her uncharacteristic quiet. She never argued, didn't join in conversations at meals, and offered no more than a perfunctory "good night" or "good morning." Samuel began to worry. This wasn't Corinne!

He forgot his own sorrow in his anxiety for his daughter. Nothing he did or said helped her. He had not expected her to bury her head in shame for so long. He kept urging her to travel, but she wouldn't hear of it.

"Cowards run away," Corinne would say and refuse to discuss it further.

Samuel prayed for something to jolt his daughter out of her lethargy. His prayers were soon answered.

"I am going to Hawaii, Father," Corinne announced a month after her wedding.

They were just sitting down to lunch, but Samuel's appetite was instantly spoiled.

"I won't allow it."

"Don't be unreasonable," Corinne said calmly. Her voice was unusually matter-of-fact. "You know you can't stop me from going. And you were the one who suggested I go away for a while."

"Not to Hawaii!"

"Why not?"

"Jared Burkett has already proved how ruthless he can be," Samuel reminded her sternly. "I don't want you crossing paths with him again."

"Don't be silly," she replied casually. "He's my husband, isn't he?"

"Oh, for heaven's sake! He doesn't give a damn about you, Cori."

"I'm still going, Father." There was a strong determination in her tone. "I think the trip will do me good. And Florence has already agreed to come with me."

Samuel leaned back in his chair and shook his head. "Why won't you let it be? Forget about Jared Burkett. I'm sure he's forgotten about you."

"It's not finished," Corinne said coldly. "Jared wanted revenge against you, but it was me he hurt. I had never done anything to him to deserve what he did to me. *He* believes in vengeance. Well, he has made a believer out of me, a wholehearted believer."

"Corinne, you can't cross swords with a man like that," Samuel warned her. "There is no way you can win. He doesn't fight fairly."

"I don't intend to fight fairly myself. And I'm not afraid of him."

"Well, you should be."

"Stop worrying," she said to pacify him. "I'm not going to do anything foolish."

"Just what *are* you planning to do?" Samuel asked. "You must have something in mind, or you wouldn't be so determined."

Corinne laughed, a wicked sound. It was a laugh her father had never heard before. "Yes, I do have something in mind. I'm going to give Jared Burkett a taste of his own medicine. We'll see how he likes facing scandal in *his* domain."

"What scandal?"

"The scandal of a promiscuous wife."

"Corinne!"

"Oh, settle down, Father," she grinned. "I'm not really going to have a multitude of lovers. I'm just going to give that impression. Jared's friends will think I am a tramp and that Jared isn't man enough to handle me. I don't care what they think about me, but Jared will. I'm going to humiliate him the way he did me, in front of all his friends."

"You think Jared will just sit back and let you make a fool of him? You think he won't stop you?"

"He can't," Corinne replied confidently. "He can't say a thing about what I do. I made sure of that before I married him."

Later that day, in her new confident mood, she agreed to see Russell when he called.

"The bastard deserves to be horsewhipped!" Russell stated vehemently after Corinne had explained everything. "How dare he slander you!"

"You tried to warn me about him," Corinne said magnanimously. "I should have listened to you."

Corinne went on to explain her immediate plans with a great deal of relish. And Russell surprised her.

"I will go with you, Corinne," he announced.

"Why would you want to do that?" Corinne asked, surprised. "I am not going on a pleasure cruise. I'm going to Hawaii with a definite purpose in mind."

"I know. But you need an escort. You can't face Burkett alone."

"My father seemed to think the same thing." Corinne was becoming annoyed. "I wish everyone would stop treating me like a child. I can take care of myself, and I intend to."

"I didn't think otherwise, Corinne," Russell replied quickly.

"It wouldn't hurt to have me along," he continued. "I could help you with your plan."

She quickly considered it. "Very well, Russell. As long as you understand that I don't intend to take any real lovers for quite some time. It will all be an act."

"I won't push you, Corinne."

"I want your promise on that," she said adamantly.

"You have it."

"One other condition," she said in a lighter tone. "You let me pay your expenses."

"That's ridiculous," Russell laughed, knowing full well

that she would insist. And thank goodness for that, because he would hate to have to borrow even more money now that his debts were already so high. "I know you must be dying to spend all that money of yours, but I won't hear of it. I'm not exactly from the poorhouse myself," he lied unconvincingly.

"I know that, but I insist. It will be as though I were hiring you as my escort," she explained.

"No!"

"I said I insist, Russell. I won't be obligated to you for helping me. I don't intend to ever feel obligated to anyone. That feeling destroys people."

"What are you talking about?"

"Never mind," she snapped. "Either I pay your way or you can forget about coming along."

"All right, all right," he sighed wearily. "If that's the only way you'll agree, then fine."

"Good," Corinne smiled, unaware of how well he had maneuvered her. "And just remember that I didn't ask you to come along. You offered. Now you had best run along and get your affairs in order. We will be leaving the day after tomorrow."

"So soon?"

"I see no reason to postpone it," Corinne answered. "The sooner I get even with Jared Burkett, the sooner I can regain my pride."

Chapter 17

SAMUEL Barrows did not stop voicing his disapproval of his daughter's decision. He tried to get her to reconsider, even at the train depot, but he knew he couldn't stop her. He did, however, make her promise to write frequently.

"And if you get into any trouble, you come home immediately."

"I will, Father."

To Russell he said, "I should have let you marry her, Drayton. I wish to God I had."

"I hope you remember that, sir, after I convince Corinne to divorce Burkett."

"Yes, well," Samuel said noncommittally. "I'm rather glad you're going along. Keep her out of mischief, will you?" He spoke to both Russell and Florence at once. And Russell replied for them both. "If that's possible."

Corinne was grateful that she had seen no one she knew on the way to the train station. It was the first time she had left her house since the terrible morning after her wedding. When she returned, she wouldn't care what people thought. She would have the satisfaction of knowing that she had gotten even with Jared, and perhaps even bested him. She could face anything after that.

The trip across country was not unpleasant. A quarter century ago it would have been difficult. But with the completion of the Union Pacific railroad in 1869, the journey took only a week. Corinne and Russell and Florence spent another week in San Fransisco, waiting for a ship.

San Fransisco was a bustling metropolis, so unlike sedate, ordered Boston, even for a city-bred girl. The three of them loved the noisy, colorful place. Corinne wondered what it was like during the gold rush. How many had struck it rich? How many died trying? That had been a time of adventure, when anything was possible.

122

In an elegant gambling house that catered only to the very rich, Corinne finally played in the no-limit game that had been her dream for so long. She won five thousand dollars. But it didn't seem to matter anymore. Jared had ruined the excitement for her, she reasoned. He had become her obsession.

No matter where she went or what she did, Jared seemed always to be with her. As the days brought her closer to Hawaii, Jared filled her mind more and more. It wouldn't have been so disturbing, except that she began recalling their wedding night. She couldn't forget it, though she had sworn to blot out the whole night.

As soon as they were out to sea she took to her bed with seasickness, and this, too, she blamed on Jared. Another mark against him, she swore.

She spent the whole three weeks crossing the Pacific lying in her bed. She lost weight. She felt terrible. And all the while she cursed Jared for every moment of her suffering. When the ship finally docked in Honolulu, she was almost too weak to get out of bed, but with a tremendous desire to touch land and Florence's help, she found her way out of her cabin and onto the deck.

Corinne was pleasantly surprised. It was December 12, a time for snow and freezing cold back in Boston, but here there were balmy ocean breezes and sunshine, and a definite fragrance in the air.

"You smell it, too?" Florence remarked. "It's flowers, all right. I learned a lot about Hawaii while you were indisposed. Visitors here are greeted with leis. It seems to be a tradition, and a nice one."

"Leis?"

"Wreaths of cut flowers to wear around the neck. This isn't Boston, my dear. Flowers grow here all year round. We're in the tropics now," Florence said, already fanning herself with a lace handkerchief. "I suppose it will take us a while to get used to the heat."

"I like it."

"You wouldn't if this were summer instead of the winter season," Florence replied. "I'm told it can be unbearably hot for *malihinis* in summer. It's a good thing we will be gone before then."

"*Malihinis?*"

"That's what the Hawaiians call newcomers," Florence explained with a touch of pride.

"My, you certainly are well-informed," Corinne grinned. "You must tell me more."

Florence didn't mind Corinne's teasing tone. "It doesn't hurt to know something about where you're going. There were quite a few passengers who had been here before. And the Captain was very knowledgeable."

"You're right," Corinne confessed. "I should have taken the time to learn something about Hawaii. After all, I could have read up on it while I was bedridden instead of moaning my sorrows to the blank walls."

"You can do that while you're regaining your strength. That's going to take a few weeks."

"Well, the sooner I get settled, the sooner I can recover. Where is Russell?"

"He's gone to see about our baggage. He said he would meet us on the dock with a carriage."

They moved through the throng of people on the dock and were greeted with *alohas* from friendly Hawaiians in bright floral clothes, bearing leis for every passenger. Other natives offered fresh island fruits. And a group of musicians were playing while local girls of dark beauty in colorful sarongs danced for the new arrivals.

Corinne was given two leis made of plumeria. She thanked the giver with a smile, but the scent of the flowers became cloying and she felt her stomach turning again.

"I have to sit down, Florence," she said, grabbing the older woman's arm.

"Come." Florence led her to a crate in some shade. "Wait here. I'll get you some of that fruit the vendors are selling. It's a wonder you can walk at all, you've eaten so little lately."

She came back in a moment with a large chunk of cut pineapple wrapped in a *ti* leaf, and a small basket with bananas, coconuts, and guavas in it.

"What kind of fruit is that?" Corinne asked warily.

"I've never seen the likes of it myself, but it's grown fresh here. Try this pineapple. They say there is nothing as delicious."

Corinne brought the yellow fruit to her lips but gagged when she smelled it. "Take it away."

"What's wrong, Cori?"

"Just take it away," Corinne moaned, turning sickly white. "I thought this nausea would go away once I left the ship, but it hasn't yet."

"Corinne—are you sure it isn't—something else?" Florence asked hesitantly. "You shouldn't be ill now. In fact, the ship's doctor told me that you shouldn't have been ill at all. People don't get sick on a smooth voyage like the one we had."

"What are you suggesting?"

"That you might be pregnant."

Corinne managed a chuckle. "Don't be ridiculous. I would know, wouldn't I?"

"Would you, as preoccupied as you have been with Jared Burkett? When is the last time you had your monthly flow?" she asked pointedly.

Corinne couldn't answer. She couldn't remember having it recently. "Oh, I don't know," she said impatiently.

"Think!"

She did, and the only time she could recall was before Jared raped her. Her green eyes widened and darkened almost instantly.

"No!"

"There's no use denying it, Cori. He sure was a virile devil."

"I won't have his child! My God, how much more is he going to ruin my life?"

"There's not much you can do about bearing the child. It's already growing."

"Well, I won't keep it!"

"That's up to you," Florence said with cold disapproval. "But right now we have to decide where you're going to have it. You can't very well go through with that absurd plan of yours now, not when you'll be showing soon. Maybe we should consider going back home right now."

Corinne grimaced at the thought. "I would die before I got back on a ship this soon. No, we'll stay here. I'm not giving up my plan. It will just have to be postponed for a while."

Chapter 18

CORINNE reclined in the shade on her large outdoor lanai overlooking the bustling city of Honolulu. She sipped a lemonade, and frowned every time the baby moved inside her. A notebook rested on her lap for the letter she wasn't really in the mood to write. She wasn't in a mood for much of anything except feeling sorry for herself.

Florence had gone down to the market, and Russell was off having fun somewhere. Corinne bitterly resented her forced confinement, but she had made the choice herself not to be seen by anyone in her present condition. She couldn't take the chance that Jared might find out. He wasn't going to know about the child, she would make sure of that.

Dear Father,

Nothing has changed since I wrote to you last. We're still living in the house I rented up here in the hills of Punchbowl. New summer blooms are everywhere, making it quite beautiful. In fact, you really can't imagine the multitude of color I have right in my own garden. I've been tending it myself, and learning about all the exotic plants and flowers here. That should tell you what an exciting time I am having.

The weather is much hotter than we New Englanders are used to. I seem to feel it more than the others, because of my condition. But being so high up on the mountain, we do get cool breezes, especially in the evenings. And Lord, how I wait for those breezes!

I am still in excellent health, so my doctor tells me, and I will deliver in another month. And as to the question in your last letter, no, I have not changed my mind about giving the baby away. It would just remind me of Jared, and I want to forget him completely once I leave here. Those motherly instincts you told me I should be feeling are just not there. I hate this baby, just as much as I hate Jared. And no, he will never know about the baby. That is one more bit of satisfaction I will have!

God, how callous she sounded. But she blamed that on Jared, too. He had introduced her to hate, and hate had eaten away any compassion she might once have had.

I am still going through with my plans, just as soon as I get back into shape. I haven't become too ungainly, so that shouldn't take long.

Jared is here in the city. Russell found out for me where he lives and also where he is working. He is building a hotel in the less populated beach area of Waikiki. He has obviously gone on with his life, without a thought for what he did to me. He has no idea I am here. I have not been seen in public since we arrived. Florence and Russell go out, but Jared doesn't know Florence, and Russell has kept away from Jared, so he assures me.

I can barely stand the waiting, with nothing to do. You know I am not a patient person. I got myself into this whole mess because I couldn't wait to get my hands on my trust. By the way, the money I brought with me is safely tucked away in a local bank, so you did not need to put up such a fuss about the large amount I wanted to bring.

I will write you again soon, Father. However, don't expect a full report on the birth of the baby. I'm not going to even look at it. It's best neither of us knows what it looks like, or even what sex it turns out to be. I don't think of it as my child, anyway. It's Jared's and only his. I have been informed by my doctor that the Hawaiians love all children. He has already found a good home for the baby, so you don't need to worry at all.

I love you, Father, and I hope you can forgive me for giving away your grandchild. I just couldn't bear to keep it. Please understand.

> Your devoted daughter,
> Corinne Barrows Burkett

Her father wouldn't like this letter. But then he hadn't liked any of the letters she sent home. She always sounded so bitter and hard. Cold, he had called her. Jared had, too. Perhaps she was. But she was strong. It was not easy to be a woman.

Corinne sealed her letter and took it into the house. Florence would mail it. The house was so quiet. Even the stern German cook they had hired had gone off for the afternoon.

With no one to talk to, Corinne became restless and went outside to work in the garden. An hour or so later, the carriage drove up the steep hill and Florence alighted with baskets of fresh meat and vegetables. She found Corinne trimming the hibiscus shrubs that formed a fence around the yard, dense green shrubs with huge paperlike flowers of yellow and red.

Florence frowned. "Look at you, Cori. You're roasting in the sun."

Corinne wiped dripping sweat from her brow with a dirty hand. "I have nothing better to do."

"When it's this hot, you could at least work in the shade, my girl. It's a wonder you don't faint in this heat. Now come along and I'll run you a cool bath."

She helped Corinne to her feet and up the few steps at the front of the house. A porch bordered the front, and potted ferns and flowers hung from the rafters and were set along the banisters. Young palms grew at the corners of the house, front and back. Such a profusion of delightful fragrances and colors made the porch a welcome place to relax.

"You wait here, Cori, while I put these baskets away and get your bath ready."

"I don't know why I let you mother me like this," Corinne complained, then smiled tiredly. "But a long cool bath does sound nice. My back has been nagging me again."

"If I didn't know better, I would think you were farther along than you are," Florence remarked, eyeing Corinne's large belly under the tentlike Hawaiian dress called a *muumuu*.

"Don't be silly." Corinne used the phrase she always used when someone came near the truth.

Florence shook her head and went on into the house. Corinne sat down awkwardly in one of the rattan chairs on the porch. It was possible, she thought sullenly, patting her belly. She could indeed give birth any day now. But even though that would end her waiting, she didn't want it to be so. Then she would have to explain to Florence about the first time she and Jared had been together, and she would rather keep that to herself.

A breeze stirred the plants on the porch and brought with it the intoxicating fragrance of gardenias from the bushes in front of the house. Corinne breathed deeply of the scent that had become her favorite, but then she held the breath as her back ached sharply again. Too much bending over, she thought angrily. She should have known better. She couldn't even work in the yard anymore without the child causing her discomfort.

How she resented it. The baby had caused her nothing but trouble, even from its conception. Corinne felt defeated, ready to take to her bed and not leave it.

"Come along, Cori." Florence opened the front door. "The tub is full."

Corinne started to get up but couldn't, and fell back with a huff. "You'll have to help me. I can't even get out of a chair anymore."

Florence chuckled and took Corinne's hand to pull her up. "You're just having a terrible time of it aren't you, my dear? It's too bad *he* couldn't be here to share in what he did and listen to all your complaints."

"If he were here right now, I think I would gladly cut his throat for this!"

"Now, now. It took the two of you to make that baby. You did want to marry him, remember?"

"Don't remind me. I didn't know he was just using me to get at my father. And he damn well didn't have to do what he did before he left! Nor did he have to leave me with a baby!"

"Now, Cori, the doctor warned you about upsetting yourself. And we've been over this time and again. You know I feel you should have left well enough alone. No good can come of vengence."

"Satisfaction can come of it," Corinne said stubbornly. Then, suddenly, she gasped and doubled over in pain.

"What is it?" Florence asked, then her hazel eyes widened. "Oh, Lord, it's not coming prematurely, is it?"

"No," Corinne said after the spasm passed. "I'm afraid it's on time. You were right about my being farther along."

"I knew there was something you were hiding from me back there before the wedding. No wonder you rushed into it so quickly."

"Florence, please!" Corinne moaned. "I will explain later. Right now, just get me to bed. My back is killing me."

"Oh, Lord, it's going to be one of *those* births," Florence mumbled to herself.

"What?"

"Nothing, love. Come on. I'll get you to your room and then go for the doctor."

"No!" Corinne cried. "You can't leave me!"

"All right, Cori, all right," Florence said soothingly. "We have lots of time anyway. I'll send the cook for the doctor when she comes back."

Eighteen hours later, Corinne fought against consciousness. That terrible pain that had wrenched her body was still too well-remembered. She just wanted to sleep, now that it was over, and forget the agony. But that awful crying wouldn't let her.

"Here, Mrs. Drayton."

Corinne kept her eyes closed. She knew Dr. Bryson was talking to her, for she had assumed Russell's name for the sake of appearances. After all, he was living in the same house with her. Why couldn't the doctor leave her alone now? He had bullied her for the last few hours, telling her what to do, coaxing her to relax when she knew she couldn't. He kept saying it wasn't time yet, when she knew she would die if the agony didn't stop.

Dr. Bryson had complained that she was the worst patient he had ever had, whereupon she had told him to go to hell. He was shocked by her language, for she had cursed Jared with every loathsome name she had ever picked up as a child visiting the shipyard. Jared's name had come to her lips every time the pressure became unbearable. Lord, his ears must have been ringing. She only wished he could have been here to receive her curses.

"Mrs. Drayton, please."

She opened her eyes. "Can't you leave me alone now? I just want to sleep."

"We're not finished yet."

"I am!"

Dr. Bryson sighed. He was a little man in his late forties, with thinning hair and large spectacles that kept falling down his long nose. He was really at the end of his patience.

"I have to cut the cord yet. You will have to hold your baby for a moment."

"No!"

"You are the most disagreeable young woman I have ever met," he scolded her. "Now stop being unreasonable."

"Let Florence hold it," Corinne said stubbornly while she avoided looking at the wailing infant. "You know I don't want to see it. I told you that beforehand."

"Your maid has gone for fresh water."

"Well, wait until she returns!"

"Do you want to risk infection?" he asked harshly. "Now hold your child!"

He didn't give her a chance to refuse again, but placed the baby at her side in the crook of her arm. Corinne turned away quickly before she saw it. She wanted no memory, no picture of it to carry in her mind.

"Hurry up, will you?" Corinne said bitterly as the child continued to wail.

It seemed to scream louder when the cord was cut and Corinne gasped. Dr. Bryson smiled.

"Relax, Mrs. Drayton."

"Did you hurt it?"

"No."

"Well, take it back then."

"Not yet. We still have you to finish with. Now push," he said and applied pressure to her abdomen.

The placenta slid from her with only minor discomfort. The infant still wailed.

"Will you take the baby out of here now?" she pleaded.

"We still have to wait for the water to wash the blood off of the little fellow."

"Blood!" she gasped and automatically turned to the baby.

"It's not his blood, Mrs. Drayton," the doctor reassured her. "No, he's a fine, healthy boy."

Now Corinne couldn't tear her eyes away. She had given this small person life! She had suffered for it, gone through the most excruciating pain imaginable so that it might live. A little boy!

"He's terribly ugly, isn't he?" Corinne couldn't help asking.

Dr. Bryson laughed heartily. "That's the first honest opinion I've ever gotten from a new mother. But I guarantee he will look better once he's cleaned up."

"Why won't he stop crying?"

"He has just been taken from his nice, warm, nourishing home of the last nine months. He is understandably upset about that and could use some comforting."

"I—I don't—"

"All he needs is your breast, Mrs. Drayton."

"I couldn't!" she said quickly.

"Well, that's up to you. I suppose it won't hurt to let him cry for a while. I'll just go and see what is keeping that water."

"Wait!"

But Dr. Bryson closed the door firmly. He found Florence in the kitchen sitting at the table over a half glass of whiskey.

"Do you have an extra glass?" he asked.

Florence looked up at him worriedly, almost afraid to ask the question. "Did it work?"

"I can't tell yet. We'll give her a little while, but then I've got to clean that baby. I don't hold with not bathing them immediately."

Florence got up for another glass and filled it. "Lord, I pray I did the right thing. But I just couldn't bear seeing her give the babe away. I knew she would be sorry after it was too late."

"If I didn't agree with you, I wouldn't have gone through with that farce."

"She wouldn't listen to reason. If leaving her alone with him doesn't do the trick, nothing will."

"Well, we'll just have to wait and see. Where is the father, anyway?"

"Oh, he went off to get drunk," Florence replied, referring to Russell. "He certainly had the right idea," she added, lifting her glass.

She had taken Dr. Bryson into her confidence, but not so far as to deny Corinne's supposed marriage to Russell. The doctor frowned on Corinne enough as it was without making it worse by telling him the truth. And Russell Drayton wasn't getting drunk because of nervousness. He was celebrating that it was finally over. He assumed the baby had come prematurely, and after Corinne had explained to Florence about the night the baby was conceived, Florence let him go on thinking that. The truth was that Russell never thought about the baby, and didn't care.

Lord, Florence didn't like that man. Russell seemed somehow different whenever Corinne wasn't near. He was like two different men. But she couldn't quite put her finger on what it was, exactly, that disturbed her about him.

Dr. Bryson finished his drink. "We had best get back in there."

"But do you think Cori has had enough time yet, Doctor?" Florence asked with a doubtful frown. "Maybe seeing the baby and holding it won't make her change her mind. She is such a stubborn girl."

"Stubborn is hardly the word, Miss Merrill! I have never met such a cantankerous, hot-headed young woman."

Florence had to grin. "She does have a bit of a temper, and very little patience."

"That's putting it mildly," Dr. Bryson grunted. "Well, come along with that water."

When they entered Corinne's room, they found her propped up in bed, gazing down at the child in her arms. When she looked up, there was no anger in her lime-green eyes.

"Be quiet," Corinne whispered. "He's sleeping."

Florence set the small tub of water down on a table and came over to the bed. "We're going to have to wake him anyway, my dear, for his bath."

"What took you so long?" Corinne demanded, though her voice wasn't harsh.

"I'm afraid that's my fault. I kept spilling the water," Florence lied. "Heavens, you were in labor eighteen hours, Cori. I haven't had a moment's rest yet. I'm plumb worn out and couldn't keep my hands from shaking."

"Why didn't Russell help you?"

"He's been gone all night. The sun's up, but he still has not come back."

"I'm sorry," Corinne replied. "I didn't know he would desert us like that."

Dr. Bryson chuckled. "That's generally the way with all new fathers, Mrs. Drayton. Very few of them stick around for the birthing."

Corinne wondered if Jared would have. But there was no point in thinking about that. Why, Jared didn't even know he had a son. A son! she thought with awe.

She watched keenly as Dr. Bryson picked up the baby and took him across the room. His wailing started again as they washed him. When they were finished, he was wrapped in a small blanket and Florence started to leave the room with him.

"Where are you taking him?" Corinne asked.

"I'll just put him in the next room for now," Florence replied. "The family who is going to take him hasn't been notified yet."

"I will take care of that this afternoon," the doctor offered. "You need your rest now. We all do. I will stop by tomorrow, Mrs. Drayton, to see how you're doing."

Corinne tried to let the exhaustion of the night take over, but though her body was willing, her mind wouldn't rest. She could hear the distant crying of the baby and the sound seemed to pull at her. Were they just going to let him wail like that?

What was the matter with her? She shouldn't care. That was Jared's child, and she hated it. What did she care if it cried itself sick? The baby would be gone soon and she would never see it again.

Corinne closed her eyes against the sound, willing it to stop. But a picture of the baby lying in her arms obsessed her. He had stopped crying when she offered him her breast. He had fallen asleep instantly, as if that had been the only thing he wanted. He had trusted her, depended on her to give him comfort.

The crying seemed to grow louder, reverberating in her mind until she couldn't stand it anymore. She fought the insistent desire to go to him.

"Florence!" Corinne called desperately. "Florence, make him stop!"

There was no answer and the wailing continued. Corinne

frowned. No, she couldn't see him again. She had to put him from her mind.

"Oh, stop it, baby. Please stop crying!"

She choked back tears that wanted to come. She got slowly out of bed. Her whole body ached. She would just make sure nothing was wrong with him, then she could sleep.

Walking was most uncomfortable, but she managed slowly. The baby had been put in the empty room next to hers. No one was there with him, either. The infant was in the center of the bed, braced with pillows on each side.

Corinne looked down at him. He did look a little better now that he was cleaned up. But he was reddish-blue from so much screaming.

"Hush," Corinne said softly, and touched her fingers to the fuzzy black hair on his head. "You have to stop this, do you hear?"

That didn't work. She opened his blankets to see if something was hurting him, but there was nothing. His poor little limbs were stiff with the effort he was making to be heard. He wasn't just crying, he was screaming his heart out and breaking hers in the process.

"Please, don't cry anymore," she pleaded. "I can't stand it."

Corinne picked him up and tried to soothe him, but still he screamed. Would nothing work? She put him back down on the bed and moved one pillow so she could lie beside him. Giving up, she opened the front of her nightgown and pulled him gently to her. When his cheek touched her breast he jerked about frantically until his little mouth clamped onto her nipple. It took a while for his breathing to settle down, but as before, he relaxed and fell asleep contentedly.

Corinne could hold back the tears no more. "Oh, God, no!" she sobbed, pain tearing at her heart. "Why did you do this to me!"

Florence looked in a while later and found mother and son both sleeping peacefully. She smiled and closed the door very softly.

Chapter 19

CORINNE examined herself critically in the full-length, mahogany-framed mirror. Her dress was azure blue, a delicate cotton poplin with white lace trimmings—very cool, yet stylish. She carried a blue parasol. She wore her golden hair in the new style as well, pulled tightly up on the sides and back into a knot on top of her head, with a curled fringe on her forehead and temples. She didn't care for the uncomfortable severity of the style. It was designed for shorter hair, not the thick long locks she was reluctant to cut. But at least it was quite cool.

Corinne had a complete new wardrobe. No more of those tentlike *muumuus* for her. She had to give the impression that she was newly arrived from the mainland, and she couldn't do that in island clothes.

"You look lovely, my dear," Florence remarked as she came into the room with a basket of fresh-cut flowers. "But why are you trying on those new dresses again?"

Corinne ignored the question and turned to catch different angles of herself in the mirror. "I did it, Florence," she beamed. "After two grueling months of exercise, I have my old figure back. The new dresses were measured from an old one, and they fit perfectly now."

"It's not too tight in the bust?"

Corinne frowned with confusion. "No, but it should be, shouldn't it?"

Florence chuckled. "You can thank me for that. I told the seamstress to enlarge that area. It's a good thing I thought of it, eh?"

Corinne couldn't help but smile. "Another bit of taking things into your own hands? Like that trick you and Dr. Bryson played on me?"

"I won't deny it."

136

"Oh, Florence, what would I do without you?" Corinne embraced her old friend, something she rarely did.

"Not nearly so well, that's a fact."

Corinne laughed, thoroughly delighted. "You know, I only have this bigger bust line and two small stretch marks to show for what I went through. Did I thank you for insisting on all those applications of coconut oil to help my skin expand without stretching? Only two marks!"

"Well, that's not all you have to show for it," Florence said quietly.

"No. I can never thank you enough for that." The two women looked into one another's eyes. They understood each other, the childless one and the new mother.

They both heard the cry at the same time.

"You want me to go?" Florence offered.

"No," Corinne grinned. "I'll bet you thought that when I came to my senses and decided to keep him, you would get to care for him all the time. Well, you can help, but I enjoy him too much to give over all his care completely."

"It's not fitting," Florence grumbled. "Why, your mother never bothered with you, except to show you off to her friends. A woman of your breeding has a nurse to take care of the changing, bathing, and feeding."

"I'm not my mother," Corinne replied. "I happen to like all those little things. Can I help it if I just can't get enough of him?"

Florence laughed. "No, I suppose not. But I still say it's not fitting."

"You're just jealous. Why, I think you love him as much as I do," Corinne said. "Come on then, we'll both go. He adores the attention anyway."

They both went into the room next to Corinne's that had been turned into a nursery. The morning sun fell across the matted floor in patterns from the screened, opened windows. A delicate breeze stirred the dangling sculptured birds hanging over the bassinet, causing the wailing to stop.

Corinne smiled down at Michael Samuel Burkett. "He's facinated by those birds you found in the antique shop. He is really starting to notice things."

"The doctor told you there was nothing wrong with his eyes," Florence replied, grinning down at Michael, who had turned toward their voices. "Babies don't see so well at first. And I'm glad to see his eyes changed from that murky blue to your yellow-green. Lord, he's going to be a handsome devil when he grows up, just like his—"

"No." Corinne cut her off. "He's not going to be *anything* like *him!*"

"If you say so, my dear."

"I do," Corinne returned firmly. "Michael is going to be special. I know he is."

"Well, right now this special young man needs changing," Florence replied and began to unwrap the diaper.

"Did Dr. Bryson leave more of that salve for his heat-rash?"

"No, he said he would drop it by today. There's nothing to worry about, though. The rash doesn't seem to bother Michael at all."

"I don't like it. Maybe I should put an overhead fan in here."

"You worry too much, Cori," Florence chided her. "Michael was born in this climate. The muggy heat probably doesn't bother him half as much as it does you and me. Look at him. He's as healthy as can be."

"I know. I just want him to stay that way," Corinne replied, and lifted Michael from the bassinet.

She smiled down at his chubby little face, all the love in the world reflected in her eyes. He was her little angel. She still shuddered to think how close she had come to giving him up. She would never forgive herself for the awful thoughts she had had about him while carrying him. She could only think that she must have been a little crazy.

Michael was no longer Jared's son, to be cast aside without a care. He was her son, and only hers. She had never dreamed that anyone could be so important to her.

"Are you hungry, precious?" Corinne fussed over him. "I suppose I should feed you again before I leave. Then you can sleep the afternoon away and won't even miss me."

"Leave?" Florence crooked a brow.

Corinne moved to the cushioned rocker by the window and opened the front of her dress to nurse Michael. "It's time, Florence. Russell told me a ship is due in late this morning. We are going down to the harbor with some of my luggage and then ride from there to the Royal Monarch

Hotel, as if I had just arrived from the mainland. I will take a room there as Mrs. Jared Burkett."

Florence shook her head. "So you're still going through with it? I had hoped you'd forget all that."

"Just because my heart has softened, doesn't mean I have forgotten why I came here. Not for one moment have I forgotten."

Florence had become sympathetic to Corinne's fury once she learned of the rape. But since then she had had time to mull over it again, and she still thought leaving well enough alone was a good idea.

"Michael is old enough to travel, Cori. Why don't we go home instead?" she suggested. "Your father is dying to see his grandson."

"I know, but he can wait a few more months. I'm not going home until I have been revenged."

"Damn and botheration! Corinne, you're going to get yourself in trouble fooling with that man!"

Corinne was surprised and a little amused. "It's not like you to use strong language, Florence," she observed.

"One picks up the habit living around you," Florence said testily. "Whatever possessed your father to let you run wild at the shipyard when you were a child, I'll never know. Some of the words you picked up—!"

"He was happy that I showed an interest."

"An interest that didn't last. But it turned you into the most unladylike lady, Corinne Barrows."

"Corinne Burkett," she reminded her old nurse. "And besides, I don't swear intentionally. It just happens when I get angry."

"Which is most of the time."

"Now, have I been disagreeable these last two months?" Corinne asked with a smile.

"No, but you will be once you run into *him* again," Florence said knowingly.

"No, I won't. I don't have to see Jared in order to make a fool of him. I may not run into him at all, and that will be just as well. But if I do, why should I lose my temper? He can't do anything to stop me. He can't play the outraged husband, not when he deserted me. I have the upper hand this time."

"I don't like it, Cori," Florence warned. "He fooled me

139

well enough with his charm, and you even more. You seem to forget how ruthless he was."

"Stop trying to talk me out of it, Florence," Corinne said firmly, her green eyes hard. "Nothing has changed. I'm not going home until I've done what I came to do."

"What about Michael?" Florence asked huffily. "Do you plan to keep him hidden in a stuffy hotel room while you parade about town?"

"Of course not. You and the baby will stay here. I am only checking into the hotel because it is a public place and I have to be seen in public. I will spend most of my time here, though no one will know it."

"And if Jared follows you here and discovers Michael? Then what will you do?"

Corinne frowned. "That isn't likely to happen, Florence. But if it does, the solution is simple. We will just say that Michael is your son, and that you are staying up here on Punchbowl because it's cooler here and you had difficulty adjusting to the heat."

"I'm not even married!" Florence gasped.

"Who is to say you're not recently widowed, Mrs. Merrill?" Corinne said. "And that Michael wasn't born in Boston, before we left? After all, we're saying that we only arrived today. And we can say that Michael is a month older than he actually is."

"You're making things too complicated, Cori. Why lie about his age?"

"So Jared can't possibly suspect anything if he does happen to discover Michael. Dr. Bryson is the only one here who knows that Michael is mine and that he was born June 14. And the good doctor knows me as Mrs. Drayton. It is doubtful that he knows Jared or will connect me with the soon-to-be notorious Mrs. Jared Burkett."

"I don't like any of it, Cori. You know I don't like lies. I never could tell one convincingly."

"You probably won't have to lie at all. I will be careful when I come and go from here. And in the unlikely event that Jared does follow me here, we don't have to let him in. So there is nothing to worry about."

"So you say," Florence replied. "But I'm afraid that does not relieve my mind in the least. Not in the least."

Chapter 20

JARED leaned back against the trunk of a large coconut palm and stared out over the ocean. He looked down at the waves breaking on Waikiki Beach. Behind him was the hotel he was building. While Jared was proud to be contributing to the growth of his island, he was also sad. The old way of life was ending.

"The job goes well, huh, Ialeka?"

Jared looked over at Leonaka who straddled a bench under the palms, paring a mango and tossing large chunks of the juicy fruit into his mouth. Leonaka Naihe was a descendant of Leimomi Naihe, as Jared was, but Leo was the truer Hawaiian, lossing his pure blood line only a generation ago, when his father took a Japanese wife. He looked pure Hawaiian, for he was a dark-skinned giant, towering well above Jared, with coal-black hair and black eyes.

They had grown up together on the north shore, gone to school together, and now worked together. Leo was Jared's best foreman as well as his closest friend and distant cousin.

"Yes, the job goes well," Jared grinned. "I don't know why I even bother to come down here. You have everything running so smoothly."

"Da successful boss no need work," Leo teased in pidgin, though he spoke perfect English. "He lay in da sun all day wit' pretty *wāhine*. No worry 'bout na'ting."

"Are you suggesting I retire before I'm thirty?"

"We manage fine without you, boss. Mo'better you enjoy life while you young, huh?"

"Thanks a lot, Leo. It's nice to know I'm needed."

They both laughed. Then Leonaka's sudden change in expression alerted Jared.

"Look who is paying you a visit," Leo said seriously,

nodding toward the hotel. "It must be something pretty important to take your uncle away from Fort Street."

Jared followed Leo's gaze. Edmond Burkett was striding purposefully toward them. "I have an idea why he's here."

"So do I," Leonaka said, frowning. "I wanted to talk to you about it myself, but since you haven't brought up the subject, I haven't dared to pry. I guess your uncle's got more courage."

"Audacity, you mean," Jared said coldly.

When Edmond reached them he was sweating profusely from the noon heat and breathing hard. The exertion of trudging through the sand had exhausted him. He collapsed on the other end of the bench by Leonaka and started fanning himself with his hat.

Leonaka rose without acknowledging Edmond's presence. "I guess I better get the men back to work now."

"Yes," Jared said tightly, and watched him walk away.

"I sent messages to you for the last two weeks, Jared," Edmond began, foregoing cordialities. "Why have you ignored them?"

"I have been busy."

"Too busy to spare me a few minutes?"

Jared stood stiffly before his uncle. "Yes. And I'm sorry you came down here for nothing, because I can't spare you any time now either. I have work to do."

Edmond became flustered. "You can't pretend you don't know why I'm here. I demand to know what you are going to do about your wife!"

"Nothing," Jared replied calmly. "Now is there anything else you wanted to discuss?"

Edmond stared incredulously at him. "Nothing? Nothing?"

"Your hearing is excellent, Uncle," Jared said sarcastically.

Edmond frowned. "Perhaps you're not aware of what she is doing."

"No, Uncle. I know all about her indiscretions. I can name you every one of the lovers she's taken in the six weeks since she arrived. I know exactly what she is doing. The difference is, I also know why."

"My God, Jared! How can you let her go on flaunting her infidelity? Doesn't it bother you?"

"If you mean that she's a whore—no, that doesn't bother me. She's not going to be my wife very much longer. She will probably divorce me as soon as she gets tired of her game and returns home."

"I don't understand any of this." Edmond shook his head. "You didn't even have the decency to tell me you had married."

"As I said, it won't be for much longer."

"I had to find out from friends, and that wasn't all they had to tell me," Edmond went on as if he hadn't been interrupted. "I couldn't believe it. I went to see her, to demand she stop passing herself off as Mrs. Jared Burkett."

"You saw Corinne?" Jared began to show interest.

"Yes, I saw her," he replied in disgust. "A trollop! With a painted face. Even after she knew who I was and had showed me her marriage papers, she had the effrontery to make a pass at me! Why, I'm old enough to be her father, let alone the fact I'm your uncle! How could you have married such a creature?"

Jared's eyes had turned slate gray. "Why I married her is not important."

"Maybe you don't mind having your name dragged through the gutter. But I am a Burkett too, and so is your sister. Have you considered how Malia is going to feel about having a whore for a sister-in-law? The whole bloody island knows about it. You've got to put a stop to this!"

"Since when are you so concerned about Malia?" Jared asked icily.

"I know how she is going to feel when this reaches her. It's fortunate she's in the country now. She probably won't ever want to leave once she hears."

"That's enough!" Jared said furiously.

"Then do something about it! The damage has been done, but it needn't continue. The political problems on this island are coming to a head. We might have a revolution soon. At least that will make people forget about your wife."

"I told you never to mention revolution to me. You know I am opposed to overthrowing the queen."

"I'm just saying that your scandalous wife won't remain the topic of conversation for very long once she's gone."

"What are you suggesting? That I ship her home whether she wants to go or not?"

"Yes. And pay her to leave, if you have to. I'll even help you if her price is too high for you."

"She's richer than you and I together, Uncle," Jared replied, watching his uncle's reaction carefully.

Edmond was surprised, but not deterred. "Damnit, Jared, you have to do something! You're letting that woman make a laughing stock of you and ruin our name."

"All right, Uncle," Jared sighed, turning to look down the beach at the castlelike structure of the Royal Monarch Hotel, where Corinne was staying. "I will take care of it."

This was the second conversation he had had about his wife since her unexpected arrival. The first had been with Dayna, the woman he ought to have married. She now knew all the sordid details of the marriage. Curiously, Dayna had recently accused him of being jealous, which was absurd. He didn't care for Corinne. Couldn't Dayna see that?

"You'll put a stop to it soon?" his uncle pressed.

Jared's mouth was set in a grim line. "Yes, soon."

Chapter 21

CORINNE was bored. The constant acting, the long drives from Punchbowl to Waikiki and back again kept her irritable. The charade was keeping her away from Michael far too much, and she hated that.

Yes, it was time to go home. The venture just hadn't been satisfying. If only Jared had reacted in some way, if he had shown her that her behavior had had some effect on him, she'd feel as though she'd accomplished something. But she hadn't seen him once. Maybe he didn't give a damn what people thought.

"I think I might just miss this island, Russell," Corinne remarked as she poured more Chinese tea into a tiny cup. "You have to admit, it's nice having summer all year round, and fresh fruit whenever you want it."

They were at a restaurant in Chinatown, a crowded part of Honolulu not far from Punchbowl. It was an exotic experience, eating pork chow mein, egg fu yung, chow fun, and a host of other delightful dishes. The courses just kept coming, seven different dishes in all, enough to feed ten hungry people. Corinne was aghast at the waste, but she did get to sample each dish.

"So you've finally decided to give it up and go home?" Russell asked.

"Yes. I should get Michael away from here before he gets too accustomed to the warm climate and has trouble adjusting to Boston."

"Michael," Russell said drily. "Everything you do now seems to center around him. When you're not acting out your little drama, you're playing with that baby, nursing him, bathing him. I hardly ever see you anymore unless it's my turn to be your lover for the day."

"Don't be crude, Russell."

"I wouldn't mind, if it were true—if I really were your lover," he replied bitterly. "But the only one you let get close to you is that damn baby."

"Russell!"

"I'm sorry, Corinne," he said quickly, taking her hand in both of his. "I didn't mean that. I'm just dispirited. I've been losing constantly at the cockfights in Kalihi, and this muggy weather we've been having is enough to put anyone on edge."

Corinne sighed. "I know. Why don't you see about finding us a ship tomorrow?"

"You're that eager to leave?"

"Aren't you? It's been ten months."

"I just thought you would settle things with Burkett first. You haven't even seen him."

"Why should I?"

"What about a divorce?"

"Russell, I told you. There will be no divorce. Jared will continue to be my absentee husband, even if we never see each other again. I happen to like the present arrangement."

"Where does that leave me?"

"Just what are you getting at, Russell?" Corinne demanded, putting down her fork and sitting back.

"I want you for my wife, Corinne." His hands squeezed hers more tightly. "*I* want to be your husband, not that rascal who doesn't give a damn about you."

Corinne sighed. "That's impossible now. I've told you that before. I never made you any promises, Russell. I don't love you and I wish you would stop expecting my feelings to change. I don't want anyone except Michael."

Russell's eyes darkened. "Maybe you wouldn't feel that way if you didn't have the baby," he said acidly. "I wonder what your husband would do if he knew he had a son."

Corinne's face turned pale. She had never heard Russell talk so callously before. Why did he seem so bitter?

"Are you threatening me, Russell?"

"I'm just curious, is all," he shrugged. "Do you think he would try to take the boy from you?"

Corinne's green eyes darkened and shot sparks. "If you told him, Russell," she said in a whisper, "I would probably kill you."

"The lioness protecting her cub, eh?" he sneered. Then his

dark eyes widened in surprise. "Well . . . the lion just walked into the den."

"What?"

"Your absentee husband is no longer absent."

Corinne felt her heart begin to pound. She couldn't bring herself to turn around and look. She glared at Russell.

"If you dare say one word about—"

"Relax, Corinne." Russell smiled warmly and kissed the palm of her hand. "I was only teasing you. Don't you know me better than that?"

"I was beginning to wonder," she said with little relief. "Has he seen us?"

"Not only that, my dear, but he is coming this way," Russell answered smoothly.

Corinne held her breath. How should she act? For some reason, the old anger at Jared wouldn't surface. Instead, she found herself worried about *his* anger, about what *he* would do.

When she heard the slow moving footsteps stop behind her, she wanted to run.

"Mr. Drayton," Jared drawled. "I trust you are enjoying my wife's company, but would you mind if I borrowed her for a few minutes?"

Russell didn't move. He replied smugly, "I do mind, Mr. Burkett. I don't believe your wife would care to be *borrowed*, as you put it."

Jared placed his palms flat on the table and leaned toward Russell. "Let me put it another way," he said in a dangerously calm tone. "If you don't leave, I am going to personally escort you out of here and beat you senseless."

Russell rose indignantly. He wasn't quite as tall as Jared, and was ridiculously slim in comparison, but he didn't appear in the least bit intimidated.

Corinne rose also. "Russell, please. We're finished here, anyway. Wait for me in the carriage. I'm sure whatever Jared has to say will only take a few minutes."

Russell looked at Corinne for a long moment. Quickly, he reached into his pocket and threw money down on the table for the bill. He then stalked angrily from the restaurant without another word.

Corinne sat down again, aware of the many eyes focused on her table. She finally looked up at Jared. A

147

spark seemed to pass between them. She couldn't tear her eyes away from his.

"You're looking fit, Corinne." Jared broke the silence and sat down opposite her. "My uncle was right, though. That makeup you wear is appalling. Didn't anyone tell you that you don't have to look like a whore to be one?"

She had expected similar words, but they stung nevertheless. "You've grown a beard," she remarked in lame retaliation, noting that his tan was darker, too. "It doesn't suit you."

"I didn't ask for your opinion."

"Nor did I ask for yours!" she retorted hotly, the old anger coming back with surprising quickness.

"What's the matter, Corinne?" he asked. "You enjoy being a whore, but you don't like being called one? Is that it?"

Corinne changed her demeanor with great effort. "It doesn't bother me, Jared," she said. "Does it you? Don't you like having it known that your wife is a whore?"

"That's enough, Corinne."

"Has it been humiliating, Jared? Tell me how you felt. Did you feel just a little bit like I did when you left your newspaper ad behind? A little bit shamed, Jared? A little bit of a fool?"

"So your behavior here was all intentional?"

"Yes, you cur!" she hissed, letting her anger show now. "You're not the only one who understands revenge!"

Jared looked down at the table thoughtfully. "Wouldn't you say we are even now? I did you a bad turn, but you have retaliated."

"Whether or not we are even is debatable. I couldn't even leave my house in Boston because of the humiliation. But I see you haven't had that problem. Perhaps you don't care about public opinion?"

"I care, Corinne."

"Well, thank you for that much satisfaction," she said coldly.

"You didn't let me finish. I care, but I don't let it affect me," he said. "But since you put such importance on public opinion, how could you degrade yourself here just to settle a score with me?"

"I don't care what these people think," she replied. "I

don't live here. Gossip here isn't going to follow me to Boston."

"I could see that it did," he tested her.

She glared at him. "If you're out for a never-ending battle, I will oblige you."

Jared's shoulders seemed to drop a little. "No, I just want to see this one ended. You've done enough damage, Corinne. I want you to call it quits and leave."

"*You* want?" she laughed derisively. "I don't give a damn what *you* want, Jared. Maybe *I* don't want to leave yet. Maybe I just happen to like it here. After all, I've been having a marvelous time."

"Whoring?" he said contemptuously.

"Yes," she grinned "*You* showed me how pleasurable love can be. But I've found that any man will do."

Jared's eyes were a steel gray. "You're going to leave, Corinne, if I have to——"

She stood up in rage. "Don't you *dare* threaten me! You lost any rights when you treated me the way you did. I had never harmed you, Jared. You are in no position to ask me anything, ever."

Jared stared after her departing figure with a murderous fury growing in him. Why was she doing this? Was she really going to stay here?

A few minutes passed before Jared decided to follow Corinne and her favorite lover. The other men had been only one-night affairs, but Russell Drayton was a regular bedmate of Corinne's. Jared wondered what Drayton thought about sharing Corinne with other men. What kind of man loved a whore?

Jared's carriage followed theirs. He was about to overtake them when they surprised him by turning off towards Punchbowl, rather than going on to Waikiki and Corinne's hotel. Jared slowed his carriage and continued to follow them at a distance. They stopped on a hill overlooking the city, and he watched as Corinne and Russell entered a house there.

Jared settled down and waited, wondering who they were visiting. As the minutes turned into hours it became clear to him. He had not been able to discover where Drayton was staying. Now he knew. Corinne not only flaunted her affairs publicly, she also enjoyed them privately. Did the woman never sleep alone?

Toward midnight, Jared watched the lights go out in the front of the house. He couldn't say why he had waited so long, hoping they would leave. Why, damnit, why did he have the urge to go in there and kill Drayton? Jared didn't care who Corinne slept with. Was he letting it get to him simply because she bore his name?

Jared rode back down to the city with one thought in mind—Corinne had to leave Hawaii. He wouldn't seek her out again. Let her come to him. When she did, he knew exactly what to do.

Chapter 22

CORINNE woke with a splitting headache. Rain was blowing into her room through the open windows. She jumped out of bed and raced to Michael's room. But his windows were closed against the downpour, obviously Florence's doing.

Michael was still asleep, so she quietly closed the door and moved sluggishly back to her own room. She shut her own windows, then pressed her palms to her temples and grimaced against the throbbing pain.

Too little sleep, she reasoned, and too many upsetting thoughts—that's why her head ached. Why had she let her meeting with Jared upset her so?

She had forgotten how handsome he was. She had lain awake much of the night, recalling his touch, their wedding night, the wild pleasure he had given her. Most disturbing, she knew that if he had walked into her room last night, she would have welcomed him.

Florence knocked on the door and poked her head inside. "You're up? Good." She came into the room without invitation. "I wanted a word with you before Michael woke and demanded your full attention."

"Yes."

"Maybe you will tell me now what was the matter with you and Russell last evening?"

"What do you mean?"

"You know what I mean. You both came home and both went to your separate rooms without a civil word to me. Did you have an argument?"

"I'm not really sure." Corinne shrugged. "You see, we met Jared."

Florence frowned and took a deep breath. "And?"

"To be sure, it wasn't very pleasant. Jared and Russell

151

almost came to blows. But fortunately, I persuaded Russell to leave."

"Well, don't stop there," Florence said with impatience. "Did you and your husband fight?"

"Yes, and I'm afraid I lost my temper."

"I was afraid you would."

"Well, how should I feel about Jared after all he did to me? And last night he called me a whore."

"What did you expect, my dear? You deliberately made everyone think you were a—" Florence faltered and grew red, unable to say the word. "—an immoral woman," she compromised. "Did you believe he wouldn't think the same?"

"I never really considered what he would think of me, only that he would be humiliated by what others thought," Corinne admitted, her eyes troubled.

"It bothers you, doesn't it?"

Corinne's chin came up stubbornly. "Why should it? I'll never see him again, so his opinion isn't important. *I* know the truth about myself, and that's all that matters."

"Then why did you lose your temper?" Florence demanded, a wise look in her hazel eyes.

Corinne bit her lip. "I guess I was stung by his bitterness. And surprised. He had no right to condemn me after all he's done. I was only getting even with him. *He* was the one who started the whole thing. He used me for revenge, then left me to face the shame of desertion. The blackguard underestimated me if he thought I would let him get away with that!"

"Cori, you're losing your temper again," Florence warned. "If you don't lower your tone you will wake Michael."

"Oh, Jared just infuriates me so!" she said in exasperation. "He had the audacity to demand I call it quits and leave here. He didn't ask me, he told me! He didn't say one word about being sorry for what *he* did. Not a word of apology. He only criticized me for what I've been doing—what he thinks I've been doing."

"Well, I hope you told him you will be leaving," Florence replied.

"No!" she snapped. "I wouldn't give him that satisfaction. I told him I like it here."

"Cori, enough is enough."

"I know," Corinne answered in a subdued voice. "I had already decided to leave. In fact, I will check out of the hotel today and withdraw my money from the bank. I was just too angry to tell Jared that. Let him be uncomfortable a little longer, while we wait for a ship."

"Thank heavens you've come to your senses!" Florence exclaimed.

Corinne smiled. "Besides being bored with the whole affair, I just can't handle the pretense anymore," she admitted finally. "I keep running into the men I've taken up to that hotel suite, and they keep pressuring me to fulfill my promises. I can't put them off anymore."

"The Lord knows it was a dangerous scheme to begin with," Florence reminded her. "You could have found yourself with an ardent rogue not willing to wait. Then what would you have done, my dear?"

"Screamed for help, what else?" Corinne laughed, then added, "I was never worried about that, Florence. Everything went smoothly. I would waltz through the lobby of my hotel with the gentleman of the day, take him to my room and ply him with wine, avoid his advances, and then make my excuses. I always promised he would find his wildest pleasures the next time. It was really so easy. Each man left with a smile of anticipation, and anyone who saw him leaving would assume he had already gotten what he wanted. Men being men, not one of them would admit defeat and say they had struck out."

"Men being men, it's lucky you were able to pull it off," Florence told her sternly.

"Well, I did," Corinne said smugly. "Now I can go home. I just hope I can avoid those men I used when I check out of the hotel today. I have really run out of excuses for why I won't see any of them a second time."

"Should I go with you?"

"No, you have to watch Michael. I'm not about to let him be seen by anyone. He has too many of Jared's features, and I can't take the chance of someone jumping to the right conclusion about him and spreading a rumor that Jared has a son. If I run into any of my so-called lovers, I will just have to hope further excuses will suffice."

153

"Take Russell with you, at least," Florence suggested. "Then there won't be any problem."

"Russell will drop me off at the hotel. But then I want him to go and see about a ship. Now that I've made up my mind to go, I want to get it over with quickly. I'll just hide out here until we sail. No more parading. No more taking the chance of seeing Jared again. Once was enough."

Florence looked closely at Corinne's expression. "He frightens you, doesn't he?"

"When he's angry, yes," she admitted grudgingly. "But only because he's so damned unpredictable."

Florence understood a bit too clearly. "You underestimated him before. You should have remembered that before you came here. It pays to learn from past mistakes."

Corinne wondered. Did she have good reason to fear Jared? She mouthed a silent prayer that the big man's rage would remain dormant until they had sailed.

The young Hawaiian attendant in bright floral shirt and flappy white trousers hailed a waiting carriage and put Corinne's few things inside. He sheepishly avoided looking at the beautiful *wahine* who tapped her foot impatiently. He knew who she was—she was the talk of the entire hotel. But the young boy didn't believe half the things they were saying about her, she who always had a smile of thanks for him whenever he helped her.

He knew her husband, too, had seen him this morning when he came to the hotel. So he knew why the lovely white-skinned lady was not smiling now, why sparks were shooting from her dark green eyes. Why did he have to be the one standing idly in the lobby when the manager ordered her bags taken out? He somehow felt personally responsible for her anger.

Corinne sat stiffly on the edge of the seat in the enclosed carriage. Her hands clenched and unclenched repeatedly in her lap. She was at a complete loss.

She had walked through the expansive lobby of her hotel, overly crowded today because of the rain. The commotion she caused amused her, women stepping well out of her way as if she were diseased, men trying to catch her eye. She had been on her way to her suite to pack the few belongings she kept there when the hotel manager stopped her.

Before she could tell him to prepare her bill, he informed her quietly that her suite was no longer available. Corinne's green eyes opened wider with every word the manager spoke. He explained that her luggage was already packed and waiting for her, that her bill had been paid in full, and that she was no longer welcome at the Royal Monarch.

"And what is the reason for this?" she had demanded, daring the cowardly little man to tell her that her scandalous activities had warranted this action.

His reply was the last thing she expected to hear. "Your husband has threatened to wring my neck if I allow you to stay here another day."

Now Corinne glared out the carriage window at the pouring rain, not really seeing the swaying palms lining the streets, or the elaborate houses. She had come to look with delight on the profusion of color everywhere, each house with its own unique garden—not formal, but with flowers and plants everywhere, framing houses and walkways, covering porches, hanging from roof edges. Bright colors were everywhere, but today Corinne wasn't seeing anything.

She was not aware that they had reached the center of Honolulu until the carriage stopped before her bank, the destination she had given the driver. Her eyes still blazed as she approached a teller, and she was too preoccupied to notice the surprise on the man's face when she handed him her account book and asked for her money.

"There must be some mistake, Mrs. Burkett."

The middle-aged teller with the gold-rimmed spectacles had her complete attention now. He had called her Mrs. Burkett. How did he know she was married? She had opened the account as Miss Corinne Burkett.

"What mistake?" she asked with growing alarm. "I have come to withdraw my money."

The man's surprised look turned to one of consternation. "But we don't have your money any longer, Mrs. Burkett. It was withdrawn this morning."

"By whom?" she demanded, though she needn't have asked. She knew.

"Why, by Mr. Burkett," the man explained.

Corinne tried to control herself. She pointed a trembling finger at her account book.

"Do you see his name on that book beside mine? How dare you release my money to him!"

"He is your husband," the man said lamely.

"How do you know that?"

Now the poor man began to sweat. "I had no reason to doubt his word. We know Mr. Burkett quite well here. He is a competitor of ours. He and his uncle own a Savings and Loan down on Fort Street."

"I don't give a damn what he owns!" she stormed, not caring anymore about the attention she was getting. "You had no right to give him my money!"

"If he is not your husband, then we have indeed made a mistake and I assure you the law will be called in. But if Mr. Burkett is your husband, then your money is also his, and he has the right to withdraw it."

Corinne turned abruptly and stormed out of the bank. "Take me back to Waikiki, and quickly!" she shouted at her Hawaiian driver.

"Da hotel we just come from?"

"No. There is a new one being built on the beach. Do you know where it is?"

"Sure t'ing, lady," he grinned. "I got one cousin work dere. Plenty work he says. Long time 'fore dat hotel finish."

She ignored his comments and got back into the carriage for the long drive back to Waikiki. A few blocks past the hotel that had evicted her was the shell of a new hotel under construction. By the time her carriage stopped there, it was already late afternoon. The rain had stopped and the sun was out. But the effects of the storm were still on the ground, and Corinne had to trudge through wet sand to reach the building.

Corinne stopped to look about the area for Jared, but she didn't see him. A monstrously tall Hawaiian of slim athletic build appeared to be in charge. She had never seen a man so tall before, and was almost reluctant to approach him and interrupt his work. She became even more reluctant when whistles and lewd remarks came her way. Construction came to a standstill. All the workers watched her approach.

The tall Hawaiian turned to see what was distracting his

men and scowled when he saw Corinne. He noted her rich dress of copper silk, the matched parasol opened to block the sun, the dark-gold hair under a stylish hat, the pale whiteness of her skin. A *malehine*, probably lost, and a stunningly beautiful one at that.

He moved towards her and blocked her way. "This is a restricted area, miss."

Corinne had to raise her head to look into the Hawaiian's dark eyes. "I'm looking for Mr. Burkett—Mr. Jared Burkett. Is he here?"

The Hawaiian was a bit surprised. "Jared didn't come in this morning. I'm Leonaka Naihe, his foreman. Perhaps I can help you."

Corinne showed her disappointment. "Only if you can tell me where I might find my husband, Mr. Naihe."

His brows raised. "Mrs. Burkett?"

"Unfortunately, yes," she answered bitterly. "Do you know where he is?"

"You might try his office on Merchant Street. Or his home on—"

"Yes, I know where his home is," she cut him off impatiently. "Thank you."

Leonaka watched her leave and let out a slow whistle. So that was Ialeka's promiscuous wife. Why hadn't he brought her home with him when he returned from the mainland? And why did she come here to flaunt her lovers in his face? Leonaka wished he knew what was going on. But he just couldn't bring himself to ask.

Chapter 23

THE red-orange glow of the setting sun lit the sky on the leeward side of the island as Corinne's carriage pulled off Beretania Street into the private lane of Jared's large, impressive house. She had already gone to his office, only to be told by an Oriental clerk that she had just missed him. Her temper was at fever pitch.

Her breasts, swollen with milk, were very painful. She pressed her palms to them to keep the milk from dripping as it sometimes did when she went this long without nursing Michael. Fortunately she wore a tight binder, but she wasn't taking any chances, and pressed harder to be sure the flow stopped before she stepped carefully out of the carriage.

For the fifth time that day, she asked the driver to wait for her. If Jared were not at home, she would have to give up for today. She hurt so badly that she almost considered doing that anyway. But her need to vent her anger was greater than the pain in her breasts or her exhaustion. Florence would have fed Michael anyway by now.

Before Corinne could pound on the front door of Jared's house, the door opened and she stared into the blue-gray eyes of her husband. He gazed at her with a triumphant gleam. A slight mocking curve to his lips incensed her beyond caution, and she took a step closer to him and raised her hand to strike.

Jared caught her wrist and held it in an iron grip. "I wouldn't try that again if I were you," he said in a deep drawl. "I just might hit back."

Corinne tried to get her hand loose, but he pulled her into the house and shut the door before releasing her. She turned to look at him. She had so many vile names to call him that she hardly knew where to begin.

Jared laughed. "I expected to see you much sooner today. Couldn't you find me?"

He didn't wait for her to answer but walked past her to a long bar in the living room and poured himself a tall glass of punch, then added a generous amount of rum. He was dressed in cream-colored pants and a white shirt, opened halfway down his chest. His casual attitude was making Corinne livid.

"Cur!" she hissed, coming further into the room.

Jared chuckled deeply. "You're a fine one to be calling anyone names, dear wife."

"You're despicable!" she gasped, her face turning redder as she looked about for something to throw at him.

How she needed to hit him, to hurt him. But Jared anticipated her intent when she went after a vase of flowers on a nearby table.

"Oh, no," he said warningly. "Either you behave yourself or I'll have to restrain you."

Corinne ignored the threat and hurled the vase at his head. Flowers and water were strewn across the room, but the sturdy vase crashed harmlessly against the wall behind Jared. She didn't see the fury on his face as he started after her. She was too busy looking for another weapon.

Before she could get her hands on a potted plant in a window nook, Jared had grabbed her from behind. He threw her down on the sofa and stood with hands on hips looking down at her sprawled form, silently daring her to get up.

"I should make you clean up that mess, damn your green eyes!" he growled at her. "Now, you came to me this time. If you're ready to talk, do so. Otherwise I will lock you in a room upstairs until you decide you can behave decently."

"You can't do that!"

"When are you going to learn that I can and will do anything short of murder? You should have realized that by now."

The rascal really would, she thought furiously. She sat up, straightened her dress, then fixed the hat that had tilted to the side of her head.

Jared moved back to the bar. "Would you care for a drink?" he offered, as he picked his up and leaned his back against the bar. "You really should have listened to me last night, Corinne. You could have avoided this."

"What have you done with my money, Jared?" she asked in a calm tone.

"It's in my account."

"Where?"

"That doesn't matter, since I made sure you can't draw on the account," he replied smoothly.

It was all Corinne could do to keep the rage out of her voice. "You had no right to do that. You *stole* my money!"

"What's yours is mine. Or have you forgotten you're my wife?" he taunted her.

"You swore you wouldn't touch my money!"

He shrugged. "So I lied. You should have remembered that I don't always play fairly, Corinne."

"But you should have remembered the signed paper I possess, stating that you will not at any time exert your will over mine or interfere with anything I do. You've done just that today."

"So?"

"So?" She couldn't understand his calm. "If you think I won't take you to court over this, then you don't know me at all, Jared Burkett!"

"Oh, I think I know you well enough," he grinned. "You're just like me. You can't stand to let someone get the best of you."

"Jared, I—"

"That ridiculous paper you had me sign isn't worth a damn here."

"What?" she gasped.

"Find yourself a lawyer and see for yourself. You're in Hawaii, Corinne, and though we're near to bursting with Americans and they have been conniving for years to have us governed by the United States, we are still a sovereign kingdom with entirely different laws."

Curse it all! Why hadn't she thought of that?

Suddenly the full meaning of what he said sank in and she shivered. The extent of his power over her was frightening. He could probably do anything he wanted to her, and the law would protect him because he was her husband.

Jared watched her changing expressions closely and grinned. "You do understand now, don't you?"

He was lording it over her. God, how she hated him!

"I understand, Jared," Corinne said coolly as she stood up and raised her chin proudly. "I understand you are beyond contempt. Keep my money if you want it so badly. I still have enough cash and jewels to last me until my father can send me more."

Jared sighed. "You have missed the whole point, Corinne. I don't want your money. I never did. I want you off this island. As soon as you decide to give it up and go, you will have your money back."

Why couldn't she tell him that was what she wanted too? Why did she have to feel such defiance?

"I won't be forced to leave, Jared," she said stubbornly. "I won't be forced into anything."

Jared's eyes darkened to a dusky gray. "That's too bad, because I have had quite enough of your whoring about town, no matter what your reasons are. You're going out of circulation, Corinne, one way or the other."

"And you're going to hell!" she yelled furiously. Realizing she had no control over her temper, she whirled and ran from the house.

If he thinks he's going to put a leash on me, he has lost his mind, she thought angrily as she ran along the walk in front of the house. He can't tell me what to do! He can't!

Before Corinne reached the waiting carriage, Jared caught up with her and swung her around to face him. She was still too angry to be frightened and struggled to get away, losing her parasol and purse in the process.

"Let go of me!" she screamed, beating at his chest with her free hand.

"You're staying here, Corinne, until I decide what to do with you," he said coldly.

"I will when you're in hell!"

Corinne tried kicking at him, but only succeeded in losing a shoe. Her hat fell off and her golden hair tumbled down into her face, momentarily blinding her. In the next instant, she found herself tossed up over Jared's shoulder, her glorious long hair hanging down to drag on the ground. Her breasts had hit against his hard back and the pain from the tender swelling was excruciating.

"Help!" she suddenly screamed at the top of her lungs. "Help me!"

"Be quiet, Corinne, before I really give you something to scream about," Jared hissed. "No one is going to come to your aid." To the driver who sat watching the scene in amusement, Jared ordered, "If my wife left anything in your carriage, bring it inside and I'll pay you for your trouble. She won't be needing your services anymore."

Jared started back to the house. Corinne sank her teeth into him. She heard his yowl of pain and her satisfaction was so great that she didn't care what he did—until he tossed her to the floor.

She fell just inside the door, bruising her shoulder as she landed. Jared stood over her with one hand pressed to his wound, his eyes smoldering.

"You damned blood-thirsty vixen! I ought to thrash you for that!"

"Go ahead," she cried defiantly. "It doesn't matter. You are already the lowest, vilest beast. Go ahead and beat me. See how much more I can hate you!"

But when Jared reached down, she shrank away. He grasped her wrist and yanked her to her feet, then dragged her up the stairs.

She held back with all her might when she saw the blood soaking the back of his shirt where she bit him. He would beat her for that, she knew he would. Was she really at his mercy because a piece of paper said she was his wife? Could he do anything he wanted to her and get away with it? The answer was terrifying.

At the top of the stairs was a long corridor. Jared opened the door of the second room he came to and pushed her inside, then slammed the door shut and locked it from outside.

Corinne pounded on the door. "You can't do this, Jared!" she screeched and pounded again.

But he had done it. She heard him walk away. Swinging around, she looked at the room she found herself in. It took a few moments for her to calm down. She located a lamp and lit it.

It was a large room, masculine in appearance, done in dark blues and browns, suede, leather, and heavy brocades. Jared's bedroom? She inspected further, carrying the lamp

with her. A large armoire revealed a man's wardrobe—
suits, shirts, robes, and shoes and boots along the floor.
Another door led to the newest kind of bathroom, with a
carved marble tub and a sink with crystal faucets.

She caught her reflection in the mirror that covered one
entire wall and gasped at her dishevelled condition. Her
dress was wrinkled terribly, she had lost two buttons at the
top of her bodice, her hair cascaded down her shoulders in
a mess of tangles, and she wore only one shoe.

The pain in her breasts was unbearable, and the pressure
Corinne applied to stop the flow didn't help anymore. She
hobbled back to the bathroom and locked the door from
the inside.

Every movement made her breasts throb and she slowly
removed the top of her dress to let it hang to her waist.
Gently, she squeezed the milk from her breasts. What a
waste, she thought bitterly. She should be home with Michael, feeding him this abundance of milk.

The process was long and tiring, but eventually she
found some relief, though not enough. She still needed
Michael. By morning, she would need him desperately.

Corinne bound her breasts tightly again and fixed her
dress, then went back into the bedroom, taking the lamp
with her. It was completely dark outside now. A cool
breeze blew in through the open window. She went to stand
there and let the fragrant air refresh her. Carriages passed
on the street before her, filled with unknown people unaware of her plight. She suddenly felt sick with apprehension and exhaustion.

Hours passed. Corinne sat in a comfortable stuffed chair
by the window and waited. The headache she had had
that morning returned. Her stomach grumbled, and her
shoulder hurt. The longer she waited, the more she forgot
her fear. Her anger grew to near bursting.

When the door finally opened, it was all Corinne could
do not to race at Jared and scratch his eyes out. He stood
there with a tray of food in his hands, her lost shoe tucked
under her arm, an unreadable expression on his face. "Are
you hungry?"

She didn't answer, but he brought the tray into the room
anyway. "I would have come sooner, but I had a difficult
time explaining that mess in the living room to Soon Ho."

She showed no curiosity, but he explained anyway, "Soon Ho takes care of me here. He cooks, cleans the house. He's really remarkable."

Corinne remained silent, seething. She watched his every move through narrowed eyes. After he set the tray down and tossed her shoe on the floor by the bed, he faced her, frowning sternly.

"Are you just going to sit there killing me with your eyes, or will you come and eat?"

Her sudden peal of deep, throaty laughter played on his nerves. "I wish to God my eyes could kill."

"I'm sure you do," he said curtly and moved to light another lamp.

Corinne stared at his back, noticing that he had changed his shirt. She also saw the faint outline of a bandage beneath it. She hoped the wound pained him. Better still, she hoped it would get infected. Perhaps he would die of blood poisoning. The thought brought a wry smile to her lips.

Jared sauntered back to the cherrywood table and picked at some fruit pieces in a bowl on the tray. Corinne frowned. Was he going to ignore her now?

"You know you really can't keep me here, Jared," she said in a calm, practical tone.

"Yes, I know," he answered coolly. "But you won't mind staying here just one night, now will you?"

"What's the point, if I can go in the morning?"

"You're not going in the morning. I agree I can't keep you here in this house. You would have to stay locked in this room indefinitely. In the morning, we will leave for the country."

"The country?" she asked in alarm. "You mean the other side of the island?"

"Yes. I can at least leave you there without worrying about you causing any more scandal. It's far enough from Honolulu to keep you out of trouble."

"I won't go!"

"I'm not giving you a choice, Corinne," Jared said calmly.

She began to panic again. He was taking her away from her baby!

"Look, Jared." She tried to keep the fear from her voice, but he could see it in her eyes. "I lied to you last night when

I said I liked it here. I had already decided to leave. I was just too angry to admit it. Russell even went to the harbor today to see about a ship. The first one that sails, I will be on it."

"It's too late for that, Corinne." He came to stand before her, his eyes inscrutable. "You had your chance to leave, but you refused."

"What do you mean?"

He smiled down at her. "I have decided I want you to stay after all."

"Why?"

"You came here to make a fool out of me and succeeded," he said, his tone turning harsh, his own anger finally showing. "I didn't mind being known as the poor, deceived husband, because I didn't give a damn about you to begin with. But when it was said that I wasn't man enough to handle my wife, well, that went against the grain. And the one way to have gossip turn in my favor is to show that I've taken you in hand."

"Do you really think people will believe you have forgiven me?" she asked, thinking quickly.

"A man could never forgive a wife who has whored as much as you have," he said cruelly, delighted to see her flinch. "But that has nothing to do with it."

"Then what?"

He put his hands on each each side of her chair and bent over her, trapping her there. "You carry my name. You should have remedied that. But since you didn't, you're going to be the model wife from now on."

"You're insane!" she hissed, green fire in her eyes. "I will never do what you want, Jared. We were even, but you're tilting the scale again. Don't think I won't make you pay for it! I promise you I will!"

He laughed and walked towards the door. "We'll see how much damage you can do isolated in the country."

"You won't get me there!"

"If I have to gag and tie you for the whole day's journey, I will," he warned her and closed the door, turning the lock firmly once again.

Chapter 24

JARED tilted the bottle of rum and took a long drink. He had gone through half the bottle since he had left Corinne in his room. But it didn't help to drown out the pounding going on upstairs that he was trying desperately to ignore. When the devil would she settle down?

He sat at his desk, pen in hand, trying to compose a letter to Leonaka explaining about his wife, explaining that he would be gone for a few days. The right words wouldn't come. There was just too much to tell.

Corinne's baggage from the carriage had been placed in the corner of the room, along with the things she had dropped in the yard. Jared's eyes kept straying to the corner. A large case, a small one, and a single hat box was all. It didn't seem to be enough. He just couldn't picture his stylish wife traveling with so few belongings.

He took another swig of rum and got back to the letter. Soon Ho would deliver it in the morning. In the end, it turned out to be just a short note leaving Leonaka in charge while he was gone. He didn't say anything about his wife.

An hour later, the bottle empty, and Jared was pacing the room like a frustrated animal. The pounding upstairs had stopped. Was she sleeping?

Her baggage still drew his attention and curiosity. He finally went to examine the contents and was even more puzzled than before when he found only two dresses and some underthings in the large case, powders, rouge, and perfumes in the smaller case, and just one hat in the hat box. Where were the jewels she had mentioned earlier? Or the dress she had worn last night?

He knew the answer. These things had come from the hotel, that's why she had them with her. The rest of her

166

clothes must be at that house up in Punchbowl, where Drayton stayed. So she had obviously spent a good deal of time there. Somehow the thought of her living with the man she seemed to love was worse than her bedding countless strangers at her hotel. But for the life of him, Jared couldn't explain why.

Jared looked up at the ceiling, knowing she was just above him. For a moment he considered going up there and having his way with her. She wouldn't like that. She had shown the whole island that she preferred any man except the one she married. He started towards the stairs, then stopped abruptly.

What was the matter with him? Corinne was the last woman he wanted. She had used her body for revenge against him, had purposely let other men have her, not because she wanted them, but just to even a score. He wouldn't touch her, no matter how damnably desirable she might be. She meant nothing to him.

"So why don't I just let her go and be done with it?" he asked himself aloud.

Jared went back into the living room and hunted out another bottle of rum, then dropped down on the sofa. After a few careless swallows he wiped his lips and his eyes returned once again to Corinne's few possessions. She would need more clothes than that to get by on. He would just have to stop by Drayton's house on the way to the country. He didn't like the idea of leaving his wife's things with her lover, anyway. But that would cause a problem, for no doubt Corinne would scream for Drayton's help.

Well, he could solve that problem at least. It was still early enough. He would go to Drayton's house now.

Jared grabbed his jacket and left the house. It was ten thirty when he stopped in front of the single-story house. Through curtained windows he could see light, so he knew Drayton was there.

Jared's lips turned up slowly in a malicious grin. He hadn't realized how much he was going to enjoy this encounter. He moved a bit unsteadily up the walkway to the front porch, regretting the amount of liquor he had consumed. But even in his inebriated condition, he could tear Drayton apart. He just hoped he hadn't drunk so

167

much that he wouldn't be able to remember tonight. It might be an entertaining evening.

Before Jared pounded on the door he heard the sound of a baby crying from inside. He stepped back in confusion. Could he be so drunk that he had come to the wrong house? He went back into the yard and looked at the house again, then at the others along the street. No, damnit, he wasn't wrong. He marched up to the porch again and hammered on the door.

Several minutes passed. The crying had stopped and Jared decided it must have been his imagination. He pounded on the door again and it opened, but only as far as a chain latch would allow.

Jared narrowed his eyes when he saw the small woman looking out at him through the crack in the door. She couldn't be more than five feet two, with fuzzy brown hair and hazel eyes. She wasn't too much older than himself, and she certainly didn't look like a housekeeper. Could Drayton be keeping more than one mistress?

"Where is Drayton?"

His tone was belligerent enough to make the woman's eyes grow round, but she obviously felt confident behind the latched door, for she answered spunkily, "He's not here and neither is Corinne. So you can just go away, Mr. Burkett. You're not welcome here."

She started to close the door, but Jared stuck his booted foot into the crack. "You know me?"

"Of course I know you. I was in the church the unfortunate day you married my Cori."

"What do you mean, *your* Cori?" he demanded.

"I've taken care of Corinne since she was five years old. I'm her maid, Florence Merrill."

Jared laughed heartily at the foolish assumption he had made earlier, but then a thought struck him. "What in the name of Hades are you doing here?"

"That's none of your business," she replied tartly.

"Open the door, Florence Merrill." His voice had lowered. "I want to talk to you."

"Oh no." She shook her head stubbornly. "Corinne wouldn't want you in her house when she's not here."

Jared's muscles tensed and his brows drew together

dangerously. "I thought this was Drayton's house. You mean to say he's been living off my wife?"

"She's paid his way, yes. She insisted on it," Florence explained quickly. "Corinne doesn't like to feel obligated to anyone."

"And did my dear wife pay for her other lovers as well?" Jared asked scornfully.

"You know *why* she came here, Mr. Burkett. She felt she had good reason—"

"Don't you dare defend that whore to me!" Jared cut her off fiercely. "Now open this damnable door immediately before I tear it down!"

"No," Florence managed, though timorously. "You have no right—"

"The hell I don't!" he growled and stepped back for one solid kick against the door.

The chain latch broke easily, and the door slammed back against the wall. Florence had moved out of the way. Horrified, she watched Jared step into the house and begin looking around.

"So this is the little love nest, eh?" he remarked acridly. "Not as luxurious as the Royal Monarch Hotel. In fact, it's downright homey." He turned icy gray eyes on the frightened woman. "No comment, Florence Merrill?"

"I—I told you I'm alone, Mr. Burkett," she stammered. "What do you want here?"

"I want Corinne's things, all of them. You can start packing them right now."

"I couldn't!" she gasped. "I really couldn't. Corinne will be furious. She—"

"—she will be grateful," he finished for her. "You see, Corinne is with me. And she will be staying with me for an indefinite period of time."

"No! I don't believe you!" Florence replied. "Cori would never agree to that!"

Jared laughed derisively. "You're so right. She's quite against it, in fact. But what she wants doesn't matter. I'm her husband and I've made the decision for her."

Florence was aghast. The man was within his rights! Now she understood why Corinne hadn't come home.

"Where is Corinne now?"

"She's at my house in the city."

"Are you sure she will be there when you return?" Florence asked doubtfully.

"You know her well, don't you?" Jared chuckled, though with little humor. "I made sure she'll be there. She's locked in my room."

"Mr. Burkett!"

"Never mind telling me how cruel you think I am," he said coldly. "It was necessary, and it is only for tonight. In the morning I am taking her to my beach house on the other side of the island where I won't have to worry about her." Suddenly he looked at Florence thoughtfully. "I suppose I should offer to take you along for Corinne's sake. I'm sure she would like having a friend with her. There are other women there, but I doubt they will take to my hot-tempered wife."

Florence found herself in a quandary. If she went along, Jared would see Michael. The baby was sleeping right now and not drawing attention to himself. Would Corinne want her to take the risk of letting her husband see the baby? She could use the story they had worked out earlier.

Jared spoke again when she didn't agree readily. "If you would rather not go with Corinne, I could pay your way back to the mainland."

"Maybe that would be better," Florence said reluctantly, praying she was making the right decision.

Jared shrugged. "That's up to you, Miss Merrill."

"It's Mrs. Merrill," she lied just in case she needed the story they'd made up. "And if you'll sit down and wait, I'll get Cori's things together."

She went off to Corinne's bedroom, a deep frown creasing her brow. Lord, why was this decision placed in her lap? If only she could talk to Corinne first. She abhorred the thought of leaving Corinne behind with the one man she hated above all others. But she had been so adamant about not wanting Jared to see his son.

Florence dragged out the traveling bags and started emptying Corinne's bureau. There was one thing she hadn't considered. Could Corinne bear to be parted from Michael for so long? Would she rather take the risk than be away from him? Just how long did Jared plan to keep his wife?

Jared appeared in the doorway. "You're going to have to hurry, Mrs. Merrill," he said impatiently. "It's a hellishly long trip to Sunset Beach, and I need at least a little sleep tonight."

"It takes time to pack," Florence replied indignantly. "Cori has quite a few belongings here."

"I can see that," he retorted curtly, looking about the room. He walked over to the open wardrobe, his eyes caught by the Hawaiian clothes there. He took out a *muumuu* and laughted heartily. "I can't picture my stylish wife in this thing. Does she really wear it?"

Florence's eyes widened in alarm. "Cori bought a few of those on impulse, because they looked so comfortable." She said the first thing that she could think of. "But she's never worn them."

She knew it wasn't necessary to lie, but she felt she had to keep anything connected with Michael a secret. She was beginning to panic.

"My wife does like to waste money, doesn't she? On clothes . . . on her lovers," Jared said scornfully. "It will take forever to pack all these dresses." He stood back, frowning. "There is an easier way," he said and scooped the entire length of dresses into his arms and started out of the room.

"Mr. Burkett!" Florence gasped, running after him. "Those dresses will be ruined, and they cost a fortune!"

"A few wrinkles doesn't ruin a dress, Mrs. Merrill," he called over his shoulder as he moved toward the door. "I told you I'm in a hurry. Now finish getting the rest of my wife's belongings into her bags."

Florence turned in a huff and went back into Corinne's bedroom. The man was impossible. How would Cori ever survive living with such an overbearing husband? Her temper would be forever on the rise, and Florence knew all too well that Cori did wild things when riled.

They should never have come here. Florence had warned Cori enough times that no good would come of her outrageous scheme.

Jared loomed in the doorway again. "You're not finished yet?"

Exasperation and anxiety made her shout, "You do it, then! But you wait and see what Corinne thinks about the mess you make of her things!"

Her raised voice woke Michael in the next room.

Florence blanched, hearing his cry. Now the lies would begin. There was no help for it.

Jared looked dumbfounded as she turned accusing eyes on him. "Now look what you've made me do," she said reproachfully and hurried from the room into the nursery.

Florence quickly picked up Michael and soothed him against her breast. Jared had followed her into the room and stood watching her for several moments before he spoke.

"Whose baby is that?"

Florence looked at him warily. His voice had been dangerously low. His eyes were narrowed, dark and menacing. He stared at Michael. Michael continued to cry, paying no attention to the drama going on around him.

"Mine, of course," she answered quickly, keeping Michael's face turned away from Jared. "Whose else would he be?"

His expression didn't change. Lord, what was he thinking?

"You mean to tell me my wife brought you all the way here with a newborn infant?"

"Michael is older than he looks, Mr. Burkett," Florence said defensively. "He was old enough to travel when we came. I would not have brought him otherwise."

"And your husband didn't object?" he demanded incredulously.

"I—I'm a widow," she explained, finding the lie difficult to get out. "And I have no family. Cori—Corinne didn't want to bring us with her, with Michael being so young. But I insisted. I wasn't about to let her come all this way without me. She's all I have—besides Michael."

"I'm finding this very hard to swallow, Mrs. Merrill," Jared said coldly. "Corinne should have had more sense than to take a newborn baby on a long journey. From the size of him, your son couldn't have been but just born. And you couldn't have been in any condition to travel, either. How could Corinne have been so foolhardy?"

"I told you Michael is small for his age, Mr. Burkett. He is five months old. He—he was two months when we left Boston. That was old enough to travel."

Florence knew she didn't sound convincing. She just

wasn't any good at lying. Please let him believe her, she prayed silently.

"Well, change him or feed him or something," Jared said harshly as Michael's wailing continued. "I can't stand to hear a baby cry."

He marched from the room and Florence let out a sigh of relief. She put Michael back in his bassinet and began to change him. She knew he must still be hungry. She had fed him ground vegetables earlier, but he didn't take well to the cow's milk she was forced to give him. He needed his mother. Now that Jared knew about him, and had apparently believed her story, there was no reason anymore for her and Michael to go back to Boston without Corinne.

After she got Michael quieted, she went back to Corinne's bedroom. She found Jared packing the rest of Corinne's things with little care, just dumping the contents of drawers into the bags.

When Jared noticed Florence at the door he growled, "Anymore damnable bags and I'll have to bring along a cart tomorrow!"

"You will probably have to do that anyway, Mr. Burkett," Florence replied. "For I've changed my mind about going back to Boston. After seeing how cantankerous and disagreeable you are, I'm not about to leave my Cori alone in your care."

"Cantankerous, am I?" Jared scowled.

"You certainly are," she assured him, determined to hold her ground.

Jared finally showed a smile. "Well, don't just stand there, woman. Get busy if you and the little one are coming with me."

A little over an hour later, the open carriage was jammed full of clothing, trunks, and bags. There was no room left for Florence, so Jared helped her up onto the drivers seat beside him. She held the baby on her lap.

Michael had slept through the packing of his room, but he was awake now, and gurgling softly, fascinated at the starlit sky above him. Jared leaned over to look down at him, though he couldn't see him clearly in the dark.

He shook his head as they started down the hill. "I still can't believe Corinne would travel with a baby," he remarked casually. "Babies require patience, and that's something my wife doesn't have."

"You would be surprised, Mr. Burkett," Florence replied, hiding her smile. "Cori has even more patience than I do where Michael is concerned. She's really quite fond of him." Then, cleverly alleviating any future suspicion he might have, she said, "Why, you sometimes think *she* is his mother, not I."

Florence was shocked at herself. The lie had been just the right thing to say. And it had come so easily. What was happening to her?

Chapter 25

DAWN was nearing, the sky a somber gray and getting lighter. But the house was still dark, and Jared carried a lamp along with the change of clothes he had for his wife when he entered his bedroom, quietly locking the door from the inside. Corinne was still asleep.

He walked over to the bed and laid Corinne's clothes down, then held the lamp high to cast a better light. He remembered the last time he had looked down on her sleeping form, on the night of their wedding. How long ago? He recalled the date and was shocked. It would be a year ago tomorrow. Would she remember?

Jared had thought about that night often before Corinne came to Hawaii. He had dwelled on the beauty of it, on her beauty, on her surprising response to him, her wild passion that had inflamed his own. During those exquisite moments, he had forgotten why he had married her. For that short time, it had been a true marriage.

But hate had rooted in him first. And so he had put her behind him, had worked desperately to forget those wonderful moments.

Corinne stirred and smiled in her sleep, making Jared wonder what she was dreaming about. Her glorious hair was fanned out behind her. Gold and copper glinted in the lamplight. She looked so innocent, so childlike. But, of course, he knew better. Yet he still had an almost irresistible urge to reach out and touch her, to feel the silky texture of her skin. His lips burned to taste hers, recalling the sweetness.

Jared's better judgement returned and, with a dark scowl, he marched over to the bathroom and started cold water running in the sunken tub. He made enough noise to wake Corinne, then came to the door to see if he had succeeded.

She was just sitting up in bed and looking around, bewildered.

Jared was furious at himself for the weakness he had almost succumbed to, and he directed that anger at her. "Get dressed!" he heard himself shouting. "I want to be on the road by sunrise!"

Corinne turned startled eyes in Jared's direction, only to see the bathroom door slammed shut. As she stared at the closed door, her eyes changed from yellow-green to sparkling emerald. Taking a deep breath, she mastered her fury. It would not do to anger Jared. She had to get back to Michael, yet she couldn't tell Jared about the baby. Somehow, she must talk him into letting her go. She had already been separated from her son for nearly an entire day.

She would reason with Jared, cajole him. She could not afford to anger him any more. Michael was at stake now, not her pride.

"You have to be reasonable, Jared," Corinne ventured, calling through the door, forcing a pleading note into her voice. "I have a maid on this island. I can't go off and just leave her stranded."

Jared came out of the bathroom wearing white trousers that molded his powerful thighs. He was still putting on a cream-colored shirt and didn't bother to look up at her when he answered.

"Your maid is here, Corinne. So there will be no stops on the way."

Corinne's eyes widened and her face turned white. Florence here? Dear God, where was Michael? Had Jared seen him?

"How?" she managed to whisper.

"I picked her up last night, along with the rest of the things you kept in your lovers' hideaway. The poor woman spent half the night sorting out the mess I made of your clothes once I got her here. Soon Ho is packing a cart now—more damnable weight to make the journey slower. You really are a good deal more trouble than I had bargained for. A maid and a baby, too! How you talked her into sailing to Hawaii with a tiny baby, I can't understand. Now hurry and get ready, Corinne. I have even less patience than usual this morning."

Corinne turned away so he wouldn't see the giddy relief on her face. Florence had done it! She had remembered their story and stuck to it! Her Michael was safe . . . and he was here! For just a moment, Corinne almost wished she could hug Jared. She had Michael again!

When Corinne and Jared approached the carriage, she saw Florence already seated, the bassinet on the seat beside her.

"You'll have to put a cover over that bed if you don't want the little one to get sun stroke," Jared mentioned to Florence as he got into the driver's seat.

"Why can't you just put the carriage top up?" Corinne demanded. "Or is it all right if we get sunstroke?"

"I don't trust you enough to put the top up, dear wife," he told her coldly. "I want you where I can see you."

"So Florence and I are supposed to just suffer in the heat?"

"Make use of those straw hats on the seat. That's what they're for."

She let it go at that, eager for him to be occupied with driving so she could talk to Florence. Florence was just as eager. As soon as they turned onto Beretania Street, she leaned towards Corinne.

"Are you all right?" she whispered.

"Yes, yes, but what about Michael? What did you tell Jared?"

Florence smiled reassuringly. "That story we concocted."

"Did he believe it?"

"Yes, I'm sure he did. He was only surprised that you would bring a baby along with you."

"Thank heavens." Corinne sighed. "Oh, Florence! I was frantic at being separated from you and Michael. Jared has been a beast."

"He wasn't none too pleasant last night, I'll tell you," Florence said huffily.

"Was Russell there?"

"No, he was out looking for you. He'll have a fine surprise when he returns and finds the house empty."

"But tell me everything you told Jared about Michael. I can't take the chance on contradicting anything."

"I will, Cori, only let's not take the risk of him over-

177

hearing us now. I'll tell you as soon as we get a moment alone."

They went slowly through the city streets, which were congested even at that early hour. But once they passed through Kalihi and rode on towards Aiea, there was less traffic. Then Michael started fussing, no longer content to let the ride lull him.

Florence dug into the basket Soon Ho had packed and drew out a bottle of sweetened water.

"I didn't feed him this morning," Florence confessed. "I knew you would be hurting. But I didn't know we would be in an open carriage. This water will have to do him for now."

"No, give him to me," Corinne ordered.

"Cori, you can't!" Florence gasped. "Jared will see you! And so will anyone we pass on the road."

"Jared and I are back to back," Corinne whispered back. "And I'll use Michael's blanket to hide what I'm doing. But I can't stand this pain anymore. I've got to nurse him."

"Very well," Florence said reluctantly. She handed Michael to her. "I just hope your husband doesn't lean over to see what you're about."

Chapter 26

STARS were winking in a blue-black sky when the carriage finally pulled off the beach road. They turned onto a sandy drive that led to a sprawling single-story house set far back from the road.

Corinne was exhausted and she knew Florence was, too. Heat had suffocated them most of the day. They were deplorably filthy too, from the red dust that had settled on them as they passed the miles and miles of cane fields.

Once they rounded the end of the majestic Koolau mountain range and started traveling on the windward side of the mountain, the view became fascinating and made the rest of the journey tolerable. The landscape was almost junglelike, and wildly beautiful on the mountain side of the road. On the other side they skirted bays, the ocean always present. Sometimes the road veered right to the shoreline. And then came the sunset in all its splendid colors, and Corinne was spellbound. She marvelled, and forgot for a short while why she was in the carriage.

Now they were at their destination, and Corinne stared at the white house, bathed in moonlight. She was relieved to find that it was not the shack she had been expecting. The house was wide in front, and set on pillars high above the ground. Tall pine trees, spaced closely together, formed walls on both sides of the house from the road all the way to the beach behind it. Only one space was open between the pines, in front of the house on the left. This space led to a small stable on the other side of the trees.

The huge long yard in front was a garden. Flowers grew everywhere—around trees in the yard, along pathways, around the house. Scents came to her through the warm salt air, scents of fruit and ginger, the blossoms a muted white, yellow, and red. Gardenia grew in profusion. There were stunted plumeria trees in full bloom, and a magnificent colvillea tree with its red-orange buds carpeting the ground beneath it. Stately coconut palms skirted the road like a gigantic fence, swaying gently in the ocean breeze.

Corinne reached across the carriage and gently shook Florence's shoulder while Jared stepped down from the driver's seat. "We have arrived."

Florence woke with a start. "Michael?"

"He's still sleeping," Corinne replied.

Michael had been a darling all day since she had fed him, not fussing at all because of the heat and dust. Corinne had been able to nurse him three times, and the pain in her breasts was completely gone now.

"We shouldn't have let him sleep so much today," Florence said as she sat up and rubbed her eyes tiredly, forgetting Jared's presence. "Now he'll keep you up half the night."

Corinne nearly choked. She looked at Jared in panic, but he didn't seem even to have heard. He was looking at the house and grinning. Corinne followed his gaze and saw the front door open slowly. Someone was peering out, holding a lamp high in the air, trying to see who the visitors were.

Suddenly, the door flew open, and the lamp was set down on the porch. Corinne stared aghast as a woman of mammoth girth came bouncing down the porch steps and, despite her size, seemed to fly toward them. Jared met her halfway and Corinne watched in amazement as he picked the huge woman up off the ground and swung her in the air.

"Ialeka, put me down!" the woman ordered sternly, then laughed as she tried to get out of his bear hug. "You break your back lifting this old woman."

Jared chuckled and let her down. "The day I can't sweep you off your feet, I'll be an old man, Aunty Akela."

She hugged him to her, then pushed him abruptly away as if the show of affection embarrassed her. She stood back and folded huge arms across an equally huge bosom.

"I like know why you no send word you coming?" the

woman asked, that stern note in her voice again. "And why you no come sooner, huh?"

"I've been busy, Aunty."

"Too busy to come home after you return from mainland?" she asked gruffly, then threw her hands in the air. "*Auwe!* Malia mad as a shook bee. You wait till she see you!"

Jared smiled tightly. "Where is Malia?"

"Where you think this time of night?" Akela said, as if the answer was obvious. "She sleeping."

"Well, don't wake her tonight. I'm too tired to put up with any tantrums. Just heat up some water for a couple of baths, then you can go back to bed yourself."

"What you mean, couple?" she asked, looking suspiciously toward the carriage.

"My wife and her maid are with me," Jared explained reluctantly. When the revelation didn't seem to surprise her, he grimaced. "You already know?"

The woman nodded with a grunt. "Now *you* know why Malia so mad. Naneki not so happy too. Good thing she stay Kahuku, visit my cousins."

Jared groaned. He had not considered Naneki. How could he have forgotten that his mistress was a servant in the very house he was bringing his wife to? Did Corinne effect his thinking that much?

"What is that the *wahine* carries?"

Jared saw that Corinne and Florence had stepped from the carriage. Florence held the bassinet in her arms.

"There is a baby—"

"A *keiki?*" Akela exclaimed and ran forward without waiting for Jared to continue.

Corinne became alarmed when the huge Hawaiian woman ran toward them and stopped next to a terrified Florence to peer into the bassinet. When she reached inside the little bed and attempted to pick Michael up, Corinne nearly pounced on her.

Florence anticipated Corinne's move and stepped in front of her. "Please, madam, he's sleeping," Florence said quickly.

"He no sleep." Akela dismissed Florence's protest. She reached again for Michael, this time lifting him from the bassinet. Florence and Corinne were taken aback when they saw tears in her eyes. She gazed down at the baby. "I wait long time to hold Ialeka's *keiki*."

Jared came up behind her, his face grim. "The baby is not mine, Aunty. He belongs to my wife's maid."

Akela looked at Jared, then back down at Michael. Then she shook her head knowingly and, against protests from Florence, carried Michael to the front porch and sat down on the step, examining Michael critically in the light of the lamp.

They all followed the large woman to the porch, and Corinne's heart beat frantically. She wanted to snatch Michael away from her. She couldn't do that, though. Nor could she say anything, not with Jared standing right there beside her, bewilderment in his eyes. She would have to let Florence talk for her, and hope that she did so quickly.

Akela was frowning. The *keiki* she cuddled in her arms was the image of the *keiki* she had helped Ranelle to birth twenty-eight years ago. Only the eyes were different, and she looked at the two *haole wāhine* and saw the eyes of the mother, and the mother was not the *wahine* she had taken the *keiki* from. The mother was the other one, the pretty one with the gold hair and anxious face.

She looked at Jared accusingly. "Why you deny this *keiki*? You think to fool Aunty Akela?"

Jared stared incredulously at her. "What in damnation are you talking about?"

Corinne pinched Florence into rapid speech. "Really, Mr. Burkett. This woman's insinuations are insulting," she said indignantly, and bent down to take Michael from the old woman.

Akela stood up, towering over Florence, and glared down at her. "Why you say this *keiki* yours?"

Florence gasped. "Because he is! Now give him to me!"

"Give her the boy, Aunty," Jared ordered, his voice cold. "I don't know what you've got into your head, but you're wrong."

"No! *You* wrong!' She pierced him with dark eyes, and then pointed a denouncing finger at Corinne. "That one is the mama, not this one!"

Jared turned to Corinne. She was hypnotized by the growing suspicion in his eyes. His face was a mask of fury and she rebelled at the thought that he might just believe this old woman.

"Don't you dare look at me like that!" she said in an offended tone.

"Corinne, if——"

"This is ridiculous!" She cut him off, then lowered her voice. "If you will just think about it, Jared, you will see how foolish all this is. That baby is too old to be yours. If I had a baby, I certainly wouldn't deny him. I wish Michael were mine. I have helped Florence care for him and I've actually grown to love him a great deal."

Jared sighed, running his hands through his hair. "She's right, Aunty. The baby couldn't possibly be mine. We were married only a year ago tomorrow." Corinne's gasp drew Jared's eyes back to her. "You didn't remember that, did you?"

Corinne's back stiffened. "Why should I?" she shrugged. "The day holds no fond memories for me."

Jared felt his anger building. Could she really have forgotten their wedding night, the night that had haunted his dreams ever since?

Jared saw that they were all staring at him in surprise. Was his rage so obvious? He would have to get a grip on himself. He had never before let his feelings be so transparent.

What was happening to him?

"Go into the house," he told them. Then he went off to unload the baggage and see to the horses while Akela led the other women inside. The house was dark and quiet. Akela carried the lamp from the porch through a large living room in the center of the house. Stuffed sofas, sandalwood tables, potted palms, and a piano dominated the room. Beaded doorways were on each side of it, and Akela went through the one on the right which showed a narrow corridor leading to three rooms.

"You sleep here," she told Florence in a whisper, opening the middle door.

She went inside and lit a lamp on a tall bureau. The room was not large. It was oddly long and narrow, but looked comfortable, with a small bed and a chair and desk against one wall. Woven matting covered the floor, and there was a large wardrobe and even a separate bathroom at the end of the room.

"Very nice," Florence remarked.

"Shh," Akela whispered. "Malia sleeping next room. No wake her, or be trouble."

"Well, I'll be as quiet as I can," Florence replied, but Akela was already leaving the room, indicating that Corinne should follow.

"I don't like that woman," Corinne whispered as she leaned over to kiss Michael good night.

"She's very astute, if you ask me," Florence replied. "But go on now. Michael and I will be all right."

Corinne left Florence and found Akela waiting impatiently at the end of the corridor. She followed her into a much larger bedroom at the front of the house. Once a porcelain lamp was lit on a bedside table, Akela started out the door.

"Who is Malia?" Corinne asked, but Akela ignored her question.

The big woman stopped at the door and gazed at Corinne thoughtfully. "I know you lie about *keiki*, but we be friends anyway, for you give my Ialeka a son and that is good. Someday he know and be happy."

It took Corinne a moment to reply indignantly, "Michael is not mine!"

But Akela had shut the door behind her. Corinne began pacing. That woman was going to ruin everything if she persisted.

When Akela came back a short while later with hot water for a bath, Corinne ignored her. She pretended an interest in the room that would be hers, noting that it was long, like Florence's, though much wider. A large bed with wooden posts sat in the center of the left wall, covered by a quilted rose silk spread. There were tall cupboards on both sides of the door, and across the room was another door, leading to the bathroom. To the right of the bathroom was a window and a big stuffed chair in front of it with a matching foot rest upholstered in dark green brocade, shot with silver. Two more windows with lacy rose curtains looked out on the front yard with all its flowers. Between them was a chaise, an odd-shaped mahogany coffee table before it.

Corinne moved to the dresser beside the bed, noticing pictures in silver frames. There were two of them, one of a man and woman, and another of a little girl with long black hair in pigtails and an impish smile. Corinne stared at the first picture, wondering if these two people were Jared's parents. The woman was stunning, with silky black hair and blue-gray eyes exactly like Jared's. Was this the woman her own father had loved?

"Your bath ready," Akela said, startling her.

Corinne turned to thank her, but the big woman with salt-and-pepper hair in a tight bun was already out of the room. Corinne didn't waste any time. That hot bath sounded heavenly. Akela had even scented it with a delicate sandalwood fragrance, and Corinne was grudgingly grateful, deciding she just might like the big Hawaiian woman after all. She quickly disrobed and climbed into the large tub, then leaned back and relaxed for the first time that day, letting all her problems drift away with the fragrant steam.

A loud thud in the bedroom shattered her quiet peace and Corinne bolted upright. When no other sounds were forthcoming, she realized that Jared had brought her baggage into the room. She relaxed again and took her time, not wanting to leave the tub even after the water had turned cold. But she was already finding it difficult to keep her eyes open.

Corinne opened the bathroom door warily, a large towel wrapped around her, but no one was in the room. The luggage was there and she opened several cases before finding a nightgown and robe. Then she found her brush, and after a few quick strokes, she climbed into bed.

She fell back on downy pillows and soft sheets and sighed, then groaned. The lamp was still burning on the other side of the bed. She reached over to extinguish it, but stopped when the bedroom door opened.

Jared stood there in the doorway, almost exactly as she had seen him that morning, barefoot and wearing only his trousers, a towel wrapped about his neck. He had shaved off the beard, and looked more like the Jared she had first met.

"What do you want, Jared?"

Ever so slowly, his lips curled. "Not a thing, my dear."

"Then why are you here."

"This happens to be my room." He closed the door and came towards her.

Corinne sat up, holding the covers up to her neck. "*I was led to this room.*"

"Of course. You're my wife."

"I won't share the same room with you!" she hissed. "Now get out of here!"

"I gave up my bed to you last night," he said in a cool tone, coming around to the other side of the bed. "I'm not about to do so again."

"Don't blame me for that, damn you!" she retorted hotly, green fire flashing in her eyes. "I didn't ask to sleep there. Nor do I want to be here. If you want your bed, you're welcome to it." She slid to the floor and grabbed the robe she had left on the foot of the bed. "I'll sleep someplace else!"

"I'm afraid that's not possible, Corinne," he replied. "There are no other rooms available."

She started for the door. "Then I'll sleep with Florence," she said haughtily over her shoulder.

Jared bounded after her and caught her arm. His grip was viselike as he swung her around to face him.

"You're not going anywhere," he said harshly, and pushed her back into the room. "Now get back in that bed."

Corinne stumbled. Her unbound hair fell across her face. When she managed to throw it back over her shoulders and look at him again, the angry response she was about to give him died on her lips. He had tossed his towel away and was starting to remove his trousers.

"No!" she gasped, her face draining. "Don't you come near me, Jared!"

He halted his movements, staring at her in bewilderment. Then he suddenly threw his head back and laughed deeply.

"I mean it, Jared!" Corinne said, her voice rising in hysteria.

"I don't sleep with clothes on, Corinne. I never have," he explained, still chuckling. "And all I intended to do was sleep."

Corinne felt her cheeks flushing in embarrassment. "You

will sleep by yourself, then." She snatched the cover from the bed. "I will use the chaise, thank you!"

Jared sobered quickly, watching her stomp away from the bed in her haughty manner. His eyes narrowed and turned a stormy gray.

"The one thing you can be assured of is that I won't touch you," he said, his voice heavy with disdain. "Your body has been used a bit too much to interest me."

He heard her sharp intake of breath and took perverse pleasure in it. She straightened her back rigidly and went to the chaise.

Damn her for looking so beautiful! He had been stunned when he entered the room, seeing her there in bed, so inviting, so damnably tempting. And then her eyes had sparkled with anger and she was even more beautiful, magnificent in her fury. But he had control of himself. He wouldn't allow her to make him feel anything.

It was only lust, but he still detested himself for feeling it, and was determined not to let her know that she could still stir his blood.

He turned off the lamp and yanked his pants off, then fell heavily into bed. As tired as he was, it was a long time before he fell asleep.

Chapter 27

WHEN Jared woke the next morning, he dressed quickly. Corinne was still sleeping, lying on her back with one arm fallen to rest on the floor, the other thrust over her forehead. Her long golden hair also dangled to the floor over the end of the chaise, and the silk spread she had used was kicked to her feet, revealing slim curves beneath her nightgown.

Jared stood looking down at her for a moment, his face set in hard lines. But he had spent half the night thinking about her. He had to get her out of his mind now. He had Malia to face.

Malia was Hawaiian for Marie, which she was never called. It was only eight months since he had seen his younger sister. But in truth, it was well over a year since he had actually paid much attention to her. This was unlike Jared, for he loved Malia better than anyone in the world. Since their mother died, he had watched over her, worried over her, and cared for her as though he were her mother instead of her brother.

But the past year had been a torment for Jared, and he had to admit that Malia's eighteen-year-old concerns had receded into the background of his thoughts.

Malia had come back here in February, furious with Jared for ignoring her. And according to Akela, she was in a worse temper now. He couldn't blame her. They had always been so close, Jared taking it upon himself to make it up to her for the loss of their mother. For him not to tell her of his marriage must have been a shock to her. He wouldn't even consider that she might have heard the sordid details about his wife. No one would bring that kind of gossip to an eighteen-year-old girl.

Corinne started to stir and Jared left quickly, closing

the door quietly. He heard voices in the kitchen and knew that Malia would be having breakfast there. The formal dining room was always ignored except when there were guests, for he and Malia both preferred the warm atmosphere of the kitchen and Akela's jovial presence.

Corinne's eyes fluttered open just as Jared left the room. Her spirits soared as she heard the door close. He would be going back to Honolulu now. And she had every intention of leaving soon after he did. He couldn't keep her isolated here in the country. She would find a way back to the city, even if she had to hire someone to take her. She still had her jewels and also a small amount of cash. No, she wouldn't be here much longer.

Michael's faint cry from the next room broke into her thoughts. Corinne got up, wincing at the kinks in her neck and back, but quickly crossed the room to pull a pink-and-white day dress from one of her trunks. Dressed, a simple ribbon tying back her long hair, she left her room and knocked softly on Florence's door, then entered.

Florence looked up from the bassinet which had been set up at the foot of her bed. Corinne joined her there, smiling down at her son.

"Did he just get up?"

Florence chuckled. "He's been awake for hours, just lying there cooing to himself. But I guess he finally decided he's hungry."

"Come on, sweetheart." Corinne picked him up, snuggling her cheek next to his. "Mama will feed you."

"You had better let me lock the door first, then," Florence suggested.

Corinne shook her head. "That's not necessary. Jared has left already."

"But that Akela is still here," Florence reminded her as she marched to the door. "There's no point in taking chances. How she could be so sure that Michael is yours and Jared's is beyond me."

"She must have known Jared when he was a baby. The resemblance is there. You and I have both noticed that Michael has too many of Jared's features."

"Well, it's a good thing Jared hasn't really had a good look at Michael in strong light."

"Oh, stop worrying, Florence. I'll be getting us out of

189

Johanna Lindsey

here today. I hope you're up to that long ride back to the city."

"Just how are you going to get us out, might I ask?"

"I don't know yet, but I will," Corinne replied. "So don't bother unpacking."

After Michael was sated and cooing contentedly in his bassinet again, Corinne and Florence started to leave the room. They stopped short when they heard loud voices.

"I thought you said your husband had left," Florence remarked.

"I thought he had."

Corinne bit her lip, wondering if she should keep out of his way. His deep voice sounded awfully angry. But who was he yelling at? Was Akela at him again about Michael?

"Come on," Corinne said reluctantly. "We'd better go see what the fuss is about."

Jared was staring at his sister, gripping the ends of the long kitchen table. Malia's small chin was set stubbornly, and he flinched from the condemnation in her striking blue eyes. The one thing he had thought wasn't possible was indeed possible. She knew everything.

He was waiting for the answer to his question, but it was not forthcoming. "I repeat, Malia. Who told you?"

"It doesn't matter how I found out!" she replied hotly. "But now I know why you didn't bother to tell me you had married. You were too ashamed!"

"I said *who!*" he shouted, pounding a fist on the table and rattling dishes.

Malia flinched, but kept her chin jutted forward. She answered petulantly. "Our neighbor, John Pierce. He felt I had a right to know, considering that it's my family everyone's talking about."

Jared leaned back, his eyes taking on a steely glint. John Pierce! He should have guessed. The blackguard had been after their land ever since Jared could remember, for his land bordered on each side and he wanted all of it. But Jared's father had refused to sell, and so had Jared. For spite, John Pierce had run to Rodney Burkett years ago with the story of seeing Ranelle on the beach with another man. Now he had done it again, stirring up trouble just for spite.

190

"How could you marry a woman like that, Jared?" Malia's question cut into his thoughts.

The hurt in her eyes made him furious. "It's none of your damned business!"

She gasped, her eyes widening. "How can you say that?" she cried. "When you married her, she became my sister-in-law. Do you think I like having a whore for—"

Akela swung around from the counter where she had been grinding poi to a smooth paste. "Malia, you watch your mouth!" she scolded her.

"Well, it's true!" Malia cried. "Isn't it, Jared? Can you deny it?" When he couldn't, she glared at him. "Why didn't you stop her? Everyone knew what she was doing. I can't believe *you* didn't!"

"That's enough, Malia," Jared said, trying desperately to calm the rage that was burning inside him. Corinne had caused this whole situation.

"But how could you let her make such a fool of you?" she continued, undaunted. "You, who never let anyone get the better of you. Well, everyone is laughing at you now! They're laughing at all of us!"

"No more, Malia," Akela warned her.

Malia came to her feet, glaring at both of them. "I'm not through yet! Do you know what you've done to me, Jared? I can't leave this house now. I would die of shame if I went to the city for the winter season. And you know I hate it here when the storms come."

"*Auwe!*" Akela threw up her heavy arms. "Malia, you make *me* shame you act so selfish. How you think your brother feel, eh? You think he like what happened?"

"He could have stopped it!"

"You don't understand how it is between Corinne and me," Jared replied.

How could he tell his sister that he didn't stop his wife from whoring because of his pride? He couldn't let Corinne know that it mattered to him. What a mess he had made of his life!

"Did I hear my name mentioned?"

Corinne stood in the doorway, looking angelic in her pink-and-white dress. Her expression was serene, her eyes bright lime-green, innocent. Jared saw his sister's shocked

191

surprise. He had assumed Akela would have warned her that Corinne was here.

He turned to the large woman, but she shrugged. "Not for me tell her," she said, having read his thoughts.

"That's your wife?" Malia asked. She had expected a painted floozy, not the stunningly beautiful lady Corinne appeared to be.

"And who might this be, Jared?" Corinne inquired as she came further into the room, leaving Florence standing nervously in the doorway.

Florence had good reason to expect trouble, for she recognized the aggressive note in Corinne's voice. So did Jared.

He said uneasily, "Corinne, this is my sister, Malia."

"Your sister!"

Jared was almost amused at the surprise Corinne revealed, until he saw her eyes darken to a deep emerald. The wheels of her mind seemed to be turning furiously, for she looked at Malia and then back at Jared.

"She is younger than I am, isn't she, Jared?"

Now it was his turn to be bewildered. What in damnation did that have to do with anything?

"By a few years, yes," he answered warily, unable to see what she was getting at until it was too late.

"You beast!" Corinne hissed. "You lied to my father just to make him suffer!"

Jared caught his breath. He suddenly knew what conclusions she had jumped to. "Shut up, Corinne!" he warned her, the knuckles of his hands white as he gripped the table.

"Not until you burn in Hades I will!" Corinne shouted furiously. "You tell me how your mother could have had *her* if she was languishing with a broken heart? I don't believe she killed herself because of my father. It was an accident, wasn't it?"

Jared had turned pale. Corinne followed his agonized gaze to Malia and saw the horror on the girl's face. She held her breath as the girl burst into tears and ran from the room.

What had she done? She was afraid to look at Jared again, but he forced her to when his fingers bit into her shoulders.

"I could kill you for that!" he said in a deadly whisper,

his grip on her becoming painful. "Malia didn't know, confound you. She was told our mother's death was an accident!"

"I—I'm sorry, Jared," Corinne stammered, never more frightened by him than she was at that moment.

"You're sorry!" he spat at her, shoving her away from him. "You meant to hurt and you did. I hope to hell you're satisfied!"

He stormed out of the room to follow his sister, leaving Corinne shaken. Florence rushed to her, putting an arm about her shoulders.

"Don't fret now, Cori. I know you didn't mean to hurt the girl."

"Why couldn't I have stilled my vicious tongue? I deserved everything he said, and more." She turned to Akela. "I really am sorry."

The old woman frowned. "Bad thing you do, Kolina, but I understand now."

"Understand?"

"Your father the one my Ranelle love too much. Ialeka hate him long time. I know why he go mainland now, why he marry you. He hurt you, huh? Then you come here for hurt him back. *Auwe!* Bad thing hate." She shook her peppered head. "Mo'better love."

"That's impossible," Corinne replied dismally, her eyes downcast.

Akela shook her head again. "Think of the *keiki* and you see love mo'better."

Corinne drew herself up defensively, but Florence urged her out of the kitchen before more damage was done. She spent the rest of the day with Michael and Florence in their bedroom. Akela brought them food, stopping to fuss over Michael for a while. Wisely, she didn't say anything more about him, or about Jared and his sister.

Corinne knew it had taken Jared hours to calm the girl down, for they had all heard the heartbreaking tears coming from the patio. If only she hadn't barged into the kitchen that morning. Damn her temper.

Jared hadn't left that day, and it was too late for him to go now. She dreaded facing him again, especially alone. But by that night, she dreaded even more the thought that he might come looking for her.

She bid Florence good night and walked hesitantly to Jared's room. He was there already, standing at the far window, looking out, his arms braced on each side of the window. He was so deep in thought that he didn't hear her come in and she had to clear her throat. Because he was in the shadows, she couldn't see his expression when he turned to look at her.

"If you've changed your mind about my sleeping in this room, I'll—"

"Come in, Corinne," he said. "You're my wife and this room is as much yours as it is mine. I told you before, there are no other rooms. And I won't have you inconveniencing your maid just because you and I would rather not share the same room."

"She wouldn't mind."

"I mind."

His voice was not harsh. In fact, he sounded terribly tired.

"Well, I won't sleep on that chaise again," she warned him. "My neck is still stiff from last night."

"Suit yourself."

"You won't—"

Corinne halted in mid-sentence and bit her lip.

"I won't," he answered.

Corinne closed the door and crossed to the bed where Akela had left her nightgown. She picked it up and went on towards the bathroom, but stopped before she got there and turned slowly to Jared.

"I—I really am sorry for what happened this morning," she said, thankful his back was to her and he hadn't turned around. "I would never have hurt your sister intentionally, Jared. I had no way of knowing she wasn't aware of the circumstances surrounding your mother's death."

"I know," he murmured, still without facing her. "It's over with, so forget about it."

How can I? she wanted to say. But she went slowly into the bathroom and closed the door quietly. She changed in what little light the moon provided as it filtered in through the row of short windows high on the bathroom wall. When she came back into the bedroom, Jared was still standing at the window, looking out at the front yard and the high clifflike base of the mountain on the other side of the road.

She got into bed, but hesitated before asking, "Do you mind if I turn the light out?"

"Go ahead. I'll be up a while yet."

Sleep was impossible. And it was indeed a long while before Jared finally left his vigil at the window and came to bed. Corinne pretended sleep as she heard him removing his clothes. When she felt him get into bed, she stiffened.

He was so close, so very close, and she couldn't help thinking of their wedding night a year ago on this day. She would never have that thrilling pleasure again, never know his strong arms holding her close, his lips touching hers, drawing her will away. Never again seemed so very long, when at this moment she wanted those powerful hands to caress her, wanted to feel the length of his body on hers. Why had they destroyed what might have been?

She felt the bed move again, and sensed that he was looking down at her. She kept her eyes closed and held her breath.

"I'm sorry, Kolina," he breathed softly and then moved back to the far side of the bed.

Sorry for what? But she knew that he had assumed she was sleeping. He believed she hadn't heard him, or he would never have spoken. Would she ever know what he was sorry for? Sorry that he had ever met her? Tears welled fiercely in her eyes and she didn't know why.

Chapter 28

CORINNE woke to find Jared's chest against her back, with one arm slung over her possessively. Her first impulse was to scramble from the bed, but she realized that would wake him and might even draw his anger. She lay still, revelling in the feel of him pressed to her.

She became unnerved by his closeness, feeling his warm breath on her neck, the weight of his arm over her, his hand slack against her breast. She could feel the excitement building in her like a live thing. Daringly, she pressed even closer to him and her eyes widened when she felt the soft bulge of him against her buttocks. She had forgotten that he was completely naked. Her own gown was bunched up about her waist.

The thrilling feel of him was almost more than she could bear. She forgot everything that had ever passed between them, everything—except his lovemaking on their wedding night, the night that he had inflamed her passion. She wanted that again, she wanted to stir his desire and make him take her again. But could she do that? Would he forget his hate long enough to satisfy his needs—and hers? Yes, she admitted that she needed Jared.

Corinne's passionate quandary was all for naught, for at that moment the bedroom door opened and a young, very attractive Hawaiian girl with light golden skin burst in on them.

"Ialeka! I see your carriage and—"

The girl stopped, her dark eyes widening as she took in the scene on the bed. Jared had awakened instantly and Corinne could feel the tightening of his body before he pulled away from her with a muttered curse.

The girl raced back out of the room with a strangled cry before Jared bellowed, "Naneki!"

Corinne watched with shock and disbelief as Jared yanked on his trousers and, without looking once in her direction, ran out after the girl. She stared at the empty doorway and felt her face grow hot with the rage that suddenly took hold of her. The girl was Jared's mistress! Nothing else could explain her familiarity with his room or her reaction to Corinne's presence.

"Damn him!"

Corinne grabbed her robe and went after them. Jared had caught up with the girl in the back yard, just outside the patio. Corinne stood bristling on the top step that led down to the sunken patio. She could see them clearly through the screened door, Jared holding onto the girl's arm, making her listen to him even though she tried to pull away.

The dining room was beside her, enclosed with latticed shelves that held all manner of colored crystal and china vases. The kitchen was directly across from this and Akela appeared at the door there.

"Leave alone, Kolina."

Corinne turned flashing emerald eyes on her. "He's *my* husband!"

Akela nodded. "But I no have chance tell Naneki you here. She hurt. Let Ialeka explain."

"What is she even doing here?" Corinne demanded, her fists clenched in anger.

"She live here, work here. She away yesterday, come back just now. Naneki my adopted *keiki*," Akela explained.

"She *lives* here? And he brought me—"

Corinne couldn't finish she was so choked with rage. She ignored Akela's staying hand and moved down the steps and across the room. But she stopped before opening the door to the patio and revealing her presence.

"Why you bring her here?" Naneki was crying. "How you can forgive her for what she did to you?"

"I haven't forgiven her for anything, Naneki," Jared said impatiently. "And I brought her here to put a stop to her whoring."

"But you sleep with her!"

"Only sleep, confound it! Nothing else."

"Well, I no stay here with her," Naneki said defiantly. "I share you with Dayna, but not with this *haole!*"

197

Who was this Dayna? Corinne wondered. Another of Jared's mistresses? Corinne started to turn around, but her attention was caught by a little Hawaiian girl who came running around the side of the house toward Jared.

"Papa!" the little girl cried and flew into Jared's outstretched arms.

Corinne gasped, watching Jared hug the child. But Naneki grabbed her angrily from his arms.

"Come, Noelani," she said roughly. "We go back Aunty's house."

Corinne opened the door. "You don't have to leave on my account," she purred smoothly, wondering how she managed such control.

Naneki looked at Corinne with loathing before she walked away stiffly, little Noelani waving good-bye innocently over her shoulder. The little girl with dark hair and eyes and golden skin was the image of her mother. But Jared also had those dark good looks. Was this really his daughter?

"So you have a daughter, Jared." She smiled. "How nice for you. I wonder why you never mentioned her before."

"Because Noelani is not mine, Corinne," he said flatly and started to walk back into the house.

"But Naneki *is* your mistress, isn't she?" she said to him, her voice rising.

Jared turned on her and said icily, "She was my mistress before I married you. But I'm afraid I haven't found any time for her since I got back from the mainland."

"You expect me to believe that?"

"Jealous?" he said sarcastically.

"Of course not!"

"Good, because you shouldn't be. You can't begrudge me one mistress," he said in a cruel tone. "Not when you give yourself to any man who comes along."

She gasped and instantly raised her hand to slap him, but he caught her wrist and held it firmly. His eyes were cold gray slits as he looked down on her.

"Does the truth hurt, my dear?" he asked unmercifully, his grip tightening. "Whores have to get used to insults, it comes with the trade. You really should have thought of that?"

"I would gladly *give it* to anyone rather than you!" she spat, wanting furiously to hurt him in return.

He paled, and shoving her away from him, marched back into the house.

Corinne turned away, fighting to control the tears. Why did they *always* have to hurt each other? She would rather he had struck her than say what he had with such venom in his voice. For an instant she was ready to tell him the truth, all of it. But she reasoned that he would only laugh at her, scorning her once more.

She had done too good a job of creating the illusion that she was a whore. No one would ever believe otherwise now —except her so-called lovers. They knew, but they would never tell! It was all so absurd.

Dismally, Corinne picked a gardenia from the shrubs that grew along the three-foot lava rock wall of the patio. She breathed deeply of the velvety white flower, then placed it behind her ear and slowly started walking through the back yard towards the beach. The yard was long and not nearly so heavily cultivated as the garden out front. There were banana trees, guava, lichee, lemon and lime trees, and two huge mango trees which cast abundant shade over lush grass. The giant mango tree on the left had a bench swing attached to it and Corinne stopped there instead of going on to the beach.

The sound of the waves beating against the shore was soothing. She couldn't see the deep blue of the ocean, for the beach slanted downward beyond the yard, but she knew it was very close. It was so peaceful here. It would be heavenly to sit in this swing and watch the sunset, to have someone she loved beside her, drawing her near, sharing the beauty and wonder of nature and the love of one another.

She suddenly felt so lonely and confused. Why had Jared's scathing remarks hurt her so much? She shouldn't care what he thought of her. He had admitted that Naneki was his mistress and, for some reason that hurt, too. And the little girl who had called him Papa. Corinne didn't believe for one minute that she wasn't Jared's child. Jared should have married Naneki, if only for the sake of his daughter. But instead he had come to the mainland and married her, for revenge against her father.

She was weary of it all. She was tired of fighting with him, of trying to understand what had happened to their one loving night. She just wanted to go home. She wouldn't even try to get back the money Jared had taken from her. Let him keep it all, she didn't need it.

A door slamming at the front of the house drew Corinne's attention. She turned in the swing just in time to see Jared cross from the house to the wall of pines and go toward the stable. A few minutes later she heard a horse canter away. So he was gone. And without even a good-bye. Instead of relief, she felt the tears begin again.

Chapter 29

CORINNE sat alone at the kitchen table, sipping the Chinese tea Akela had made earlier. It was the first of November, three weeks to the day since Jared had returned to the city. Her efforts to get back to Honolulu herself had been frustrated over and over again.

She had found out quickly enough that the stable was off-limits to her. *Kapu*, the big Hawaiian who tended the few horses had shouted at her the day she went there. Jared had left orders that she wasn't to use the carriage, nor could she have a horse. And each time she had sneaked into the stable to try and get a horse anyway, she was discovered by the big Hawaiian and had another exchange of shouts that neither of them understood, for he hardly spoke a word of English, and she understood only a few Hawaiian words.

Corinne had had only one other opportunity for getting away, when the iceman stopped to deliver ice, as he did periodically. She had quickly asked him to give her a ride to the nearest town, shoving what little cash she had into his hands. But Akela had overheard, and warned him that Jared would come after him with a club if he took his *wahine male* anywhere. The poor man's eyes had bulged. He couldn't get away fast enough.

"Kolina no leave," Akela had said to her afterwards. "Ialeka say so."

Corinne had been furious with her, but the huge woman only clucked her tongue and walked away. That had been more than a week ago. Corinne couldn't bribe Akela. She'd been with Jared since he was a baby. Akela would never sell her loyalty.

"Why did you marry Jared?"

Corinne caught her breath at the sudden intrusion into

her thoughts. She looked up to see Malia standing across the table from her. It was the first time the girl had spoken to her in three weeks, in fact, the first time she had even come near her. She had always left a room whenever Corinne entered, and she took all her meals in her own room, avoiding Corinne.

"Well?"

Corinne couldn't blame the girl for her hatred. "There were several reasons why Jared and I married," she answered, hoping the girl wouldn't press her.

"Did you love him?"

"No."

"Did he love you?"

"No, he certainly didn't." Corinne heard the bitterness creeping into her own voice.

"Then why?"

Corinne felt as if she were being backed into a corner. "It really . . . isn't any of your business."

Malia rested her hands on the back of a chair and leaned forward. "He is my brother," she said, nearly pleading. "I asked him why he married you, but he said the same thing you just did. I am asking you now to help me understand."

Corinne lowered her eyes from the beseeching look on Malia's face. She tried to put herself in this young girl's place and realized how terribly bewildered she must be.

"Your brother promised to give me what I wanted out of a marriage—no husband."

"What do you mean?"

"He was not to interfere in anything I did. We were to lead separate lives."

"If you didn't want to live with him, then why did you come here?"

"I don't think you would really care to know the answer to that," Corinne said in a hard tone. "It does not say much for your brother."

"My brother has done nothing wrong, except to choose you for his wife!" Malia came to Jared's defense, quickly hostile again.

Corinne matched Malia's anger with her own. "Jared is not the paragon of virtue you think he is, my dear. He lied about his reason for marrying me. He claimed it was a matter of honor. You see, your dear brother had raped me. He offered to save my reputation through marriage."

"You lie!"

"Ask him and see if he can deny it. That was his excuse for marrying me, Malia. But it *was* only an excuse, for your brother has no conscience. The real reason he married me was this; he thought that as my husband, he could control the stock I owned in my father's shipyard. He wanted to ruin my father. He found out too late that he couldn't control my stock at all. It must have been a terrible blow."

"Your father is . . ." Malia couldn't finish.

"Did Jared explain to you about my father? Or did he only tell you his side of the story?"

"He—he said my mother died—that my mother killed herself because she couldn't live without Samuel Barrows," Malia said brokenly.

"Yes, she loved my father and he loved her. She wasn't strong enough to go on without him. But my father never knew how badly their separation affected her. All these years, he had thought she was alive and happy with her life. He was crushed when Jared told him what had happened, for he still loved her. Remember, she originally sent my father away from here."

"But Jared said he was to blame!"

"No one can be held responsible for the weakness of another." Corinne replied. "Jared never saw it that way, though. That's why he went to the mainland, and that's why he married me, all for revenge. He used me, Malia, when I had never done anything to him to cause such treatment."

"Is this why you came here then?" Malia asked. "You wanted revenge too?"

"You sound as though you don't think I was justified, Malia," Corinne said quietly.

"You were not! You got what you wanted. Jared came home—he left you to lead the separate life you wanted."

"Yes, he left me, but there's more to it than that. You see, he deserted me publicly, Malia, the very day after we were married and he learned that he couldn't use me to ruin my father. He ruined me instead, with a formal announcement in all the newspapers that his wife had proved unsatisfactory and he was deserting her. It was not true. Your brother found no fault with me. He meant only to hurt me. And if you think you have been humiliated by what I did, think about how I felt after the public announcement."

"I don't believe you! You say all this only because Jared is not here to deny it! And nothing could excuse what you did—nothing!"

Corinne lost all patience with the girl. "I haven't done anything to be ashamed of. I created a scandal, but it was all an act."

"What are you saying?" Malia demanded. "Everyone knows you've slept with a great many men!"

"Everyone *thinks* I have!" Corinne replied furiously, not caring anymore what she revealed. "I entertained men in my hotel suite, but not in my bedroom. It wasn't necessary to go that far to humiliate Jared, not when people jump so easily to the worst conclusion. It was all a farce, Malia. The only man who has ever touched me is your brother!"

Malia drew herself up. "I should never have come to you for the truth."

Corinne stood up, her eyes reflecting exasperation. "And I should have known better than to tell you the truth. It's easier to think I'm a whore, isn't it? You can go on thinking that, because I don't give a damn what you believe."

"You—you're horrible!" Malia cried. She ran from the room in tears.

Corinne slumped back in her chair. She had hurt the girl again. Why the devil couldn't she keep her temper? She had told Malia that her brother was a cad, and had tried to make herself appear blameless, when she knew she wasn't.

Corinne glanced out the windows at the storm clouds gathering. The sky was as dark as her mood.

Chapter 30

JARED stood at the window in his uncle's office, looking down at the busy street below but not really seeing it. He was listening with embarrassment while Edmond reprimanded his young assistant Marvin Colby for some real or imagined mistake. Edmond Burkett was forever finding fault. It was a wonder anyone worked for him. The young Miss Dearing had quit long ago, a prim Mrs. Long taking her place.

"I won't tolerate your ineptitude any longer, Colby," Edmond was saying. "You know that the final approval of all loans is made by me!"

"But you weren't here, sir, and the man desperately needed the money yesterday. It was a small loan, and he had ample collateral."

"That is no excuse for ignoring the policy of this company, *my* policy! And this is the last blunder you will make here, Colby. You're fired."

"You're being unreasonable, Mr. Burkett." Marvin Colby dared to let his temper show.

"Get out!"

After the door had closed, Jared turned to face his uncle. "Don't you think you were a bit hard on him?"

"You don't know the facts, Jared, so don't presume to interfere."

Jared sighed. He had enough problems of his own. And he had learned long ago that it was pointless to argue with his uncle over anything concerning the Savings and Loan.

"Just why did you send for me, Uncle?" Jared asked impatiently.

"Don't be so defensive, my boy," Edmond smiled, congenial now. "I thought we might have lunch together.

There's a new restaurant on King Street that serves excellent shrimp Canton."

"You called me here to invite me to have lunch with you?" Jared asked incredulously. "I don't have time for leisurely lunches, Uncle."

"Nonsense," Edmond scoffed. "I happen to know that your hotel job is running smoothly. And you've told me enough times that you couldn't find a better *luna* than your friend Leonaka Naihe. Let him do the job you pay him for. He must get better results from your local laborers than you do since he's a local boy himself."

"I happen to like the work," Jared said stiffly. "I thrive on work."

"You mean you lose yourself in it," Edmond replied knowingly. "That won't make your problems go away. In fact, you shouldn't have any problems left to deal with. You handled the situation with your wife admirably. I told you the talk would die down if you just put a stop to her outlandish affairs. She has been forgotten because of the coming revolution."

"Uncle!"

"The fact won't go away by ignoring it, Jared. There will be another revolution, and soon. Only this one will have more results than the revolution of 1887, which won our constitution. This time, the queen will be overthrown. No one is pleased with Liliuokalani's reign. She's too hotheaded and wants too much power."

"She *is* the queen," Jared reminded him. "The old monarchs had absolute power. Queen Liliuokalani just wants a return to the old ways."

"It's too late for that. Too many foreign interests are involved here in Hawaii."

"Too many greedy interests, you mean."

"Can you deny that annexation to the United States would benefit these islands? And better America than some other foreign power like China or Great Britain."

"The Hawaiians should rule their own islands, Uncle," Jared said in exasperation. "I've always felt that way, and nothing has made me change my mind. These islands belonged to the Hawaiians, but bit by bit *haoles* have taken them away."

"The fact that you have a touch of Hawaiian in you influences you, Jared," Edmond said harshly.

"I just can't condone a race being destroyed for the greed and benefit of another."

"Good heavens, man. I'm not talking about war! It certainly won't come to that. It will be a quick revolution."

"I'm talking about a culture dying. More than half of the Hawaiian peoples have lost their lives to foreign disease, the rest are intermarrying and forgetting the old ways. The number of pure Hawaiians left is few. Their beliefs have been stripped from them, and their land, and now you would take away their last bit of pride."

"Can you approve what the queen is doing? Nothing gets accomplished anymore at the palace. She does nothing but fight with her ministerial advisers. The legislature is completely blocked because of opposing parties. Resignations have been forced. The queen no longer hides the fact that she wants to do away with the present constitution we all fought so hard for. She wants to proclaim a new one that would give her unlimited power and give only Hawaiians and foreigners married to Hawaiians the right to vote. Can you really condone such tyrannical behavior?"

"Perhaps she is overdoing it a bit, but I certainly can't blame her for trying. Her reign has been a mockery. She bears the title of queen, but she has been robbed of her power by the foreign interests you side with. They have made the decisions for years. Can you blame her for wanting her people to rule their own islands?"

"The islands have prospered because of foreigners!" Edmond said defensively.

"At the expense of the Hawaiians, who have nothing left!" Jared replied furiously. "Now *pau!* I don't want to hear anymore talk of revolution."

"Jared, wait!"

But Jared was already halfway through the outer office. If Edmond wanted to talk politics, he would have to find someone else to do it with.

On the ride back to his own office on Merchant Street, Jared finally took notice of the storm that was brewing overhead. He grew uneasy. Judging by the strong winds, he knew that this would be one of the destructive storms. And the windward side of the island always suffered worst. On the north shore, devastating waves would wash right through houses and flood roads. Trees toppling and roofs blowing away were common occurrences during this kind of storm.

Malia had always feared such storms. And Corinne? She wouldn't know that she was safe where she was. The waves might reach the yard, even flood the patio, as had happened many times, but she would be safe. Only she wouldn't know that. Akela would reassure her, but would Corinne believe that the winter storm wouldn't last long and the sun would shine again tomorrow? Or would she be frightened by a natural occurrence that came often in the winter rainy season?

Jared turned his carriage toward Beretania and whipped the horses on. He suddenly felt an irrational desire to protect and comfort his wife. He knew it was absurd, but nevertheless he rode home recklessly. He quickly saddled a horse and then set out again with a growing urgency that bordered on panic.

Jared made excellent time until he reached Wahiawa. He changed horses there, but before he set out again he could see the rain approaching in solid sheets. It swept over him in a matter of seconds. The rest of the ride went much slower, for many parts of the road were washed out, leaving gaping holes that could easily cause his horse to stumble.

He rode down to the sea, but the view of the ocean was lost in the blinding storm. Once he passed Haleiwa he saw evidence that this storm had been building for days, with frequent showers. Fields and roads were already flooded. Wagons and carriages were abandoned. Twenty-foot waves came up to meet the road in many places, slowing his progress even more.

It was night when Jared finally reached the beach house. He had made no better time on horseback than he would have with a carriage on a clear day. He was drenched to the bone, and it was still pouring steadily. The front yard was swamped and Jared knew that if the ocean waves rose another five feet the yard would be drenched with more than just rain water.

The front of the house was dark, but there was a light in the kitchen. Jared could see that the patio had been closed off with heavy shutters to keep the wind out. All of the patio furniture had been moved into the living room. Akela had everything in hand, as usual, but Jared was still anxious about Corinne.

He went directly to his bedroom, but found it dark and empty. He stopped only long enough to grab a couple of towels from the bathroom before he went to the kitchen. But Corinne wasn't there either. Akela and his sister sat at the table sipping hot chocolate.

Malia saw him first and jumped up to run into his arms. She began crying immediately, moaning his name over and over as she had done as a child.

Jared tried to hold her back from him. "You're getting soaked, Malia." But she clung to him that much harder and he quickly relented and held her soothingly. "It's only a storm, dearest. You've been through enough of them to know that we are safe here. It has never gotten so bad that we had to desert the house."

"It's not the storm, Jared!" Malia sobbed. "It's your wife!"

Malia only called him Jared when she was angry or upset with him, so he knew that she and Corinne had fought.

"What about her?"

"That—that *woman* is horrible! She told me terrible things about you. But she lied! I know she lied about everything. And she tried to tell me she wasn't a whore!"

Jared grabbed his sister's shoulders and held her away from him. His whole body had grown rigid.

"What did she tell you?"

Malia repeated the story she had sobbed to Akela earlier, but in greater detail. A murderous gleam grew in Jared's eyes. Akela saw it, but Malia went on, unaware.

"She was so spiteful," Malia finished. "And she shouted at me, when I did nothing to cause her anger. I hate her!"

"Where is she?" Jared asked in a deadly whisper.

Akela stood up apprehensively. "Ialeka, no. No see her now."

But Malia answered, "She is with her maid and that brat who keeps me awake at night with his squalling."

Jared left the room. Akela felt like boxing Malia's ears. "You *lolo!*" she said angrily. "Why you make so much out of nothing, Malia?"

209

"It wasn't nothing!" Malia cried.

"Kolina no hurt you, girl. But because of what you tell your brother, he hurt her. And you to blame!"

"I am not! She is—for all the mean things she said to me!"

"Puā no ka uahi, he ahi ko lalo!" Akela spat, and turned away in disgust.

Malia grimaced and said no more. Akela was right. "When smoke rises, there is fire below," she had said. When angry words are used, there is a cause. Yes, she had instigated the whole scene with Jared's wife. She had sought Corinne out and said spiteful things herself. But that didn't change anything. Corinne was still a horrible woman, and if Jared beat her, it would only be what she deserved.

Even with the rain pounding on the roof, they still heard a door crashing in against a wall, and Malia said quickly, "I think I will have some more hot chocolate. I never sleep when it storms, anyway."

Akela grunted. "What wrong, Malia? You no like go your room where you can hear the trouble you cause?"

"Quiet. I only told the truth. Can I help it if Jared got so angry?"

"You as quick with your tongue as Kolina. You should both learn when to keep silent."

Corinne stared incredulously at Jared when he barged into Florence's room without knocking, startling all of them. She had been holding Michael, walking him about the room because the storm and the thundering roar of the ocean frightened him. But as Jared came at her with purposeful strides, she quickly handed Michael to Florence.

"What is the matter with you, Jared?" Corinne asked fearfully, backing away from him.

He didn't answer her, but grabbed her wrist and started to pull her from the room. Corinne held back, terror gripping her now, but Jared gave her a yank that almost sent her crashing into him.

"See here—" Florence started to protest.

Jared glared at her and the words that had sprung to her lips died there. "Don't interfere," he warned her harshly. "She's my wife. Remember that."

"Interfere with what?" Florence questioned, but Jared was already out of the door.

Florence held her breath. But there was really nothing she could do. Cori *was* his wife and furthermore, he wouldn't hurt her. No, he wouldn't, she told herself.

When she heard their bedroom door slam shut, she quickly left her room with Michael and went to the kitchen on the other side of the house. She couldn't stay where she might overhear what was going to happen.

As soon as Jared shoved Corinne into the room and released her long enough to close the door, she raced across to the bathroom and locked herself in. Her heart beat frantically as she pressed her ear to the door. She had never seen Jared like that before, not even on the night he had raped her. He had been determined then, but not violent.

She could see a light from beneath the door and held her breath. What was he doing? Why had he come back here in the middle of a storm and in such a rage?

Corinne could hear Jared just outside the bathroom door now. He turned the handle, but found it locked. And then he slammed a fist against the hard wood, making her jump with the explosive sound.

"Open the door, Corinne."

He didn't shout. In fact, his voice was deadly calm.

"Not until you tell me what you want, Jared."

"Open it!" his tone raised menacingly.

"No!"

"Then you had better stand back!"

She jumped away from the door quickly, and just in time. The bolt gave way under Jared's kick and the door crashed open. He was silhouetted in the doorway with the light behind him, making it impossible for her to distinguish his features. Her own face was a mask of fright.

When he reached out for her, she gasped. He caught her arm and dragged her back into the bedroom, then swung her around to face him. He let her go and she felt a second of relief. She was unprepared for the stinging slap that followed, so forceful that it knocked her sideways. She fell against the coffee table, nearly tumbling over it.

Tears sprang to her eyes. She brought her hand up to cover the spot, while she kept her shocked eyes on Jared, still standing several feet from her.

"What in all damnation is the matter with you?" she shouted, her temper rising, despite the fear and shock.

His face was black with rage, and when he took a step toward her she panicked and scrambled around the coffee table, her eyes wide with fear.

"Stay away from me, Jared," she warned, though her voice was too timorous to carry much weight. "I'm not going to take your abuse, especially when I don't know what's bothering you."

"You'll take whatever I give you," he snarled, his fists clenched at his sides. "I should have taught you to keep your mouth shut a long time ago!"

"What am I suppose to have done?" she begged desperately.

"You drove my sister to tears again! You told her what a blackguard I am, didn't you?"

Corinne struggled for breath. "Why should I take all the scorn when no one but you knows *why* I did what I did? She insisted on the truth and I gave it to her!"

"And you tried to paint a picture of innocence for yourself!"

"Not entirely," she said through tight lips.

"Not entirely?" Jared repeated with a cold sneer. "You *lied* to Malia! Will you try to tell me that you're not a whore?"

Corinne winced. "I'm not," she said defiantly.

Jared's eyes blazed even more. "I know half the men you've been seen with, and they are not the kind who will be shrugged off by a tease."

"That's all I did, Jared. I teased. I made promises to them that I didn't keep," Corinne said simply. "It wasn't so difficult to put them off. I never saw the same man twice."

"And of course Russell Drayton only pretended to be your lover?"

"Yes. He knew I wanted to get even with you and he helped me."

"He just went along with your so-called sham, never touching you? Never asking for you, even though he knew you loved him and would be willing?"

"What?"

"You admitted to me once that you loved him," Jared reminded her.

"I—I lied to you," Corinne stammered, groaning inwardly that he should remember that. "You would have thought me callous if I told you the truth. After all, I was planning to marry Russell. I didn't love him anymore than I did you when we married. Russell and I had an arrangement."

"You're incredible. You have an answer for everything, don't you?" Jared's eyes narrowed and he growled ominously, "I'm tired of your playing me for a fool! I hope you got your pleasure out of using that viperous tongue of yours on my sister, because now you're going to pay for it!"

He started toward her, but the green fire that shot into her eyes stopped him. "What about my feelings, damn you? I didn't mean to hurt Malia, but she wouldn't leave well enough alone. And I have never been able to take insults without getting angry."

"Your temper has caused trouble ever since I met you!" he stormed.

"If you strike me again, Jared, I'll—"

"You'll what?" he cut her off virulently. "An errant wife deserves a beating, and yours is long overdue."

She ran for the door again. It was locked, and before she could throw the bolt, Jared's fingers bit into her forearm and he pulled her to him. She saw him raise his hand to strike her again, his eyes without mercy. She couldn't stand pain, and she couldn't bear the realization that if he beat her, she would never be able to forgive him for it.

"Jared, no!"

Without hesitating another second, Corinne threw herself at him and wrapped her arms tightly about his chest. She could feel the sudden tensing of his muscles and knew he was about to push her away.

Jared was thoroughly jolted by Corinne's unexpected reaction. But his fury didn't lessen. It was not entirely rage over what had happened with Malia, it was also the lies she had just told him. He knew she wasn't innocent—he knew it! And for her to attempt to convince him otherwise showed her utter contempt for him.

"Let go, Corinne!" he breathed through clenched teeth, and started to pull her arms away.

Corinne tightened her hold on him, desperately locking her fingers together behind his back. She looked up at him, but could still read no mercy in his expression. And then she felt his hands in her hair, gripping the curls arranged in a high sweep, and he began to pull her away from him that way. She resisted, even when it became terribly painful, her eyes glistening with tears.

"Jared . . . please!" she cried, feeling her hair coming out by the roots. "Please . . . don't . . . hurt . . . me!"

Corinne felt his grip slacken slowly. And then suddenly he let her go, and she buried her face against his chest. Her sobs came naturally, a mixture of pain, the humiliation of being forced to plead, and relief that Jared had mastered his fury. She held to him and sobbed.

When Jared released her hair, his arms remained outstretched, inches from her back. He didn't know whether to drop them at his sides or put them around his wife. The terrified look he had seen in her eyes had unnerved him. He remembered his reason for coming home—to comfort her during the storm. The storm still raged outside, but Corinne wasn't frightened of the storm. She was terrified of *him*.

What in God's name had come over him? He had never struck a woman before, yet he had wanted to strangle this one, to throttle her senseless.

Jared felt her trembling against him and shrank from her heartbreaking sobs. His arms ached to hold her, and at last he did. He smoothed the silken hair that had tumbled down her back because of his cruelty, cursing himself for the pain he had caused. She cried and cried and the sound tore at his heart.

"I'm sorry," he murmured. He cupped her face in his hands, but she wouldn't look at him, and the tears still fell. "Please, *makamae,* don't cry anymore. I swear I won't hurt you again."

He kissed her eyes, her cheeks, and then her lips, gently. Slowly he raised his head, waiting for some sign from her, a sign of relief, anger, anything. When she opened her eyes they were sparkling green pools that still seemed to plead with him, but in a different way. And suddenly his own eyes blazed again. Not with anger, but with the fire of passion.

He brought his mouth back to hers, but this time his kiss was demanding, devouring. He couldn't get enough of her. And her responses matched his. She did not resist. She was wholly his. She released his back in order to grasp his neck and draw him down to her. She raised herself up on tiptoe to press even closer. Their kiss became savage, even painful, and Jared finally broke away to bury his lips in the silken hollow of her neck.

"I want you, Kolina," he breathed huskily. He raised his head to look down at her and started to unfasten her dress. "I'm going to make love to you."

"I know," she whispered, her eyes meeting his directly. "I want you to."

Jared nearly ripped her gown in his urgency to remove it. At the same time she unbuttoned his wet shirt. But when he started to lift her shift she stopped him.

"Turn the lamp off first, Jared."

"No," he said forcefully. "I want to look at you."

"Please, Jared."

At that moment he couldn't refuse her anything. As much as he wanted to gaze on her beauty, he did as she asked.

As soon as the lamp was extinguished, Corinne quickly removed the rest of her underclothes and the binder on her breasts that she had been so afraid Jared would see. God, how he stirred her blood! She didn't care what had happened earlier. None of that mattered anymore.

He wanted her, needed her. The knowledge made her own desire build to a warm ache, and she was the one who pulled him to the bed and pushed him down on it. She followed him and brazenly rubbed her body against his, then teasingly pushed him down when he tried to rise. On her knees, she touched him where he throbbed and heard his gasp. She revelled in his desire for her. Then she ran her hands up his chest, to his face, through his hair. Her lips found his.

Jared's reaction was immediate. He couldn't wait any longer, and neither could she. Their passions had been denied too long. He pushed her down on the bed and mounted her and she opened for him, her body starved for him. They moved together, wildly, savagely, as the climactic moment neared. And then it was upon them and Corinne cried his name as her thighs widened, drawing him deeper into her, savoring the blissful throbbing he had caused.

It was over too soon, and the time for remembering returned. But Corinne thrust memory aside. She was too happy to let anything spoil this.

"Corinne—" Jared began.

"Jared, please, don't say anything. Let us both keep silent," she answered quickly. "Can't we at least have this night?"

His answer was to draw her near to him. She fell asleep like that, her head cradled on his shoulder, a blissful smile on her lips.

Chapter 31

JARED stopped in the doorway to the kitchen and stretched the sleep from his body. Akela was at the counter making poi, a morning ritual that dated as far back as Jared could remember. Poi was made from the taro plant, from the bulbous root which Akela cooked once a week and then pounded to a hard consistency so it wouldn't spoil. Each morning she took what was needed for the day and mixed it with water and pounded it again, this time to a smooth paste. Jared thought the sticky gray starch rather bland, but Akela couldn't live without it.

"How about some breakfast, Aunty? I haven't eaten since yesterday morning."

"Auwe!" She gave him a sharp look over her shoulder for startling her. "I no hear you come in, Ialeka."

He laughed. "It's a wonder you can hear anything, with all that noise you're making."

"You like poi?"

"Not for breakfast," he groaned. "I'll take some banana pancakes, though."

"No more bananas," she chuckled. "The *keiki* Mikáele think they *ono*. He eat one mashed every day. No more on our trees. You go up the mountain today, bring some stalks down, huh?"

"We'll see. How about those papayas on the ledge? Are they ripe yet?"

"Go see. Kuliano bring them with some sausage. I fix you eggs, huh, with sausage?"

"Kuliano's blood sausage?" Jared shook his head. "Just the eggs will do," he said. He found one of the green and yellow papayas on the windowsill ripe enough. "And fruit. And maybe some toast with guava jelly." He slit the papaya in half and took it to the table. "How is Kuliano?"

217

"My nephew just fine. That Japanee wife of his keep him jumping. But he complain he no see Leonaka long time. He say you work his boy too hard."

Jared grinned. "I guess I'll have to give Leo some time off to visit his father, or Kuliano will end up disinheriting me from the family. I'll send for Leo today. The rain is going to slow the hotel job anyway." He paused to take a large chunk of papaya in his mouth. "I haven't seen Kuliano for ages. Maybe I will stop by when I go for those bananas."

"Why you no take Kolina too?" Akela suggested, looking at Jared closely. "I think she like the view from up high."

"Do you?" Jared said, his lips turning up slowly at the corners. "Maybe I will. Has she given you much trouble while I was gone?"

"Kolina? No!" Akela replied emphatically. "She all the time play with little Mikáele, take care him. She always stay with the *keiki*."

Jared ignored the emphasis she put on her words. "She didn't try to leave here?"

"Only few times. Kolina lonely, I think. Maybe she miss you, huh?"

"You can get that hopeful look off your face right now, Aunty. Corinne and I may have reached a temporary peace, but I'm sure it won't last."

"*You* make it last," she said sternly.

"Good morning, Mr. Burkett." Jared turned to see a stiff-lipped Florence coming into the kitchen. "I didn't hear Cori stirring about in her room," she said in a manner that demanded reassurance.

He grinned. "Didn't you go in to check on her?"

Florence squared her back, her hazel eyes glaring at him. "I didn't want to disturb her if she was still sleeping."

"She probably still is." Suddenly Jared laughed. "Sit down, Mrs. Merrill, and have some breakfast. And stop looking at me as if I had committed some abominable crime. I haven't. Your Cori is just fine."

Florence relaxed and even smiled a little. "I didn't really think she wouldn't be all right."

She joined him at the table, noting his good spirits. The

hard lines were gone from his face, leaving him younger-looking and decidedly more handsome.

"Would you care for some papaya?" Jared offered. "This is the only one that's ripe yet."

Florence accepted a piece of the yellow-orange fruit, but set it aside. "I'll just save it for Michael, if you don't mind. He loves fruit."

"And poi," Akela added proudly.

Florence grimaced, wondering how anyone could like that moldy-looking starch. "Remarkably enough, he seems to thrive on it," she conceded.

Jared laughed. "I've been told I was raised on it myself. If Akela has been stuffing poi into your baby, I imagine he's fattened up some. He did seem awfully tiny when I first saw him."

"You should have a good look at that *keiki*, Ialeka," Akela said slyly. "Maybe you see what I see."

Florence rose quickly to distract Jared's attention. "You certainly have unusual weather conditions on this side of your island, Mr. Burkett," she said as she crossed to the window overlooking the left side of the house. "I have never known such a violent storm as we had yesterday. But today the sun is shining and the winds are calm."

"That's not unusual weather for the islands, Mrs. Merrill. It's not so bad here on the end of the island, but this is the rainy season and we do tend to get a few violent sea storms. On the windward side it generally rains at least once a day, every day, for a few months. But that's further up the coast, where the mountain draws clouds to it."

"That doesn't sound too bad, compared to a gloomy winter in Boston," Florence commented before she went to the other kitchen window. It was now just an opening onto the patio. "I see the waves didn't reach the house, after all. I'm afraid I had visions of waking to find my bed floating in the sea."

Jared chuckled. "A highly unlikely possibility. The ground level is high here, and the house is elevated for further protection. The patio serves as an added blockage, to cut the force of any waves that might reach the house."

"You have such an unusual house, Mr. Burkett," Florence said as she turned back to face him.

"I suppose it is," he agreed. "My father built it as a summer retreat. It was only three rooms then, two bedrooms and the living area."

"No kitchen?"

"The cooking was done outside, in the Hawaiian tradition," he explained. "But my mother liked it so well here that she decided to stay. My father then set about enlarging the house. A kitchen was added, and the dining room. Later the bedrooms were lengthened."

"And the patio?"

"At first it was a garden area for my mother, enclosed with the three-foot lava rock wall. But she was more interested in cultivating the front yard, and so a roof and floor were put in there to make it a patio. Still later it was enclosed completely with windows and screens. With all the windows open, it still has the outdoor effect and is the coolest room in summer."

"You like it best here too, don't you?" Florence remarked.

"I suppose I do," Jared replied. "I grew up in this house, and helped build some of it, once I was old enough. But I haven't spent much time here in recent years. Taking over my father's business has kept me quite busy."

"Has your work slowed, then?" she asked. "I mean—well, you're here now." Jared frowned, and she quickly added, "Forgive me, Mr. Burkett. I didn't mean to pry."

Jared fell silent, thinking about his reason for coming back here so soon, and what it had led to. He had to admit to himself that ever since he had left Corinne here, he had done nothing but think about her. He had wanted so often to tell her how sorry he was, sorry about so many things. But he couldn't bring himself to say the words.

He hated what she had done, but still he wanted her. The sight of her reminded him of all the men who had had her, but he still wanted her. The storm and wanting to comfort Corinne had only been an excuse to bring him back here. He knew that. And look what it had led to. He wanted her more than he had ever wanted a woman. The mere touch of her made him forget what she had become.

He knew in his gut that he could never really forgive her for being with all those other men. But, after last night, he also knew that he didn't want to let her go. It was crazy and could never work, yet he hoped the truce they had reached last night would continue, if only for a little while. He sighed. A lot would depend on Corinne, though. And Corinne could be very difficult.

Jared did not notice how carefully he was being watched by the Hawaiian nurse and the nurse from Boston.

Chapter 32

CORINNE stared pensively at her reflection in the mirror hanging over the dresser. She was mesmerized by the swollen area of her cheek with the slight tinge of blue. If she did not bruise so easily, there would be no telltale reminder of what had happened last night. The swelling would last a few days, and the bruise would fade to brown, then yellow.

She wondered what Jared would say when he saw the mark. Surprisingly enough, she wasn't in the least angry about it. What had happened after Jared struck her was well worth anything that had gone before. She didn't hate him anymore, she knew that now.

But she wasn't quite sure what she did feel. There was a powerful physical attraction, but anything more than that was frightening to admit. It wouldn't do to fall in love with him. He hadn't believed her confession, and never would. And the disgust he felt for what he thought she was would destroy any relationship they might have had. No, it was hopeless. She would be better off gone from here as soon as possible.

The door opened, but Corinne was reluctant to look around. She held her breath, waiting for someone to speak, but when no one did, curiosity got the best of her. She turned to see Jared standing by the door, looking just as shy as she felt.

He came forward slowly, and stopped abruptly when he saw her cheek.

"Oh, no—did I do that?" Jared didn't give her a chance to answer, but was in front of her in an instant, gently lifting her face up to his. "I'm sorry. What is it about you that makes me lose control? I've never hit a woman before, I swear it. I'm . . . . sorry."

Corinne became unnerved. He was standing so close. Her pulse quickened, and her face flushed. She lowered her eyes, embarrassed.

"Does it hurt?"

"Not very much," Corinne answered, looking up at him again. "It looks much worse than it really is."

Jared moved away, discomfited by the soft words that were passing between them. "Akela suggested that you might like an outing. I'll be going up into the hills today to bring down a few stalks of bananas. I understand Mrs. Merrill's son has a passion for them."

"I hope you don't begrudge him the fruit growing on your grounds," Corinne said stiffly.

"Not at all," Jared replied, looking at her curiously. "You *do* like that baby, don't you? I understand you've been spending a good deal of your time with him."

"Is there anything wrong with that?" she demanded, a bit sharply.

"No, I suppose you needed some diversion to fill your time." He took a step closer, his brow furrowed. "But why do you get so sensitive every time I mention the boy?"

"I don't know what you mean," she said evasively, turning away from his penetrating eyes.

"Do you think it's wise to form such a close attachment to another woman's child?"

"Florence is not just another woman, Jared. She's been a mother to me, a sister, and she's my only true friend. She's been with me all my life and I love her. There would be something wrong with me if I didn't care for her child."

"That's good enough logic for most people, but I was under the impression that you were different. Didn't you want a life free of attachments? That's not possible when you love, Corinne. Then you need love returned."

"Perhaps I've changed," she whispered.

Jared wasn't quite sure he had heard her correctly. "Have you?"

"You don't know anything about me, Jared, you really don't. But then, I didn't know myself."

"And do you now?"

"I think so," she replied slowly, thoughtful. "I've found that I have a lot of love to give, but very few people that I care enough about to give it to."

"You seem to have spread it around recently," he said unthinkingly, and immediately regretted his words.

"You had to bring that up again, didn't you?" she said angrily, her hands on her hips. "Our marriage was a farce to begin with, but must I remind you that you deserted *me?*"

"I didn't come in here to fight with you," Jared said. "I'm sorry for that remark—it was uncalled for. I was hoping we could continue the truce we started last night."

"So was I, but—"

"No buts." He cut her off with a grin. "Will you come with me today?"

She hesitated, wanting to go, yet thinking that she hadn't nursed Michael. "How soon? I haven't even eaten yet."

"You'll have plenty of time. We'll leave in a couple of hours."

"I'll be ready then," she smiled.

Corinne was disappointed later to find that Jared had a long walk in mind. She brought along a parasol, for the sun persisted throughout the day, and Jared had warned her to wear comfortable shoes. She found out why after they left the road a good half mile up the coast and started over the rough terrain.

The path they followed was narrow, and still quite muddy from the storm. There were ditches to cross, and dried-out thicket and leafless trees to skirt. This area looked nothing like a tropical paradise. The only color was that of the wild kalamona shrubs, with clusters of bright yellow-orange flowers, and the green and brown of the *koa*, rubbish trees.

They walked along silently yet companionably, with Jared holding her hand to pull her along behind him, helping her over deep ditches. She was at ease with him, perhaps for the first time.

They passed between craggy hills, and the landscape suddenly changed drastically to green splendor. It was beautiful here, like an enclosed valley. An upward climb led through thick wildflowers and lush trees.

Finally the path leveled off and they came to a patch of banana trees, where Jared stopped. While he searched for likely stalks, Corinne looked back the way they had come.

She gasped at the view. It took in the entire length of the north shore.

"It's lovely, isn't it?"

Jared had come up behind her and now she felt his arms slip around her waist and pull her back against him. At that moment, Corinne was undeniably happy.

"Yes, it is lovely," she said with a sigh. "Thank you for bringing me."

"My pleasure."

When Jared didn't move away, but instead brought his lips down to the side of her neck, Corinne felt the stirring of desire. She wanted to scream at him for arousing her when there was nothing they could do about it up here. She tried to pull away, but his grip tightened about her.

"Jared," she began in frustration. "Jared, shouldn't we be going back now?"

"We'll have to go on a bit," he said into her ear. His manner was unhurried. "The bananas aren't ripe enough in this spot."

"How much further?"

"My cousin has a good patch of trees behind his place. I meant to stop by for a visit, anyway."

"Your cousin?" Corinne asked, surprised. "You have a cousin—up here?"

"Don't look so astonished," Jared said. "Lots of people like the seclusion of the mountains."

"But I'm not dressed to meet your relatives."

"You're dressed just fine. But I like the idea of your being *not* dressed."

The devilish glint in his eyes gave her warning even before he reached to unfasten the buttons at her neck. She moved out of his reach and started backing away from him, shaking her head slowly from side to side.

"Jared, no."

"And why not? You're my wife."

"You're crazy," she said, unable to keep from smiling.

He shrugged and reached for her, but she turned and started running down the path. Jared caught up with her before she got more than a few feet away. He tumbled them both to the ground. He began to raise her skirt and she laughed, even as she protested weakly.

"Not here, Jared."

"Yes, definitely here, and definitely now," he said, and kissed her soundly to silence her.

Corinne lost herself to the moment. She wanted Jared. He had the power to arouse her with just a soft word, an impassioned look, a touch. Why him and no other man? Other men had desired her, but the fact that Jared did thrilled her.

With the heady scent of wildflowers surrounding them, they made love with a savage urgency that suddenly overcame them both. Corinne was left feeling decidedly wicked, yet utterly pleased with Jared's impulsiveness. She wanted to stay there all day, making love again and again. How she wished they could. But now that Jared was satisfied, he would want to go on.

But Jared surprised her. He made no move to rise, but propped himself on his elbows, easing his weight from her. His eyes were bright blue as he gazed down at her, then touched her lips with a featherlight kiss.

"You are magnificent, *makamae*."

"Well, thank you, sir," she said impishly.

He smiled. "I think I'll take you for a walk on the beach tonight. Walking with you is quite enjoyable. The night will be perfect, with the stars and the moon out to touch your beauty."

Corinne sighed. "I think I'm going to like this truce, Jared."

He kissed her again lazily, then sighed. "We'd better go now, before I'm tempted to forget all about bananas and everything else."

Reluctantly, she let him pull her to her feet and help her straighten her clothing.

Twenty minutes later and further up the cliff, they came to another leveled-off area where a crude shack made of thin wood and metal scraps huddled beneath thick trees. Animal pens were all around, yet small pigs and chickens ran about freely, unpenned. Ferns and plants abounded, covering the hillside. There were mountain apple trees, a huge mango tree which shaded the shack, and the banana patch Jared had mentioned not far from the shack.

Corinne clung to Jared's arm. "Surely your cousin doesn't live here?" she whispered.

"Why not?" Jared looked down at her in amusement.

"He likes it up here. It's like living in a past century. He has never taken to the modern world and what the *haoles* have done to his island."

"*His* island? I don't understand."

At that moment a huge Hawaiian stooped through the doorway and sauntered over to them. He was immense, with a mat of black hair and a beard, and warm brown eyes. He wore only a pair of yellow flowered baggy shorts. Even his feet were bare, but he didn't seem to feel the sharp twigs he walked over.

"Ialeka!" He gave Jared a bear hug before he released him and turned a curious eye on Corinne. "*Wahine male?*"

"Yes," Jared answered with a note of pride. "This is my wife, Kolina."

"Aunty Akela tell me you marry, Ialeka. When you make *luau*, celebrate?"

"It's rather late for that," Jared said.

"*Auwe!* Any reason good reason for *luau*. But come. You no visit long time. Kikuko!" he yelled, and a small Oriental woman in a faded kimono appeared in the doorway.

She was a solemn creature, shy, and so tiny compared to the big Hawaiian. She scurried back into the house without even a greeting.

"She put more *laulaus* in calabash. You stay have *kau kau* with us, huh?"

Jared didn't have a chance to answer before the big man ambled back to the house, motioning for them to follow.

"We've been invited for dinner," Jared explained.

Corinne began to relax after the initial discomfort of meeting strangers. The little house was quite comfortable inside. The two cultures blended well, mixing Hawaiian tapa cloth, gourds, and artifacts with Japanese idols, statues, and silk screens.

Kuliano Naihe was a jovial man and easy to like. He entertained them throughout the afternoon with Hawaiian chants and songs, accompanying himself on the ukulele. His wife Kikuko was very quiet, staying in the background. Jared explained to Corinne that it had nothing to do with their presence. It was just her way.

They ate a delicious meal in the back yard, where a magnificent sunset of red, orange, and purple hues lit the sky below them. *Laulaus* were made of pork wrapped in taro tops, which looked like thick spinach but tasted much better. The *laulaus* were steamed in a large calabash, first wrapped in *ti* leaves to protect them. The meat was tender, with a unique taste from the taro tops. Of course, poi was served too, and fresh papaya and unusual little mountain apples. Like nothing Corinne had ever eaten before, they had a soft, thin skin and one large brown seed in the middle.

Once the sky darkened, Kuliano lit a fire in the back yard and began to sing again. Jared, in no hurry to go, leaned back against a colvillea tree. Its tremendous bunches of red-orange buds, like clusters of grapes, hung from the tips of branches down around them. Corinne sat near him, enjoying the music and the company.

"How long have you known Kuliano and his wife?" she asked casually.

"All my life," Jared answered. "You met Leonaka, my foreman, or so he told me."

"Yes."

"Kuliano is his father. Leonaka and I grew up together, more like brothers than cousins."

"Wait a minute, Jared. When you say cousin, you mean it only as a term of friendship, don't you?"

"No. The Naihes are my distant cousins by blood."

"But they're Hawaiian."

"You noticed," he said playfully.

Corinne found herself quite confused. "Would you mind explaining?"

"Leonaka and I have the same great-great-great-grandmother, Leimomi Naihe. So you see, I do have some Hawaiian blood, though little of it is left. Do you want to hear about it?"

"Yes."

"Leimomi was a beautiful young woman who lived on Kauai, the first island landed on by Captain Cook in 1778. You've heard of Cook, haven't you?"

"Yes."

"Well, he was considered a god when he first came, and the Hawaiians, a friendly and free-spirited people, couldn't do enough for him and his crew. Leimomi gave herself to one of the English sailors, a man she knew only as Peter.

He sailed away, not aware that she would soon bear his son. She had a male child she named Makualilo.

"Leimomi later married one of her own people, and bore him a son and two daughters. Her husband accepted Makaulilo and raised him as his own. But the boy grew up feeling that he was an outcast. Cook's visits ended in bloodshed, and there was much resentment of the white man for quite some time. Makualilo was too fair-skinned, a constant reminder of the disliked white men, who continued to visit the islands.

"In 1794, when he was only fifteen, he sailed for the mainland on a whaler. Five years later he returned with an infant son, born to him by an American prostitute who wanted nothing to do with the child and would have sold it if Makualilo had not claimed the boy."

"That's terrible!"

Jared glanced at her, then continued. "Makualilo brought the baby, Keaka, to his mother. She raised him on the island of Oahu.

"But he didn't stay in the islands. In 1818 he sailed to England, and then on to Ireland. There he married, and in 1820 Colleen Naihe was born. Keaka settled in Ireland. Colleen was raised there, and in 1839 she married a French trader, Pierre Gourdin. A year later my mother was born."

Jared's voice softened as he began to talk about his mother. "Ranelle spent her youth in France. In 1850 she sailed with her parents to San Francisco."

"Wasn't that when gold was first discovered there?" Corinne asked.

"Yes. But they had no luck there, and Pierre was a trader at heart. They took to the road and travelled across America for three years, finally settling in Boston, where they opened a small store."

"That's where Ranelle met my father?" Corinne ventured tentatively.

"Yes. She felt she couldn't stay in Boston after your father broke their engagement. Her parents were no longer living, and, since the Civil War was imminent, she felt she was better off leaving the States altogether. She knew she had relatives here, though distant ones, and she came here to find them. She found Akela and Kuliano, who also knew the story of Leimomi and her first son, Makualilo. Akela and Kuliano are descendents of Leimomi's other children.

"Ranelle taught school until she met my father and they married. And you know the rest."

"So you're mostly English and French, with just a little Irish and even less Hawaiian."

"Does the Hawaiian blood bother you?"

"Why should it? And I think it's nice that such a complicated story has been passed down from generation to generation." She paused, then asked, "Do you still hate my father, Jared?"

"The feelings I have for Samuel Barrows have been with me for a long time, Corinne."

"In other words, you do still hate him," she stated with a frown. "And me?"

"For quite a while you and your father were one and the same to me. That's why I felt no compunction about using you to get at him."

"And now?"

"I don't hate you, Corinne." He hesitated, and she could feel his tension. "But I hate what you did when you came here."

"But—"

She started to profess her innocence again, but stopped. It would only lead to an argument, and the day had been too nice to end it that way.

"Shouldn't we be getting back?"

Jared shook his head. "It's too dark now. We'll wait until morning."

"You mean spend the night here?" Michael had already missed his afternoon feeding. "But we'll be missed, Jared. Florence will be frantic with worry."

"They won't miss us for one night. Akela will know what happened. When I come up here, I usually spend the night."

"I want to go back now, Jared. It's not that late," she protested.

"Go ahead, then," Jared shrugged. "But when you miss your footing and tumble down the side of the mountain, don't expect me to come to your aid."

"That was uncalled for," she said tartly.

"Then be reasonable, and stop fussing. There's nothing back at the house that can't wait until morning." He

230

grinned then, and pulled her up against his chest. "Unless you're thinking about that walk on the beach I promised you."

"I was not!"

"No?" he crooked a brow, his teeth flashing in the firelight. "Just the same, you'll still have that walk, if not tonight, then tomorrow night. But right now, I know a nice little spot a little farther up the mountain where we can—"

"Jared, stop it," she said, giggling even as she pushed to get out of his warm embrace. "We've already frolicked today."

"As I recall, you took an active part in that frolic. And that was only the appetizer. I'm ready for the main course."

"You can be crude sometimes."

He laughed and began to fondle her breasts.

"Now stop it." She tried to sound angry but failed. "Besides, what would your cousin think if we just disappeared?"

"Kuliano will laugh and remember his younger days." He looked down at her devilishly. "He might even join us there."

"Jared, you are incorrigible!"

He rose, pulling her up with him. "Come on." One arm wrapped around her waist, he lifted her face with his free hand and brushed her lips lightly. "I can't seem to get enough of you."

Corinne put Michael from her mind, knowing that Florence would take good care of him. At the moment, only Jared mattered.

Chapter 33

THE sun was high overhead as Corinne walked along the beach, kicking at the hot sand with her sandaled feet. She smiled, thinking of that morning. She and Jared had walked into the house to find that no one had missed them. Michael was happy with his diet of solid food.

It had been such an enjoyable time away. Jared was not the charmer she had known in Boston, nor the enraged husband she had known recently. He was himself—relaxed, easygoing, a pleasure to be with. And what pleasure she had had last night, when he made love to her, slowly, sensually, prolonging the ultimate until neither of them could bear it anymore. He was a magnificent lover, this husband of hers.

"Hello, ma'am."

Corinne looked up to see a tall, barrel-chested man waving a white straw hat at her from about ten yards away. He started to approach her. She watched him warily, realizing she had walked a good distance away from Jared's property.

"The name's John Pierce," he said, stopping a few feet from her and flashing a smile. "You must be the new Mrs. Burkett."

"Yes, but how did you know that?"

"Heard tell that Jared found him a beautiful little woman in Boston, a real society girl. That must be you, cause I ain't seen anyone as pretty in a long time."

"Well—thank you, Mr. Pierce," Corinne said hesitantly, wondering what else he had heard about her. Probably everything. Would she ever live down the sordid reputation she had built for herself?

"Call me John, my dear. I'm your nearest neighbor of any consequence. Been meaning to pay Jared a visit, but just can't seem to find the time." He paused, wiping his brow with a checkered handkerchief. "I expect he's in the city?"

"No. He came home just the other day. He's over checking out his vegetable fields right now."

"You don't say," he returned thoughtfully. "It's not like the boy to get out this way in the winter season."

Corinne smiled. The "boy," indeed! John Pierce looked to be in his late forties, with brown hair and long brown side-whiskers that were graying. He seemed a nice enough man, and certainly friendly.

"Perhaps you would like to come back to the house with me?" Corinne offered. "Jared should be back for lunch by now."

He looked thoughtful, almost wary. "No—no, but perhaps another time."

"Well, I had better be getting back before Jared misses me."

"He keeps a close eye on you, does he? Well, who can blame him, with such a pretty wife."

"Good day to you."

Corinne turned and started back. She felt his eyes on her as she trudged through the warm sand. Her face flushed as she realized the double meaning in his last remark. Of course he knew about her. Everyone did.

"Hold up a minute, Mrs. Burkett."

Corinne started, for he had come up behind her silently. "Yes."

"You wouldn't happen to know anyone might like a little spaniel pup, would you? One of my dogs whelped four a couple weeks ago and they're ready to be given away. I got me five dogs running about the place already."

"I don't think so."

"You're the first one I asked. You could have the pick of the litter."

She hesitated, picturing Michael playing with a little long-eared spaniel. He was a bit young right now, but he could grow up with the dog.

"As a matter of fact, I do know someone who would adore a little puppy."

"Good! My house is just right over there, behind those

palms. The pups are in a shed out back. It would just take you a minute to come and pick one out."

Corinne nodded and followed behind him. Through the trees she was soon able to make out an old, peeling, ramshackle house. The yard leading down to the beach was hardly a yard at all, with very little grass, but an abundance of sand and dirt. It wasn't exactly a homey place, and Corinne wondered if there was a Mrs. Pierce.

"Right in here." He held open the door to a storage shed and waited for Corinne to step inside.

Sunlight filtered in through cracks in the ceiling and walls and dust motes swirled riotously, as if the shed had not been entered for months. There was the rank smell of mold and mildew and Corinne held her breath.

"Where are the puppies?" She turned around, but the door slammed shut in her face. She stared at it stupidly for a moment. "Mr. Pierce?"

No one answered. It took another few seconds for the confusion to wear off and uneasiness to set in. Corinne stepped over to the door, but there was no handle on the inside. She pushed gently, and when it didn't budge, she used more force. At last she threw her shoulder into it, but it still remained firmly shut.

Fear was beginning to take hold now. "Mr. Pierce! Where are you?"

There was no answer, and she started pounding on the door with her fists. "Let me out of here! Do you hear me?"

John Pierce must be crazy, she thought wildly. She turned back to look around the shack for something to use to get the door open. All she could see were old crates, two wheelbarrows, and a pile of wet dirt. She searched in and around the empty crates, but could find no tools. She did discover one thing though. There were no puppies in this shed. What the devil had she gotten herself into?

Malia turned back from following Corinne after she left the beach with John Pierce. Her lips curled smugly as she hurried home. She had been prepared to provoke another scene with Jared's wife, and now she had something to tell him. Corinne and John Pierce—ha! Jared would be livid. He would not be so quick to forgive his erring wife this time.

She found Jared in the back yard, rinsing off under the pump their father had made so that the sand would not be tracked into the house. It was hooked up to a huge rain barrel on the other side of the trees.

"Did you go swimming?" Malia called, wondering whether he had seen Corinne.

"Just a quick dip to wash off. The storm gave the fields a good soaking. It's quite muddy over there."

Malia waited until he released the water pump and grabbed a towel hanging over a branch on the lichee tree. He was wearing only a pair of shorts and she saw that he had lost a good deal of his bronze tan. Too long away from the beach, away from home, ever since their father died. Malia resented that. She missed the swims and rides they used to take together, and the attention her brother had given her.

"Did you want something, Malia?"

"I was wondering if you knew where your wife is," she said in a tone that made Jared go tense.

"Isn't she in the house?"

"No, she's with John Pierce."

"Oh?"

Jared's calm response infuriated her. "She met him on the beach and went with him to his house. Doesn't that bother you?"

"Why should it? I may not like John very much, considering his obnoxious determination to get our land, but he is our closest neighbor." Jared looked at his sister. "It's time Corinne met our neighbors."

Malia's eyes flashed angrily. "You talk as if she will live here permanently."

"Maybe she will. Who knows?"

"I don't understand you, Jared. How could you forgive her after she made a cuckold of you?"

His eyes narrowed. "Where the devil did you learn such a word?"

"I read a lot," she said defensively. "With no one my age out here, there is nothing else to do. Naneki was the only friend I had, but your wife drove her away!"

"Naneki chose to go back to Kahuku," Jared said, unperturbed. "It was her decision. And as for my forgiving

235

my wife, that is none of your business, Malia. I will thank you to not mention it again."

"You don't care, then, if she still consorts with other men?" she demanded. He was treating her like a child.

"John Pierce?" Jared laughed at the absurdity of it. "Don't be ridiculous, Malia."

She chafed. "I saw them together! I saw her flirt with him and entice him. If you think they're sipping tea right now, then you are a bigger fool than she made of you in Honolulu!"

Jared's eyes turned a stormy gray as he watched Malia run into the house. He looked down the beach, but there was no sign of Corinne. Damn Malia for planting suspicions in his mind.

Jared waited only an hour before he couldn't stand it anymore. He saddled a horse, preparing to ride up the beach road to Pierce's. He had worked up a fine head of steam during that hour, imagining the very worst, yet furious with himself for doing so. He was not prepared to find Johen Pierce trotting up to the stable just as he was mounting his horse. Jared eyed the older man suspiciously.

"What are you doing here, John?"

"I've come about your wife."

"Has something happened to Corinne?" Jared asked in alarm.

"No, no, nothing like that," John Pierce assured him, looking ill at ease.

"Where is she, then?" he demanded. "I understand she paid you a visit today."

"You know, it's not a very nice thing you've done to that poor girl."

"What the hell are you talking about?"

"It's well-known why you brought her here, Jared. The rumor is that you keep her under lock and key. I was surprised when I met her out walking earlier, but not so surprised when she asked my help."

"Your help?"

John hesitated a moment. "She wants me to take her to Honolulu."

"What?"

"Your wife seemed terribly upset," John said quickly. "She—she said she couldn't stand the restrictions you placed on her. For that matter, she said she could not bear living with you."

Jared's eyes narrowed. "What else did she say?" he asked, with deadly control.

John looked at Jared nervously. The idea of holding Mrs. Burkett had come to him on the beach. He had acted impulsively. Now it was too late to do anything but see it all through.

John cleared his throat. "Your wife promised me a good deal of money if I would take her to the city."

"And did you agree?"

"Not yet," John replied. "I told her I would have to think about it first."

"What is there to think about? The woman is my wife. She married me of her own free will." Jared took a step closer. "I'll tell you now that if you interfere, you will regret it."

John moved his horse back. He was sweating profusely, but not from the heat.

"Now see here, Jared." John tried to sound indignant. "There's no need for threats. I see your side of this."

"Then what are you doing here?"

"Well now, I also see your wife's side. I mean, the little lady seemed quite desperate, desperate enough to pay whatever I asked. It would be downright ungentlemanly of me to ignore such a plea."

"You mean it wouldn't be to your advantage," Jared said sarcastically. "Just what are you getting at?"

The time was at hand. "I thought you and I might make a deal. Although I would like to help the little lady, she *is* your wife."

"And you would like to help yourself as well, is that it?" Jared asked coldly.

"I didn't create this situation, it was dumped in my lap," John said defensively.

"What do you want, Pierce?" Jared demanded, his patience growing thin.

"Well, you know I've always wanted this little piece of land you have here, my boy. And I'm still willing to pay you double what it's worth if you will consider parting with it now."

"Let me get this straight," Jared said softly. "You will return my wife to me if I sell you my land?"

"That's right."

"And if I don't sell the land, then you'll take Corinne away where I can't find her?"

"Right again," John beamed.

It was such a good plan! Why hadn't he thought of it sooner? Of course, once the wife was returned, she would explain that he had locked her up, that she hadn't asked his help at all. But it would be her word against his, and he would own the land by then, so what did it matter?

"Where is my wife?"

"Come now, you don't think I would be fool enough to divulge that information, do you?" Then John added quickly, "She's not at my place, if that's what you're thinking. We're wasting time. What's your answer?"

"You amaze me, Pierce. Did you think I would agree to this blackmail?"

"Don't you want your wife back?" John asked, his confidence ebbing.

"Not particularly," Jared replied in a deceptively casual tone. "Not if she is so desperate to get away from me."

"But—but—" John stammered, unprepared for this turn.

Jared laughed, though the humor didn't reach his cold gray eyes. "You seem confused, Pierce. Didn't my wife tell you she was only here on a temporary basis?"

"No, she didn't," John said sourly.

"Well, she's welcome to leave, since that's what she wants to do. And if she will pay you to take her to Honolulu, that's fine too. You might as well get something for your trouble. And, that way, I won't have to take her."

"You really don't care, do you?" John asked incredulously, shaking his head.

"I'm sorry to disappoint you, but no, I don't give a damn anymore what she does. I wash my hands of her."

"But she's your wife! Tell you what, I'll give you a day or two to think it over."

"Suit yourself, but I won't change my mind. And by the way, my wife has a servant here. You're welcome to come get her before you leave for the city."

Jared turned to ride his horse back into the stable. Only when he heard John Pierce riding away did he let his true feelings surface. In the quiet of the stable he let out a bellow of rage that shook the rafters and frightened the horses into bucking against their stalls.

Chapter 34

LEONAKA sat across the kitchen table from Jared, clasping a cool glass of rum punch between his large brown hands. It was late afternoon, and he had only just arrived from the city. His welcome was not what he had expected. The only one to show him any warmth was Malia, who alone was cheerful in a household of gloom. Even Akela, Leonaka's great-aunt, had only said a few words to him before she went back to banging pots and pans.

"It didn't take you very long to get here," Jared commented.

Leonaka smiled now, encouraged that his friend had finally said something. "When I am offered a week's vacation with pay, I'm not going to sit around and think about whether to take it."

Leonaka expected a rejoinder, but none was forthcoming. Finally he could stand it no more.

"What in damnation is going on here?"

Jared couldn't meet Leonaka's imploring gaze. He got up and stalked from the room without another word. Leonaka turned to Akela for explanation.

"His wife gone," Akela said, showing her own anger and disappointment.

"What you mean, gone?" Leonaka asked, slipping into pidgin English, as he always did with Akela. "Where she wen' go?"

"That John Pierce come here this morning, say Kolina ask him take her to Honolulu, say she pay him plenty money. He hide Kolina so Ialeka no can find her."

"What?"

Akela grunted. "You ask me, I say that no-good *haole* lie!"

"Who? Pierce?"

She nodded. "Kolina happy since Ialeka come home this time. They no fight. I watch them. I say to myself, is good, they will have good marriage. They just stubborn, no yet ready admit they love each other."

Leonaka looked skeptical. "Maybe you just see what you hope to see, huh, Aunty?"

"You ask Ialeka!" she snapped. "You ask him if things not better between him and his wife these last days." Then she paused. "No, mo'better you no ask him now. Right now he mad like hell."

"And what if Pierce's story is true?"

Akela shook her head stubbornly. "Kolina not run away without her *keiki*."

Now Leonaka was truly surprised—and hurt as well. "Ialeka and me used to tell everything about each other. Now he keep everything to himself. He no tell me about his wife, he no tell me she give him *keiki*."

"He no tell you about the *keiki* because she tell him the *keiki* not hers, but belong to her *wahine* servant."

"So you only suspect—"

"I know!" she cut him off emphatically. "I tell Ialeka, but he no believe."

"This is too complicated." Leonaka sighed. He got up and walked to the door. "Is Ialeka just going let her go?"

Akela finally let a grin cross her lips. "He say he no care, but I know better. That's why he so mad."

Corinne sat on the wet earth with her back propped against a crate. She was exhausted and her hands were blistered and filled with splinters from trying to pry open the boards in the wall that had cracks wide enough to get her fingers through. She had failed. Though the shed was old, it was sturdily built and she didn't have any tools at all.

She had wracked her brain all afternoon trying to figure out why she was here. The only conclusion she had reached was that John Pierce was a madman. If that was true, then she had more to fear than just being locked up. Her life might be in danger.

All matter of horrors came to mind. Her imagination went wild over the different ways he might try to kill her.

Each murder she envisioned was more gruesome and terrifying than the last.

When the door to the shed finally opened, Corinne was a nervous wreck.

Rigid with fear, she stared up at the man. She was utterly unprepared when he said, "There's no point in keeping you locked up. You've no place to go anymore."

She had to struggle for the courage to ask, "What—what do you mean?"

"Your husband doesn't want you back, madam."

The anger in his voice frightened her more than his words did. "You spoke to Jared?"

"I went to make a deal with him. I told him I'd bring you back if he'd sell me his land. But his land means more to him than you do."

What he was saying sank in slowly, and finally Corinne realized that she wasn't facing a madman after all. She was facing a plain greedy crook who had held her for ransom.

But that ransom wasn't going to be paid. Her fear was gone instantly, replaced with hot anger. She got to her feet.

"I'll have you put in jail for this!"

"No, you won't," he said harshly. "No one's going to believe I kept you here by force. It's your word against mine. And your reputation is no good, Mrs. Burkett."

"Jared knows you kidnapped me!"

He laughed. "Don't be absurd. You came to me to help you get back to the city."

"That's a lie!"

"Yes, but it doesn't matter because your husband believed it."

Why would Jared be so quick to believe that?

"Now what?" she asked herself softly. And suddenly she knew the answer. Pierce had left the door open, and Corinne simply dashed through it and, picking up her skirts, ran as fast as she could run.

She knew exactly what she was going to do. She wasn't frightened anymore. She was so angry that she hardly felt her own fury any longer. The fighting between her and Jared had gone on long enough. In the last few days, everything had changed between them. Yet here was this repulsive fellow informing her that Jared *believed* she wished to leave him.

It was too much. She was sorry for the wrong she'd done her husband, but when was he going to remember the good about her instead of the bad? When, if not right now?

Corinne ran on, having forgotten all about John Pierce.

Chapter 35

LEONAKA found Jared sitting on the beach, bathed in the red glow of sunset. He sat staring pensively at the ocean, so wrapped up in his dark thoughts that he wasn't even aware of Leonaka until the big man spoke.

"I can remember finding you like this many times after your mother died," Leonaka said hesitantly. Jared didn't even look up. "You want to talk about it, Cousin?"

"No."

"We used to share all things," Leonaka sighed. "What has happened to us?"

Jared finally looked over at him. "Shouldn't you be letting your father know you're here?"

"Is that your way of telling me to mind my own business?" Leonaka asked.

"Look, Leo. There's nothing to talk about. I got myself into a deplorable marriage that isn't worth discussing, and I would just as soon forget it."

"If your marriage is so deplorable, why are you so upset?"

"Who said I'm upset!" Jared growled.

"You're not?" Leonaka raised a brow.

"All right," Jared said testily. "I am a little upset. But not because she's gone," he added quickly. "I would have let her go soon, anyway."

"Would you, Ialeka? Maybe she is in your blood already," Leonaka said quietly. "Maybe she is the woman you must have to be happy."

"That's ridiculous," Jared replied adamantly. "But even if it were true, she wants no part of me. She proved that well enough today."

"Perhaps you gave her cause? You have a violent temper," Leonaka pointed out. "I know this. Does your wife know it too?"

Jared's eyes grew mournful as he remembered how terrified Corinne had been the night he struck her. Was that why she had left at the first opportunity? Was she still frightened of him? But no, a woman terrified of her husband could not put on a performance of such willing compliance and keep it up for a couple of days.

"Corinne has seen my temper and she has one to match it."

"Ialeka," Leonaka began earnestly, "if you want her, go after her. She is your woman. I think you love her, and—I only met her once, but isn't that your wife?"

Jared turned quickly and stood up as Corinne approached them. Elation hit him first, but the old anger and bitterness soon took over.

"Did you forget something?" he asked sardonically. He was taken completely by surprise by the stinging slap she dealt him.

"By God, you had better have a good explanation for that," he growled menacingly.

Corinne was exhausted from running, but she found her voice. "Explanation? I hate you—that's explanation enough! But if you want more, there's the little fact that you abandoned me to that horrible man next door."

"You went to him for help."

"You fool!" She cut him short. "Didn't it occur to you to doubt the word of a man who had made you an unsavory proposition? I know what he told you and it was nothing but lies!"

"So you say," Jared replied and turned away from her in disgust.

Corinne grabbed his arm and managed to stop him. "Don't you dare walk away from me!" she shouted at him. "I've spent the afternoon locked in a damp, dirty storage shed, thinking all the time that Pierce was a madman and was going to kill me. I worked my hands raw trying to get out of there, but I couldn't."

"Is that the best story you could come up with, Corinne?" Jared asked with heavy sarcasm. "What really happened? Did Pierce refuse to help you after I turned down his offer?"

"Oh!" She grabbed her skirt and started to the house, but stopped again and swung around to face him. "I didn't ask John Pierce to take me away from you, Jared." She marvelled at the way she was able to bring her voice under control. "When I met him on the beach, he said he had puppies to give away. Thinking of Michael, I went with him to pick one out. Once I was in the shed where the puppies were supposed to be, he slammed the door shut on me. I didn't find out why until he let me out."

"And you expect me to believe that?"

She clenched her fists. "I don't care. But since I know Pierce lied to you, I want to know if he lied to me as well. He told me that your land meant more to you than I did, that you didn't want me back. Is that so?"

"Yes, that's what I told him." Bitterness kept him from explaining why he had said so.

A long silence fell while Corinne fought to swallow the painful lump in her throat. She had hoped it wasn't true. Pierce had lied to Jared, why couldn't he have lied to her too? But he hadn't. "I see," she said evenly. "In that case, you may arrange for someone to take me back to the city tomorrow."

Jared watched Corinne walk away, and heard the patio door open and close. He stood there silently, fighting his own emotions.

"What if she was telling the truth?"

"She wasn't," Jared replied gruffly.

"But what if she was?" Leonaka persisted, forcing Jared to listen. "It would mean that she had the chance to ask Pierce to take her away, but she didn't ask. It would mean she didn't really want to leave."

Jared turned abruptly and walked off down the beach. His friend watched him go.

It was late. Corinne sat in Florence's room on the narrow bed, while Florence worked her needle on the splinters in Corinne's hands. She had told Florence the whole story while she fed Michael. He was sleeping now. Florence had already agreed to give up her room for the night, saying that she would use Naneki's room, which was empty.

"Law, will you look at the size of these blisters," Florence clucked.

"Just drain them and get it over with," Corinne said tiredly.

She felt depleted of strength and sick with resignation. Akela had brought her a large meal, but she couldn't eat. Her stomach churned. She would be going back to the city, then back to Boston. Wasn't that what she wanted? The answer didn't come readily. It didn't come at all.

"I just don't understand Jared," Florence remarked angrily. "You mean to say he still didn't believe you, even after he saw the condition of your hands?"

"He didn't see them, Florence. But even if he did believe me, it wouldn't make any real difference. He admitted that he didn't want me back."

"That was probably just his pride talking," Florence reasoned.

The door opened without warning and they both turned. Jared stood in the doorway, his hand still on the doorknob. He didn't say anything, but just stared at Corinne with an inscrutable expression.

Florence broke the silence first, her tone indignant. "Now look, Mr. Burkett. It's not seemly, you coming into a lady's room without knocking. And you've got no business in this room a'tall."

"I'd like to speak to my wife privately, Mrs. Merrill. Would you please leave us for a few minutes?"

He had just come in from the beach, after spending hours trying to sort out his feelings. He was certain of only one thing. He wasn't ready to let Corinne go.

"You stay right where you are, Florence," Corinne said while she kept her eyes on her husband. "I have nothing more to say to you, Jared. And the only thing I want to hear from you is what time I should be ready to leave in the morning."

"You're not going anywhere—not yet, anyway," Jared replied in a quiet tone. "That's what I want to talk to you about."

Corinne was incredulous. "You mean you're not going to take me back?"

"No."

"Why?"

"Because I said so," he replied childishly.

"Why?" she demanded again.

"Never mind why, damnit!"

Michael started crying and Corinne rushed to him. "You see what you've done with your shouting?" She glared at him furiously.

"You shouted first," he reminded her. He took a few steps into the room. "Leave him to his mother, Corinne. We're not finished yet."

"Oh yes we are," she replied, turning her back on him and soothing Michael against her breast.

"You had best leave now, Mr. Burkett," Florence stated firmly, standing solidly between husband and wife. "Cori will be sleeping here tonight. That's her own choice, and I will thank you to respect her wishes."

"And I would advise *you* not to interfere," Jared told the older woman sharply.

Florence didn't back down. "After the deplorable way you have treated my Cori today, I'm not about to turn aside and let you abuse her further. What she told you was the truth."

"Mrs. Merrill, you would undoubtedly believe anything she told you," he replied coolly.

"You insult my intelligence, sir, and you seem to be lacking any of your own," Florence said stiffly. She heard Corinne's gasp at the impertinence, but she continued anyway. "You were nothing short of a fool to doubt Cori's word when the truth was right there in her hands. I removed nine splinters, Mr. Burkett, and there are also five blisters. You can see for yourself. Tell me how her hands could have come to that condition if not in the way she claimed?"

Jared was no longer looking at Florence, but at Corinne who stood facing him again, Michael in her arms. His eyes narrowed as he brushed passed Florence and strode over to Corinne.

"Let me see your hands."

"No."

He didn't ask again but grabbed one hand and turned it palm up. There were cuts and abrasions and two of the blisters Florence had mentioned. A grimace passed over Jared's features and deepened when Corinne yanked her hand away. He looked up at her slowly and met her fiery green eyes.

"Corinne, I'm—"

"Don't you dare say you're sorry! Don't you dare! It's too late for that." Michael started crying again. "Will you leave now, Jared? Just leave me alone!"

Jared turned quickly and left. This was not the time to make amends. Outside the room he stopped, his shoulders slumping. Would she ever forgive him for doubting her, for saying he didn't want her back when that wasn't the truth at all? How could he have let things get so messed up? Would they never believe each other about anything?

Chapter 36

CORINNE settled back in a wicker chair. Michael was on a large rug in the center of the patio where she could keep an eye on him. A tiny brown puppy was sniffing around him and making the baby squeal with delight.

The pup had been an unexpected surprise. He was just a mongrel, or poi pup, as the Hawaiians called dogs of mixed breed. But he was darling, with floppy ears and short tail that never stopped wagging. Jared had found him for Michael, or so Akela had said.

Corinne hadn't seen Jared. He had been gone all morning, returning with the present. It was his way of making amends, she supposed, his way of letting her know he was sorry for not believing her story. But it was too late for that. Her heart was hard once more, tightly sealed so he couldn't hurt her.

Voices from the kitchen drifted out the open window to the patio. Florence was there, helping Akela make taro biscuits. Florence's curiosity about the islands was never quenched. She was constantly grilling Akela with questions. Corinne listened with only half an ear to the history lesson in progress.

"There were maybe sixteen *Kahunas* in old days before missionaries come."

"But I thought you said the *Kahunas* were like priests and every community had one," Florence interrupted.

"Yes, they were *Kahunas* who spoke with gods. I talking now about other *Kahunas,* men who knew history, other men who read stars and tell future. Have *Kahunas* for healing and magic. All things important rested in hands of these wise men."

"And to think you were called savages," Florence

250

laughed. "It sounds rather civilized to me. It must have been very peaceful back then."

"Was good life, but not so peaceful. We have many wars, just like rest of world."

"There, you see! You really *were* civilized."

Corinne could imagine Akela grinning. "With each new king, lands were given to favorite chiefs of new ruler. This uproot the old chiefs and sometimes make civil war. Bad thing, civil war. Kalaniopuu, the old king who ruled when Cook came to islands, was king because of such a war—when the rightful heir, Keaweopala, was murdered."

Corinne shut out the voices when she saw Leonaka crossing the backyard, coming up from the beach. He dropped the long board he was carrying and came into the patio. He wore only shorts, and these were wet. He smiled when he saw Corinne.

"We meet again."

"Yes, it looks that way, doesn't it?" Corinne returned his smile. "How are you?"

"Enjoying my vacation while it lasts." His eyes were drawn to Michael on the floor and he came over to him and squatted down for a better look. "So this is the baby." Corinne watched as the giant young man scrutinized her son. Leonaka put out one long finger and Michael latched onto it and giggled as he tried to shake it.

"When are you going to tell your husband the truth about this little fellow?"

Corinne gasped and nearly jumped out of her chair. Leonaka saw her frown and stood up.

"I'm sorry. It's none of my business. I won't mention it again. I came up here to ask if you would like to learn how to surf."

He had dropped the subject of Michael as quickly as he'd brought it up, and Corinne let it go at that. She silently cursed Akela and wondered who else she had told.

"It's nice of you to ask, Mr. Naihe, but I must decline." There was a slight note of stiffness in her voice.

"We're going to be friends, so you call me Leo. And you can't come to Hawaii without getting your feet wet at least once."

"No, I couldn't."

251

He frowned. "I suppose you never learned to swim, living in a cold city?"

"As a matter of fact, I'm a good swimmer," Corinne answered, and a smile came to her lips. "I learned when I was a child and went with my father to the shipyard. When he was busy with the workers, I went out into the street and found other children to play with. At first they were shy because my father owned the shipyard, but after a while they taught me all their games. We used to swim under the docks—Florence never could understand why my hair was damp when I got home, because I never told anyone. They would have stopped me. One of the kids, Johnny Bixler—he must have been about eleven—took me under his wing. I learned quite a lot from him."

Corinne suddenly laughed. Why on earth had she told him that? She hadn't thought about little Johnny Bixler for a long time. She used to wonder what had become of that tough kid who had taught her to swim, swear, and use a knife during that one wild summer when the harbor became her fascination, and her playground.

Leonaka was grinning at her. "So you took up with a gang of street toughs, huh?"

"Heavens, I was only ten. And it was only for one summer. But you know, I never forgot the freedom I had that year. It was marvelous."

It was also what had made her determine to be independent all her life, Corinne reflected. But for some reason that didn't seem too important anymore.

"Since you know how to swim, you have no excuse for not learning how to surf. The waves are good today," Leonaka encouraged. "Jared and Malia are both surfing."

So that's where Jared was—out playing. Corinne felt her anger rising. So he had dropped off the puppy, thinking that would pacify her, and had then gone off to surf without giving her another thought.

"Well?"

Oh, how she wished she could show Jared that it didn't matter to her, either, that they were at odds again.

"I'm afraid I don't have anything I could wear into the water."

"Nonsense," Leonaka scoffed. "My aunty can get you a sarong from her sewing chest."

Corinne reddened at the thought. She shook her head. "No."

Leonaka shrugged. "That's too bad. Jared said I wouldn't be able to get you into the water, but I thought you had more daring."

Corinne stood up instantly, never one to ignore a challenge. "Please give me a few minutes to change. I would be delighted if you would teach me how to surf."

Leonaka grinned as Corinne left the patio, calling Florence to come watch the baby. Jared hadn't said anything to him about Corinne not wanting to swim. In fact, he hadn't said more than two words all morning.

It was too bad about the trouble John Pierce had caused. But what better way to make a truce than for Jared to see his beautiful wife in a wet sarong? Let desire bring him to his senses and realize what Leonaka already knew—Jared wouldn't be complete without this woman.

Corinne blushed as she peered at herself in the mirror over the dresser. With the sarong, she might as well not be wearing anything at all. Her arms, shoulders and half her legs were bare. And the rest of her shapely curves were outlined in vivid detail.

"I just can't wear this, Akela."

"Why?"

"It—it shows too much."

Akela shook her head with humor. "You see Malia wear same thing. All *wāhine* wear that to swim," she chuckled. "Even me. This not Boston, Kolina. You stay Hawaii, where we have fun."

Corinne grinned.

"Good thing you no wear breast wrapper no more," Akela was saying as she took Corinne's clothes to hang up. "Or the sarong no stay up so good."

Corinne swung around with rounded eyes. "I don't wear any such thing!" she snapped, wondering at the same time how on earth Akela knew.

It was true. She didn't have to wear the binder anymore. She still had ample milk for Michael, but it was under control now and her breasts didn't leak.

"Why you no tell Ialeka the truth, Kolina?" Akela asked reproachfully. "I see where your friend put the breast wrapper after she wash clothes. She put them in your room,

253

not hers. I could show Ialeka, but I keep quiet. You have to tell him."

Corinne bit her lip. Deciding to trust the other woman, she said, "Don't you see? Jared is better off not knowing. I'm going back to Boston eventually, with Michael. Jared will never see either of us again."

"You wrong, Kolina. Ialeka not let you go. And one day he will know you lie about Mikáele and he be plenty mad. Mo'better you tell him now."

"I swear there's just no point in talking to you!" Corinne said in exasperation.

She picked up a towel and left her bedroom. The woman was impossible. Would she never give up?

Leonaka was waiting for her in the back yard. Corinne put Akela from her mind and decided to enjoy herself. Riding the waves would certainly be something to tell her friends about back home.

Jared and Malia were both still in the water. Corinne kept her eyes averted from her husband as she listened to Leonaka explain what she had to do.

"Perhaps you should watch for a while first," Leonaka suggested, wondering now if he hadn't been a bit hasty in pushing Corinne into it. The sport wasn't without risk.

She shook her head adamantly, her long golden hair floating about her waist. "Let's go."

It took Corinne about an hour to get the knack. She was afraid at first that she might have forgotten how to swim after so many years, but that came back. And riding the waves on a sleek long board seemed easy too, with Leonaka behind her calling out support and instructions. Jared had left the water and was sitting on the beach watching her progress. That made her determined to master the sport. She would show him what she could do.

"I'm ready to try it alone."

They were far from shore, each treading water and holding onto the board.

"Are you sure, Kolina?" When she nodded, he added, "Ride the first few waves lying prone until you get used to the board."

"I will, teacher," she grinned and climbed on top of the flat board.

Malia was only a few feet away, sitting confidently on

her board. She caught a big wave and rode it expertly to shore.

Corinne gritted her teeth, scowling. Damnation! Malia was showing off!

"Don't mind Malia," Leonaka was saying. "You will surf as good as her soon."

I will do it now, Corinne vowed to herself. She waved to Leonaka as her board started moving toward shore. She helped it along, paddling with her arms on each side of it, gaining speed. Finally she felt it was time, and inched herself very slowly to a crouched position. Slowly, she straightened her legs with one foot forward as Leonaka had shown her.

She made it! Her spirits soared. She was riding the waves, just as the ancient Hawaiians had done, as well as Jared and Malia. But Corinne's triumph was short-lived. Her balance deserted her and she tumbled sideways, plunging into the surf. Then just as she broke the surface, sputtering and coughing, another huge wave rolled in from the sea, crashing down upon her. The current pushed her toward the shore, scraping her along the ocean bottom in the process.

Corinne fought to reach the surface again, but she was tangled in her own hair and in seaweed. Stronger currents kept pushing her down, until her lungs were on fire. Just when she couldn't stand it anymore, strong hands yanked her to the surface and she was crushed against a hard chest and lifted out of the water. She coughed spasmodically, gulping air. Her eyes burned from the salty water and she kept them closed as tears mixed with salt. Her whole left side was on fire.

"You crazy fool! What the hell were you trying to do?" Jared! So he had saved her.

Jared didn't put her down on the beach, but carried her all the way to the house. Corinne managed to wipe her eyes with one hand so she could see, and as soon as Jared entered the patio she protested.

"Put me down, Jared, this second! There is nothing wrong with my legs."

He didn't answer.

She started to squirm, but Akela and Florence rushed out of the kitchen to demand what had happened. Jared explained as he passed them, and Corinne's pride was doubly crushed. What a fool she had made of herself!

Jared laid her down on his bed, then stood back and looked at her. "Are you all right?"

"Of course I'm all right!" she cried. "You didn't have to carry me all the way up here."

Akela came into the room then with a jar of ointment and Jared took it from her. "I'll do it."

"What's that for?" Corinne demanded and started to sit up, but moaned and eased herself back down slowly.

When Jared lifted her left arm she grimaced, seeing the red welts all over it. Her left leg, too, was bright red. And her cheek was burning.

"You took a pretty bad scraping, but this mixture will take the sting away and the red should be gone in a few days. If you didn't have that sunburn, it wouldn't be so bad. You're too fair to stay in the sun that long, especially in the water, where the reflection is intensified."

He was right, of course. The rest of her body was just as red, though without abrasion on the right side.

"I can do that," Corinne said as he sat down on the bed and started to rub the ointment on her arm.

But Jared held the jar out of her reach. "Would you just be still and let me take care of you?"

Corinne leaned back and closed her eyes, grudgingly letting him have his way. His fingers were gentle as they massaged the ointment into her arms and legs. She suddenly felt very sensual. His every touch was a caress that took away not only the pain, but her anger as well.

He turned her over. She sighed. But when she felt her sarong being loosened, she tensed.

"What are you doing?" Corinne demanded, the mood broken now.

"You'll catch cold if you stay in that thing much longer," Jared explained, and there was humor in his tone when he added, "Not that you don't look adorable in it."

She looked around and caught him grinning. "I can undress myself, thank you."

Jared shrugged and stood up. "I was only trying to help, Corinne."

"I can well imagine what you were trying to do," she answered tartly.

"Would that be so terrible?"

She caught her breath. Did he really think yesterday didn't matter?

"Making love is not going to make everything all right. Last time was different, Jared. I thought you cared then, but now I know you don't."

"If I didn't want you, I would have let you go home a long time ago. Don't you see that?"

"Wanting and loving are not the same."

"What do you want from me?" he shouted. "I only said what I did to Pierce because he told me that you couldn't stand living with me any more. I didn't mean it, Corinne."

Corinne stared at him with wide eyes. What had Florence said? "It was only his hurt pride talking." Was that so? *Don't believe him*, a tiny voice whispered. *He'll only hurt you again.*

"Why should I believe anything you say, Jared?" Corinne asked softly. "You didn't believe me when I told you I hadn't really slept with other men. Don't ask me to believe you when you won't believe anything I say."

"Corinne, I'm sorry. What more can I say?"

She got up, crossed to the bathroom, and closed the door on him. With the click of the lock tears sprang to her eyes. It would have been so easy to forgive him, to make love and call a truce again. But she never again wanted him to hurt her. She had been hurt too much."

"So why does it *still* hurt?" she whispered brokenly.

Chapter 37

IT was an absolutely beautiful morning. The sea, deep blue and shimmering, formed a perfect background for the flowers in every imaginable color. The sun was warm and welcome, not hot as it would be later. Even so, Corinne wore a wide straw hat over her golden curls as she strolled through the fragrant garden. She was wary of the sun now, after getting burned so easily. Her skin had turned brown and then peeled a few days ago. But it was smooth again now, and she had a light golden tan.

Corinne stopped by a gardenia bush and picked a fat, velvety white bloom to place in her hair. She smiled, thinking of the bouquets of gardenias that Jared had brought to her room each day.

Corinne was finding it very difficult to stay angry with Jared. He was so generous and considerate. He didn't push her or even make any overtures, but he was obviously trying to make amends.

"Kolina!"

Corinne looked toward the road and saw Leonaka standing between two of the coconut palms, waving at her. Then he shook one of the trunks until a coconut fell. She laughed as he jumped out of the way, then scooped up the fallen coconut and brought it to her.

"For the *keiki*," he grinned.

"And how is he supposed to eat that with only two teeth?" She laughed, her green eyes sparkling.

"Just tell Aunty to make a coconut pudding. I guarantee he will love it."

"Thank you," Corinne said, and took the heavy fruit to cradle in her arms. "Are you looking for Jared?"

"No, I spoke with him last night. I came to get my horse and say good-bye to you."

"Your vacation certainly went by quickly. We'll miss you."

"You'll have to tell Jared to finish your surfing lessons," Leonaka suggested.

"Well, I don't know . . ." she began.

"He will be glad to," the big Hawaiian assured her. "He was put out about my having you out on my board. He thought you should have been on his."

"Did he say that?"

"He didn't have to." Leonaka and Corinne started toward the stable. "I know Jared. I know his moods and I know what he feels even before he, as stubborn as he is, realizes it." Softer, he added, "I know that he loves you, Kolina."

Elation hit Corinne, but she forced it away from her. This was only Leonaka stating his opinion. She knew better.

"It's nice of you to say so," Corinne said quietly.

Leonaka smiled knowingly and bent to kiss her on the cheek. "You will hear him say it one day, and then you will have no doubts. *Aloha*, Kolina. Be happy."

He disappeared into the stable. She stood for a moment, looking after him, then turned slowly toward the house. Jared met her at the door.

"So there you are!"

"Were you looking for me?"

"Yes. Here, give me that." He took the coconut from her. "I thought you might like to go on a picnic. You've been past Waimea Bay, but you haven't seen the valley. Some of the most beautiful plants on the island are there."

"How far is it?"

"Far enough that we'll have to ride."

She smiled. "I would love to go, and I'm sure Florence will, too. How soon would you like to leave?"

"Hold on. I meant just the two of us."

"Why?"

"I wanted to be alone with you for a while," he said softly.

Corinne slowly shook her head, her eyes locked with his. It was too soon. She simply didn't want to be alone with him yet. "I don't think so, Jared."

"You mean you won't go unless you're chaperoned?"

259

She nodded and he sighed. "Then by all means, invite the whole household. We'll leave as soon as everyone is ready."

Waimea Valley was breathtakingly lovely and like nothing Corinne had ever seen. The entrance to the valley was bordered by high rocky cliffs, with huge banyan and other lush trees fronting the cliffs. A little way into the valley was a creek. Corinne and Jared, on horseback, rode beside the creek, while Akela, Florence, and Michael rode in the open carriage. Malia had rudely refused to come, but that didn't dampen Corinne's spirits. She was determined to enjoy the outing.

Jared had been right about the beauty of the plants. There was quite a variety of trees, short and tall, sandalwood, kukui nut, and the giant monkey pod, not to mention mango, guava, papaya, and breadfruit. But the flowers outshone everything. Every color was there. From the bright orange-yellow of the kalamona shrubs to the exotic purple ginger plant, the valley looked like a painting.

They rode only as far as the carriage could go, and then Akela unloaded a large basket she had filled with food. Jared started a fire to roast a chicken and yams. Then he settled back under a banyan tree to watch the women cook. Akela had included her delicious taro biscuits and a banana pie she had made for lunch. Corinne poured lemonade from a big jug for everyone, then announced that she would take the job of keeping Michael out of mischief. He wasn't crawling yet, but the little devil certainly managed to get around and into things. Everything that found its way into his little hands went straight into his mouth. Corinne almost screamed when she saw he had found a dead cricket.

Jared couldn't help laughing as he watched Corinne try to get the insect out of Michael's fist without actually touching it herself. She finally succeeded, then put the boy on her lap and cuddled him.

Jared sobered, seeing how natural she looked with the child. The baby didn't mean anything to him, so he had never really paid much attention to him. But Michael certainly meant a lot to Corrine. She fussed over him more than Michael's own mother did. And it was absurd that the baby was sleeping in the same room with Corinne. He had wondered why Florence didn't move the child in with her. Granted, Naneki's room was small, but still . . .

Akela motioned Corinne over to the fire and she took Michael with her, unwilling to put him down again after the incident with the insect.

Jared sat up impulsively and called, "Bring him over here, Corinne."

She turned around very slowly and stared. She didn't move, but held the boy against her breast.

Jared's brow furrowed. "For God's sake, I won't hurt him."

Very slowly, Corinne walked to him and then reluctantly handed Michael over. She stood before Jared for several seconds before finally walking away. Every few steps, she peeked over her shoulder at him.

Michael squirmed in his lap and Jared laughed. "You must be mighty special, little fella, to have my wife wrapped around your little finger. What's your secret?"

Michael seemed surprised by the deep voice and looked up at the man who was talking. Jared sucked in his breath as he looked at Michael's eyes. They were bright lime green, exactly the color of Corinne's eyes. Why hadn't he noticed the eyes before?

The more he looked at Michael, the more thoughts crowded in on him. He could see now why Akela was so sure the baby was Corinne's. It was the eyes. Obviously, Florence's husband had had green eyes. It was an unusual shade, but hardly rare.

Jared was satisfied with that conclusion. To reassure himself, he considered the child's age. He would be six months now, even though he looked small. Five months?

Jared quickly calculated and his eyes darkened to a smoky gray. If the child were really only five months old, he could have been conceived on the night they'd been in the gambling house. But if that were so, it would mean Corinne had left for Hawaii almost immediately after the child was born. The baby would have been too young to travel.

Angrily, Jared shook the suspicions from his mind. He chided himself. Corinne would not lie to him about his own child.

Michael was climbing up Jared's wide chest. Face to face, he warily reached out and touched Jared's cheek, then

261

giggled. The sound was infectious and soon the baby settled down and confidently laid his head on Jared's shoulder.

Jared was touched more than he cared to admit. God, what he wouldn't give to have such a son! Those eyes haunted him. And the black hair, just like his own. He quickly resolved to write to the one person who could lay his doubts to rest. He hated to ask the man for anything, but Samuel Barrows would know if his daughter had had a baby. It would take at least two months to receive an answer, but that would give him an excuse to keep Corinne a little longer. For now, he would forget about it. It would do him no good to brood about it.

"Come on, I've got something I want to show you."

Jared's voice brought Corinne's eyes open. She had been lying in the shade, listening to all the different bird songs around her. She sat up now and stared up at Jared. "What?"

A smile curled his lips. "If I told you, then it wouldn't be a surprise. Come on, I gave Michael to his mother and told the others we would be back later."

"I don't really care for surprises, Jared," Corinne said hesitantly.

"You'll like this one. Come on." He offered his hand and pulled her up.

"Where is it?"

"A little way up the valley. There's a trail, so we can take the horses."

"We won't be gone long, will we?"

"No."

They set off, following the creek. It widened in places, and divided in others, joining again on its path to the bay. The cliffs weren't as high here, and the landscape was much denser, like a jungle.

The farther they went, the more the valley narrowed and the louder the noises around them became. There were many more birds in this thicker part of the forest, and even the running creek sounded louder.

Suddenly Corinne saw why. The valley ended abruptly before them with a tall concave rock wall that formed an almost perfect curve. And right in the center was a breathtaking waterfall, at least forty feet high, that cascaded into a large green pool of sparkling water.

Jared had been watching her delighted reaction, and she finally looked at him and smiled. "It's absolutely beautiful."

"I wish you could see it in the spring, when the royal poinciana and orchid trees are in bloom. The ferns are even greener then, too."

He helped her down from her mount and they walked over to a flat blanket of fine grass. Jared stood behind her, breathing in the fragrance of her hair.

"It's like an Eden here," Corinne remarked.

"Yes, and just as private. Would you go for a swim with me?"

Corinne shied away. "I couldn't."

"It's just the two of us, Kolina. Are you afraid I'll take advantage of you?"

She *was* afraid of that, but she wouldn't admit it. "I didn't bring anything for swimming."

Jared grinned. "You didn't come prepared, but I did." He walked over to his horse and opened a satchel tied to the saddle, pulling out the sarong Akela had given her for surfing. "Will this appease your modesty?"

"You had this all planned, didn't you?" Corinne said with amusement.

He tossed the sarong at her. "I knew you'd enjoy a swim. And I promise not to peek while you change."

Corinne stood behind her horse to disrobe. It was just hot enough to make the round pool look inviting.

With her sarong tied in place, her clothes thrown over the back of her horse, Corinne jumped into the water, not waiting for Jared. He had gone off to cut some vines and was surprised to hear her splash. She surfaced quickly and glared at him. "Did you know this water was like ice?"

He chuckled. "It usually is."

"Why didn't you warn me?"

He was taking off his shirt. "You might have changed your mind. But it's not so bad once you've dunked yourself completely."

"I suppose so," she conceded grudgingly. After swimming a bit and warming up, she moved closer to the edge of the pond. Jared was just stepping out of his pants, revealing shorts beneath. She grinned mischievously. His attention was on what he was doing, so the splash she sent his way caught him by surprise.

"Hey!"

Corinne squealed with laughter and immediately set off with quick strokes for the opposite side of the pool. She heard him enter the water and turned around to see him coming straight for her. He was a much better swimmer, with years of practice in the ocean, and before long he grabbed her foot.

"So you want to play, eh?"

He had both her feet now, and turned her over on her back, making it difficult for her to stay afloat.

"Jared, let me go." She couldn't help but giggle. "I just couldn't resist doing that."

"Well, I can't resist doing this."

And he raised her feet until her head submerged. Then he let go of her, and when she broke to the surface, she saw that he was swimming rapidly away from her.

"Coward!" she called after him. They were acting like children and she enjoyed it thoroughly.

Jared swam toward the falls. He climbed up on the rocky ledge beside it and sat down. He motioned for her to join him, but she shook her head, floating in the center of the pool, watching him.

"Can you dive?" he shouted, but she shook her head again. "Want to give it a try?"

"No, thank you," she shouted back.

Jared stood up and faced the solid rock wall. The cliff slanted upward. Corinne watched in amazement as he started to climb up beside the roaring falls.

After he had gone about ten feet Corinne became alarmed. "Just what do you think you're doing?" she shouted. He didn't answer. "Jared?" Still he said nothing and continued on his way. "You fool, you're going to get hurt!"

He turned then and boyishly threw her a kiss, then continued his climb. Finally reaching the top, he stood arrogantly right in the center of the falls. And then he spread his arms and propelled himself away from the tumbling water, diving gracefully, beautifully, into the pool. But he didn't surface, and Corinne became frantic as the seconds passed. She didn't know how deep the pool was. He might have hit his head on something.

When his hands grabbed her waist and pulled her under

the water she wanted to scream. They surfaced together and she quickly wiped the water from her eyes and glared at him.

"That was stupid! Absolutely childish!" Corinne snapped, her heart still racing. "You could have been killed!"

Jared grinned, still holding on to her waist. "You were really frightened for me, weren't you?"

"Of course—" Then she caught herself. She refused to admit it. "—not."

"That wasn't the answer I wanted to hear."

He dunked her again and she came up sputtering and grasped his neck.

"So it takes torture to get you in my arms, eh?" Jared chuckled.

She wriggled until she was at arm's length, then brought her feet up, planted them against his stomach, and pushed away from him. She knew she hadn't hurt him. He was too firmly built. But she did reach the edge of the pool before he could catch up to her.

She climbed out, ready to quit while she was ahead. Jared let her go, swimming by himself while she lay in the grass and let the sun dry her off.

The day had turned out to be quite enjoyable, more than Corinne would have guessed. Were it not for those few agonizing moments at the picnic, it would have been perfect. God, how terrified she had been when Jared had asked for Michael! It was the first time he had showed an interest in the boy. What if he had seen what Akela saw? But apparently he hadn't noticed the resemblance.

And Michael had actually been reluctant to leave Jared. It almost broke her heart to see how naturally they took to each oher. Oh, *why* couldn't it have been different? She could have had a blissful life with Jared. She really loved being with him when he was the way he had been today. And she loved his lovemaking. She could not deny that to herself anymore.

But it really was hopeless, she knew that. There was just too much between them, too many things that neither could forgive in the other.

She lay there musing wistfully, and didn't hear Jared move quietly out of the water and come to sit beside her. He took her hand, slowly and tenderly.

"We've had a truce today, you and I. Haven't we, Kolina?"

"What good is another truce?" she sighed, near tears. "You know we can't stay together. You've said you'll never forgive me, Jared, and I'm tired of trying to convince you of my innocence."

"Don't bring that up again, Corinne."

"You see? You're too pig-headed to even listen to my side. I want you to let me go, Jared. There's no reason for us to remain together anymore."

"No."

His face was set.

"When, then? When you get tired of playing with me? I'm not a toy!"

"You're my wife, damnit!"

"Your *wife* is a whore—remember?"

She watched his eyes turn slate-gray and instantly regretted her taunt. He reached out and grabbed her shoulders.

"Yes, I remember. It eats away at me every single day of my life." He stared hard into her face for a second, then abruptly released her and stood up.

"There was a time—" He would not let himself dwell on their wedding night. "—when we were able to enjoy each other even though there was anger between us. Why can't we enjoy each other any more? Why do we always have to reopen old wounds?"

"Everything's different now," she said brokenly.

"Since when?"

"Since—"

Oh, God! Since I fell in love with you!

She turned her face away from him and finally allowed the tears to fall. She sobbed openly. She loved him. But she couldn't tell him. Never, never would he know he had that much power over her.

"You didn't answer me, Corinne." He knelt beside her again. "Why does it matter now?"

She stumbled to her feet and ran for her horse.

"Will you answer me?" Jared had come up behind her, but she wouldn't look at him.

"Stop being so damn childish." Anger was unmistakable in his voice.

She turned and met his eyes. "Will you allow me the privacy I need to get dressed?" Understanding that she wouldn't answer, Jared turned and left. Corinne quickly dressed and mounted her horse. She started back down the valley without waiting for him. She no longer noticed the beauty all around her. Tears blinded her.

Jared was cruel without realizing it, arrogant, and much too proud. But didn't those used to be her own traits? Was she paying for her own sins? Sins she saw in the man she loved?

She was still shocked by the sudden realization. She loved Jared, but that love could only make her miserable.

Chapter 38

THE next morning, after feeding Michael, Corinne dressed with particular care, choosing a frilly morning gown of soft yellow, which made her eyes seem almost golden. She tied her hair loosely with a matching ribbon. Yellow was one of her best colors.

Satisfied with her appearance, she went to the bassinet and kissed Michael, then went to the kitchen. Akela was there alone, shredding the coconut Leonaka had shaken down yesterday morning. She looked up and smiled.

Corinne came over to the table and asked casually, "Have you seen Jared?"

Akela looked back down at what she was doing. "He gone, Kolina."

"Oh? Did he say what time he would be back?"

"He no be back today. Not tomorrow either, I think. Don't know when."

Corinne felt her heart sinking. "Don't you know? Where did he go?"

"Back Honolulu."

Corinne's shoulders fell and she asked hesitantly, "Did he say anything before he left, Akela? Did he leave me a message?"

Akela shook her head. "I sorry, Kolina."

"Not as sorry as I am," Corinne whispered. Shocked, she left the room. She moved through the day like a sleep-walker.

Jared entered his offices on King Street and went directly to the safe next to his file cabinets. He withdrew two long, slim boxes and one square box from his coat pocket. He put them in the safe and locked it. He had returned

268

to the city too late yesterday to make the purchases, but he had gone to his jewelers the first thing this morning.

In a long box were gleaming white pearls for his sister. Presents always cheered Malia, and her mood needed a drastic change. He was sure the pearls would improve Malia's disposition.

In the same way, he hoped to please Corinne. For her he had been more extravagant in purchasing hundreds of the finest opals in long double strands.

Jared had also bought her a solid gold heart on which he had asked the jeweler to inscribe, *I would marry you again, and without regret.* He knew what that meant. Would she understand the depth of his feelings? He prayed that she would, and that they could begin all over again. Was it possible?

There was an abrupt rap on the door and Jared looked up to see Russell Drayton enter the room. Jared realized that he shouldn't be as surprised as he was. Why had he assumed Drayton would be long gone by now?

"So, you finally decided to show up again," Russell began.

Jared was too amazed at the man's rudeness to speak for a moment, but at last he demanded, "What are you doing here, Mr. Drayton?"

Russell was standing directly in front of his desk, glaring at him. "Corinne's been missing for a month and I finally figured out that you have her hidden somewhere—I want to know where," Russell said, placing his fists on the desk and leaning forward. "And it's no use denying it. I want to know where she is."

Jared smiled, but it wasn't a warm smile. "And you really expect me to tell you?"

"By God, you'd better, Burkett!" Russell shouted. "You've ruined too many of my plans. I'm going to make sure you don't interfere again."

Jared was actually becoming amused. "Maybe you have forgotten that Corinne is my wife."

Russell sneered. "She can't stand you, Burkett. She'll thank me for making her a widow."

Too late, Jared saw the gun Russell pulled from his coat pocket. He expected to hear an explosion, but there wasn't one. He realized that Russell was planning on savoring his triumph.

"So you're not the spineless coward Samuel Barrows thought you were, eh?"

"Hardly." Russell was glad for a chance to clear himself. "That was the only kind of man Corinne would show an interest in, so I played the role. She will meet the real me once we're married."

"If she'll marry you."

"Oh, she will. She may not love me, but I'll convince her that she needs me. It's really too bad my aim was off when I shot at you at the church. It would have saved so much time if you had died then, and I would have had Corinne's money a long time ago. Speaking of money, I'll take whatever you have here. The landlord came around a few days ago."

Jared let his words sink in. The man was broke. He was also the scoundrel who had tried to kill him the day of his wedding. Jared cursed himself for passing that incident off as an accident, meant for someone else.

But right now he had to stall Russell and manage somehow to get the bottom drawer of his desk open. He kept his own gun there and would feel a lot better with his hands on it.

"I'll have to disappoint you again. I'm afraid I don't have but a few dollars on me."

"Don't try that with me." Russell scowled. "There's always money in a safe, and you have a large one right behind you. Open it."

"There's nothing there but business papers," Jared said calmly. He couldn't afford to leave his desk. "Contracts, account books, that sort of thing. No money."

"Show me, damnit!" Russell growled impatiently.

Jared got up and slowly opened the safe. Russell had followed him around the desk and now motioned him to open the safe door wide so he could see inside without getting too close to Jared. There were the boxes Jared had put in earlier, two stacks of business documents, and, on the bottom shelf, two stacks of petty cash amounting to less than a hundred dollars.

"I thought so," Russell snarled. "Hand it over."

Jared took the money out, but he held onto it, still kneeling, while he closed the safe.

"Being careful even though you're about to die?" Russell chuckled as he waited for Jared to straighten up. "Maybe you don't think I mean business? But you'll see. Now I want to know where Corinne is."

"And why should I tell you, when you plan to murder me anyway?"

Russell grinned. "You're right, of course. No matter. She'll be back in the city as soon as she learns of your death. Now hand over the money."

Jared extended his arm, and when Russell reached for the money, he dove straight for Russell's feet, lifting them out from under him. The thinner man was stunned by the fall and that gave Jared time to yank the gun from his hand.

Jared stared at the weapon for several moments, itching to point it at Russell and fire. The urge was almost overpowering, but he fought it.

Russell watched Jared as he debated whether or not to use the gun. His eyes bulged with terror, his gut turned sour. But finally Jared tossed the gun aside, grabbed Russell by his coat, and pulled him up. He drove a ramrod fist against Russell's nose, knocking him down again. Russell scrambled to his feet, realizing the man had decided to kill him with his bare hands. His nose was broken, and he didn't duck quickly enough to escape the next blow. He felt his jaw snap, and then a fist slammed into his middle and ribs cracked.

He moaned as he tried to get up, stumbled, landed on his face, then tried again. Finally Russell was on his feet, but two viselike hands were around his throat, and though he fought with all his might to break the hold, he couldn't. Lights shot through his eyes and oddly, he thought of God just before he died.

But he wasn't dead. He was in a broken heap on the floor and a giant stood over him with a rope in his hands.

"I'm not going to kill you, Drayton, but I will if I ever see your face again."

His wrists and feet were bound and through a mist of pain he still heard that cold, merciless voice. "I will give you a free ride to the docks, where you will be dumped on whatever ship is leaving first. You can work off your passage, cause I'm not feeling that generous."

Russell was picked up and thrown over Jared's shoulder, then taken out of the office and dumped in a carriage. Icy gray eyes bore into his.

"Consider yourself lucky today, Drayton—I really wanted to kill you." And then, "Don't ever come back. The moment you set foot on this island I'll know it and you'll be a dead man."

The carriage took off. Russell believed the threat. He wouldn't be back, not ever. He wanted Corinne's money and had expected to get it for quite some time. But no fortune was worth that kind of risk.

Naneki returned to Jared's north shore house, fully intending to remain there. Florence had to leave Naneki's room and return to her own, which forced Corinne back into Jared's. Naneki did not like Corinne's presence in Jared's room, not one bit.

Corinne assumed that Jared had sent for his mistress. It wasn't improbable. He had probably given up on Corinne after their last encounter at the waterfall, and wanted his mistress to warm his cold bed.

Naneki fell into a routine, spending time with Akela in the kitchen. But most of her time was spent with Jared's sister. The two became inseparable, and Malia acquired a new, superior attitude.

Then strange things happened that Corinne couldn't manage to ignore. Food occasionally made her sick, while no one else was affected. She couldn't help but wonder about that. And then one evening, when she returned to Jared's bedroom, she found a large centipede crawling out from under the bed. The size and ugliness of the poisonous creature made her scream and run from the room.

Fortunately, Michael was still with Florence. Akela came running in with a broom and killed the creature, and at Corinne's insistence, searched the room. There were three others, one in Corinne's bed. Corinne didn't sleep that night.

She might not have questioned one centipede, for Akela said they did sometimes sneak into the house. But four? And all in her room?

It took a long time before Corinne could enter her room without going over it thoroughly.

Time passed and she grew even more miserable. Why didn't Jared send her a message? But there was no word from Jared. It was as if he had forgotten all about her and his north shore home. What was keeping him in Honolulu?

Chapter 39

CORINNE had become quite good at surfing. She had gotten into the habit of going out every morning when the waves were reasonably high, and going back to the house as soon as Malia and Naneki brought their boards into the water.

She had begun to openly dislike Malia, though she realized it was Naneki's influence that had turned Jared's sister into a shrew.

One bright, clear morning Florence brought Michael out to watch his mother surf. Corinne smiled at him sitting on the beach, slapping at the sand. He was over six months old already, and so adorably chubby. Michael was the light of her life.

She was writing again to her father, but she had yet to receive any mail from him, and knew it would be more than a month before she could expect any. She had told him about her dilemma. She'd mentioned nothing about being a prisoner, for she knew her father would come to rescue her if he knew that. But she told him that she had fallen in love with her husband. He was, after all, her parent. Could he help her? Probably not.

Lost in her thoughts, Corinne had not noticed when Malia and Naneki entered the water. But their giggling beside her drew her attention and she grimaced. She looked to the beach and saw that Florence was still there with Michael. Noelani had joined them. That was one suspicion Corinne no longer harbored. Akela had assured her that the little girl was not Jared's daughter. She told Corinne about her daughter's husband, Peni. It was sad that the girl had lost her husband after so short a time, but her wanting Jared made it hard for Corinne to sympathize for long.

She waved to Florence and started paddling to shore.

Through the corner of her eye, she saw that Malia was going to catch the same wave. Corinne didn't pull back. She had a nagging suspicion, but she was fed up with Malia's pranks.

The two stood up at about the same time, but then Malia started crowding her, cutting purposefully toward Corinne's board. When the two boards hit, Corinne lost her balance and tumbled to the right. The surf took her straight down and then something struck her from behind and she was no longer aware of the ocean, the sun, and the sand.

Someone was crying. It sounded so pitiful. Not the sobs of a child, but a young woman crying. Who? Corinne started to open her eyes, but a stabbing pain shot through her head and she clamped her eyes shut against it. The pain throbbed viciously. She thought surely she would faint, but she didn't. Through a haze she still heard the sobbing, and now voices that she recognized.

"I've never seen anything so surprising as the way those two surfboards collided." That was Florence.

"Which boards?" Corinne recognized Akela's deep voice.

"Why, Cori's and Malia's," Florence answered. "When the boards hit, Cori fell off to the side and Malia tumbled backwards, away from the large wave they were riding. And then one of the boards shot straight up in the air and, God! I was terrified when I saw it coming down right where Cori had fallen. When I didn't see her come up, I started right in after her, but it was Malia who pulled her to the surface. She probably saved Cori's life."

"I—I didn't mean for her to get hurt," Malia sobbed.

"Of course not, dear," Florence soothed her. "It was an accident."

"I wonder!" Akela growled darkly.

Corinne was so surprised by the anger in Akela's voice that she managed to open her eyes a little. The two older women were standing at the left of her bed, facing Malia, who stood on the right, sobbing, with her head in her hands. Akela pointed an accusing finger at the girl.

"You go too far this time, Malia! You make me shame, cause I raise you. But you no learn right from Aunty!"

"What are you saying, Akela?" Florence whispered, shocked.

"Not accident. Malia not have accident in water. She ride board all her life."

"I didn't mean for her to get hurt!" Malia was crying hysterically again. "I only meant to frighten her!"

"She maybe die, and why? Because you jealous of your brother."

"My God!" Florence gasped.

"And I think maybe this not first time, huh, Malia?" Akela went on, voicing Corinne's half-realized suspicions. "I no like believe you put those centipedes in Kolina's room. I say, no, my Malia not that bad. But I wrong!"

"Naneki said—there would be no danger." Malia tried to catch her breath. "That's why we found the largest ones we could, so she would be sure to see them."

"*Auwe!* My own daughter help you? You both need the stick against your backside. This terrible thing!"

"We only wanted to scare her so she would leave!"

"She leave? Your brother the one keep her here."

"What?"

"You hear good, Malia! She want to go, but he no let her."

"But she is not good enough for Jared. She—"

"Malia, you blind just like Ialeka!" Akela snapped. "Can you no see Kolina not bad?"

"That's right, Malia," Florence spoke up. "Cori was so furious with your brother that she planned the whole charade before we came to Hawaii. I told her not to do it, but she was very headstrong back then. It was all an elaborate ruse to make people think—she was a—" Florence paused, still unable to say the word. "—an immoral woman."

"She took men to her room."

"Yes. She got them drunk, and then sent them home with promises for the next time. But there were no next times because she never saw the same man twice. The only man she's ever been with in—in that way—is your brother."

There was a silence and then Malia said weakly, "She told me, but I didn't believe her."

"Your brother wouldn't believe her either. That's the tragedy."

"Jared must actually love her then if he still wants to keep her even when he thinks—"

Florence sighed. "I believe so, yes, but no one really knows what's in his mind."

"I'm so sorry." Malia started sobbing again.

"Mo'better you tell Kolina that," Akela said gruffly.

"I will. I didn't understand. And I never meant for her to get hurt."

"It's all right, Malia," Corinne whispered from the bed. The three faces turned to her. "So you're awake?" Florence said.

"So it seems."

"Don't try to get up. You've got a pretty mean bump on the side of your head, but that seems to be the only injury. You don't hurt anywhere else, do you?"

"No."

"I sent for doctor. He live Haleiwa, so be a while yet 'fore he come," Akela said.

"That wasn't necessary," Corinne protested.

"Of course it was. You gave us all quite a fright," Florence said sternly. "I don't know if I'll let you do any more surfing."

"Don't be ridiculous. It was an unusual . . . accident." They all fell silent. Corinne looked at Malia. The girl was standing with her head lowered, afraid to face her. "It really is all right, Malia. I've been awake for quite a while and heard everything. And as far as I'm concerned, it *was* an accident. We will forget it."

Malia looked up sheepishly. "I'm so sorry, Corinne."

"I know. Maybe we can be friends now."

Malia smiled faintly, then turned away and left before she started crying again.

Akela started after her. Soon, Corinne turned to Florence. "You have got to do something for me if the doctor says I have to stay in bed a few days."

"Of course, dear."

"Tomorrow, get Akela to take you to the nearest store. There were a few stores in Wahiawa, remember? Or maybe Akela knows if there's one closer. Anyway, I want you to buy Jared a Christmas present for me. Something really special."

"And just what am I to use for money?"

"Take my rubies—no, the diamonds are more valuable. Take all of them, the necklaces, rings, the bracelets."

277

"Cori, really! Those diamonds are worth a fortune!"

"For God's sake, I don't care about the money. And you won't be able to get what they're worth anyway. But whatever you can get for them, spend it all. This is Michael's first Christmas. Get him lots of toys, and some clothes if you can find readymade. He's outgrowing things so quickly."

"As if I hadn't noticed!" Florence chuckled.

"And get something for Akela and Malia, and—oh, find a little something for Naneki and her daughter too—Christmas is no time to be carrying a grudge. And don't forget yourself. But make sure you get a perfect gift for Jared."

"I've never bought anything for a man before."

Corinne frowned. "If only we could get to the city. Look for a ring maybe, or a—a sailboat!"

"Cori!"

"No, I don't suppose you would find one in Wahiawa. Oh, I don't know. Just find something special. It's got to be a gift he will like."

"I'll try, dearest. Now you rest."

Florence shook her head as she closed the door. It had been ages since she had seen Cori so excited. Who would have guessed she would have fallen in love with the very man everyone thought she hated?

Chapter 40

JARED sent word to the house, that he wanted to give a Christmas *luau*, and preparations kept everyone busy all week long. After the two days of bedrest the doctor ordered, Corinne joined in the work. Everyone pitched in to help, including the men who worked in Jared's fields. Kuliano brought a cart filled with bananas down from the hills.

The pig was delivered on Wednesday, a mammoth animal yet to be slaughtered. The fish and pineapple arrived Friday in two wagon loads, with kegs of beer in a third large wagon. Extra chickens were brought in, and coconuts were gathered from up and down the coast, along with seaweed, which would be eaten raw. Corinne was astounded by the mountains of food.

Long, squat tables were brought out of the stable and cleaned, to be set up and covered with *ti* leaves on Christmas morning. Huge pans came out of the storehouse. The cooking began on Saturday, the day before the *luau*. All of the fish, *opihi*, crab, squid, and salmon, would be served raw, but it still took hours to cut up and prepare the fish, especially the *lomi* salmon, which was marinated with chopped onions and spices. The chicken boiled all day long. The pineapple had to be cut, then packed in ice. Corinne helped make *haupia*, the coconut pudding that would be served as little cakes.

What was most fascinating, though, was the cooking of the pig. This was started early on the day before the *luau*. Akela supervised the men who dug a hole for the back yard oven. Wood was placed in the bottom of the pit, then stones were piled on top, and a fire started. After the stones were hot and the fire died down, hot stones were placed inside the pig, and the carcass, already wrapped in fragrant leaves, was lowered into the pit-oven and covered. Small amounts of water were added from time to time to produce steam that would tenderize the meat.

On Christmas Eve, Corinne and Florence decorated a small pine tree in the living room. Malia helped tie bright ribbon and a few store-bought wooden decorations to the tree.

Wrapped gifts were placed beneath the tree, including a finely worked Spanish saddle for Jared.

Corinne went to bed that night feeling quite anxious. She didn't even have Michael to soothe her for, thinking Jared might return at night, she had let Florence take him back.

She was afraid. Why had he stayed away so long? Because of his work, or because of her? Would he still be angry?

"Come on, Cori, some of the guests are arriving."

Corinne stirred in bed and turned to see Florence poking her head in the door. "What did you say?"

"Heavens, it's almost eleven."

Corinne grimaced. "I had a bad night."

"Well, you'll have a nice day to make up for it, so come on. Some of the neighbors are here, and so is Jared."

"Jared's here?" Corinne sat up instantly.

"Yes, and he brought some of his workers with him, about twenty. And his friend Leonaka, too. Just like men, they all headed straight for the liquor. This is going to be some wild party tonight, after they've been drinking all day."

"Come help me, then."

"Oh, no," Florence said. "Akela has Michael in the kitchen and I've got to rescue him before he falls into one of those vats of poi. My God! She filled five huge pans with that gooey stuff!"

"Oh, stop," Corinne giggled, excited now. "I've seen you eating poi when you thought no one was looking. So you can stop pretending it doesn't appeal to you."

"Well, I guess it's not so bad with a little cream and sugar mixed in," Florence conceded. "But you'd best hurry, my love. Akela wants you to pick some flowers to put on the tables."

Florence closed the door and Corinne jumped out of bed. She already knew what she was going to wear. It was the beautiful red, white, and green *muumuu*, Akela's Christmas gift, that she had presented ahead of time. It fit Corinne snugly and had a low neckline bordered in delicate white lace. And Corinne had the perfect necklace to wear with it, a large single ruby on a long chain. She had rings, bracelets, and earrings to match, but she wore only the bracelet and her wedding ring. Her hair, washed yesterday, sparkled with coppery and golden and lemon highlights. She left it loose and flowing, since that seemed to be the style the local women preferred.

She left her room and went straight to the patio, where she could see outside without being observed. She saw Jared instantly, standing with a group of young Hawaiians at the end of the yard near the beach. He was wearing a white lawn shirt, opened halfway down his chest, and a tan coat and breeches. He was dusty from the ride, but he looked so handsome her heart fluttered.

This was a man she would never get her way with unless she used all her womanly wiles, a man of strong will, dominating. Yet she was in love with him. What had happened to her?

She knew very well how much love could hurt. But she had never known anything as exciting.

Yes, her feelings had changed. But would his?

A few of the men had already started for the beach, but Jared had yet to get his shirt off. And then Corinne saw Malia run to him and grab his hand. She began pulling him toward the house and Corinne could hear her excited voice.

"Come on! I want to open my presents. Your wife made us wait till you came."

"My, but you're in a fine mood, aren't you?"

"And why not?" she reproached him. "It's Christmas. Did you bring me something?"

Corinne was suddenly afraid to face him, afraid he would still be angry, even though she wasn't. She went quickly into the kitchen. It was crowded and bustling with activity. Naneki was there cutting the *haupia*, and some of Akela's cousins had come from Kahuku to help. Akela was cooking the chicken long rice and baking sweet potatoes.

Corinne was just in the way there with so many already helping. But where else could she go to avoid Jared? And then Malia poked her head inside.

"Aunty, come take a rest," Malia called excitedly. "Kolina, come, Ialeka's home!"

Jared appeared in the doorway and their eyes met. But his expression was unreadable. She still didn't know how he felt. And then Malia grabbed his hand again and pulled him toward the living room, and Akela was pushing Corinne out of the kitchen after them. Florence and Michael were already there, gazing at the little pine tree.

"Whose idea was that?" said Jared, looking at the tree.

"Kolina suggested it," Malia supplied. "It's nice, isn't it?"

"A tree? In the house?"

"Oh, stop being so gruff," Malia chided him. "I like it and we're going to have one every year from now on."

"And where did that come from?" He pulled the saddle out from under the tree.

"That's for you, from Kolina."

Jared straightened up slowly and looked directly at Corinne. His expression was clearly readable—hard and accusing. What had she done wrong? His look brought tears to her eyes and she ran from the room.

A few moments later Jared strode into their bedroom. When he saw the tears, he said, "Why in damnation are you crying?"

She tried to pull away, but he held her fast. "I don't know why I'm crying. I thought you would enjoy the Christmas tree, but you didn't. I thought you would like my gift, but you don't. And you've been gone well over a month, but you didn't even come to say hello to me when you arrived."

After a long silence, he said softly, "I didn't come to you because I wasn't sure whether you wanted me to." Jared's tone surprised her. "And I do like the saddle." Abruptly his voice grew cold again. "But it's the finest leather I've even seen and that's expensive. I want to know how you paid for it."

Suddenly what he was thinking became clear to her. She gasped. "Do you really trust me that little?"

"I know you didn't have any money, Corinne, because I

have your money. How did you buy that saddle if not—"

"Don't you dare say it, Jared!" She stopped him furiously. "Don't you dare! For your information, Florence found the saddle for me because I was bedridden. Are you going to accuse my maid now of bartering herself? Your mind runs to the gutter!"

He flinched at her words. "What do you mean, you were bedridden?"

"Don't change the subject, I beg you!"

"Answer me!"

"It was nothing. I had a small accident and ended up with a bump on my head, that's all."

"And you're all right now?" He was obviously relieved.

"Yes, but why this sudden concern for my welfare after what you just accused me of?"

"For Christ's sake, what was I supposed to think? I know you didn't have money because I took yours out of the bank before you came here."

"I sold some of my jewels," she snapped. "I have more than I need, anyway."

Her words were like a physical blow and Jared paled. "My God! Corinne, I'm sorry."

She was too hurt to be mollified. "No, you're not! You'd rather think I sold myself! I wish now that I hadn't parted with my diamonds, even though I didn't care at the time. I only wanted to buy you something nice. I guess I'm a bigger fool than you are, Jared Burkett."

"Confound it, Corinne, how was I supposed to know? I never would have dreamed you would part with any of your jewels. You wouldn't wear any to the gambling house for fear of losing them. I thought your jewels were important to you."

"They were once, when my father controlled the purse strings. But I'm rich now. I don't give a fig about the jewels I have. I can always buy more."

He let her go and turned away with a strained expression. He left the room and returned quickly with a long box, which he tossed on the bed.

"It's just something I thought you would like. But I made a mistake. We had the same idea—I'm just sorry they both turned out so disastrously."

Jared left the room and Corinne walked hesitantly to the

bed and opened the box. Brilliant opals gleamed up at her in a rainbow of fiery colors, and tears sprang to her eyes again. Very slowly, she took off her ruby necklace and put the opals on. Then she clasped them in her hands and brought them up against her cheek. They were cold against her skin.

"Oh, Jared, why do we have to have these stupid fights all the time?"

The day had started out so badly. But it was Christmas. She would make the rest of the holiday better. Thinking of Michael and the presents he had yet to open, her spirits began to rise.

Chapter 41

DRINKING and eating went on all day long, and the guests kept coming. Many went swimming, and there was even a little surfing competition. Corinne met so many people that it was impossible to remember names. She was given *lei* upon *lei* until she was nearly buried under the fragrant wreaths and was forced to take most of them off.

A group of Hawaiians with string instruments played continuously, a steady flow of beer keeping them happy. Everyone was very gay, and Corinne found herself laughing constantly. The actual feast, where everyone sat down to eat together, didn't begin until late afternoon. Nearly all of Jared's friends were there, but Corinne didn't feel awkward. Many looked at her curiously, wondering about her and Jared, but she didn't let it bother her.

The food rated unanimous praise and Akela beamed proudly. Corinne tried everything, and surprised herself by enjoying some of the raw dishes. The chicken long rice was delicious, but it was the *kalua* pig that Corinne couldn't seem to get enough of. She went back three times for more of the tender, shredded meat.

Jared sat next to Corinne at the table, but they said almost nothing to each other.

The drinking and merriment continued after the feast. Jared moved on, but Corinne stayed at the table with Florence and Michael. Hawaiians loved children and Michael went from lap to lap, getting enough cuddling in one day to last him several months. Leonaka joined them for a while to watch Malia and some of the younger girls dance the *hula*. They wore skirts made of shredded *ti* leaves and *leis* around their heads and necks. The instruments used for *hula* dancing were gourd drums and coconut rattles.

After sunset, an entertainment in itself, *tiki* torches were set all around the yard and the *luau* went on. Some were still swimming, others surfing by moonlight, and Corinne discovered that a *luau* was an all-day, all-night affair.

While Corinne was watching the surfers, a slightly older woman sat down next to her and introduced herself as Dayna Callan. A few years younger than Jared, she was quite lovely, with light brown hair and blue eyes. Corinne was flustered, wondering what to say, when suddenly Dayna surprised her.

"I suppose you've heard that everyone thought Jared and I would marry?"

It took Corinne a moment to answer. "No, I hadn't heard—"

"Oh dear, I am sorry. You must think I'm terrible to just blurt that out, but I thought surely you must have known. I only meant to get it out of the way, in case you felt uneasy talking with me."

Corinne tried to find her wits. "Did—had Jared asked you to marry him?"

Dayna smiled. "Heavens, no! Ours was more or less a silent understanding. He always put off asking me. And frankly," she lowered her voice, "I dreaded the day he would."

"I don't understand."

"You see, I grew up with Jared. My family had a beach house up the coast and we spent half of every year out here. Jared and Leonaka were like my brothers. Can you imagine the prospect of marrying a man you think of as your brother?"

"So you didn't want to marry him?"

"No. I was relieved when he returned from the mainland and told me about you. I believe I'm the only one he confided in. In fact, he told me all he had done. He was miserable after he returned, and I am sure he regretted his behavior. When the stories reached him about you, I knew he was frantic with jealousy. He tried to hide his feelings, but I knew."

For the very first time, Corinne felt a hot embarrassment because of her charade. "You must think I'm a horrible woman."

"I really didn't know what to think. But you see, I knew what Jared had done, so I couldn't blame you. And besides, it was only rumor, and one has to be skeptical where rumors are concerned."

"Jared wasn't."

"Well, Jared often reacts with pure emotion instead of sense. I knew the moment I saw you that you couldn't have done what they say. But Jared doesn't have a woman's intuition. And jealousy can distort one's thinking."

"You have to care in order to be jealous," Corinne replied.

"Exactly." Dayna emphasized the word and smiled. She gazed directly at Corinne.

Corinne understood. "I'm certainly glad I met you. I only wish it had been sooner." She smiled wistfully and sighed.

"Has Jared been difficult?"

"Oh, it's not so much Jared's behavior. It's the constant doubts and suspicions. I guess I'm prone to jealousy, too."

Corinne's eyes moved to Naneki, who was dancing solo now, and Dayna followed her gaze. The Hawaiian girl was dancing beautifully, seductively. Her attention was entirely on Jared, who was standing nearby, watching her.

"Oh dear."

Corinne turned back to Dayna. "What is it?"

The other woman was frowning. "I assumed Naneki had given up on Jared, but I see she hasn't."

"She was his mistress, wasn't she?"

"Well, yes, for a while. But that was before he married you. I would have thought—well . . ." She trailed off.

"Jared and I aren't a honeymoon couple," Corinne said.

Dayna faced her squarely and said, "I must be rude now and ask you something that is none of my business. Do you love Jared?"

"Yes."

"Well then, you will have to fight for him," Dayna replied, a twinkle in her blue eyes.

"What do you mean?"

"You're a very beautiful woman, Corinne. If Jared knows you want him, he won't look elsewhere. Another woman wouldn't have a chance with him."

"Do you really think so?"

"Of course. Why don't you start now? Go get his attention away from Naneki. It's late, and no one would think it odd if the two of you retired soon."

Dayna winked and Corinne blushed.

"What about you?" Corinne asked, hoping she would see Dayna again. "Will you be leaving soon?"

"Heavens, no. One of the best parts about a *luau* is finding a place to bunk down for the night. Just about everyone stays until morning and then helps clean up."

"I didn't know that."

Dayna laughed. "You'll have people sleeping all over your house, and in the stable, too," she smiled. "Now go on. I'll see you in the morning before I leave. You can meet my escort, Mark Carlton, then."

Corinne left the table and approached Jared slowly. She still didn't know what to say to him. She nervously fingered her necklace, then realized she had the perfect excuse to speak to him.

"Jared." It took him several moments to take his eyes off Naneki, but he finally turned to her. "I wanted to thank you for the opals. They're beautiful."

"If you like them, I'm glad. If not—" He shrugged as if to say he didn't care.

"I do like them, Jared," she said quickly, and added, "Honestly."

He took her arm and walked her to the bench swing, a few feet away. Oh, why was she so nervous?

"The opals suit you," Jared said casually without looking at her. "They compliment your coloring. You have picked up quite a tan while I was gone."

"I'm sorry if you don't like it."

"Oh, but I do. Your skin has darkened, but your hair has lightened. You look very exotic now."

"Is that good?"

"Good Lord, woman, nothing could hurt your beauty. Are you just being naive, or are you fishing for compliments?" Corinne's chin rose perceptibly and Jared chuckled. "Don't get your dander up. I was only teasing."

She relaxed and decided to broach the subject that had worried her so often of late. "Why did you stay away so long?"

He glanced at her curiously for a moment, but then looked out over the ocean.

"There was some trouble with the hotel job. One of my workers nearly lost a leg in a bad fall. I couldn't very well take off with him laid up in the hospital, not knowing whether he would lose the leg or not."

"Is he all right?"

"Yes. He'll have a limp the rest of his life, though. A few other things kept me in the city after that."

"What?"

"It's personal, Corinne."

She drew up. "You mean because of me?"

"No, damnit," he said with exasperation. "If you must know, I was looking for John Pierce. He and I had some unfinished business."

"Did you find him?"

"He's left the island."

"For good?" she asked.

"Apparently," Jared said, frustrated. "I also learned that his land is up for sale." Then his tone lightened. "But enough of that. Akela tells me you helped quite a bit with the *luau*. I appreciate it. Things must have been pretty hectic around here all week."

"I enjoyed it."

"You must be tired after such a long day."

He was looking at her again with those piercing blue-gray eyes. Was he asking her or telling her?

"I'm ready for bed."

She smiled. "I am, too."

They bade good night to their guests and went inside. Walking through the patio was difficult. Children had already been bedded down there on the big rug and the sofas, and a few adults, too, were already sleeping. Jared led her over and around little bodies and big ones, and when they reached the top of the patio stairs, they saw that the living room was already filled.

The corridor to the bedrooms was quiet and empty. Florence had gone to bed much earlier with Michael. Malia hadn't lasted long, either, excitement having caused her to be up at dawn.

Jared stopped at Florence's door to bid Corinne good night. He had decided not to press her. He had made a terrible blunder that morning, a stupid blunder, and he was sure Corinne was still angry. But Corinne went on to his

289

room and entered. Jared stared after her in surprise. She went to the dresser and lit a lamp, then removed the gardenia from her hair, breathing deeply of it before putting it down.

Jared came into the room slowly, watching her. "You moved back in here?"

She glanced at him demurely. "I hope you don't mind."

"No, of course not," Jared answered, wondering how on earth he would get through the night without touching her.

Corinne went on nervously as she took off her necklace. "Naneki is back. She has been since you left, so there are no extra rooms. And I don't think Florence and I would be too comfortable sharing her small bed."

"Corinne, I said I didn't mind," he interrupted. "Anyway, you belong in here."

She turned away from him, moving her long hair aside. "Would you unfasten my *muumuu?*"

He started to unfasten her gown and slowly her slender back was revealed. Her neck was so tempting, he wanted to lean forward and caress her with his lips, to taste her silken skin. Would she jump away from him and be enraged? He kept his control and then turned away and began undressing.

Corinne crossed to the closet and stepped out of her *muumuu* and her underthings. Naked, she took a long time searching for a nightgown, hoping Jared would at least look at her. Finally she could stall no more, and withdrew a dark green negligee of luxurious satin.

Corinne turned towards Jared before she put the gown on, and found him staring at her as if mesmerized. She smiled to herself and averted her eyes. Ever so slowly, she slipped the gown over her head and pulled it down.

Jared stood motionless as he watched Corinne walk enticingly to the bed and slide under the covers. Didn't she know what she was doing to him? She was tempting him beyond endurance.

"Aren't you coming to bed, Jared?"

Corinne's voice was seductively sweet, and he realized he hadn't moved for several minutes. He tore away the rest of his clothes and walked over to the bed.

"Confound it, woman, do you know what you're doing to me?" he demanded harshly. "I can't stand it anymore!"

She was silent. Then slowly she wrapped her arms around him and laid her head on his chest.

Corinne thought she would die with wanting him, with the need to have him drive into her, claim her. It was the only assurance she had that he felt something for her, even if it was only desire. She tore off her gown and tried to pull him down with her, but he held her back.

"No, *ánói*," he said huskily. "I want to savor you. God, how I've longed for you, dreamt of you." Slowly, he pushed her down and lay down by her side with one leg over hers, possessively.

And then he began to torture her with sweet, exquisite kisses that drove her wild. His lips pressed hers with tender passion, while his hand scorched her skin. Her body demanded release, but still he prolonged the delicious torture. At last she could bear it no more and grasped his hot, steel-like shaft and urged him to her.

Jared groaned at her touch and moved on top of her. "Oh, my Kolina—" he breathed.

He buried his lips in the curve of her neck at the same time he buried his throbbing manhood within her. In only seconds Corinne was swirling, spiraling upward to the climactic moment of explosion. Her fulfillment was complete because Jared joined her in that instant of bliss. The shattering moment was theirs together.

Corinne sighed deeply when Jared moved to her side and pulled her close. No words were spoken, but none were needed.

PIRATE'S WILD

out back. It would... too long now. But, as midnight came, finally she went to see about.

Jared put the heart necklace in his pocket and smiled as

Chapter 42

CORINNE woke late to discover that she was alone. She dressed quickly and made the bed lovingly, remembering each moment of what had happened there the night before. She picked up the clothes Jared had left lying on the floor. They were a mess. He hadn't even bothered to empty his pockets. She laid some coins and loose pieces of paper on the dresser, then pulled a small box from another pocket. It was a jewelry box, and she couldn't resist opening it. The solid gold heart that gleamed up at her was lovely. Slowly she read the engraved inscription.

Corinne quickly closed the box and put it back in the pocket. Then, quickly, she replaced the other items in the clothes and hung them up. He mustn't know she had seen the necklace.

She was trembling. What did it mean? *I would marry you again, and without regrets.* Of course he regretted the first time. But now? *Without regrets.* Could it mean he loved her?

"Then why didn't he give me the heart necklace?" she whispered to herself.

The answer was obvious. He had changed his mind. It was only lust that had prompted the inscription. Not love. He had realized that he didn't love her. Therefore, he was not planning to give her the gold heart.

Corinne spent the rest of the day waiting for Jared to approach her. But there were guests to attend to, and he was kept constantly occupied.

After dinner, when Jared went out to the stable, Corinne got a shawl and went out to the backyard. She sat in the bench swing, hoping Jared would join her when he finished. It wasn't too long before she heard him cross by the front of the house and enter there. Akela would tell him she was out back. It wouldn't be long now. But he didn't come, and finally she went to seek him out.

Jared put the heart necklace in his pocket and smiled as he left the bedroom. He had hoped to find Corinne there, but then assumed she had gone for a walk. He waited for her in the living room. It was peaceful, their guests having departed long ago.

Jared grew impatient when Corinne didn't return. He paced the room, then opened the front door and stood there gazing out at the bright moon. It reminded him of that long-ago promise he had made her, of a walk on the beach, and the added promise of making love under the stars, with moonlight shining down on her.

Then he smelled the strong fragrance of gardenia behind him, the bloom Corinne always wore in her hair. Her arms slipped around his waist and Jared smiled and turned to capture her lips. But the lips parting beneath his were not Corinne's.

Jared drew back, his eyes growing dark. "What are you doing, Naneki?"

She pouted. "Well, she not only one who can wear the gardenia. Why you no come to me anymore?"

"I am married now, and my wife is more than enough woman for me."

"She no good."

"That's enough, Naneki," Jared said coldly, pushing her away from him.

"You love her then?"

"Yes, damnit, I love her!" Her hurt expression made him soften his tone. "Look, Naneki, I told you long ago to find a husband. Why don't you give Leonaka a chance? He cares for you."

"Leonaka?"

"Yes, didn't you know?" When she shook her head, he continued. "That's because you never gave him any encouragement. But he loved you even before you married Peni."

Her face brightened. "Leonaka good, strong man."

"Yes, he is."

"I think I take him *laulaus* tomorrow. That encourage him, huh?"

293

Jared laughed. "It certainly will. Now go on to bed."

Jared should have been hurt that Naneki could transfer her affections from him to another so easily, but he wasn't. He loved Corinne. He couldn't stand waiting any longer, and he left the house to find her. He would tell her how much he loved her.

But Corinne wasn't outside. She was locked in their room, crying on the bed where just last night she had found such joy. That was all gone now, and would never return. Why did she have to come in when she did, and see Naneki and Jared embracing? Corinne had felt her heart wrenched from her, and without waiting to see any more, she had run to the bedroom and locked herself in.

She was a fool ever to believe in happiness. The love between Jared and Corinne was a thing of the past.

Jared returned to the house after a futile search outside and went to their room. It was locked.

"Corinne?"

"Go away, Jared."

He shook his head, baffled. "Open the door."

Corinne jumped off the bed and came to the door so he could hear her clearly. How dare he come to her after just leaving his mistress?

"I told you to go away, Jared. Last night was a mistake, and it's not going to happen again."

"What in damnation has got into you?" he roared in disbelief.

The anger in his voice made her answer, "I've come to my senses, that's what! I had forgotten how much I hate you, but I won't forget again."

God, it wasn't true—it wasn't! But it was better if he thought so.

Tears flowed again, just when she thought she had spilled them all. "I do mean it, Jared. You can have your room back in the morning. Tonight—go sleep with your mistress! I don't want you, but she certainly does."

"Corinne—"

"No!" she stopped him. "I've had enough, Jared. You either take me back to the city in the morning or I'll walk!"

Jared backed away, bewildered and furious. Then anger took over completely.

Twice. She had made an utter fool of him twice. She had always hated him and she always would. There would not be a third time. He would take her back to the city. He would escort her right to a ship. He would see that she got on it. To hell with Corinne!

"On Aldrich Street."

"Very well," he replied. "But I want you to come downstairs with me. With both of you fussing over the boy, you're probably frightening him. He—"

Chapter 43

JARED went to summon Corinne. The carriage was waiting and a cart was attached to carry the luggage to the harbor. In a very short while Corinne would walk out of his life. He ought to be glad to be rid of her and the rage she inevitably caused him. But he didn't feel glad. He felt lost.

The baby's cries drew Jared to Florence's room. He knew he would find his wife there. Both women were trying to soothe the child at the same time, obviously without success.

Jared shook his head as he came into the open room. "If everything is packed, ladies, I'll start taking your things downstairs."

"Not now, Jared," Corinne answered curtly without looking his way.

"Well, it will have to be soon. Your ship leaves in about three hours."

"I don't care about the damn ship!" She turned to him. Her eyes were wide. "Michael is sick."

"You know there won't be another ship until the fourteenth."

"Whenever," she said absently and turned back to Michael.

"Have you sent for a doctor?"

"I was just going to go," Florence answered.

"Nonsense," Jared replied. "Your place is with your child. I'll send Soon Ho."

He started to leave the room, but Corinne stopped him. "Jared. I want Dr. Bryson. Michael knows him. And tell him it's an emergency."

Jared frowned. "Where is his office?"

"On Alakea Street."

"Very well," he replied. "But I want you to come downstairs with me. With both of you fussing over the boy, you're probably frightening him."

"No, I'm staying here."

"Go on, Corinne," Florence said sternly, with a meaningful look.

"All right," she agreed reluctantly. "But only until the doctor comes."

After Soon Ho was sent on his way, Jared joined Corinne in the living room. "You look as if you could use a drink," he offered.

"I could, thank you."

She sat on the edge of a chair, clasping her hands in her lap and keeping her eyes on the stairs. Jared watched her as he made the drinks. She seemed terrified.

"The boy will be all right."

"Of course he will."

He handed her the glass and noticed her hands trembling. "What's wrong with him?"

"We don't know. He's burning with fever, and he won't stop crying."

"That could be any number of minor things, Corinne," he tried to reassure her.

"It could also be serious!" she snapped. "I'm sorry, Jared. I'm just worried about him."

"I can see that."

Corinne lapsed into silence and Jared watched her. He wanted to soothe her. Damn, he wanted to offer her his love.

"Corinne, there is no reason for you to leave on the fourteenth, or ever." She wasn't listening to him, but to the crying that continued upstairs. "Did you hear me?"

Finally she glanced his way. "What did you say?"

"I said there is no reason for you to leave. You can stay here."

"With you?"

"Yes."

Her eyes focused on him now. They were a dark emerald. "And share you with Naneki and God knows how many other women? No thank you."

"Share me?" he asked in surprise. "I haven't had another woman since I married you."

"Spare me, Jared," she said bitterly, and her eyes darkened even more. "I happen to know differently."

"What?"

"I saw you!" she shouted, all the pent-up pain and anger coming out. "You and your mistress kissing!"

Jared stared at her several moments, but then it all became clear to him. He laughed. "That was nothing. She came up behind me that night, but I thought it was you. I kissed her without looking, but stopped as soon as I knew I didn't have you in my arms."

"I don't believe—" Corinne jumped up when Michael's cries grew louder.

She ran to the stairs, but Jared stopped her. "I don't want you up there, Corinne."

She tried to yank her arm free, but he held her fast. "Stop it, Jared. He needs me."

"Don't be ridiculous, Corinne. Florence can take care of him."

"I want Michael."

"If it's serious, then you could get sick as well. I won't have it."

"I don't care what you'll have!" Her voice rose frantically. "Now let go of me!"

"Corinne, stop it!" Jared said harshly. "All that boy needs is his mother. My God, you've become obsessed with that child. Can't you see that?"

"Obsessed!" she screamed and started crying. "Yes, I'm obsessed. Because Michael is my baby! Do *you* understand now? He—is—mine!"

Jared released his hold so suddenly that she stumbled. She didn't stop to see the pained look on his face as she ran up the stairs.

He is mine—Jared heard her scream again over and over in his mind. Not "ours," but "mine," she had said. It didn't occur to him that she was simply upset. No, this proved what he had once suspected.

The baby was Drayton's, all right. That was the only possible explanation for Corinne's keeping the truth from him. If the child were his, Corinne would have told him the truth.

Corinne fell back in a chair and sighed deeply. She was exhausted and looked it.

"Here, I think we can both use some of this." Florence came into the room with a bottle and two glasses.

"Did you see Dr. Bryson out?"

"Yes."

"You know, I don't understand why I did it." Corinne sighed. "After all the trouble and the lies to keep Michael a secret from Jared, I just screamed the truth at him. And it wasn't even necessary! There was no danger. Michael wasn't seriously ill at all."

Dr. Bryson had been amused when he discovered that the "emergency" was teething. Michael was simply cutting molars.

"Don't worry about it, Cori. It's time he knew, anyway."

"Don't say that, Florence." Corinne shook her head from side to side. "What if he tries to keep Michael now?"

"You have more money with which to fight him in court if it comes to that. But I don't see why you two just don't settle your differences."

"It's too late for that," Corinne said quietly. "I couldn't live with him, knowing he doesn't love me—not even a little bit."

"Who says he doesn't?" Florence asked huffily.

"I do." Corinne sat up and moaned. "Oh, I wish we hadn't missed that ship today."

"There will be another, if you're really set on going."

"Yes, but what's going to happen in the meantime? What am I going to say to Jared when he demands to know why I kept the truth from him?"

"You tell him the truth, that's all."

But Jared stayed away all that night. Nor did he return the following day. Corinne waited nervously, frightened of a confrontation, but wishing to get the inevitable scene over with.

But Jared stayed away from the house until the fourteenth. By then, Corinne had given up hoping.

Chapter 44

"WE certainly didn't pick a good day to be leaving this island."

Corinne turned, putting on her bonnet. "Why? It's a nice day."

"Haven't you been reading the papers, Cori?"

"Whatever for? News is too depressing."

Florence shook her head. "There has been nothing but talk of revolution."

"You mean war?"

"I don't know. But there seem to be a good many people on Oahu and all over Hawaii who want to get rid of the monarchy. It will all come to a head very soon. And today is important."

"Why?"

"Queen Liliu—Oh, I just can't pronounce the name. She's planning to throw out the present constitution and introduce one of her own. The foreign citizens here, mostly Americans, are set against that. It's all a test of strength between the revolutionaries and the monarchists—and between the foreign settlers and the Hawaiians."

"Then it's a good thing we decided to leave early today. We can take a roundabout way to the harbor and stay well clear of Iolani Palace."

"You're still not going to wait a little longer to see if your husband will come home?"

Corinne didn't hesitate before answering. "No. It's been a week. He's either too angry with me for keeping Michael a secret from him, or he just doesn't care."

"I can't believe he doesn't care, Cori."

"I can. I know Jared better than you do. Now let's go." She picked up her gloves and purse, and left the room to get Michael. The luggage was already in the cart. After perfunctory good-byes to Akela and Malia, they set out for the harbor with Soon Ho driving.

Before long, another carriage came bounding after them. Both carriages stopped. Corinne tensed when she saw Jared. He left his carriage and approached hers.

"I didn't think you would be leaving this early. I almost missed you."

He was so casual about it! "Why did you bother?"

"I came to escort you to your ship. There may be trouble today. Already people are fired up in the streets—a bunch of hot-heads."

"We know about the trouble, Jared. We had planned to go around the palace."

"The trouble is everywhere, Corinne. There will undoubtedly be street fights."

"And you're worried about me?" she muttered sarcastically.

He didn't answer. He ordered Soon Ho to take his carriage home, while he climbed up on theirs. Corinne simmered silently. Jared hadn't said one word about Michael. He must have seen the child on her lap. Not one word! Why had he come? Probably to make sure that she left.

The streets were more crowded than Corinne had ever seen them. There was a great deal of noise, mostly shouting. People were running in the direction of the palace, and Corinne spotted several weapons. She became frightened, then, especially for Michael, and put him down on the floor of the carriage. Then she began to worry about Jared, sitting high up in the driver's seat, in plain view. He hadn't even brought a gun, although he'd known what was happening. Just as she was wondering why he hadn't, shots rang out from in front of the carriage and Corinne screamed. The carriage stopped slowly, and Corinne screamed again as she watched Jared slump over on the seat.

She jumped out of the carriage and climbed up to the driver's seat. When she got there, Jared was sitting up, breathing heavily. "Are you all right?"

"I only got a little dizzy," he replied roughly. "I'm fine."

But she saw the blood on his side, and her heart stopped. "You've been shot, Jared!"

"It's only a nick."

"I don't care, I'm taking you to a doctor."

"I don't want a doctor."

But he swayed as he spoke, and she grabbed the reins he had dropped and started to Alakea Street.

Luck was with them. Dr. Bryson was at his office and he helped Corinne get Jared inside. She refused to leave the room while he examined Jared, but stood by helplessly, anxiously watching the doctor probe his wound, while Jared tried to hide his pain.

Dr. Bryson peered over his shoulder at her. "Why don't you wait in my outer office? This will take a while."

She shook her head firmly. "Not until I know he's going to be all right."

"I can assure you of that right now. The bullet has not damaged any vital organs. It's just a matter of removing it. He'll be as good as new in a week."

"Very well," she said, not wanting to get in the doctor's way.

But Jared sat up, his face a stony mask. "Never mind waiting, Corinne. You go on and catch your ship."

"Don't be ridiculous, Jared!" she cried. "I can't leave you like this."

"You will, damnit!" His voice rose harshly. "I'm not going to be responsible for your missing your ship. You wanted to leave today—just get out of here and do it!"

She thought he would say *something* about their son before she left. "What about Michael?" she ventured.

Jared closed his eyes against the pain and anger. Love for Corinne was driving him crazy. And she was mocking him with Drayton's child! She must surely loathe him! Jared said coldly, "You take your son and get out of my life. Go back to Boston where you belong. And you damn well better get a divorce this time, Corinne, or by God I will!"

She turned blindly and ran from the office. So! His own son meant less than nothing to Jared.

Jared slumped back on the examining table, drained. It had taken all his strength to tell her to go when he really wanted to beg her to stay.

"Don't you think you were a bit harsh with her?"

Jared opened his eyes and stared at Dr. Bryson. He had forgotten the man was in the room.

"It was necessary."

"You mentioned divorce. I don't understand. I thought—"

"Yes," Jared interrupted sharply. "I understand. You thought she was Mrs. Drayton. But you see, she's my wife, although the baby you treated is Drayton's child. It's a very . . . complicated story," Jared finished wryly.

"Well, well." Dr. Bryson was thinking rapidly. "This explains a lot. You're the 'Jared' that pretty woman cursed up and down when she was giving birth. I never did understand why, if her husband was called Russell."

After a pause, Jared asked, "How would you know? Corinne had her child in Boston. Were you there?"

"I don't know what misconception you're under, Mr.—"

"Burkett," Jared supplied impatiently.

"Mr. Burkett. Your wife delivered her child here on the island. I saw her the first time in December before last, shortly after she arrived, and regularly after that until she delivered in June. At her request, I even had a family ready to adopt the child."

Jared sat up abruptly. "My wife arrived here in August of last year!"

Dr. Bryson did not wish to argue with such a large and belligerent man, wounded or not. He shrugged. "If you say so."

Jared scowled. "But you say otherwise?"

Dr. Bryson nodded hesitantly.

Jared shook his head as if that would help him to understand. "You said she gave birth in June. When in June?"

"I can check my records for the exact day, but I believe it was in the middle of the month."

Jared calculated quickly. "You mentioned an adoption. She didn't want the child?"

Dr. Bryson frowned, remembering. "She certainly didn't. It was unnatural the way she seemed to hate that unborn baby. I never could understand it."

Words came back to Jared, words of long ago. "I certainly wouldn't keep a child of yours."

"What did Drayton think about the coming child?"

"Well, that was puzzling too, since he was the husband, or so I'd thought. He didn't want the baby either. Now I understand about that situation. Why, they didn't even share the same room, not even after the birth."

303

"How would you know?"

"I was called on often enough before and after the birth. This was all happening too quickly for Jared. "Why didn't she give the child up?"

Dr. Bryson chuckled. "That was Miss Merrill's doing."

"You mean Mrs. Merrill?"

"Oh dear, is she married?"

"Never mind," Jared replied curtly. "Go on."

"Well, Miss Merrill convinced me that Mrs. Burkett would regret giving away the baby. She said she was obsessed with other things and wasn't thinking clearly."

Jared grimaced. *He* was the other thing. She hated him so much that she couldn't bear to keep his child.

"Are you all right? I really should be getting that bullet out."

"It can wait a bit more. I want to know what happened."

"Well, Miss Merrill and I arranged it so that Mrs. Burkett was left alone with her new baby for a while. That was all it took. It was love at first sight, you might say. I rarely see mother love any stronger."

Jared sighed and lay back on the examining table. He was hurting badly. It was time to remove the bullet.

Just before the doctor administered pain killer, Jared realized everything fully. *My, God, I have a son!*

Chapter 45

CORINNE'S homecoming had been pleasant in one
way. Her father was waiting for her when she stepped
off the train in Boston, and his delight in Michael was
heart-warming. From the moment of their reunion, Samuel Barrows doted on his grandson.

Corinne had been to a few parties in the two weeks since
her return, and to teas and other social functions that
Lauren had dragged her to during the days. She didn't
mind. It kept her busy so she couldn't dwell on Jared too
much.

The gossip about her reasons for leaving the city were
now considered misinformation, for Lauren let it be known
she had been living happily with her husband all this time,
and was only in Boston for a visit. Lauren had acquired a
great deal of sophistication and was now able to handle
nearly everything with aplomb.

Corinne went along with her cousin's lie, because it was
easier than telling the truth. But people's curiosity caused
her much pain. Naturally, questions were asked about the
exotic, fascinating island she had been living on. Corinne
was barely able to hide her melancholy when she described Hawaii.

Corinne was saying, "You've never met a more friendly
and fun-loving people than the Hawaiians." She sighed.

How was it possible that Hawaii had become her home
in such a short time? Why, she had spent her whole life in
Boston, walked among its stately homes, played on Boston
Common, watched the rowers on the Charles River, and
fed the ducks on Jamaica Pond. But all these things now
seemed like old, outgrown friends. Boston just wasn't her
home any longer.

Would she ever stop expecting to see the bright flowers

305

of Oahu? Would she stop hearing in her mind the rushing waterfall she and Jared had seen that day? Would she ever see a Boston sunset without being disappointed?

It was her turn to entertain, and seven women, old friends, sat in her parlor sipping tea before the fire. Lauren and her mother were there. Heavens, how her cousin had grown up while she was gone!

"You must be eager to return, Corinne," one of the women remarked. "I certainly would be. We really didn't expect you to come home so soon."

"Well, my father hadn't seen Michael yet and he couldn't get away to visit us there."

"Your husband must have been reluctant to let you leave," Mrs. Hartman commented. "Look at the extreme measures he took when you were married."

"Extreme measures?" Corinne asked.

Lauren leaned forward and grinned. "I hope you don't mind, Corinne, but I confided to Mrs. Hartman why your husband put that outlandish notice in the newspapers before he left. I told her that it was his way of making sure you followed him without delay."

Corinne was astounded by Lauren's ingenuity. "Yes, well . . ." She groped for words. "My husband has a rather dry sense of humor."

"I can't imagine my Harold doing something like that," said Mrs. Nautily.

"Nor could we," Lauren laughed.

Corinne smiled. Harold Nautily was a timid man, a good five inches shorter than his large and imposing wife. He never said anything to his wife except "Yes, dear." Before Jared, that was the type of man Corinne had thought she wanted!

"How is that adorable little boy of yours, Corinne?" Mrs. Turner wondered.

"Michael is fine, though he's had a slight cold ever since we arrived."

"Nothing serious, I hope."

"No. It's just taking him a while to get used to the colder weather."

"That's understandable, since he was born in the islands," Mrs. Hartman said. "I'm sure he will be glad to get back, and you too, of course."

"Yes," Corinne whispered, her eyes on the floor.

She wondered what she would say to these women when it became apparent that she and Michael wouldn't be returning to Hawaii. Lauren and her father both knew what an effort it was for Corinne to pretend she had a happy marriage and a devoted husband waiting for her to return. But no one knew the real depth of her misery. Not even Florence. How long would she have to bear this aching pain before it began to fade?

The knocker sounded on the front door and Corinne saw Brock pass the open parlor door on his way to answer it.

Lauren smiled regretfully at Corinne. "That will be Cynthia. I ran into her yesterday and she said she would try and stop by. It looks like she's here."

Corinne grimaced. She dreaded the catty questions Cynthia would ask. Cynthia had probably never forgiven Corinne for snaring Jared.

Just as Corinne was bracing herself for Cynthia's appearance, Brock came to the doorway, looking quite put out. And then Corinne saw why.

"Well, heavens me!" Mrs. Hartman exclaimed. "It seems he couldn't wait for your return after all, Corinne."

Corinne stood up very slowly, hearing only the pounding of her heart and nothing else.

"Corinne? Corinne?"

She turned toward her aunt, but didn't really see her.

"Well, it looks as if you're as surprised as we are! Shame on you, Mr. Burkett. You have rather too much flair for drama."

Jared tore his eyes away from Corinne and turned on his most charming smile. "It was a spur-of-the-moment decision, Mrs. Ashburn. But you're quite right. It was most inconsiderate of me."

"I think we should be going, ladies." Lauren motioned to the other women. "I'm sure these two have missed each other. The honeymoon must not be over yet."

She winked at Corinne, who barely noticed. What was Jared *doing* here? And then suddenly she and Jared were alone and panic rose to choke her. Michael! That's why he was here! He had come to take Michael away from her!

"Hello, Corinne."

307

She sat down again with as much composure as she could muster and her hands gripped in her lap to keep them from trembling. "You—you look well, Jared."

She imagined that she was as white as the china tea cups left scattered on the tables. She plunged into talk so he wouldn't notice her nervousness. "I hope your wound has healed."

He shrugged. "After a week it was only a minor discomfort. It's just an ugly scar now." He grinned. "Would you like to see it?"

"No!" she gasped.

How could he be so calm, as if they hadn't parted in anger? As if it were perfectly natural for him to be sitting here in her house, halfway around the world from Hawaii?

Corinne lowered her eyes. "What happened after I left? Was there a great deal of fighting?"

"Hardly. It had to be the most peaceable revolution in history."

"And the queen?"

"She no longer rules," Jared said with a touch of bitterness. "There is a provisional government now, under the American flag. And men were sent to Washington to petition for annexation."

"How did that happen?"

"January 14th, the day you left, Queen Liliuokalani went ahead with her plans to abolish the constitution. She tried to force her cabinet to sign her new constitution, but they wouldn't. A Committee of Safety was formed, made up of some of the most prominent men on the island, and given the power to keep order. They took possession of the government building and issued a proclamation that the monarchical system of government was abolished."

"Just like that? By proclamation?"

"They had the majority of the citizens behind them," Jared answered. "The queen was made a prisoner in her palace quarters and the American flag was raised." Jared sighed. "It was a sorry day for a proud people."

"You sympathize with her, don't you?"

"Perhaps she did overstep her bounds, but to me she is still the queen. It's ironic, but it's only been a little over a hundred years since Hawaii was discovered by foreigners.

That's a remarkably short time for a culture to become lost to other civilizations."

"It's not completely lost."

"Perhaps not," he agreed, then rose and gazed at her intently. "You haven't asked why I'm here."

Corinne turned away. "To be honest, I'm afraid to know."

He looked pained. "You have nothing to fear from me, Corinne."

"Don't I?"

Jared gazed at her thoughtfully, then joined her on the sofa. "Are you afraid I have come for Michael?"

"Yes," she whispered.

"Is that why you didn't tell me the truth about him?"

"Yes." She looked at him with wide eyes. "*Is* that why you're here, Jared? Because if it is, I won't give up my son. You would have to kill me first."

"*Our* son," he corrected her gently. "And I would never take him away from his mother."

Her eyes opened wide. "Do you mean that?"

"Yes." He moved closer to her, but she still moved away diffidently. He sighed. "I have a letter from your father in my pocket."

When she remained silent, still fidgeting nervously, he went on. "It arrived a few days after you left Hawaii. It was his answer to the one I wrote him . . . asking about Michael. He explained everything."

"He had no right!" Corinne began angrily.

"You had already told me, Corinne," he reminded her gently.

"Yes, and you said nothing! Nor did you say anything that last day!"

"I was still getting used to the idea," he lied.

He wasn't going to tell her of his suspicions about Drayton. She wasn't going to know how foolish he had been.

"It was a shock to learn I had a son," he continued. "And that you had kept it from me."

"Jared, I—"

"No, I know why you did. Your father's letter helped, and I already knew a good deal from Dr. Bryson."

Corinne blushed and looked around the room, unable to meet Jared's gaze. "You have to understand that I hated you then, Jared. I was obsessed with hating you, or I could never have done what I did."

"I know. Just as I was once obsessed with hating your father. I hope we have all learned from this. I don't blame your father anymore, and I will tell him so while I'm here. I know now what cruelty hate can drive people to."

"What are you saying, Jared?"

He reached out to take her hand. "I know you hated me when you left, Corinne, and you probably still do. But if it takes me the rest of my life, I'm going to make you love me instead."

Her eyes began to fill. "Why?"

"Why?" he echoed. "Because I love you, damnit!" Now that the words were out, he was able to say softly, "Yes, I love you, more than I ever dreamed possible."

Corinne shook her head slowly, wanting to believe him, yet still afraid to. "You're saying you love me regardless of what you think I did?"

"I knew months ago that I loved you. And yes, regardless of what I thought. I was going to tell you that Christmas night, but you shut me off again."

Her face brightened. "Then what you told me about Naneki was true?"

He nodded. "I wasn't sure you even heard me."

"I heard, only I didn't believe you."

"I can hardly blame you for that, as often as I've doubted you."

"Oh, Jared, I love you too!"

And she threw her arms around him. If she had her way, she would never let him go again.

He cupped her face in his hands and looked deeply into her eyes. "Do you mean that?"

"Yes! Oh, yes! And I swear I'll never lie to you again. You will never have cause to doubt me again."

"God, what fools we've been." Jared sighed and held her closer. "The misery we have caused each other!"

But then he felt Corinne stiffen and push away from him. "We are still fools, Jared." Her face held utter desolation. "It would never work. You will never forget what I did— what you think I did. That will always be there between us."

He got up and walked to the window. "Corinne, I know the truth now."

She froze. "What truth?"

"I paid a visit to a few of your ex-lovers."

She groaned. "Did they lie, and give you explicit details?"

Jared chuckled. "On the threat of being torn limb from limb, they gave me the truth."

"Really, Jared?"

"Each story was exactly the same. I didn't need to see more than a few in order to convince myself." Suddenly he laughed. "My God, you certainly had a clever scheme." Then he sobered. "It was too clever, for you fooled me completely, I'm sorry to say. Can you forgive me for believing you capable of that?"

"Now that you mention it," she began, her eyes darkening. But before she could build her fury, he quickly moved to the sofa, grabbed her, and kissed her deeply.

When Jared released her, her anger was gone and he was grinning devilishly. "That is a sure way to avoid a fight. I'll have to remember it in the future."

She smiled up at him, her eyes sparkling. "Never mind the future. You started something right now and you'll have to finish it, my love."

He crooked a brow. "Is your father home?"

"No."

"Then what are we waiting for?"

Chapter 46

THE ship glided along smoothly in the water. They were only a few miles from home and Corinne stood on the deck with Jared, waiting for the first sight of land.

This voyage to Hawaii was nothing like the first one had been, with Corinne in her cabin, sick and miserable.

This trip had also been spent in the cabin—but with Jared, who kept her occupied with loving. She was secure in her happiness, and in the knowledge that she was just where she belonged.

Jared wrapped his arms possessively around her and pulled her back against him, hugging her tightly. "Are you glad to be coming home?"

"You know I am."

"Dayna will be thrilled to see you." He chuckled, remembering the stormy encounter he had with her before he left for Boston. "She treated me to quite a spectacle when she found you had gone. She called me thirty-two different kinds of a fool for letting you go."

Corinne laughed. "I liked Dayna the moment I met her. We'll have to have her and her doctor friend over for dinner soon. I believe she's a bit in love with him."

"Yes, I know. We'll have to invite them to the wedding."

She turned in his arms and gazed up at him questioningly.

"Invite them to their own wedding?"

"No, to ours," he murmured. 'Will you marry me again, Mrs. Burkett?"

Corinne touched the golden heart she wore around her neck. It was warm from her skin.

"Without regrets?"

"Yes. Neither of us meant our vows the first time. I want to say them again, Kolina, and this time there will be no doubts—no regrets."

"I'll marry you a hundred times if that will make you happy," she said seriously, her green eyes intent on his.

He chuckled. "Like you promised me a dozen children to make up for missing Michael's early months?"

"Yes. You know I'll give you anything you want, as long as you keep on loving me."

"I'll never stop loving you, my Kolina. And one more wedding will do. One—to last us forever."

There was a distinct throat clearing going on behind them and they both turned at once to see Florence standing there with Michael. "Someone wants to join you two."

Jared laughed and took Michael from her. "He let you know that, did he?"

"He did," Florence said. "He noticed the island and wanted to show you. See?"

Michael was pointing to the long stretch of land suddenly in view. He was bouncing excitedly. "See!" he echoed Florence.

They all laughed. "Say 'home' now. Home?" Jared prompted.

Michael looked at his father, his lime-green eyes shining brightly like his mother's. Then he looked back at the island. "See!" he beamed.

"He's certainly made a better seaman than I've been," Corinne said, laughing. "I was hoping I would be the first to notice land, but he beat me to it."

"He did indeed," Florence remarked, suppressing her laughter. "It's a wonder you notice anything when that husband of yours is around."

"And that's the way it had better stay," Jared said in mock sternness.

Seconds later, after the word should have been forgotten, Michael chimed "home," and Jared squeezed him proudly. They all turned toward the island. Diamond Head crater with its stately beauty came well into view. And further inland, they could see the majestic Koolau mountain range.

Jared pulled Corinne closer. Together, with Michael between them, they sailed home to Hawaii. Home. A word as wonderful as family, which the three of them were now.

And as beautiful a word as love.

pau

**BESTSELLING ROMANCE
by Johanna Lindsey**

PARADISE WILD　　　　　77561　$2.95

From high-bred Boston society to the wilder shores
of Hawaii's blazing tropical sands, an impetuous
beauty and a man of smoldering anger meet head-
on in a battle of wills, revenge and love. Corinne
Barrows and Jared Burkett find a love so violent, so
reckless, that it must either destroy them—or give
them completely to the wild abandon of tropical
nights in paradise!

FIRES OF WINTER　　　　　75747　$2.50

Abducted from Ireland across an icy sea, the lovely
and dauntless Lady Brenna vows vengeance on her
Viking captors. Though slavery is the fate of women
captured on raids, Brenna swears she will never be
owned. But the Viking leader Garrick claims her,
and between them is forged a bond of desire—until
a rival Norseman challenges Brenna to defy Garrick,
whom she despises as a master . . . but loves as a
man.

A PIRATE'S LOVE　　　　　75960　$2.50

From sun-blazed beaches to star-lit coves, languid
Caribbean breezes sweep a ship westward, carrying
the breathtakingly beautiful Bettina Verlaine to fulfill a promise her heart never made—marriage to a
Count she has never seen. Then the pirate Tristan
captures Bettina's ship. Many days—and fiery nights
—pass, while he casts his spell over her heart, and
their passion blossoms into the fragile flower a
woman can give to only one man.

CAPTIVE BRIDE　　　　　75978　$2.50

Recklessly following her brother from London to
Cairo, beautiful Christina Wakefield is abducted by
an unknown stranger who carries her off to his hidden encampment, where she is made his prisoner.
There she shares his bed, learns to know his touch,
and grows ever closer to the man who owns her as
a slave. And soon she learns to want the desert
sheik as he wants her—and to submit to a stormy
and passionate love.

Available wherever paperbacks are sold, or directly from the
publisher. Include 50¢ per copy for postage and handling,
allow 6–8 weeks for delivery. Avon Books, Mail Order Dept.,
224 West 57th St., N.Y., N.Y. 10019.

(Lindsey 6-81) (1-B)